Praise for *The Lotus and the Storm*

"*The Lotus and the Storm* is part beautiful family saga, part coming-of-age story, part love story, but above all a searing indictment of the American campaign in Vietnam and its incalculable toll on generations past and future. A powerful read from start to end."

—Khaled Hosseini, author of *The Kite Runner*

"A profoundly moving novel about the shattering effects of war on a young girl, her family, and her country. In sensuous and searing detail, Lan Cao brings Saigon's past vividly to life through the eyes of her child narrator, Mai, following the girl and her father halfway around the world, to a suburb in Virginia, where forty years later, Mai's trauma unravels. In this fractured world where old wars, loves, and losses live on, *The Lotus and the Storm* is a passionate testament to the truth that the past is the present—inseparable, inescapable, enduring." —Ruth Ozeki, author of *A Tale for the Time Being*

"The ambition of *The Lotus and the Storm* is evident from the first page. . . . The experiences of the American soldier in Vietnam have been explored deeply in film and fiction. What remains considerably rarer are stories from the Vietnamese perspective and particularly those of Vietnamese emigrants whose lives span two cultures. . . . Cao's young protagonist, once again named Mai, links the mythic pair to her vision of her parents, lending her own narrative an epic backdrop that extends beyond the war and later years in the U.S. when, psychologically tormented, she finds herself alone and caring for her ailing father, Mr. Minh." —*The Daily Beast*

"Dazzlingly, Lan Cao captures Vietnam's dichotomy as both an enchanting realm and a place of carnage. . . . *The Lotus and the Storm* is both epic and intimate . . . offering a rarely discussed perspective on the Vietnam War."

—*Shelf Awareness*

"Be prepared, readers, to travel an emotional roller coaster from the most profound joy to the most devastating sadness in an astonishing journey in and around Saigon. . . . This is a stunning historical novel. . . . Cao has written a spellbinding work about life and death amid turbulent times. A must-read!" —*Historical Novels Review*

"A heart-wrenching and heartwarming epic about war and love, hurt and healing, losing and rediscovering homelands. Through the mesmerizing voices of a Vietnamese-born father and his daughter resettled in Virginia's

'Little Saigon' after the fall of Saigon, Lan Cao dramatizes landmark battles in the Vietnam War and the toll such battles take on winners and losers. *The Lotus and the Storm* establishes Lan Cao as a world-class writer."
—Bharati Mukherjee, author of *Jasmine* and
*The Middleman and Other Stories*

"Lan Cao is not only one of the finest of the American writers who sprang from and profoundly understand the war in Vietnam and the Vietnamese diaspora, but also one of our finest American writers, period. *The Lotus and the Storm* is a brilliant novel that illuminates the human condition shared by us all."
—Robert Olen Butler, Pulitzer Prize–winning author of
*A Good Scent from a Strange Mountain*

"Written with acute psychological insight and poetic flair, this deeply moving novel illuminates the ravages of war as experienced by a South Vietnamese family. In a rewarding follow-up to her well-received debut, *Monkey Bridge*, the author returns to the conflict that shaped her own destiny before she was airlifted from her native Saigon to live in Virginia. Here, she shows what happens to a family of four—a South Vietnamese airborne commander, his beautiful wife, and their two young daughters—as the war challenges loyalties with betrayals. . . . A novel that humanizes the war in a way that body counts and political analyses never will."
—*Kirkus Reviews* (starred review)

"For all that has been written about the Vietnam War, little has come from the perspective of the South Vietnamese whose lives were shattered in the conflict. Cao looks to rectify that imbalance in this complex tale of a father and daughter who fled to America, forever marked by the war and its aftermath. . . . Evocative and elegiac, *The Lotus and the Storm* is a stunning accomplishment."
—*Booklist* (starred review)

"It is when she describes moments of surprising intimacy that Cao shines. . . . She chronicles her characters' lives with clarity and suspense."
—*Publishers Weekly*

"A novel about reconciliation, and about that generation of Vietnamese for whom the future supersedes the past. . . . An impassioned and powerful attempt to understand a chapter of history."
—*BookPage*

PENGUIN BOOKS

THE LOTUS AND THE STORM

Lan Cao is a novelist and a renowned expert in international law, trade, and economic development. A professor at the Dale E. Fowler School of Law at Chapman University, she lives in Southern California.

*The*
# LOTUS
## AND THE
# STORM

## LAN CAO

PENGUIN BOOKS

PENGUIN BOOKS
Published by the Penguin Group
Penguin Group (USA) LLC
375 Hudson Street
New York, New York 10014

USA | Canada | UK | Ireland | Australia | New Zealand | India | South Africa | China
penguin.com
A Penguin Random House Company

First published in the United States of America by Viking Penguin,
a member of Penguin Group (USA) LLC, 2014
Published in Penguin Books 2015

THE LIBRARY OF CONGRESS HAS CATALOGED
THE HARDCOVER EDITION AS FOLLOWS:
Cao, Lan
The lotus and the storm : a novel / Lan Cao.
pages cm
ISBN 978-0-670-01692-1 (hc.)
ISBN 978-0-14-312761-1 (pbk.)
1. Vietnamese Americans—Fiction. 2. Family secrets—Fiction. 3. Vietnamese
diaspora—Fiction. 4. Vietnam War, 1961–1975 I. Title.
PS3553.A5823L68 2014
813'.54—dc23        2013047861

Set in Haarlemmer MT Std with Aptifer Slab LT Pro
Designed by Daniel Lagin

146119709

*For Harlan Margaret Van Cao,*
*In every way, always.*

*Who is the third who walks always beside you?*
*When I count, there are only you and I together*
*But when I look ahead up the white road*
*There is always another one walking beside you*
*Gliding wrapt in a brown mantle, hooded*
*I do not know whether a man or a woman*
*—But who is that on the other side of you?*

—T. S. Eliot, "The Waste Land"

# I
# A SMALL COUNTRY

# 1

## *The Tale of Kieu*

### MAI, 1963–1964

O ur mother drives with an elegant, carefree manner, one hand
casually on the steering wheel. My sister and I picture her driving through the streets of Cholon in our Peugeot, a hulk of sleek
black metal winding its way through this spark plug of a city filled with
open-air markets. Cholon is where we live and where she conducts her
business. She alone is in charge of our family's finances. She keeps the
records and maintains the books. It is in this unprepossessing Chinese
city adjacent to Saigon that she makes our family fortune.

We have a chauffeur, but our mother often drives herself. Demon-
strations organized by monks have begun to disrupt the city, but she is
not afraid. She is intimately familiar with these streets, even the
unmarked ones that dissolve into begrimed dead ends. The Chinese
merchants trust her. Perhaps it is because she is herself part Chinese,
although you would have to go back several generations to prove it.

Tonight she has just returned from an evening out with our father.
The Peugeot is parked in our driveway, its black paint highlighted by
swags of molded silver and chrome. Mother is resplendent in her satin
*ao dai* as she arranges its folds on her lap, then sits with her back against
the headboard of our bed. Her hair, shiny and black, is tied in a chignon
at her neck and she is wearing pearl drop earrings. Daylight slowly

extinguishes itself and a lavender darkness creeps through the window. The streetlights have come on. We are inside the meshed enclosure of white mosquito netting. I don't allow any whiteness to touch my head. White is the color of death and mourning, levitating above me even as I sleep.

Our mother reaches into a straw bag and pulls out a book. But she will not need to read from it; these are well-waxed passages she knows by heart. I lean against her body and ready myself to listen. She and our dad recited these verses to each other when they first met. It is hard to imagine a time when they existed without us, but still, I try to picture their time together before my sister and I were born. The sound of their laughter as they walk hand in hand. The velvet green uplands of rice fields, waiting to greet them.

She smiles, ready to share a great national epic with us. Kieu, beautiful and learned, loves Trong, the young scholar-hero, and Trong loves Kieu. They are bound together by the threat and promise of love. We know that they suffer years of separation because of Kieu's decision to sell herself as a concubine and a servant to save her family. But what I love most is the part where he longs for her. Our mother runs her hand along the length of my back and, in one long breath, recites Kieu's heroic renunciations and Trong's grief. Every child in our country grows up with this story.

> He drained the cup of gloom: it filled anew—
> one day without her seemed three autumns long.
> Silk curtains veiled her windows like dense clouds,
> and toward the rose within he'd dream his way.

Her voice has a quieting effect on us. Trong and Kieu, I say out loud. Minh and Quy, I add, pairing our father's name with our mother's.

> Both wrote a pledge of troth, and with a knife
> they cut in two a lock of her long hair.
> The stark bright moon was gazing from the skies
> as with one voice both mouths pronounced oath
> Their hearts' recesses they explored and probed,
> etching their vow of union in their bones.

Once in a while, my mother will lengthen the story with paper and pen if I demand some similar evidence of her bond to our father. Her pen makes swift, scratching sounds as it inks out the strokes of her signature. It combines her name with our father's, his name first, attached to hers after. Our father's signature similarly conjoins his name with hers, in reverse order. We know—it is impossible not to—that our parents are linked in many inward and outward ways.

Our mother's eyes rest on us. My sister, Khanh, smiles back but I know her attention is elsewhere. She is fixated on the book's pagination, on the tiny numbers tucked in the upper-right-hand corners. Numbers captivate Khanh. She dwells in a world of equations and straight-spined rules that are constant and predictable. Mine is a world of fantasy and mystery, words unloosing themselves, producing secret, tangled lives that float into my imagination. Still, I am certain at that moment that my sister and I share the same lustrous dream. Around each of our necks is an identical chain, fine gold with a circlet of jade, now a pale apple green that over time will mature into a deep dark luster.

It isn't long before Khanh, fired up and fidgety, nudges our mother to turn the page again. My sister, four years older, is convinced that she will win the Nobel Prize in Physics when she grows up. She looks at page numbers and does mathematical calculations in her head, showing off virtuosic accomplishments with giddy delight. I begin to nod off to sleep. Our mother whispers our names. "Khanh." "Mai." Khanh's breath is warm against my face. *Khanh,* a name I have known before speech, before memory. Hers is a presence I take on trust. Four years apart, but we are twinned. I hold my sister's hand, comforting myself with the softness of her palm as she turns this way and that. Soon, our mother's impeccable chignon begins to loosen, her hair falling with liquid ease into a thick cascade that rests on her shoulders. At that moment of reverential silence, when we are poised to sleep but yet awake, her touch softens. She waits for us to doze off. Inside this coveted sphere, the world is filled with happiness even as the bashful sun disappears.

Sometimes in the evening, we gather among the ravenous vines that meander through our mother's garden. There, in an unruly tangle of fernlike shrubbery, are clumps of plants with feelings. The mimosa is sensitive and shy, reluctant to offend, my sister says. It clasps its leaves inward against its chest when touched. I brush my legs against the leaves. All at once, as if they were fully on beat and part of a well-disciplined choir, the entire being of the plant, stems and leaves alike, reorients itself to bend modestly toward the ground. Tonight, against the green stretch of ground cover is an explosion of small, fluffy pink flowers that bloom like stars.

A declivity of earth and bluestone pebbles surrounds the mango tree, and I crouch there behind a giant earthen jar—my favorite place to hide. Next to the mango is our star fruit tree, its branches bearing green fruits the shape of a five-point star. It is how starlight tastes, my sister says. Our mother told us she herself had planted it from an original cutting when she and Father first moved into our house. Khanh has etched her initials and mine on its brindled trunk.

I am still hiding. Tendrils coil and brush against my bare legs. The air smells of frangipani blooms. Khanh leans against me and together we draw into our lungs their flowery fragrance. A violet twilight swaddles us in a benign glow. I love the evening most of all—the ritual, at least when our father is at home, of hiding in the murky night and waiting to be found, his giant black military boots trudging through the brambles and ground cover. From where we hide, he cuts an imposing figure. The jungle green on his military fatigues ripples. Our swing set squeaks. Ordinary noises startle us as we settle into a hushed silence to practice invisibility. Fire crickets rustling their wings. Fireflies flicking dots of umber. Street vendors peddling bean cakes with their syncopated voices. I make myself small behind the jar, holding my breath as if my life depends on it. But of course our father will soon be upon us, swooping us into captivity, cupping my belly with his large hand and flinging me onto his shoulders. I rub my bare legs against the stubbles of his cheeks. His arms, lithely muscled, will hold me in place, perched high above his head.

He is away from home most of the time because there is a war going on and he has to fight in it. On those occasions when he is with us, I love the sight of him, the halo of thick black hair, the symmetry of his body, the tumble of tight, compact muscles shifting quietly under his uniform. His omnipotence is palpable, though not suffocating or overpowering. He is beautiful but his beauty is modest.

In my father's private room is a framed photo of a lotus flower. The flower, our father once explained, is a reminder of life's eternal progress toward a simple purity. A plant that grows in mud yet manages to produce a stunning flower that floats pristinely above the water. One night I stood at the doorway, looking at the picture and at Father. He was sitting diagonally across the daybed, cross legged, studying a book, running his index finger across the page. Closing it to caress its leather spine; reopening it as if to contemplate its mystery. My forehead burned with the realization that this was where our father came to fully occupy himself. He let go of his book and sat in seemingly unremarkable stillness. I listened to the smooth intake of his breath. Something was happening and I felt suddenly like an interloper. I wanted him to need my presence. But everything, the water running through the faucet next door, reckless sounds from the kitchen below, the neighbor's hammering, was happening outside of him. I wanted to reclaim him, make a noise, claw through the hard distance to pull him back. But I could not imagine how. Here was our father, baffling, elusive. But at that strange moment, he was not. Not our father, nor a soldier fighting in a terrible war. Nor a paratrooper who jumped out of planes. He was instead this new person, even-tempered, with liquid eyes. An almost unbodied presence.

As a child, I want to talk about the satiny eggplant color on our father's face when he returns home after months away. I want to talk about his boots, muddied and nicked. I want to talk about old wounds, puckered scars that glisten like mother-of-pearl against his sun-browned abdomen, strange griefs of delicate luster, hidden from view. I never know what exactly he does during those intermittent months. Our father cups his other life away from us inside himself. Khanh and I want what he wouldn't give us. His stories, his explanations. Rampant and obstreperous, like firecrackers. I know they are inside his skin.

Every time he vanishes into some remote province of our country, I ask my sister, "Why does he have to go? Doesn't he want to stay here with us?"

"He has to go where he is ordered," my sister answers.

"The war is far away and he goes to it?" I ask.

My sister stoops over and pulls me toward her. "Yes. But he will come back soon." There she stands in front of me, rocking on her toes and heels and offering me her promises and reassurances.

"Will it come to us, right here, where we are?"

"The war? No. It won't come here. That's why he goes away to fight, so the war can be kept far away."

She tells me the names of places where the war supposedly is taking place—Qui Nhon, Binh Gia, and more—but they blend together like distant shadows.

Our mother's side of the family is Catholic so we celebrate Christmas. Every Christmas Eve, Khanh and I place our father's military boots outside our door. With profligate coatings of thick black polish, they look beautiful, hefty, and brand-new. Santa Claus, we are assured, would leave our presents next to them.

On the map, Cholon is a separate city from Saigon, but in reality, the two cities are twinned and hardly anyone knows where one ends and the other begins.

Cholon's commercial district is several blocks from our neighborhood. Our house is tucked away in a more residential area. Here it is, a French colonial–style villa, painted in yellow ocher, the same color as all the other French colonial villas, the same as the grand Opera House on Rue Catinat, as our mother still calls it, although it was changed after the French left to Tu Do Street, *Tu Do* for "freedom."

Here I am with my sister. Here is the place where everything that has yet to occur will occur. I do nothing without running it by Khanh; I live my life under her protection. From the window in our bedroom I can see our terrace where our parents go for their after-dinner drinks. More often than not, my sister is permitted to join them while I am sent to bed early, merely because I am younger. In our country a child is one year old when she emerges from the mother's womb. Although I insist for the sake of argument that I am therefore older, this fact is lost on our mother. She shrugs off my protest with a declaration of her own.

"Time to nest for the night," our mother would say, tossing her hair. Aggrieved, I would beg our father for more time. Our mother would utter "Anh Minh" and place her hand preemptively on his, as a restraint against his tendency to indulge. They are now a united front. Our nanny, whom we call our Chinese grandmother, would scoop me up and hustle me out. On this bed, I am left to mull over their unconsidered act. The view from the window is partially covered by an adjoining building. Its brick wall cuts a vertical line and creates a narrow, elongated frame through which I can glimpse but a swath of our terrace and garden—a beguiling sliver of an image. Sometimes a full, socketed moon positions itself inside this enclosure, hanging low, as if within reach. From this vantage point I can hear voices, faint but clear enough through the rush of air. Even as they think I have dropped off to sleep, I listen.

Today, Khanh put up a giant poster of Galileo on our bedroom wall. Already my sister has a plan, an ambition, and Galileo is her inspiration. Khanh turns herself with stubborn conviction into someone who will someday win the Nobel Prize. With implacable hunger she devours books, not those about magic carpets or evil genies, but those with equations and proofs about the fundamental principles of the universe. Hers is an intricate vocabulary of numbers. Each new day brings with it a modulation of magic outside the world of Euclidean perfection.

Yes, my sister reads books about matters that lie beyond the norms of conventional understanding. She believes in infinity. Her fingers peck at reality. She draws the mathematical sign representing infinity for me. There is no time in her world. Hers are stories that evoke the balance between science and magic. When a giant star dies and a black hole is created, both time and space stop. In the black hole, the gravitational pull is so strong that nothing, not even light, can escape. Our planet was birthed during a cosmic explosion of dappled colors that hurled matter in all directions. Distant galaxies are still moving away from us at great speeds. I am astounded that such a wistful and scary epic of the universe inspires her.

"Do you understand?" she asks with a proprietorial gaze. She wants me to love what she loves. Stars, especially. She shows me a picture of Van Gogh's *Starry Night*. She sees motion in the brushstrokes, swirling patterns of subatomic particles beneath the appearance of solid mass.

I nod. I understand. I wish for my own personal planet. For a genie to grant me my every wish.

When I confide my wishes, she says with a show of exaggerated exasperation, "What an imagination you have, little one."

In the kitchen, we prepare a smorgasbord of delicacies. We practice eating a well-known Swedish specialty—*surströmming,* fermented canned herring. My sister has researched the ritual. It cannot be performed indoors. We go to the open-air terrace. She ties a cloth napkin around the tin can, places it on the table, and opens it. The cloth is not included to create an aura of formality but rather to soak up the liquid that spurts from the can due to pressure built up during fermentation. The can, bulging with gas, hisses. We wait for a strong smell to be released. My sister scoops the herring from the briny liquid and spreads it on paper-thin hard bread. We each take a bite. I swallow mine quickly without chewing, pretending it is no more stinky than our traditional nuoc mam sauce of fermented anchovies.

My sister wants to acquire this taste. The Nobel Prize is given in Sweden and she has many ways to prepare for this heroic future awaiting her. Already she is graceful. There is an eloquent flex, an arch to each foot as she positions one lightly in front of the other; she is on a stool, her stage, to deliver her acceptance speech. I stand sheltered, next to her. Ours is a world of mathematical grace. It is alive with possibilities. I lean into Khanh's body as if the enormous resolve inside her were solid mass.

Hours later, we eat dinner with our Chinese grandmother, who has been with our family since my sister was born. She comes from a family of Chinese traders and speaks fluent Vietnamese.

She is wearing her usual tunic and trousers. Her hair is tightly coiled and held together by pins. We call her Grandma when we talk to her. When we talk about her to others, we call her our Chinese grandma or our Chinese grandmother. Our real grandmother lives in Saigon, not far from our house, although we rarely see her.

We swirl about the trees and grass, raising ourselves ecstatically skyward, diving with winged arms like planes dodging rocket fire. We take turns. We taxi and take off, swoop and swerve. Our Chinese grandmother grows impatient. A crease of disapproval lines her bark-colored face.

She wipes her mouth with her upper arm and grunts. "Is it possible for the two of you to stop moving and sit down to eat?" she asks as she clops down the garden path in pursuit of us. When she's excited, a Chinese cadence is unloosed into her Vietnamese, giving it a peculiarly choppy rhythm.

My sister smiles. I hear a giggle as she speeds up and vibrates her wings. I too am flying and doing clever aerial turns. I know our Chinese grandmother wants us to hurry. She wants us to be on schedule. Eat, play (a little bit), then sleep. Once we fall asleep, she will be able to settle, at last, into her nighttime routine of betel nut chewing and reading.

"Stop and eat. Chew. Swallow. Have I not taught you manners?"

She is not pleased that we have developed a habit of bunching our food in the back of our mouths. I want to accommodate our grandma's demands but I do not want to antagonize my sister.

"Don't walk away and ignore me when I'm talking to you," our Chinese grandmother says, enunciating each word.

My sister walks away and ignores her. I too take a few steps before turning back to look. We get no more than a few meters down the garden path before we are collared.

"Huh," she says, satisfied with her success.

I stand still, to let her know I have succumbed. My sister twists herself loose but then stops and smiles.

"Grandma," my sister pleads. "I am sorry. I want to make up."

There is only silence.

"We will sit still and eat, I promise."

To demonstrate, my sister sets herself on a rock and does not move.

Immediately our Chinese grandmother responds. She can be placated with the right move. "All right then. You can sit right . . ."

"But we will need to have some Coca-Cola," my sister says sweetly. "Please?"

Our mother doesn't allow us to drink soda pop, but once in a while our Chinese grandma rewards our good behavior with a few sips of Coke.

Today my sister is trying a new experiment. She is asking for the drink in exchange for good behavior that has yet to come.

Perhaps because she is exhausted, our Chinese grandmother consents.

I am astonished. Khanh runs to the kitchen, finds a bottle, and takes a good, long draw. Her face is radiant.

We quickly finish eating and then return to the task of piloting our planes. As we hover in the air and look down, making sputtering sounds with our mouths, the rice fields below are alive and voluptuous, a glorious green. We take care to avoid the rain-collecting cistern that sits squarely against our wall, positioned just so to be gravity fed, its open mouth ready to intercept the rainwater that flows off our roof. Our mother harvests the rain and redirects it for our garden. During the monsoon season, she puts out an additional four or five cisterns under the eaves of our house. When they are empty, my sister and I use them for games of hide-and-seek.

I lift the lid and dip my hand into the cistern, spraying my sister with water. We run out the front door with Grandma in tow. "Not so fast," she says. Her face is brown and weathered. She can be crotchety if challenged. She is bestowed a degree of authority over us but doesn't possess any intrinsic authority of her own. Khanh and I listen to her, but only enough so that she does not complain about us to our mother. Grandma sighs at our impudence. I glance nervously at Khanh who is busy placating her.

"We're very careful," my sister says, glancing back to give our Chinese grandmother a compliant nod.

We do not want to lose time. We are in a hurry. Khanh and I head straight to the front gate, make a right turn, and race down our block, Ngo Quyen Street, named after a Vietnamese general who decisively defeated the Chinese in the tenth century and declared Vietnam's independence after one thousand years of Chinese rule. Our street is lined with tamarind trees. Tamarind pods, fully ripe and plump, lie scattered about. Their shells are dry and brittle. I pocket a few to crack open later. With a sprinkling of sugar, their brown juicy pulp, normally acidic, becomes sweet and tangy.

We walk by an ornate moss-covered tomb, its stone marker engraved with Chinese calligraphy. The tomb is in our neighbor's garden a few houses down from ours, and although it is not his ancestral tomb, he is reluctant to remove it for fear that something bad might result from dislodging ancient spirits. We turn left into a side street with Khanh leading the way. I am learning how to snap my fingers. We snap our fingers in unison as if in doing so we button our parts together to make a corresponding whole.

As usual, we are hoping to find the American soldiers who gather every day in and around the South Vietnamese military police compound, a modular building with a roof made of galvanized iron sheets.

A guard-duty station stands at a corner, and as we round it, the Rolling Stones thump "Tell Me" accompanied by a strong slide guitar and driving bass. We are surrounded by coils of concertina wire. Because the South Vietnamese military police is headquartered here, this is a secure and well-guarded street, always patrolled by soldiers.

It isn't long before James Baker catches sight of us. James is our special friend. He is an American serviceman whom we often see with the South Vietnamese units at the military compound. We found him about a year ago when we followed the thumping bass line and the squeal and transport of electric guitars emanating from his portable cassette player. We were coming home from school. My sister, running after the music, caught up with him, tugged at his shirt, and grinned. "Mick. Mick Jagger." He pointed to the music box and winked.

"We love it," my sister said, speaking for herself and me. We didn't want delicacy. We wanted the big sound of rock and roll. James turned the volume up and offered us two sticks of Wrigley's gum.

We have learned his routine. We know when he is off duty.

"We're here," he says when he sees us this evening. "Me and the Rolling Stones." My sister beams. James is eager to show off his liquid moves. There is no getting around the music. It pulls you into its center, coaxes you to take leave of the ordinary world. There, in the midst of the acoustic guitars and bass drums, is a new kind of sound, loud and enormous enough to assault and liberate at the same time. You can feel it up your spine. James throws more music on the turntable. It erupts with life, snaps and crackles with a bigger and bigger bang. Grandma grimaces. I jump into the shrill, raucous rumble as the music rises. James strips down to his white undershirt and begins to shift his feet, sway his body. His back is long and lean. He reaches for Khanh and me and swings us each a half-turn. The three of us hold hands by hooking fingers. Our private ritual.

Rock and roll has its way of gathering momentum, of transcending barriers and demanding acquiescence even in this smoldering heat. We watch James, his James-ness, as he shakes his shoulders and lowers his body to the drum's beat, lower, lower, lower, until he is squatting against pronounced resistance on his haunches, the Vietnamese way.

James had told us about his family. His parents come from a long line of potato farmers in a place he calls the East End. I imagine the same flatness of farmland we have here, absorbing the same iridescent green, extending infinitely from plot to plot. He likes to tell us about his two-story clapboard house sitting on a flat field overlooking the Long Island Sound. That is where he played soccer. The game the entire world loves, James calls it. We nod in agreement.

I look at his distinctive chin, the way he thrusts it outward, the way the dimple dances when he moves. A low growl rumbles from the record player. We are all still caught inside its grip. I see Grandma out of the corner of my eye. She shakes her head. She likes James but she does not like his music.

"It's time to go home," she declares.

We protest; we have barely arrived. Khanh picks up an album cover and studies it. The singers have long hair and stare sulkily into space.

"Don't ignore me when I'm talking to you," Grandma says.

Khanh keeps her eyes on the album cover. She feels the drum's beat underfoot. I see the pursed lips, the palpable defiance. Her hair, knotted and tangled, is plastered in sweat.

"Do you hear me?" Grandma asks. "You still have homework to do and it is almost your bedtime." A definite Chinese-ness has insinuated itself into her Vietnamese.

Khanh pretends sudden interest in her watch, doing quick multiplications and divisions with the numbers, a stalling tactic. She shoots our grandma an imperious look, juts out her jaw defiantly. Grandma scowls. James prudently intercedes.

"One more song," he says cordially. A perfect voice, soft and melancholy, fills the air. "Yesterday," sung with aching abandon. Grandma, becalmed but still petulant, begins to relax. The hardness she affects is usually short-lived. Most of the time she can be jostled out of it. She allows herself to enter Paul's loose, liquid voice. I slip into her arms and stay there while the Beatles sing.

James winks. Despite her outward displeasure, Grandma is inclined to indulge him. His weekly volunteer work at the orphanage in the neighborhood behind our house gives him a gravitas that his youth alone does not. James often buys chocolate and gum from the American PX and hands it out to the children there.

"He is a nice young man," Grandma often says with an intonation meant to convey not just affection but also admiration.

James pulls a camera from his knapsack and fiddles with it. He aims it at us and maneuvers the lens into focus. "Just point and shoot," he says, then mimics what he wants to convey by pushing his index finger toward the camera's button. He hands it to our Chinese grandmother and asks her to snap a photo of him and my sister and me. So that the camera's lens will take me in and I will not be cut from the picture's edges, I lean as deeply as I can into my sister and James.

Our Chinese grandmother looks through the viewfinder and pushes. I hear a click. The shutter is released. James tells her he is sure the photo will be just fine.

# 2

## *For I Remember Yet*

### MR. MINH, 2006, 1963

I wake from a long night's sleep to discover that it snowed heavily overnight. Wind has blown a swell of snow onto my windowsill. The shimmering expanse of white covering the grass reflects the sun's glare. Roofs, trees, cars—everything is covered in snow. Beyond them, against a stretch of acquisitive white, a steeple dances in the mist. A pure silvery world has been created, separate from the world of yesterday.

Once I used to wish for the infinite beauty of a snowfall. As a child in Saigon, I read about it, the wind-whipped powder, the geometric flakes, tree branches sheathed in white. So different from the tropical swelter I was born into.

Virginia is not a state that gets heavy snow. Cars stall or slip aimlessly in the whisper of frost. Those who do not dare to wander out will stand by their windows to watch the snow lash soundlessly toward them.

The clock on my bedside table shows that it is still early morning, but in this weather, my daughter might already have left for work. I run my thumb over the tips of my fingers, shriveled in the cold. I exhale and watch the uneasy vapor drift. Reflexively, I touch the familiar patch of abdominal scar tissue. How long ago that was, that dark rainy night when I parachuted into enemy territory, crawled through black earth crowded with underbrush of thorn and thistle and rotting trees. The wound on my stomach had turned necrotic and I had no antibiotics. The medical kit was lost in the storm that downed the helicopter. I knew how to improvise. Luckily, a swarm of flies was buzzing about, attracted to decayed flesh. I dropped to my knees, unbuttoned my shirt, and proffered my wound to them. The next day the bandaged area teemed with an infestation of maggots. I kept it covered up, checking only once in the morning to make sure the maggots were eating abscessed tissue, not healthy pink flesh. I could feel them wriggle and swarm. The stench of blood lingered, refusing to be fanned away.

What I need is a lighter tread into the past. I take in a deep breath.

I am what you can call lean. One American neighbor in this building sometimes calls me Bob. His American mouth, the muscles of his tongue, cannot form the sort of sounds that our Vietnamese names demand. Neither my first nor my last name starts with a *B*. So I know Bob is not a pun on my real name. Of course I eventually figure it out. Bag of bones. He means it affectionately, I think.

I touch the skeletal outline of my body, its softness, its diminishing musculature. It is hard to eat prepackaged convenience food—Jell-O, hard-boiled eggs, toast. Once your tongue has known a more belligerent, embellished flavor, it yearns for what it once had. Cloves, cinnamon, peppercorn, ginger, fennel. I crave the pinch of five-spice powder that blends sour with sweet, bitter with savory and salty, the many-layered coatings of *char siu* seasonings on pork that turn the meat a dark lurid red, burned and charred along the edges, tender in the middle. The sweetness of honey, the sharp bite of salt. Their aromatic dust drifts about, teasing, winking for memory's sake in this subdued January light.

Against the wall opposite my bed is a sideboard with a television set and a row of photographs. I stare at the one of a little girl with wide inquisitive eyes, long black lashes, black hair that curls and loops. She must have been six when the picture was taken. I close my eyes. I remember when I first felt the kicking of her foot against her mother's rib cage. I see her as she came out of the womb, to the sound of prayers accompanying her birth, with a tuft of spiky black hair on her newborn head. She is still connected to her mother by an umbilical cord. Her skin is warm, suffused with heat from her mother's body.

After all these years, let me say who I am still: a father. A husband also. I call up lines from a poem by one of France's most romantic poets, Alfred de Musset. *"The first love, and the tenderest; | Do you remember or forget—| Ah me, for I remember yet."*

Surely, I remember yet. Here, in this room I am inside the rattle and rush of history. I remember "La Nuit de Mai," that beautiful poem dedicated to Alfred's doomed love affair with George Sand, the woman he lost but never forgot.

In another photograph, next to the one of my little daughter, a young woman looks back at me, her neck long and slender, her face slightly tilted, as if in contemplation. This is how I remember her, as she was when we first met. She is here, but not.

If we are fortunate, all of us find, at some point in our lives, the one special person for whom everything is possible, for whom love itself rearranges one's entire being. That is how it all begins. My wife, Quy, was that person for me. I am still there with her.

I am reminded of the quiet, inward beauty of yin, a feminine, peaceful acceptance that is but the other side of yang. I lie back to enjoy the whisper of falling snow. There it is, a strange beauty, equal parts loneliness and equal parts poetry. I watch the translucent specks and imagine their desire to let go and drift carelessly toward the earth. Here is the irresistible compulsion to float and fall.

A muffled groan lodges itself inside my chest, followed by a series of fitful coughs. Pert footsteps stop at my bedroom door. My child? Yes, though not a child any longer, of course. A grown woman who must get to the office in the snow. I see the faint creases on her face, creases that deepen when she is deep in thought.

"Mai?" I ask tentatively.

She nods. I smile. She can be sweet and caring, if on occasion distant. We do not always speak to each other in our language. Sometimes it is easier to speak a new language. Dispensing with normal courtesy— How are you? How do you feel today?—she comes straight over to inspect me. With a certain theatricality, she rolls up my shirtsleeve and peeks at my upper arm. Revealed thus, I can see my own true unprosperous thinness. As if in grief, there it is. The dull, mottled skin. The angular wrist. The brittleness of bones. The ache inside.

"It is better," she announces reassuringly, working her hand around my neck to prop me up.

What is better? And then I remember. Sometime, a few days before, perhaps, I had fallen and scraped a patch of skin from my arm. A searing pain registered through my arthritic joint. A tingling feeling radiated from my nerves. I can still hear the hushed chorus.

It could have been serious. An old person's broken tissue can easily become ulcerated.

A punctilious vigil was maintained. Mai paid the Korean housewife in the ground-floor apartment to watch over me while she worked and when Mrs. An could not be here. I cooperate. It is important in a place like this to be pleasant. Nothing happens here that is not noticed.

Mai and I live in an apartment in Sleepy Hollow Manor, a small complex housing an amalgam of transplants displaced and dislocated from the world over. In the evenings, I hear the clash and clangor of Hindi and Tagalog, Korean and Chinese, and of course the familiar and comforting elocution of southern Vietnamese. Much of life spills forth and is conducted outdoors here. Pleasantries and gossip as well as business exchanges and proposals are discussed in the front yard and back garden, on sidewalks and stoops. Women in saris may work as receptionists or nurses during the day but after hours they double as gold merchants or moneylenders willing to finance under-the-table businesses for the ambitious—ticket scalping, catering, hairdressing, marriage brokering. At Sleepy Hollow Manor, New World ingenuity combines with Old World desires and networks to spin a furtive, anarchist version of the American Dream.

Still, no one here knows how things were for me. Years ago, my now-crooked fingers were made to perform wondrous feats. Through these fingers ropes and cords were passed through tangles and loops and emerged as knots that came with names: the double Blackwall hitch, fisherman's bend, Turk's head, cat's paw. It was all part of the training. We rehearsed every contingency while blindfolded. Cyanide pills were sewn inside shirtsleeves and trouser hems. I practiced the motion with my hands tied. Body curled forward to receive the end to suffering, I bit open the seams. The pills would be within tongue's reach if a mission failed. I could swallow death.

It is almost eight in the morning, but the light is beginning to darken under the weight of hanging clouds.

Mai seems shaky, perhaps because she dreads having to drive in this weather. She searches for her handbag, a huge leather pocketbook that contains her wallet, books, papers, and other miscellaneous items that she often cannot find because they are buried at the bottom.

"Your cell phone is over there." I point to the chest of drawers by the door. "Where you left it last night."

"Thank you," she says. She picks it up and starts thumbing messages on the tiny keyboard. She usually sticks it in the back pocket of her pants but I notice that these trousers have no pockets.

There is the sound of a key jiggling in the lock. "Hello, hello," a voice calls from the threshold.

It is Mrs. An. The high cheekbones, knife-blade sharp, make her stand out in any setting. She has been in this country almost as long as I have but, unlike me, she escaped by boat after the war. She still dresses conspicuously native, in silk shirts and sparkling gold threads. She is rather slender, but she knows how to position her body for leverage and can lift me with one hand. She floats my way and wedges a pillow behind my back, exuding benevolence. I have known her for decades and am comfortable speaking my language with her. It is lucky that she lives with her family on the same floor, only two doors down from us.

"I'm sorry I'm here so early, but I am on my way to work earlier than usual. I'm worried the road will turn icy," Mrs. An explains. She sputters. When she feels overwhelmed, her facial muscles pull. I watch the left half of her face dance upward. She pushes her palm against it as if to press it into submission. "Argghh," she lets out a fierce sigh. The tick continues, up, down, sideways. She is losing patience with its incalcitrance.

"Oh, good, you are still here!" she exclaims when she sees Mai.

Mai nods.

Looking at my daughter, I can sense the mass of unarticulated feelings hovering about her. She is small-boned, almost deceptively delicate, her skin smooth and supple. Her thick hair falls in sheets and shines in almost lacquered blackness. Her eyes are charcoal black, like the seed of a longan. I fed longans long ago to my daughters. Dragon eye, literally. The fruit is round with a thin, brown shell. Its flesh, white, soft, and juicy, surrounds a large black seed.

Mrs. An cranes her neck and looks toward the kitchen, checking to see if there is food on the counter for me. She manages a derisive laugh when I ask her who is working the shift with her today. "The young ones won't bother to get out of bed on a day like this." She sulks, though with a discernible degree of satisfaction. "The nursing home has a lot of trouble finding reliable aides."

She and Mai give me my meals on most days, although I can manage by myself more than they believe. She is the one who noticed my swollen feet and hands and worried about my ability to breathe. A month ago, at the hospital, they removed one gallon of water from my lungs. Even now my breath comes out in serrated gasps like a fish out of water. I close my eyes, separating myself from my physical body.

"It's all right, Aunt An, I can stay home awhile," Mai says. "I am not going in for another two hours." Mrs. An is not really her aunt. It is simply the Vietnamese way of bringing close friends into the family fold.

Mrs. An nods. A long effervescent hiss comes out of the coiled pipes.

I glance at the basket on the credenza. There is a plate of sticky rice, dried shrimp, and Chinese sausage. A bag of persimmons, unskinned. I also smell simmered catfish and rice, even though both are in a tight-lidded stainless steel tiffin box. There are four canisters stacked one on top of the other, held together by latches and fitted into a metal frame with handles on top. Each box contains a different treat.

Mai subscribes to what we traditionally call *com thang,* monthly rice. Her subscription entitles her to home-cooked Vietnamese food made by two women who have over the years developed a steadfast following. We now dine on whatever the two women choose to prepare and deliver each day.

They typically bring comfort foods. Fried vermicelli; catfish caramelized in soy sauce, fish sauce, and melted sugar; potbellied tomatoes stuffed with minced pork and onions; a clear broth soup that is so delicate it tastes more like tea than soup; eggs scrambled with bitter melon. Today there is also a thermos of tea and sticky rice.

Although I can do it myself, Mai feeds me, scooping the sticky rice from the plate with her fingers and rolling it into a ball. I open my mouth and swallow what she slips into me. Time floats, then curls and curves backward into itself. Coaxed by the lure of memory, my mind drifts into an imagined world from years past. The distant chant of an itinerant peddler hawking food swims in my ears. Tamarind pods fall on the misshapen sidewalks, cracked open by the Saigon heat.

I shake my head, almost too violently. Saigon still wraps itself around me and squeezes with sudden force.

Mai turns on the television. A weather map shows precipitation remaining in our area, which, combined with the cold temperature, is certain to mean more snow. I see arrows and lines and a shaded spectrum of pink and red that looks almost ornamental.

"Are you cold?" she asks as she hands me a tissue for my runny nose. Her narrow shoulders slope inward, giving her a meek, seemingly serene appearance, but I know better. Poor child, I think. Memories course through both of us and sometimes they short-circuit inside her. My hand trembles as I try to protectively clasp hers.

I nod. "This is so good. I love that you order this food. Remember how your sister loved caramel pork?"

Her face darkens but she gives me a tentative smile and offers me a cup of tea poured from the thermos. The thick, smoky flavor of a full-bodied black tea rises. She tilts the cup at just the angle that makes the flow manageable. I am touched by her tenderness.

On television, the undulating green of a rice field grabs my attention. I can almost taste the succulence of a blade of rice, green and sharp, against my tongue. Pagoda roofs slope with architectural deliberateness against the Saigon skyline. Above, a helicopter hovers. Conical hats ruminate, bowing toward black earth covered by a shimmering liquid green. I reach for the remote control and raise the volume notch by notch. Tanks roll, truckloads of soldiers hop into chaos, voices emerge brittle with anxiety and sorrow. The number of dead is chronicled, one by one. How quickly they are counted. A precise tabulation of American dead, American wounded.

Scraps and remnants of glistening green present themselves to me, from a distance. Many layers of forests, thickly canopied. I can see the earth where death is interred. The scarred trees, the dark shades of green that spill over from branch to branch, as each overgrown layer fights off vines and tendrils in search of sunlight, space, and growth.

I take a deep breath and look again, though I wish to forestall insurgent introspection. Over and over, newscasters recall Vietnam from the American consciousness.

Quagmire.

Now stretches of monochromatic orange and brown desert sand tremble in the sun's haze. Desert towns are besieged against a drifting landscape of sand and sloping plateaus. I hear of continuing fights in embattled cities along the Euphrates. Basra. Nasiriyah. Najaf. In the background, outside the focus of the camera's lens, a cactus blooms amid the sunburned sagebrush. I see the crumbled sections of mosques, the traveling dust storms, the treacherous movement of shadows against gentle date palms. There is no assurance of order here in this self-canceling landscape where sand obliterates sand. Everything now occurs *here,* the way it occurred *there* so many years ago. A disputed town is controlled by a clutch of government soldiers one day, unofficial militias of one religious sect or another the next. A soldier's body is found floating in the Euphrates. Armies slip across borders, attack, and retreat. I think of Phnom Penh, Cambodia; Vientiane, Laos. I might have been echoing them in my sleep.

The names that once ignited high passion have changed, but the ends of the earth were once found there, as if they had been there forever.

I lie still as she takes my hand and places it on her knee. I know what she is doing but my mind is on the screen. I take in a deep breath and hold it inside me before letting it out. I can feel the squeaky lungs bucking and rebelling. But still, after a few minutes I manage to find a rhythm of alternating inhalation and exhalation. The body still hurts and disobeys but I am learning to ignore it. I can move on. I look into Mai's face. She starts with my baby finger and clips her way to the thumb. The clippers make crisp, snappy sounds, sending the jagged edges of my nails flying. As I slip back into the slow pulse of that place from long ago, I hear the tart scraping sounds of the broom against the floor. It must be a Vietnamese broom by the full throaty contact it makes on tile. The rice straws, bundled and bound together by vines, scrape and scratch. I feel a tear run down my cheek. I listen to the sweeping motions, left to right, left to right. My nails are being recovered and swept into a dustpan.

A television announcer asks about exit strategies, that pernicious little phrase. I know the calamity of being this country's ally. The unleashing of warring factions, of fire and chaos, and then the declaration of victory. The escalating cost is proving to be too much—too much blood, too much treasury, all adding up to a pointless generosity. I can see politicians in Washington, D.C., preening for the next news cycle. How can they be blamed! They didn't know things would turn out like *this.* I watch what is going on as someone who was born in a poor country. I see how they swing the wrecking ball. I know how the weak country has to wheedle.

With each successive moment they are deeper into the very war from which they wish to exit. It is familiar, a shadowed history that stalks and does not recede.

It has been more than thirty years since Vietnam fell. But 1975 is still here, held to enormous scale inside me.

It is now 2006. The year hardly matters. Why would it be different now? They continue to cartwheel from one disposable country to the next, saving the masses and abandoning them.

Mai has returned to my bedside and wipes my face with a washcloth. She does not seem to mind my occasional lapses; she has her own phantoms and demons. I know that she makes private but regular sojourns to the Vietnam Veterans Memorial in Washington, D.C. I know that under her neatly folded shirts are pamphlets and booklets about the history, conception, and construction of this haunting structure. Once, I happened upon her stash when I folded the laundry. The mere photograph of it on a book's glossy cover tugged at my heart. Two black triangular granite walls coming together to form a V, sunken belowground like a scar in the earth. Names of American dead are etched row by row on its shiny surface. A diamond next to the name means the person was killed; a cross means the person is missing.

Mai props me up and plumps several cushions behind my back. She has become the keepsake of my memory. "Tell me," she says. And inevitably, I do.

It is 1963 and I am back in Saigon—the suffocating haze of heat. One day before the coup.

It was late afternoon and I had awoken from a long nap. I thought of nothing, not of motives or consequences, and that itself was of enormous consolation and satisfaction. I lay in bed staring at the ceiling, a calm beige. There was a lightness in my body, an abiding sense of possibility, merely because for that singular moment I hoped for nothing. Perhaps the lightness would stay. But at the very moment I wished for it to remain, the feeling collapsed inside me. The door opened and a sliver of half-light entered the room. My wife slipped into bed and positioned her head on my chest. I whispered, "Em, darling. Quy." She breathed softly into my neck. Her hair floated, its long soft strands brushing against my face. She wore loose clothing that flowed. The cotton fabric was so thin I could almost feel the full nakedness of her body pressed against mine. Ours was an old-fashioned courtship that continued right through the domesticity of marriage. Her mouth rested on the nape of my neck; her skin settled into mine. I shifted her body and allowed my palm to ride the length of her back. I closed my eyes. If only I were a painter, I'd have been able to capture her form and essence with a few brushstrokes, a fluid line here, another there.

My wife pulled me closer. She hummed the slow, cantabile passage from Chopin's *Fantaisie-Impromptu*. We were surrounded in each other's warmth. I exhaled. A feeling of contentment worked its way slowly into my being, the same feeling that had entered me when I first walked alone with my wife not long after we met. I hoped for nothing; I was already certain that we would spend our lives together. All around us was a vast rice field, the single point of access into the country's soul. I loved its opalescence, rich earth redolent of harvest; the froth and swell that churned and roiled when the monsoon swept through the country, draining off years of accumulated wrongs and faithlessness.

The first time I kissed her as we stood by that field had surprised us both. She tasted faintly of sugar. I did not quite know what love would feel like, but in that moment, I believed I understood everything. Something moved inside me. "Anh," she had said, softly. "My love." Her voice was polished, like a stone rubbed smooth by a river's flow.

"I have never kissed before," she whispered. She called my name. "Minh."

Right through my heart surged a thrill so fierce it made me desire not consummation but restraint. I wanted to prolong the moment. I wanted to fall to my knees in complete surrender.

"How old are you?" she asked.

"Twenty-two."

She hesitated. "I am not yet twenty."

I said nothing.

She drew herself closer to me, her face against my shirt. She too was holding back, leaning against me, but not quite. Her breath danced against my skin. I felt the *ping ping ping* of my nerves dancing up and down my spine.

I would not reveal any of this to her. I knew these protesting facts—the ways of old Vietnam. Status mattered and I had none. I was an errant son from a distant land. My parents were Vietnamese but made their living as shopkeepers in Vientiane, Laos, where I was born. I was only traveling through Vietnam, panning for gold in the tributaries of the Mekong River.

Still, over the course of weeks, months, she convinced me that we would find our way into the world by love's intuition alone, the way each day inevitably followed the next. We hung on to this belief, even when her parents disapproved of the marriage and disowned her.

If I could be granted one wish, it would be this: to go back to that time when I first fell in love by the rice fields. I would return to the place I had left and it would still be there, waiting. Just as my wife would be. There, among a profusion of green, in a flowing purple *ao dai*.

How did a small, skinny country clinging to the coast of the South China Sea attract the attention of a great power?

I see the cursed geography of Vietnam. A conquered country cleaved into two halves, the northern half under Ho Chi Minh and the southern under Ngo Dinh Diem. The differences between the two were stark. The North was tightly clasped inside the iron-clad scaffold of the Communist Party. The South was a loose archipelago of centrifugal impulses, each spilling away from the center, each seething with its particular desires, fractious babble, and fierce passion.

Our efforts to forge a national identity out of the South's divisions were opposed by a tangle of local, religious, and secular interests. President Diem himself was impeded by his own police and secret service, all of whom had split loyalties. From the Hoa Hao to the Cao Dai to the Binh Xuyen sects, each commanding its own sprawling army, from the biggest to the smallest landlords, from the French to the Chinese monopolists with coffers of silver and gold, everyone had something to fear from the president's ambition for a strong, centralized national government. And everyone in this group did what could be done to sabotage this dreaded possibility. The rest simply waited.

Saigon in 1963 was battered down by factional rivalries and conspiratorial politics. It was a city driven by appetites, afflicted with vertigo. Plots were recklessly hatched. A common desire ran through the city, to charge and push outward, to enlarge the sphere of influence.

One November day, our collective fate would be redirected. After that, everything faltered and changed.

I was in a government-issued jeep driving to the military headquarters. The streets of Cholon, sloped and tilted, were slicked with spilled diesel. Still, as if to defy, trucks, cars, motorcycles, assaulted the concrete landscape. Here, in this traffic, was where the highest level of gamesmanship would be played out. Everyone believed he had right-of-way and no one yielded to anyone. Drivers turned their steering wheels wherever they needed to go and blasted their horns.

My jeep was stuck among ox-drawn carts, construction trucks, cars, and bicycles. This section of the road was under repair and traffic converged into one lane. Everyone was heading home for the afternoon nap or lunch. High school girls floated in their virgin-white *ao dais*. The acrid smell of diesel and tar lingered in the air, trapped in the earth's steam. My eyes smarted from the sting of smoke. A persistent sourness like the odor of damp laundry lifted from the street. It had rained and a certain unpleasant moistness remained trapped inside the black asphalt. Vendors thrust wedges of green, unripe mangoes toward me, their sourness to be tempered by chili-spiced salt wrapped in plastic. I bought a glass of sweet jelly grass cubes mixed with syrup and hand-shaved ice. The midday sun hovered fiercely above, suspended against the bruised sky. On the sidewalks shoeshine boys squatted, running their rags over rows of military boots just like mine. Perhaps it was the military boots that triggered it; suddenly I could feel it, the way you could feel your throat tighten and your heart clutch when you sense the beginnings of danger.

I drove the jeep onto the main boulevard of Saigon, heading toward the Presidential Palace. I had received the order to attend a routine meeting at the Officers' Club in the General Staff headquarters. Such meetings were necessary to maintain an esprit de corps among the president's officers.

During those chaotic, troubled times, forthrightness was neither prudent nor desirable. People presented impassive faces and learned to produce oblique answers that were ambiguous enough to satisfy the country's many competing factions. But I was not a political man and, unfortunately for me, saw only what was right before my eyes, not what was brewing underneath.

Months before, I had watched as flags were hoisted along the major streets of Saigon. The mood was celebratory. Multitudes were expected to gather for the Buddha's birthday. Against the indigo sky the flags luffed and billowed. I noted with some trepidation that all the flags were Buddhist flags and not one was the national flag of three red horizontal stripes against a background of yellow. It was a fact worthy of observation because the government had ordered that religious flags could be flown only in temples or churches and political flags only in political headquarters. The government had decreed that national flags must be bigger in size and hoisted above all other flags. We were trying to forge a common identity and a sense of duty to the nation, after all.

As I stood that day watching events unfurl in Saigon, something similar was happening in Hue, home of the most militant and organized Buddhist hierarchy in the country. Among the ancient, mildewed sidewalks in that old imperial city, along the banks of the Perfume River, Buddhist flags were being hoisted. It was there, in Hue, that fate conspired with politics to spin complications. In a country of Buddhists, President Diem was Catholic. All his brothers were Catholic, including the archbishop, whom the Vatican had appointed to Hue.

Hidden in the gray-hued shadows of the royal citadel and the tranquil tombs of the emperors, the Hue monks, committed to their transcendental quest, conspired to remake the country's political fortunes.

As they flexed their muscles, rumor had it that the increasingly desperate archbishop of Hue turned to his brother the president for commiseration. And so the president ordered that government regulations regarding national and religious flags be strictly observed, even in Buddhist Hue.

This was of symbolic importance, but it had an immediate effect.

The defiant snap of Buddhist flags could be heard around the country. There, right there, was the tug of opposing forces, the struggle between central control and religious expression. After several years of fighting and finally quelling armed rebellions by the religious sects, the government opted decisively for national identity over religious autonomy.

Even the most obstinate and thick-skinned official in Hue could sense the stirring of whipped-up discontent. Far from Saigon and surrounded by a sea of angry monks, government officials succumbed, turning a blind eye to the president's directive. They watched as Buddhist symbols were tacked on doors and Buddhist flags hoisted, in historical centers among crowded shops, along the river's old-fashioned promenade and the boulevards winding through the old city.

In city after city, passions spilled over. A venerable old monk doused his clothes with kerosene and set himself on fire. Radio stations were seized. Buddhist leaders issued fiery sermons denouncing the Catholic presidency, authoritarian rule, and, most searingly, the arrogance of the president's brother and the supercilious dragon-lady style of his flashy sister-in-law. The newspapers were full of stories about Hue. Day after day, security forces with batons and guns stood clench-fisted, facing broad, patient rows of razored heads and fixed, unforgiving eyes. Over time, university students joined the monks to jabber about injustice. At barricaded intersections, they locked arms. A few lobbed stones at scorched vehicles. As the crowd became animated, soldiers tapped their nightsticks and prepared to unleash water jets.

Armored cars sputtered, clearing the way, and troops advanced in frontal formation toward a radio station, where two big explosions ripped through the hyperkinetic heat. In the dense orange haze, the crowd swiftly dispersed. The scent of blood and charred flesh lingered in the heat.

Much later, it was determined that what the soldiers carried, MK III grenades, could not have killed and maimed so many. MK IIIs are used for training only and do not have the power to shred arms and legs. The smell of conspiracy hung in the air. Was it a Vietcong grenade? Did the Vietcong possess such a weapon in their arsenal so early on, even before receiving massive Soviet and Chinese aid? Could the explosives have been part of a twisted CIA plot? To turn the population against a president who no longer met its needs?

A few weeks after that terrible explosion, elements of the government's Special Forces attacked the famous Xa Loi Pagoda in Saigon. Monks and nuns were beaten and rounded up. The president's supporters shuddered. I knew this new government of ours was stumbling badly.

I looked at my watch, worried that I would be late for the scheduled meeting at the Officers' Club. I had learned to become wary of bottlenecks, stalled traffic, sputtering scooters that slowed down just enough to hurl a bomb into crowded intersections. Anything could be hidden under the buckled sidewalks, inside the sewers beneath the road's surface.

Finally I lurched the jeep into a patch of shade in the parking lot and hurried to report to the General Staff headquarters. Soldiers with fully loaded M1 assault rifles stood guard. An M66 machine gun pointed from a guard tower surrounded by concertina wires and fortified with sandbags.

I was ushered along with fellow senior officers into the cavernous conference room. Others were directed straight into the Officers' Club down the hall. This was not routine. Next to me was the commander of the Special Forces, Colonel Tung. I stared at his blank, broad face, the fierce, narrowed eyes, the short bristled crew cut. He was as unsure of what was happening as I was. His eyes blinked in nervous tics.

After a while a man wearing a military police uniform opened the door. His voice was matter-of-fact. "Please follow me, sir. Colonel Tung, sir. The general is waiting for you." Colonel Tung was then swiftly hustled out. The MP's hand stayed detectably insistent on Tung's lower back. I searched for signs of normality. Diesel fumes leaked into the room through the door's crack. Saigon dust, dry specks of grittiness, blew in through the partially open window. Silence. Then laughter down the long hallway in the direction of the Officers' Club. And then, cutting through the November evening, the sound of gunshots.

I stood up, braced myself for whatever would happen next. Another knock at the door, and the same MP appeared before me. "Please, Colonel," said the voice with eerie formality. "The general would like to meet with you now."

I followed him out of the conference room, down the familiar hallway toward the office of the chief of the General Staff. From behind, a sudden pounce. Big rough hands, several, in fact, squeezed my wrists into handcuffs. Utter panic passed over me.

General Minh motioned me to come in. On instinct, I tried to snap him a salute. The general proceeded to inform me he was orchestrating a coup d'état against the president. He looked me over, then asked, "Colonel, we would like to know your view. Will you be with us? Will you mobilize the troops under your command?" His voice was flat, uninflected.

The general's aide-de-camp, the MP who had led me here, stood still. His fingers moved ever so lightly over the unholstered pistol against his thigh. I heard the sound of the safety clicking off. The general fingered his pearl-handled pistol and rattled off names, explaining the convergence of events that made the planning of an elaborate coup possible.

For every gesture of trust, there is, is there not, a countervailing gesture of betrayal?

General Dinh, a close friend of the president who had been put in charge of organizing countercoups, had himself joined the plot. He had sent the Special Forces out of Saigon to address a supposed Vietcong buildup, leaving the Presidential Palace vulnerable. If General Dinh had turned against the president, the matter was practically hopeless, I feared. Another of the president's most trusted officers, the one he relied on to counter intrigues, chief of the General Staff himself, was recuperating from lung cancer treatment. Bad luck. His temporary replacement, General Don, had taken over, led the charge, and also joined the coup. Other generals entrusted with the task of commanding the areas north of Saigon had also turned. The list of cohorts willing to shift allegiance grew. I was astonished to hear the names. The coup had been punctiliously planned. These very generals had convinced the president to let them move troops into Saigon as a massive show of force to frighten potential coup plotters.

Blood rushed to my head. It was now clear that there were two camps: those in the Officers' Club who were aware of the coup and supported it, and those in the conference room who were gullible and believed this to be a routine meeting.

I could feel a primitive rage rise through me, spiraling inward into itself until it turned inexplicably and with effortless delicacy into something else altogether, into a deeper reserve of calm, a subterranean well of steady, shadowless tranquillity. I could disappear, unstretched, unbeset, into its bottomless comfort—even standing before the mouth of a .45-caliber pistol.

"General, this is a matter of enormous magnitude. I was not contacted beforehand. I cannot join you now while under threat."

It was straightforward in its own strange way, this direct threat of death. I felt no fright, no grief, no terror. And I certainly felt no courage.

The chief of military security requested that I make an announcement on the national radio in favor of the coup. I refused.

"In that case I'm afraid we have no choice." The general's voice hardened.

I was dismissed, arrested, and returned to the conference room to be sequestered. I thought of what had happened to Tung and waited.

The booted thump of MPs sounded on the tiled floors outside. I was under guard, waiting to be executed. From the window of the darkened room I could see the courtyard, and above it clusters of forlorn clouds. Below, standing next to General Minh on an outstretched patch of earth, was one of my closest friends—Phong. How many evenings had we spent together sipping coffee and playing Chinese chess until our wives insisted on an end to the game? How many arguments had we had, how many times had we surfed the ocean waters of Vung Tau together and felt the tug of its undertow? How many meals had we shared? And now suddenly, the dependable, trustworthy side of him, that which defined him to me, could have been altogether inauthentic. Phong's body shook. I recognized the familiar wheezy cough, the quickening steps that signaled private turmoil, the cigarette loosely held between his fingers, flicking ashes.

A church bell sounded mournfully. I blinked and looked away, my heart seized by a fierce, vengeful pinch. I did not want to see Phong standing next to a coup leader.

Yes, blunders had been made and had been left uncorrected. But President Diem had also managed a series of reassuring accomplishments. The disciplined resettlement in the South of almost one million North Vietnamese fleeing Ho Chi Minh's Communists. The crushing defeat of the warlords' militia controlled by an array of wayward factions. Assembling with surprising swiftness a strong central government.

Once upon a time, President Diem had made the construction of a centralized government free of local feuds and factions a national priority. It had to start with a desire and a will and a commitment to implement it—to butt heads with opponents, to be forceful, to take unpopular steps, to take away privileges, to threaten. Diem broke conventions and gave offense. At what point did power become too concentrated? When did he become a dictator? Somewhere between a measure to clamp down on the press and another to muffle dissidents, somewhere between what we had imagined and what we ended up with, I too began to have doubts.

But much more than his actions or inactions, his blunders or virtues, it was his character that touched me. He was frugal and uncorrupted. I understood him. He was an unmarried man drawn to a spartan lifestyle and uninterested in the accumulation of personal wealth. His sin was an overinflated sense of loyalty to his family. But who among us in this land of Confucius could not understand such a sense of duty?

My eyes returned to the courtyard. An MP walked toward the general, conveying a message furtively. My friend Phong remained at the general's side.

Hours later, an apocalyptic darkness was settling in, bringing with it its own noises and surprises. There were red ribbons of tracer rounds, lolloping curves, each sizzling against the moon's molten silhouette. Metal fire streamed from every corner of the city. The Saigon skyline glowed. A rocket shot straight up, pulling lilies of white phosphorus that intertwined, then scattered across the sky. The sounds were overwhelming. I hated to think it, but the sky looked beautiful.

The fighting continued into the night. Tanks and cannons would fire into the Presidential Palace. The Presidential Guard's headquarters would be subjected to an intense artillery barrage. I waited for the MP's return. And for my own death.

I could see into a row of windows across the courtyard where Phong stood, making grand gestures with his hands. Facing him was General Minh, large and imposing. One talking, quickly, almost pleading, the other listening, then nodding in apparent agreement. Phong smiled. He pulled the cigarette's end from his mouth and smashed it triumphantly into an ashtray. He looked up and for one instant I thought our eyes locked. I stared unblinking until someone pulled a curtain.

There were crescendos of massed voices in the hall, rising and falling. But the MP never came. The passing hours clicked by. One day passed, then the next. Finally the door swung open, and I was released into a new day.

Never had it been as clear to me as it was at that moment: For every act of betrayal, there is also a simultaneous act of friendship. I knew full well to what I owed my life. To the mere chance that Phong, one of the coup's leaders in the Revolutionary Military Council, was my friend. How fragile the rules of survival were. These were the elemental calculations of loyalty and treachery. He had betrayed the president but had saved me. The poignant incongruity of it all stayed with me.

A fine crimson dust coated the windshield as I drove home, encumbered by a new and heavy debt. I maneuvered my way toward the labyrinthine decrepitude of Cholon as the radio announced the revolution's success. It was reported that the president and his brother had committed suicide. Nobody would believe such a story, of course, as they were Catholics. When published photographs of the president's corpse showed his hands tied behind his back, the official cause of death was amended to "accidental suicide."

From the beginning there was the word. *Murder.* Murder that was being passed off as revolutionary wonderment. What awaited the country now? Something had changed irreversibly. Fighting had stopped but a sense of emergency persisted. An unprosperous future lay ahead of us.

I let the jeep sputter in the back lot by the bedroom before turning the ignition off. I resisted the urge to rush to the house, to shake off the ghostly fog that cast its long shadow over me that late afternoon.

"Is it you?" The voice was frantic. "Minh?"

My wife was at home. Of course she would be home when Saigon was still seized by the aftermath of a military coup. I negotiated my way up the front steps and came into the room, eager to throw off the stale uniform and undershirt. She ran toward me. "You're safe," she whispered, pushing her body against me. I felt the fluttering beat of her heart. The world was full of mistakes and punishment, but here, in the sanctuary of her arms, I would be safe. I dropped to my knees, from exhaustion and relief. My arms wrapped around her legs as I pressed my face against her flesh.

I scanned the room, searching for my daughters. "They are with their Chinese grandmother," she said reassuringly.

There were radios on both night tables, each tuned to a different station. I could make out snippets of the news reports: The emphasis was on change but also continuity. A new prime minister would be appointed. The country would embark on a strong, steady, newly charted course. Corruption and authoritarianism would be yesterday's problems. The Revolutionary Military Council had seized power to build a strong regime and to terminate the fake anti-Communist policy of the prior government, which was aimed not at winning but at engaging in an illicit peace dialogue with the enemy. And to top it off, the new regime, the announcer assured, had also been promised continued American support.

Of course.

The statement carried within it a dreadful truth. Its gravity ran right down to my core. American support for the coup had been secured not after its success but before its attempt.

My wife clicked both radios off and let out a muffled groan. She wanted to insulate me from reality. She wanted to console.

I heaved myself up. "Of course the Americans are behind this coup," I said.

"Shhh. All that matters is that you're home and safe." Her voice came out as a long, low moan. She flicked specks of dust from my face. She stood on tiptoe and pressed her cheeks against mine. Touched my hair. Pinched the fabric of my uniform between her fingers and thumbs, as if to test the authenticity of my physical presence. I felt the soft fluttering of her eyelashes against my face and heaving sobs against my chest.

"I am here," I whispered, suppressing my own emotions in order to soothe hers. I reached for her hand and held it.

My wife headed for the bathroom and ran a hot bath. I lowered myself into the water and relinquished my body to the steaming heat while she sat on the edge of the tub.

"Let it go," she finally said. Three limpid words. I looked at her. I wanted to be blotted out, erased.

"Let it all go," she said again, as if to herself this time.

I leaned against the tub and allowed my wife to scrub my back with a sponge. "Quy," I said, not knowing what else would follow. "Quy." I merely wanted to call out her name. Her fingers worked my shoulders, massaging the complications of muscle and bone. I wanted to collapse into something, the rampaging thump of love renewed, the unashamed confession of fears and failures. But for the rest of my time in the tub, neither of us talked. We both gave each other the gift of silence.

Outside the phone rang. I could see a flutter of shadow through the door's crack. My body went rigid. Yesterday's experience had made me watchful.

The nanny knocked on the door.

"It's Mr. Phong," she said.

What does he want, I wondered, and reached for the towel.

My wife rushed toward the door. "Stay," she said emphatically. "You lean back and rest. I'll handle it."

I obeyed. In fact, I was relieved that my wife took the initiative to handle the phone call herself. I would not know what to say to him and I needed the time alone to mull over and allay my suspicions.

Later that evening, my wife surprised me by initiating our lovemaking. The surprise was not the initiation but the timing. I was settling myself and trying to fall asleep. The neighbor's cat yowled. A tree branch jumped against the moonlight. My wife cleared her throat softly and leaned over to kiss me. I allowed myself to be kissed, to catch up with her desires and abandon myself to her care. I raised my head off the pillow and kissed her back. As I pulled her closer, I felt a slight resistance from her that I registered but swiftly flicked away.

# 3

# *Two Sisters and One Thousand and One Nights*

## MAI, 1964

Outside the wind blows steadily and drives sheets of rain against the walls and windows. Once again our mother reaches into a straw bag and pulls out a book. Khanh is skeptical but our mother smiles and pulls her into the circle of folded arms. The overhead fan briskly stirs the air as our mother reads one story after another. It all began once Scheherazade was in the sultan's chambers. "Shahriyar," I whisper. Shahriyar, the sultan who out of spite married a virgin each day and beheaded her the next. Scheherazade volunteered to spend one night with Shahriyar, to save herself and her sister, knowing that her sister too would eventually be next in line to be the sultan's wife and then his murder victim.

Our mother fixes her attention on us. I wait to discover how Scheherazade would save her own life by telling one thousand and one enthralling tales to the sultan, each one a story within a story, hypnotically interwoven. Scheherazade asked if she could be permitted to bid her last farewell to her beloved sister Dunyazad by recounting a story to her. The story would be fantastical, alluring. The sisters would take the whole of the night and, under the entirety of the moon's glow, spin each detail until it was fully stretched, drawn and twisted, like a magical yarn whose filaments looped and enveloped, seduced and ensnared. At dawn, the cluster of knots that kept the story's mystery suspended would not unravel. It would still be there, the complexity of cross-grained nodes that intersected and entangled, that Scheherazade would not undo until the next night and the night after that.

And so every night brought with it another night, every moon another moon, until a thousand and one nights were strung and webbed and desire and faith conquered death. I know each story by heart, but still I yearn for every additional half hour, every quarter hour, of our mother's time, to hold and stretch like a ribbon around us. I put my hand over my mother's to keep her from turning the pages, hoping to slow her down, to fix her in the infinity of our present. I hold my breath as one story, then another, loops back upon itself, like a serpent swallowing its head.

Our father works all day almost every day. My sister and I love to watch him put on his starched, crisp uniform and polished boots. They give him an air of gravity. Sometimes I wear one of his uniform jackets around the house. Bury my face in its folds and taste our father's valor, witness the majestic eloquence of his flight. A paratrooper's emblem is stitched on the sleeve. You have to have a certain confidence to take your body and fling it from the sky toward the earth, to let the parachute catch and billow in an updraft of air, with nylons and canvas answering wind. I am not courageous, certainly not—I make no move without my sister's approval—but I believe that I have the possibility of courage in me. Inside our father's jacket, I am something else altogether.

Almost every morning before school, we take his hands and walk him to his jeep. He calls us by our names. "Khanh." "Mai." He calls us good little girls, and because of his prophetic powers and triumphant glance we would become so. I am sure of it.

But our father also has fears. He fears that wrongness would insinuate itself into our flesh and blood. Not our own wrongness, but the world's.

He speaks to us sweetly but with conviction. "You must not trust easily. Trust has to be earned," he says. "The person who can harm you the most is the one you mistakenly trust." Judas kissed Jesus and in so doing identified him to enemy soldiers. Brutus, who was made governor of Gaul and allowed into Caesar's inner circle, led the plot to assassinate him. Oda Nobunaga, one of the greatest military geniuses of all times, had harbored the singular dream of uniting Japan under a single sword but was thwarted by his most trusted general. Nobunaga hid in a monastery and disemboweled himself.

We listen to our father more to indulge him than to try to understand his warnings. I abandon myself to the certainty of his protection. I remember how he would toss me in the air and inevitably catch me in his arms.

He pushes us to study. For me, the world is full of facts to be learned. For Khanh, it remains full of mysteries to be solved, beautiful mathematical rules to be discovered. Our father believes that education offers a hope, even if it is an obscure hope, of allaying life's dangers. He warns us about love. "You must not trust a man to support you." Love is independence. Love is self-reliance. There is no Prince Charming and Cinderella in our house. Our father does not allow it.

When Khanh asks if he trusts our mother, he says simply that it is less important whether a man trusts and depends on his wife. It is more important that a woman not find herself dependent on her husband.

Why? Khanh asks.

A boy's life would not be ruined if his love is a mistake, but a girl's life would be.

Why? Khanh asks again.

Boys start life on one side of the equation and girls on another side, our father explains. The boys' side has additions and the girls' subtractions. Girls have been unfairly pushed onto the margins where human failings will harm them more. "That," he said, "is human history."

For a moment I feel afraid of him and wish to take flight from his warnings. Until his stories curl back to where they started, to the yearning toward that which is good in the world. Our father always returns to what matters. His face shines with happiness when he kneels to kiss our faces.

Our mother too works almost every day but her work does not always take her out of the house. Because our mother comes from a large landowning family, her fortunes have become the foundation of our future.

She speaks triumphantly of what the shimmering stretch of her family's land—pungent black earth—faithfully yields, an accumulation of harvest dawns. But despite the vastness of the land, it is no longer of any use to us. The land, boundless acres of it, is all in unstable territory—government control by day, Vietcong by night. Without the steady rhythm needed to prepare the land for tilling, it can no longer reward us with the fruits of its fertile soil. And so our mother cannot afford to inherit the life of comfort that has been her birthright.

Our father often speaks of her resilience. The loss of the family's wealth has not undone her. She has given us a revised but undiminished future—one that depends not on land but on ideas. She has a discerning eye. A piece of land here, in a modest, marginal locale on the outskirts of Saigon, is likely to become prosperous in a moment's time. Under her ministrations, an ill-fated enterprise can be turned around with a modest infusion of cash.

Our mother is a businesswoman, our father often says with pride. She has her Peugeot driven all over the city to the houses of Chinese merchants. They also come to our house. Ours is one of a few Vietnamese families in this Chinese-dominated city of Cholon. While feasting on elaborate meals prepared by our cook, our mother and her Chinese friends contemplate new ventures. Their success is based on astute commercial calculation, but also intuition. Among them are many years of experience. Buying and selling rice. Building and renting houses. Putting money in this and taking money out of that.

There is in our Cholon villa an almost daily chaos of visitors. My sister and I can barely keep everybody straight. We do not call them by their names, first or last. It is impolite to call adults by their names. In order to create an atmosphere of familiarity, it is customary to address family friends as Younger Uncle Number Three or Younger Aunt Number Four, Older Uncle Number Six, and so forth. What each person is called depends on whether he is older or younger than our father or mother and his birth order in his own family. To be accorded a number is to be included in an intimate ritual—to be inside an orbit of enumerated family members and special friends, first, or second, and so forth, among a brood of just so many. A number conveys a relationship within a particular order. By contrast, a name is impersonal and commonplace, available to strangers, proffered to the world at large. And so we children do not use names when we refer to those embraced within the circle.

Khanh and I refer to one visitor as Younger Aunt Number Three the Rice Seller, a pasty-faced, plump woman who smiles compulsively, and another as Older Aunt Number Three the Pharmacist, a tall, slender woman who presses coins into our palms and asks our mother for Coca-Cola, not tea, so that my sister and I might partake of the forbidden drink. When Older Aunt Number Three the Pharmacist comes to our house, she bears gifts for my sister and me, plastic swords and daggers and mentholated oils. Sometimes we dump out the oils but keep their tiny glass bottles with the long necks and curved bodies.

Today we come home from school to find the usual congregation of Chinese aunties impeccably dressed—black slacks, colorful silk blouses, shiny black sandals. I take my cue from my sister, who hovers near them. She has made eye contact with our mother, who then offers us an unopened bottle of Coca-Cola. The women are sitting expectantly around the table in a seating area near our family room, waiting for our mother to preside as host. "Our capital account is large enough to move forward with the deal," our mother declares. The aunties all nod approvingly. Our mother smiles. "We talked about this last week, but here are the papers I've prepared for you to examine," she says. "This is actually your idea," she adds, turning graciously to Older Aunt Number Three the Pharmacist.

Aunt Number Three the Pharmacist sits up straight and nods proudly. She owns a business that makes tiger balm, a concoction of eucalyptus ointment that cures everything from headaches and stomachaches to nausea and the common cold. "Taiwan is a good market for us," she explains. "A Taiwanese businessman I've known for years needs an infusion of cash to grow his herbal medicine business. He's had to divert his attention to deal with family problems and the business has struggled a bit. This is an opportunity to help his business grow for him and for us."

"Look at the charts I prepared and you'll see why this is a good idea," our mother chimes in. Columns of colorful numbers and arrows crisscross the pages.

The Chinese really know how to make money, our mother has often noted admiringly. A small part of her is Chinese, perhaps a

Chinese grandmother or great-grandmother. She believes with a profound sense of conviction that the Chinese are trustworthy, that they
work hard but expect only modest rewards, that, surrounded by non-
Chinese, they have to turn inward and depend on themselves alone.
They do not use contracts but instead rely solely on trust. They work
with one another whereas the Vietnamese work against one another.
Being a foreigner means learning how to share burdens, to trust and
depend on others of one's own kind. Somehow she has gotten into their
inner circle, perhaps because we are almost foreigners ourselves, part
of the Vietnamese minority in heavily Chinese Cholon.

Younger Aunt Number Three the Rice Seller heaves herself up
from the table and reaches for the papers our mother is handing out.

"This is quite good," she says. The visitors share a vocabulary of
commerce. All the Chinese aunts speak Vietnamese with a particular
Cantonese or Fukienese twist and cadence. Some speak with the delicate undulation of upper-class Northerners who fled the Communists
in 1954 when Vietnam was divided at the 17th parallel into a Communist North and a non-Communist South. Even now their voices carry
traces of nostalgia for faraway places.

"Yes, then, right?" our mother asks.

Once the aunts agree, their attention turns to card playing and eating. The cards are small and narrow, no bigger or wider than an index
finger and imprinted with Chinese ideographs. A hand consists of
twenty cards. All twenty are stacked between the thumb and index finger of one hand as the other slowly spreads them out like a fan. We hear
laughter. Our mother slaps a card against the table and grins with satisfaction. The Chinese aunts shake their heads and sigh. "Sister Quy,
she's lucky today," they say, laughing.

"Luck plus skill," our mother replies lightheartedly.

Khanh and I sometimes bet if a particular business deal is likely to
make money. "This one will," Khanh assures. "I looked at Mother's
charts," she says. I am wide-eyed and impressed that my sister can tell,
simply by looking at the numbers, when our mother's sure-footed prophesies and firefly intuition are going to pay off, when guesswork and luck
are likely to materialize. "According to the numbers, in a year, Mother
will double what she puts in. All of them will."

While our mother and the Chinese aunties play cards downstairs, my sister takes me by the hand and leads me toward our parents' room. I sense that we are engaged in something forbidden. She stops abruptly at the landing, tilting her head toward the bottom floor and pulling her hair behind her ear, presumably so she can better hear. "They're still down there," she declares.

I am not afraid. She leads me on tiptoe toward our parents' closet and opens the door. I see nothing out of the ordinary. There are, on one side, dangling trousers, shirts, and jackets, military uniforms in jungle-green camouflage; on the other side, women's blouses, silk pants, long flowing *ao dai*s that our father always admires when worn by our mother.

Khanh touches my shoulder. "You wait and see," she says. With both hands, she parts the heavy curtain of clothes to the side. I see, at the very back of the closet, a square-shaped box covered by an olive-colored military blanket. There it sits: an emanation of the forbidden and the mysterious. She nudges me forward. I creep inside the cavernous enclosure of the closet. An eagle, buoyed by a parachute, stares down at me from the South Vietnamese Airborne insignia stitched on our father's jacket. Khanh ignores its electric-black eyes. The closet door makes a firm, solid thud. She yanks the blanket off the box to reveal a metal safe. My sister turns the dial left, then right, then left, and clicks the door open. "I figured out the combination. It's their anniversary date," she says.

Khanh shows me packets of banknotes and gold bars wrapped in plain tissue paper. "Take this to the window and look," she says, handing me a bar of pure yellow gold. Urged on by my sister, I inhale its metallic smell. "Better than money printed on paper," she explains.

I nod. My sister returns the notes and gold bars to their rightful place. When she shuts the door of the safe, it clicks securely into place.

Our father's military salary is meager. And so our mother's natural anxieties are aggravated by her mother's indelicate opinions about his modest beginnings. Having married him instead of someone with the possibility of a more prosperous future, she must be the one to rebuild the family's fortune. The only other option is to reclaim Grandmother's acres of lost land, flat stretches of inert green at a distance beyond our powers of intervention.

At times our mother is plagued with a quiet, slow-moving sense of unease, even in the midst of noise and commotion. Our father believes its source is news that came years before I was born, news that her father, a wealthy landowner, had been captured by the Vietcong and held in a secret hideout. Villagers friendly to the government had leaked news of his captivity and the general whereabouts of the secret hiding place. But no one knew the exact location. It was a place of phantom enemies, sniper fire, crushing vines, and overgrown jungle. A place without borders. Vietcong would attack then retreat, come then go. Our father went on a secret mission to try to rescue him but his helicopter was downed. He was badly wounded and the mission failed.

It was there, in that unknown place, that our grandfather was decapitated, his head sewn onto a pig's body staked by the trapdoor's entrance. A photograph of it was later delivered to our house, into our mother's hands. It was carefully framed to suggest the details of his death. There was a plastic pail. Knife against whetstone. Bloodied ropes. I wasn't there but I could almost hear the infernal howls of agony inflicted and prolonged. Imagination can be a terrible thing. Our mother has been haunted by what might have happened to her father. The only girl among a brood of three boys, she was the one most coddled by our grandfather. I can see her clearly, even years later, stilled by sorrow and anxiety.

Since our grandfather's death, chicken and ducks are no longer served in our household. I am told our Chinese grandmother once bought live chickens from the market and killed them right in the garden. That is how chicken is eaten in our country. But our mother cannot bear to hear the futile flapping of wings trying to escape death. She cannot allow our cook to wring a feathered neck or to cut it and let the blood drain over a bowl. Our cook was offended at first. He took it to mean that our mother lacked faith in his skills. Of course it had nothing to do with skepticism on our mother's part and everything to do with grief. For our mother grief can appear in midsentence and leave her altogether inconsolable. Even the most ordinary objects and events can bring about her grief. A hard, unpeeled green mango, the kind our grandfather liked to eat. A sickle moon on a starless night. But some things are certain to provoke it. Definitely a knife's blade against the neck.

And definitely Uncle Number Five's visits as well. Uncle Number Five is our mother's younger brother and he calls her Big Sister Number Four. His presence represents the complications of family and signals the confluence of loyalty and betrayal. For her, his impromptu appearances mean that the awful war that our father has to wade into every few weeks is indeed fully alive and capable of entering this sacred space of house and home. Uncle Number Five rarely arrives at our house except when it is dark and always for short, surreptitious visits. He always arrives unannounced, carrying with him the sediments and smells of faraway places. Of our mother's siblings, Uncle Number Five is the closest in age to our mother. She wants him to come home but dreads his return.

The photograph of our dead grandfather is becoming damaged, worn, sullied from repeated handling. Our mother does not know the exact date he died but, based on the timeline of his capture, she picked a day to commemorate the anniversary of his death. On that day, my sister and I are allowed to see the terrible picture of a half-pig, half-man figure. The clear lines and edges of objects, torso, animal—they have faded and become smudged. But in our mother's memory they have become all the more clear, as the days pass and she is able to add imagined details, telescopic and microscopic, to his final hours. She can see and hear what is right in the picture and what is not. Her protracted agony is, in that way, self-inflicted.

And so that is why our mother dreads Uncle Number Five's return. He evokes their common childhood as well as the war's unbearable brutality. He is a Vietcong and, hence, surrogate assassin. Youthful delinquency taken to the utmost extreme. Worse yet, although he is saddened and deeply affected, our uncle remains an unwavering Vietcong even after our grandfather's death. His explanation—if one could call it that, our mother says, sighing—is merely that evil itself is not the province of any one group, any particular ideology. This continued loyalty to the other side and the claim that the Vietcong is the true nationalist, the peasant hero fighting American imperialists, almost cleaves our family apart, although after so many years we have settled into long periods of acceptance and calm.

There will be trouble if it is discovered that our family harbors Uncle Number Five in our house. Our parents warn us not to say anything to anyone about his dark presence. There are to be no politics discussed when Uncle Number Five is in the house. Our father prefers to meditate alone in his private room. You can tell by his forced smiles that he struggles to accept Uncle Number Five for our mother's sake.

When they are together, our mother tells stories archived since their childhood and Uncle acquiesces in listening to them over and over, delighting her by adding his own dead-on details. "Do you remember when," Mother asks again and again. "Do you remember when we ate *com chay* and you broke your front tooth?" *Com chay* is what my sister and I covet as well. Rice left to simmer on low heat after the water has boiled off will form a charred crust at the bottom that sticks, carbonized, to the pot. Our Chinese grandmother would pry it out delicately with a spatula and it would emerge sanctified as a flat, crispy layer topped by a thin fluffy coat of soft cooked rice. The best finishing touch is a few spoonfuls of oil garnished with sautéed scallions and garlic.

Reminiscing, there is no judgment, no condemnation. History and familiarity usher in tenderness and expand our capacity for forgiveness. Sometimes our mother and uncle communicate with their eyes, as if the language of silence were the best evocation of their ties. Perhaps they fear that words could be misunderstood. Our mother clucks and pulls her little brother's ear lovingly as if to chastise him. They talk animatedly into the night, gesturing with their forks and glasses, winking at each other. Happy childhood stories are what they both choose to remember. The rest they forget.

Sometimes they have arguments, but those are tolerated because they are not centered on the war or the Vietcong. One such fight started when our uncle made a remark about our Chinese grandmother.

"Big Sister, how long will she stay?" our uncle whispered.

"Who?" our mother asked.

"The Chinese woman."

"The children love her. She's like family now."

Our uncle made an "um" sound, as if to fill in the ensuing silence with some sound.

"I'm only your younger brother," he said in a self-deprecating voice. "And you know I am not the type to hold anything against foreigners or even the Chinese."

It was then our mother's turn to make her particular "um" sound, demurely suggesting that she knew better but was too polite to say more. Our uncle continued, staring into our mother's eyes with a steely expression. "You should not trust these Chinese too much," he cautioned. He said "Chinese" in the tone of one trying to repress an unpleasantry. "The Chinese are seldom harmless. There is a reason why they are called the Jews of Asia. It's one thing that they are here and seem to have no interest in being one of us. It's another thing that they want to own and control everything. We should not put up with profiteers and speculators."

"She is from a family of poor shopkeepers in Tra Vinh. They are hardly profiteers. They have very little," our mother answered, arching her eyebrows for emphasis.

Uncle Number Five sighed. "You live in Cholon, which is practically a Chinese city. It has warped your perspective. As usual, you see only what is right before you. I'm talking about the big picture." He wore a steadfast look on his face and patted our heads. He was the one who had to keep in mind what was important, in the long run, for our sake.

"And I," our mother insisted, "prefer the little picture. We love *this* woman, who happens to be Chinese." She turned to us and smiled. "Do you love your Chinese grandmother?" she asked us. She scooped my sister into her arms and caressed her long hair with her palm. Khanh was all too happy to submit to the powers of our mother's attention.

"We love her," we answered in unison.

Our mother flashed a sharp, cutting look in our uncle's direction. She planted a loud, exaggerated kiss on Khanh's forehead. As if that were too meek a show of maternal love, she then pressed her face against my sister's hair and inhaled Khanh's very essence into the depths of her own being.

Presumably to cut off any further talk about the Chinese, our mother pushed a bowl of rice and a clay pot of braised fish toward Uncle. The fish had simmered all day on a low fire. Its sticky caramel-and-fish-sauce liquid was dark and russet-colored.

"Eat," she ordered, with both maternal velvetness and authority in her voice. He obeyed.

Even though our uncle mainly visits with us and our mother, he sometimes pays a short call to our father in his private room. Our mother agonizes over the possibility of friction between husband and brother. She finds the muffled whispers emanating from Father's study excruciating.

"But why, Mother?" Khanh asks. "Why is it not possible for Uncle and Father to just talk?"

Our mother shakes her head. "They are too serious to enjoy themselves bantering."

Uncle Number Five is rarely serious with us, however. He is prone to spontaneous laughter. Once he comes into our house, he enfolds us in his arms, large wings that spread like those of a white crane over our shadows. He accommodates and indulges. Galileo, our uncle proclaims, is not just a genius but a constellation of genius. The sun is but one in a river of stars. And the earth orbits around it. Imagine saying that then, he says, playing to my sister's ardor for all that is Galileo.

Once, during one of our uncle's many visits, my sister and I were playing hide-and-seek in an upstairs alcove around the corner from our father's room. Our game happened to coincide with Uncle's private meeting with our father. In retrospect, perhaps Khanh had timed it that way. From the perfect stillness, I could hear an occasional whisper, a stirring of words, but never enough to make out what was actually said. Underneath the muddle of a word here and another there, we could make out the tone, hushed yet heavy. A claustrophobic intimacy. I crouched behind a cluster of potted plants in the corner of a long hallway to wait for my sister to seek me out. I watched as she tiptoed toward the stairwell near the door. I wanted to run after the purple ribbon of her ponytail but instead froze in place. My sister crept across the tempting stretch of tiles and pressed her ear against the door to our father's room.

Khanh's eyes widened. After a few moments, my sister quickly slid away and ensconced herself next to the potted plant and me. The door opened and our uncle walked out. With a slight backward glance, he said, "Trust me," and again, "Trust me," before heading down the stairs. My sister and I held our breath. Our father was staring at us.

"What are you doing?" he said, uncharacteristically gruff.

"Nothing," I said, feigning innocence.

"Not you," our father said. "You," pointing his chin at Khanh.

Our father plucked Khanh up and held her by the waist. My sister dangled from his arm, fingers splayed as she struggled to escape. Not knowing what to do, I kept quiet, sifting through the bewildering lines of allegiance I felt toward each of them.

"No," my sister hollered in spittled fury. Our father put her down gently but firmly. I had rarely seen her this flushed, this petulant. I lingered on the edge of tears, watched as our father led her by the ear, even as she flailed, into his room. I could see the glare of her astonished eyes. The door closed with a bang. I suspected she was being punished but still I felt excluded and miniaturized. I hovered nearby, working up a heightened sense of danger and dreaming up ways to rescue her.

It was hours later when Father emerged with sister in hand for dinner.

That night before bed my sister and I engaged in our usual ritual of raiding the cupboard. I had become addicted to the rush of doing that which is forbidden. There, waiting for us, was a feast forged from leftovers. I imagined it before I even got to the cupboard—a lick of the tongue along the rim of a clay pot still filled with morsels of pork and caramel, more concentrated in sugar and salt after sitting in a dark cupboard than when first brewed on the stove. By midnight, the evening's intensely earthy flavors had commingled and deepened. We scraped the bottom of the pot and poured spoonfuls of scallions and garlic on rice left over from dinner. I loved the burned and slightly smoky sugar drippings sprinkled in fish sauce that still coated the cast iron pan. I ate while my sister stood watch by the slit of a half-opened door.

But I was in a hurry this time and my sister knew it. "Come," she said. We crept back upstairs to the sanctuary of our bedroom. Our Chinese grandmother was still asleep, head off the pillow, mouth wide open, her body tightly curled on the bed across from ours.

"So you want to know what happened?"

I eagerly nodded. "When I had my ear against the door, I heard Uncle Number Five tell Father in a very serious voice, 'I am warning you to be very careful, Anh Minh.'" My sister lowered her voice further. "I find that so strange, don't you?" she murmured. "Uncle said something else but I couldn't hear it. 'There's going to be a big . . .' or something like that."

We are always worried when our father goes on his missions and we always want him to be careful. It turned out that Uncle Number Five shared our feelings. I also knew that our father and Uncle Number Five were on opposite sides of the war. I edged closer to my sister's side.

"It's so . . . ominous," my sister whispered.

"Maybe Uncle is just concerned. He's our family."

"But why would Father be so upset that I overheard a family conversation, if that's all it is? He put me in a corner and made me kneel for an hour, facing the wall, as punishment." We were amid a sprawl of pillows and blankets but suddenly I felt vulnerable. My sister's anxiety became mine. Sensing my concern, Khanh affectionately rubbed my head. "Sh, sh, it's okay," she said. "Close your eyes."

Before falling asleep, we hooked and locked our index fingers into a double chain that was meant to signify inevitability and finality. My sister whispered that she would always protect me. We declared that we would always be each other's topmost rung on the tallest ladder. My sister reached over to run her fingers ever so lightly on my bare arms and face and then under my shirt, caressing, lingering on my belly and chest. Night after night, I fell asleep this way, with the delicate tickle of my sister's touch on my puckered skin. Through the flare and flicker of our common lives, through the disappointments and deceits our father warned us about, I knew we would always belong to each other.

# 4

# *Little Saigon*

## MR. MINH, 2006, 1945

It is always the tremors of home that are most deeply felt. Here in Virginia, I often find myself lying awake at night, watching the illuminated clock flip its numbers, seconds, minutes, hours. I lie in wait for the light of dawn, watching the present curve into a distant past. I lay my thoughts out in a straight line of reassuring sentences. "She loved me." "I did the best I could." My inner voice floats up to me like a filigree, soft and faint.

Once when I walked beside her on the edges of the green rice fields, my wife asked, "Who would you most like to be if you could be anyone you want in history?"

I had several apt answers but none that would qualify as one I wanted *most* to be. And so I asked her to reveal her choice instead.

"Chopin," she said without hesitation.

In the distance that now separates us, I can only wonder. Fate stares me straight in the eye as I lie here in bed, waiting to be with my wife again, somehow. I inhale deeply. I feel the full sensation of each breath as it enters and leaves my nostrils.

The sun glares, although a chill remains in the air. I can feel it in my bones. I touch the scar on my abdomen. My wife once loved it, the puckered tissue like a mother-of-pearl fixed in lacquer. She used to run her lips over the slight indentation of scooped-out flesh that stored a reservoir of war's pain.

I know the doctor's warning. My heart is weak. My hands and feet are swollen. There is fluid buildup in my lungs. I am supposed to be more active. Walk up and down the hall of the apartment building. I am torn between ignoring her advice and heeding it.

Mrs. An walks in. She has a key to our place and has full access to it. She is ever vigilant. She can sense distress and discomfort and does what she can to rectify things quickly. I think she is temperamentally suited to care for the elderly at the nursing home where she works. Although she is normally sturdy and vigorous, today her body is slumped under the weight of sweater and coat. She gives me a few pills, then closes the bottle and puts it away.

I hear breathing and movement on the oversized armchair across from my bed. Mrs. An takes my hand and in a voice of quiet authority says, "Mr. Minh, no one is there."

I nod and pretend to agree.

When Mrs. An leaves, I prop myself up and look. I can almost see a chest's rise and fall on the overstuffed chair. Black hair spills in a shiny monochrome onto the cushion. I know her back, its slender length, the deep groove of her spine. There is a hollowness by the smooth slopes of her shoulders. It always made an impression when she wore the *ao dai,* its sleek folds of fabric delicately sewn together to fit her slender figure. The *ao dai* is all about allusion and suggestion. The flare of its fabric, the provocative slit. That is why its movement in the wind is so beguiling.

I close my eyes. I see her as I first saw her, in soft lavender silk, in purple gloss. That day of our meeting, I glimpsed a sliver of bare midriff. The *ao dai*'s body-hugging top splits sensually, slightly above waist level. From the waist down, it flows daringly, the way rivers flow, with desire and intensity, into two streams that float over wide satin trousers. It reveals and conceals, like a confession.

Even after years of marriage and separation, my heart quickens. I am still undone by the sight of her. The first time we met, she spoke without once turning toward me. Why was I even in the same room with her? I, an impecunious wanderer passing through the land of the Mekong? Someone must have introduced us. We were seated at the same table. There was the porcelain face, almost masklike, unconquerable and untouched by the ravages of sun and weather. She glanced in my direction only in quick flashes, a detachment that I first took as arrogance and later as something more. I tucked the moment away, to be retrieved when I was alone.

As she dabbed her lips with a napkin, her manners revealed centuries of exquisitely honed breeding. Her *ao dai* had an open boatneck that dared to show cleavage. Around us, French was aggressively spoken, sometimes translated for my sake, sometimes not. At one point, she rolled her eyes at the excessive use of a foreign language by those wishing to signal their upper-class starchiness. She flashed an aristocratic sneer, turned away, and at that moment noticed my own similar reaction. Our eyes locked and we smiled at each other. She did not say a word to me and turned to speak to someone else. In French, presumably to keep me from understanding, she asked someone my name. A toast to celebrate some occasion was called. Her lips parted as she raised the glass to her mouth. Only when she was getting ready to leave did I make a point of saying a few words to her, first in Vietnamese, then in French.

I smiled. I bade her farewell. "Miss Quý," I said. "Je vais sans doute vous revoir." *Quý* pronounced with a rising tone means "precious." I had boldly declared I would see her again. My hand lightly touched her wrist. For a few seconds, she did not answer. Nor did she withdraw her hand. Her eyes gleamed. She turned her head, looked up at me, her chin jutting out in an apparent show of disapproval and defiance. Because she was sitting and I was standing, her neck arched scandalously. "One might have thought you would have spoken up *sooner*," she finally said, almost mockingly. *Sooner.* She stretched it out to produce a sense of stickiness or elongation in a word that ironically suggests the opposite— a shortening of time. She too was leaving. I kept my eyes fixed on her even as she turned her back and walked toward the door. I noted her excellent carriage. As she craned her neck toward me, raising her eyebrows to signal she knew I had been watching her, I gestured a farewell.

I had been wholly unprepared for anything as extreme as that first meeting.

When the day comes, and it will, when everything, even memory, of people, of earth and water, of history, has gone from me, this is what will remain—the dreaming colors of purple evenings, a lavender *ao dai* that flows this way and that, and a rice field that illumines earth and sky in a shimmer of liquid emerald.

Mrs. An has prepared me for an outing, made me presentable to the outside world. I am dressed in a collared shirt, a thick cardigan, and neatly pressed khaki pants. I give the belt a tug and notice that its buckle gleams. Footsteps come toward me. "Ba," a voice calls. I nod. I like the sound of the word. Father.

I lift my head and see her eyes fixed upon me. I look at the knot of tightly wound hair on my daughter's head. Mai is made up. Brown eye-liner, a dab of rouge, and glossy pink lipstick. She sports a buttoned white shirt and black trousers. She flashes me a big smile. "Are you okay, Ba?" I nod. She slips one arm under my shoulders and helps me to my wheel-chair. The act of bending down momentarily shifts her scarf, revealing a brilliant bruise on the side of her neck. I have not seen bruises on her for some time and their reappearance startles me. I know the hurt she carries but I work to keep what is so unsayable about it deep inside my own self.

"Little Bao," I say, a nickname I first used when she was a child. It means *little treasure* or *keepsake* when pronounced with a gentle dipping-rising tone. "Bảo," treasure, like her mother, "Quý," which means *precious* when spoken with an upward lilt. "My Bao Bao?" I repeat. Fear and tenderness fill my heart.

With a flicking motion, she waves the sound of this name away. For a moment she looks achingly little but that moment quickly dissipates. "No," she answers with polite firmness, or rather, exaggerated patience. With a shake of the head, she pivots into the present and in the process reverts to adulthood. Our eyes meet, unblinking. Her body stiffens and she diverts my attention with a series of coughs and a question. "Are you looking forward to our outing?" she asks in her usual obliging way. Her voice takes on a tone of utter normality.

"Yes, very much. It's a nice day to be out." I look at her with tender devotion. I know the gamut of her emotions—reserved and reticent, dutiful and steady, but also occasionally stormy.

As she wheels me through the kitchen and toward the front door, Mrs. An looks up from the kitchen table and calls out to her, "Don't forget to send money home for me."

"Aunt An, I will take care of it for you," Mai promises. "I've got the envelope you gave me." Mai fixes her scarf, flipping it nonchalantly around her neck in a manner meant to simulate carefree ordinariness.

Mrs. An nods. She walks briskly to my side and kneels down so her face is at the same level as mine. "How nice you look all put together, Mr. Minh. Have a good time out." Pointing to Mai, Mrs. An says, "She's going to help me with an errand while she's out. She's so skilled at these things." And she is.

Here in this external universe my daughter is clear-eyed and straight-backed. "Hullo," she answers when a young Korean man hauling a thirty-pound bag of jasmine long grain rice greets us in the ground-floor lobby. A young Indian boy fingers his collar and lapel, revs his motorcycle engine, and winks at his girlfriend to hop onto the back-seat. "Hi, Dinesh," Mai says breezily. Dinesh nods at Mai and gives me a deep bow the Vietnamese way—arms folded across chest, head down. I recognize Dinesh. Slicked-back hair. Copper-colored tone. He lives with his father and grandmother across from us. He and Mrs. An's son are best friends. Both are charmers.

Mai manages the car smoothly, neither too slow nor too fast, pilot-ing it along Sleepy Hollow Road and Leesburg Pike. When she makes a turn onto Wilson Boulevard, I see the dramatic Lion's Arch gate with sloping red roofs that marks the beginning of Little Saigon's Eden Cen-ter. Almost immediately I feel a sense of relief. Leaving behind the hooks and snares of life in this new country, we come here for the com-fort of pho noodle soup and other aromas from home. I can almost feel its recuperative powers, the full-throated pleasures promised by the simulation of familiar sights and sounds. Authenticity is not the point. Although the car windows are all the way up, I hear Vietnamese music coming from loudspeakers. A beguiling complexity of shops and res-taurants lies before us, promising an abundance of nostalgia. Even the food in all its varieties of northern, central, and southern fares, is inci-dental. For it is nostalgia, the vehement singularity of nostalgia, more than anything else, that brings us here.

Mai glides the car into a tight parking space. She unpacks the wheel-chair and positions it by the passenger's side. I am able to walk by myself, with the occasional help of a cane, but I indulge her insistence that I be wheeled instead. I pivot my bottom and sidle onto the wheelchair. The sun is high and the sky is clear, though the grounds are still wet. Mai rolls me toward several sidewalk carts piled with papayas and rambutans, each labeled with a placard that advertises the price accompanied by exclamation marks in bold black markers. ONLY ONE DOLLAR EACH!!!! and ONE DOLLAR A POUND!!!!

"Do you have longans?" Mai asks the vendor in a convent-schooled voice typical of well-bred Southerners. I note the ease with which she navigates the world.

"Yes. Only one shipment came in this morning. I have not even unpacked the carton," the vendor replies.

Mai beams. The longans are fat and plump. Swiftly, almost greedily, she picks out several bunches. She does not comparison shop nor does she haggle. "We'll get more than you need so you can share with Aunt An," she says, leaning close to me.

"Yes, isn't that lovely," I tell her. I am pleased.

"Goodness," Mai exclaims when a man accidentally elbows her in his haste to hand out leaflets. She protectively grips the handles on my wheelchair. The man smiles apologetically and asks if we would sign a petition protesting Hanoi's human rights violations. He points to a poster board covered with photographs of mock trials of dissidents. I see color pictures of priests and monks with duct tape over their mouths and military police at their side. A man in the role of judge holds a gavel, pointing it at the accused. Adrenaline charges through me. In this part of the parking lot people walk together in twos and threes, holding banners denouncing Hanoi's repression. There is no paucity of passion or goodwill here. Little Saigon needs the perpetual buzz of Vietnam, even if it is to condemn. Everything before me, Little Saigon itself, is part of war's debris. We are here to reminisce and sometimes to denounce. We are here to salvage something from the ruinous disorder of defeat.

Mai doesn't stop, although I would like her to so I could peruse the leaflets. She pushes my wheelchair, using it to part the crowd. The man persists, rushing ahead and stretching out his arm to slow us down. "Miss, excuse me," he says agreeably, while his fingers dig into her upper arm. "These are calamitous times in Vietnam. Please. We need your signature."

His persistence takes me by surprise. "You too," he says to me. The "you" he uses to address me is a respectful "you." I take the pen he gives me and sign a petition addressed to our congressman. Mai smiles and speaks in a breezy, conversational tone. "Yes, Uncle," she says. "I am sorry. I was rushing to a shop before the owner leaves for lunch." She signs the petition too.

A voice booms from the loudspeaker. There will be a demonstration at a neighborhood high school to protest plans to fly the current Vietnamese flag in the school's hallway on International Day. The demonstrators will insist that the flag of the now-defunct Republic of Vietnam be flown instead. "We did not flee the Communists in search of freedom only to be confronted with the Communist flag here," the voice continues. The Vietnamese in Virginia have become unapologetically political. I do not know when this happened. It was not so when we first arrived in 1975; we had worried more about how our children fared in school or whether we should relocate to warmer locales in California or Texas. The younger generation's interest in the political embattlements of Vietnam surprises me and sometimes fills me with renewed hope.

Mai has locked my wheelchair to keep it from rolling off. Nearby, she talks in a soft voice to the man with the loudspeaker. After a certain amount of back-and-forth, she says with finality, "It's a good idea but I won't be able to join you, unfortunately." Her face flushes pink. She fixes her scarf methodically and tightens the knot. She is eating a doughnut and sucking frosting from her thumb and finger. In the light her face reflects a startling childlike quality that endears. Still, I am watchful. My child has had her share of suffering and I can sense the fury and spit of darkness that still cling to her. I always understand more than she thinks.

"All right, we can go now," she says to me.

"How about we stop at the *banh mi* store?"

She looks at her watch, and then nods. "Okay, but we need to leave time for Aunt An's errand."

*Banh mi* is a Vietnamese sandwich that is a favorite of mine. We head toward a nearby bakery. There is the whole French baguette, perfectly crunchy, and the usual colorful spread of vegetable slaw—daikon radish and shredded carrot marinated in salt and vinegar. There is a variety of fillings to choose from—fatty roast pork, pâté, grilled chicken, meatballs, red pork, marinated tofu, and fried eggs. I opt for pâté and a profligate slather of aioli, topped with jalapeño peppers and cilantro sprigs. The bakery has a buy-four-get-one-free policy, which has attracted an ardent following. Sometimes the line is out the door, Mai tells me.

I chew slowly, savoring the sweetness of earthly comforts. Mai reaches over and dabs my mouth with a corner of the napkin. She does not eat lunch and so she waits patiently for me on a counter stool, her hands calmly folded across her lap. I offer her a bite of the sandwich but she recoils and utters a fastidious "No."

"Your sister would love this pickled daikon," I say to myself, though in a voice meant to be heard. A moment passes. I persist. "Has she visited you lately?" Mai briefly looks up, her face flushed. She opts instead to read a Vietnamese paper, occasionally pausing to relate a story to me.

She shows me a front-page picture of a demonstration in Little Saigon in Orange County, California. A video store owner had put up a poster of Ho Chi Minh on the store's window and refused to take it down despite widespread protest and condemnation. The gaunt, goat-bearded, tubercular face of the Communist leader has sparked scuffles outside the store. To compound matters, plastered next to his picture is an oversized Communist flag of the current regime. A higher-court judge will soon rule on whether the store owner is provoking the more than 300,000 Vietnamese Americans in the area with "fighting words," which would not qualify as constitutionally protected speech.

"Free speech," Mai says. A lower court had issued a restraining order for the poster's removal.

Whose? I want to ask. The insane Ho Chi Minh sympathizer who owns the store or the equally insane, easily goaded protestors whose intemperate display of political passion provoked sneers from Americans admonishing Little Saigon to get over it?

"Free speech," Mai repeats. I cannot tell if her voice lilts upward, like a question mark, or if it is flat, like a declaration. "Of course," I say, though I am hardly convinced. Still, I can see the relevant legal point, but less well than Mai. She has a law degree. She is trained to see both sides of everything. I suspect she is not wholly devoted to either side. Her back is straight, her demeanor proper. Outwardly she can always retain her poise. You have to, to function in this country.

She grows increasingly animated as she reads the story aloud to me. One hundred fifty police in riot gear. Fifteen thousand protestors spawning sympathy and solidarity protests some four hundred miles away in San Jose. Effigies of Ho Chi Minh hung from lampposts. Some slept outside the video store in homemade replicas of the cages used to house political prisoners in Vietnam. Two mock coffins, representing American and Vietnamese war dead, were paraded along the frothing perimeter of the parking lot. It did not help that Hanoi, through its Los Angeles consulate, called for the protection of the store owner's First Amendment rights. The crowd outside the video store surged with this news. Insults were screamed, vengeful chants lobbed. Punches were thrown, demonstrators hustled into custody. The police swung their black baton sticks. This is America? Little Saigon in Westminster, California, is on the verge of conflagration. I wince when she tells me about violence and arrests.

Mai glances at her watch. "All set?" she asks. I know we still have the important errand to do for Mrs. An.

About ten stores away is a shop that sells curios and Vietnamese CDs and DVDs. I have always liked its collection of pre-1975 music, the sort that follows the bent of one's soul and its deepest longings. The door releases a loud chime, announcing our entry. There is a familiar tune, plucked from a guitar. The proprietor stands up and greets me cheerfully. Her jaw drops in a feigned look of surprise. "How nice to see you out and about at last," she exclaims. I cannot recall her name but I know she is a friend of Mrs. An. "How are you?" the woman says, presumably to me, but Mai answers.

"Fine, fine," she says. And after a momentary pause, "Busy."

"Who isn't."

Mai nods. And then without any further preliminaries, she comes to the point. "Mrs. An wants to send money home to a relative."

"Oh, sure," she says comfortably. "How much?"

"Two thousand," Mai says.

After a long pause, the woman declares curtly, "We are all up next month for the *hui*. That includes Mrs. An."

*Hui*. Money club, I say to myself.

"Yes. I am sure she is aware of that," Mai replies. There is a quiet attentiveness in her demeanor, a defense of what she takes to be an implicit questioning of Mrs. An's reliability and her commitment to the *hui*. She turns toward me and fixes her scarf.

"Well, she will still be responsible for the usual one thousand," the woman insists. "If she sends two thousand home now, will she be able to make her one-thousand-dollar contribution?"

Mai nods. "Of course." The shop is sparse and the surrounding white walls make things stand out. Awkward moments can't be hidden or tucked away here.

The woman walks toward the cash register and flashes me a questioning look. I quickly nod, as if to back up Mai's assertion. Her eyes catch mine and soften. "I don't mean to offend. You understand that I'm the organizer of the *hui,* so if anything happens or someone defaults, I'm responsible," she says, defensively.

I am familiar enough with the *hui* to know that it is an informal rotating credit association. This one has ten members, including Mai, Mrs. An, and the shop owner. For years, Mai had made monthly deposits of the requisite amount, to be mutually determined by the members. How much the pot is worth depends on the members' collective decision. The *hui* meets monthly, like a book club or Weight Watchers. Each member deposits her dues once a month, which for some might be half of their monthly earnings. And everyone has a chance to draw from the *hui* pot once until the rotation is complete and a new *hui* rotation begins. The current pot is worth ten thousand dollars. It is supposed to rotate ten times, giving each member a chance to collect.

Mrs. An has apparently collected her ten thousand already. The defining feature of any *hui* is the commitment even of those who have drawn the entire amount from the pot to continue contributing until every member has had a chance to draw. Once the *hui* has rotated among all the members, a new cycle begins.

In this tightly knit community of Little Saigon, has anyone collected and then failed to contribute? No, even suggesting such a thing is ludicrous. So why is the woman concerned that Mrs. An will not make her payment?

The *hui* is a venerable arrangement of ingenuity and trust. When we first came in 1975, it was clear none of us would qualify for a bank loan. This is our way of saving and lending to one another. With the *hui*'s help, we became fluent navigators of the American landscape. Over the years, withdrawals from the *hui* have been used for so many purposes—college education, home renovation, weddings, funerals. It is the *hui* that allows people with no collateral or credit history to nurture their largest dreams and tenderest hopes, by leveraging the circuitry of friendship and social connections for financial purposes.

"With that no-good son of hers saddling her with his debt, of course sometimes we have to worry," the woman explains, squinting to gauge my reaction. "Even if she's been with the *hui* so many years."

This is all news to me. I am not aware of these details of Mrs. An's life.

"Of course I'm not telling you anything you don't already know. She's practically a member of your family. You must be so worried," the woman says, masquerading flagrant gossip as care and concern.

I keep my face neutral, showing no reaction. "There's no contract, nothing. Just trust and honor," she continues, half musing, half lecturing. "Don't you think that as organizer I am supposed to be vigilant?" she prompts, looking to me for affirmation.

The organizer is not reluctant to wield communal power to ensure compliance with *hui* rules. I sympathize with her but my allegiance is to Mrs. An. "You're right. Completely. But I'm sure Mrs. An is honorable," I say as casually as I can. Still, I am stupefied.

"Oh, sure, honor." The woman shrugs. "The *hui* is supposed to make you save, not spend." She purses her lip up, baring teeth. A gold crown flashes. "But too bad she's cursed with having a leech of a son. Her husband works two shifts and is never home. Mrs. An herself works nonstop. But no, not the boy. The boy drinks and lives a jolly life. Gambles. Wears fancy clothes. Hangs out with hustlers. There's only so much money she has to spread around. And she doesn't have the guts to cut him off. Everyone here knows it."

"Well, *I* don't know anything about it," Mai says.

"I *do* know something about it. Her business is my business. I am liable if she defaults." The woman shakes her head disapprovingly. Still, she accepts the envelope that Mai hands her. She counts out loud, one hundred, two hundred, until she gets to two thousand. I watch from the corner of my eye. I am relieved. I know it is important to Mrs. An that this transaction goes through. Wiring money through the bank or some other official channel leaves a record, and Mrs. An's relative does not want the authorities in Saigon to know she receives regular transfusions of cash from America.

"Just to be sure, let me write the address down again," Mai says. "When will the money arrive?"

The woman gives Mai a quick, penetrating look. "Tomorrow. Is that fast enough?"

Mai nods. "That is splendid," she says. "Thank you."

We call this flying money, an ancient remittance method resurrected to evade Hanoi's repression. This is how it works: Mai gives the woman cash, in dollars, plus commission. The woman calls up her counterpart in Vietnam. The counterpart delivers the equivalent amount of money in dong, using a more favorable exchange rate than the official rate, to the designated recipient, in this case, Mrs. An's sister, who is entitled to claim the money if she provides the correct password. There is no actual physical transfer of money. The woman and her counterpart will settle up later. Both are part of a subterranean import-export network. This proprietor in Virginia will sell goods to her counterpart in Saigon but under-invoice them by two thousand dollars to pay off the debt.

Given its need to control, Hanoi can't be too keen about flying money. But the American government would not appreciate such transactions either, I imagine, given their strict banking regulations, especially after September 11. The flying-money business is not shared with outsiders.

Mai buys a CD and hands it to me. "Here, Ba. It has those singers you like." It is a collection by an eclectic group of pre-1975-era singers, Thanh Thuy, Thanh Tuyen, Khanh Ly, and Thai Thanh. I am not particularly fond of the new crop of singers who mouth meaningless lyrics in mediocre voices camouflaged by a surfeit of synthesized drums, electric keyboards, guitars.

I smile broadly on my way out and wave my hand over my head to the proprietor, who returns my smile.

"Overbearing," Mai mutters.

"She's probably worried."

"So she gets to spread nasty rumors about people?"

It is true that what she said was unkind. "Is it only rumors?" I ask.

"People talk. You know that. What else is there to do in a tiny little community like this?"

As Mai pushes me from the warmth of the shop into the brisk air outside, I look around. The sun is out, its rays shining full tilt through the lot. Mai still has some more shopping to do. She will buy *pâtés chauds,* a French pastry filled with meat, light and flaky on the outside and crispy at the edges. There will be bags of *banh tieu,* a Vietnamese doughnut that is round, puffy, and slightly sweet with a hollow center. I admit it is not as rich or tasty as a Dunkin' Donut, but it tugs at an old longing. I remind her to get Mrs. An a bag of roasted watermelon seeds. My teeth are no longer strong enough but I love to watch others maneuver teeth and tongue just so to crack the shell and get at the flesh, which has a salty and slightly nutty taste.

There is activity all around: heels clicking on the pavement, doors opened and banged shut, muted laughter, children's cries, greetings. Through closed eyelids, I imagine Mrs. An's tightly rolled washcloth pressed against my forehead on cold nights, her hand cupped gently under my chin as she repositions my head on the pillow. And then I think of what the woman at the music store said about Mrs. An's son and wonder if Mrs. An has been quietly suffering. I see her face, her long hair pinned back by combs, the tilt of her head, the open gaze of her eyes when she enters my room, and a wing beat of sadness flutters and settles in my chest, refusing to let go.

The day is almost over. I enjoyed the outing with Mai but it has also worn me out. I experience fatigue as a creeping, physical sensation moving from one part of my body to the next until it takes over completely.

I turn my head toward the door. "Mrs. An, are you still here? I thought you would have gone home by now."

She grins. In the refracted light, her face shows lines of worry I hadn't noticed until now. I feel some responsibility to look at her carefully, to search for clues I might have missed.

"I popped home and put something in the oven. But I want to hear about your day and to thank you for the longans."

I nod. "We also sent your money home to your sister."

"She needed more than the usual amount this month because of the doctor. If I send a little bit each month, she can even live off the interest. Banks over there have been paying over twenty percent interest, can you imagine?"

"Isn't it already late?" I ask.

"Mr. Minh, it's only four in the afternoon. It gets dark early now, don't you know that?"

"Still. You should go home and rest," Mai interjects.

I don't know how long Mai has been in the room. "You're still here too?" I ask.

"I can stay for a little while," she says. "I don't have to be at work until later in the evening." My daughter sometimes takes the evening shift at the law firm, which goes from six P.M. to midnight. Her face beams with pure affability. I smile. The sun has gradually tucked itself behind the distant church steeple.

"Let him rest, okay?" Mrs. An tells Mai. "I'm going home to check on the roast chicken and then I'll return to give him his pills."

I hear the front door open and the sound of boots trudging down the hallway. "Leaving so early? No one has minded me one bit today," a woman's voice complains in the distinct accent and tone of someone from the Indian subcontinent. I recognize the voice of the crazy old woman from Bengal whose apartment is across from mine. Mrs. Amrita Amar. Her door is usually left open and the nickname Mai gave her when we first moved in has stuck. "A Door Ajar." She thinks she is already in a nursing home and has been abandoned by her family. Mrs. An's voice replies, "No one is leaving you. Your son is coming home at six. Your grandson Dinesh only went out for dinner with his girlfriend." "Liar. Liar." A wheelchair shoots swiftly across the floor and a door slams shut.

I struggle to find a comfortable position on the bed. Although I am thin—I have never been fat, but thin is something new—I do not feel agile or light. My ankles are puffed out. Mai murmurs something as she hesitates by the foot of the bed. I turn my gaze to the ceiling, letting my eyes drift in the sea of white above.

I can hear the deep murmur of voices outside the window where people congregate to smoke. But the ocean beyond continues to beckon through the fog and eclipse of a life from long ago. A high wind blows through the room. I struggle to draw breath. I have been given morphine to open my veins. Red pills to make my heart strong. White pills to drain excess fluid from saturated tissues. I lie back, my body drugged and duped.

I know life can only be, should only be, lived in the present.

I squeeze my eyes shut, then open them. Mrs. An has come back. She catches me looking at the empty space near the overstuffed arm-chair.

"Are you looking for something?" she asks.

I hesitate.

"There's no one there," Mrs. An says authoritatively.

"Yesterday there was," I answer. The stolen image of a woman's body, quietly curled into itself, a soft lavender petal, lingers. I close, then open my eyes to discover it has vacated.

She looks at me and shakes her head. I hear a sigh.

How did I get here? From my house in Vietnam to this apartment complex in America? she wants to know.

I am willing to tell her the essential story that has been all too easily mistold.

I watch her dark, flickering eyes, and the face that turns toward me, waiting.

"I will tell you," I whisper. "Soon."

# 5

## *Salted Lemonade*

### MAI, 1965

Mick Jagger growls against a raucous surge of drums and electric guitars. This is music, the kind that imparts unlimited possibilities. That is why it is addictive. My sister and I move to its beat, knowing that boys and girls all over Saigon move with us.

While the music blares, we take turns walking on James Baker's back. James has blond hair that sparkles against the sun's glare. His neck turns red, not a honeyed brown, when exposed to the searing heat. James swears he has never in his life had his back walked on. I find that hard to believe. Certainly it is a back to be admired. I can feel with the balls of my feet the two solid mounds of muscle rising under the swell of his shoulders. Carried on this back alone is a mass of muscles, regal and arrogant.

A back walk is an uncommonly effective form of massage. When I make my way up the plates of his back and press my heels against a stray knot, James lets out a long, low moan. Sometimes it is a painful grunt—"Ouch!"—which James tells us is what Americans say when they feel pain. My sister and I laugh. What a funny word, we both think. I wonder why people from different countries produce different sounds of hurt, when what comes out of our mouths when pain is inflicted is purely reflexive. Why would pain, universally felt, not have its own universal expression? When James asks us what the Vietnamese yell out when we are hurt, we teach him the word, *oui yaaah.* It is more open-mouthed, more emotional. "Oui yaaah," he would mutter, and chuckle when I step on the knots along the length of his back.

I practice my elementary English with him when I make my way up and down his back. "Where are you from?" I ask in as casual a tone as I can. We watch an array of American shows on the English language channel—*The Wild Wild West, The Beverly Hillbillies,* and *Combat!, Combat!* being our father's favorite. I try to emulate the breezy American way of talking.

Sometimes he answers in Vietnamese. "I am from New York."

"Where in New York?" I ask, although my sister and I already know the answer. We are learning the rudiments of conversational English.

"Long Island," he says, making a motion with his hands to describe something long and narrow. Switching to English, he explains, "I grew up on a farm. Faaarm."

"Moo, moo. Oink, oink?" I say.

"No, no. Po-ta-toes. Long Island potatoes are famous."

Sometimes my sister and I sing a song about a boy who herds buffaloes that roam the green rice fields. Sometimes James tells us about a man named Old MacDonald who has a farm. We love the sound he makes. "Ee ai ee ai oh." He points to the tip of Long Island, the southern fork, where the family farm is located. He points to the ocean he crossed to get to Vietnam. Ocean travel, even if it is by air, on a plane flying over an ocean far below, changes a person, James says. "If you ever travel across an ocean, you will see what I mean," he says.

We have never crossed an ocean. According to James, it makes some people crazy or afraid and others curious. He has become curious, longing to learn our cries, our language. James doesn't speak our language fluently, by any means, but he does speak it enthusiastically. He has managed to make himself understood, in an elementary way, in our mother tongue. My sister considers it a most impressive feat. James has command of quite an inventory of practical, serviceable words. In addition, he has mastered our six tones, though not in the back-and-forth necessary for smooth conversation. In conversation, his Vietnamese becomes atonal. But in controlled moments of recitation, James enthralls us with his skill, unleashing the six tones of the word *ma,* which, depending on how it is uttered—with a level pitch, a steep rise, a soft curve or a sharp one, a slow fall, a deep drop—may mean *ghost, mother, graveyard, horse, but,* or *seedling.* When he finishes, he takes a bow and we applaud, especially when he makes a mistake.

One day I am home early. Our mother is at the table in the upstairs dining area with Uncle Number Two. He is not my uncle by blood, unlike Uncle Number Five. But as my father's close friend, he is entitled to this honorific. We call him by a word that signifies not just a familial relationship to our father—a brother—but also an elevated status: our father's elder brother.

Our mother loves the foods of many countries but especially those of France. The pastries on the table are from the famous Givral bakery, consecrated by the hands of a master chef trained in a top restaurant on the Left Bank in Paris. I smell the creamy, ambrosial scent of whipped butter and sugar; fresh croissants, perhaps; the slightly smoky caramelized sweetness of crème brûlée; the sustained bitterness of dark chocolate, undoubtedly of the famous Menier brand, simmering in a fondue bowl. There is an extravagance of flavors delicately balanced on one silver tray—even an imaginary taste would do.

I sneak up the stairs and stand at the top of the staircase, peering through the screen door, coveting the feast before my eyes. The top of my head barely touches the bottom of the meshed screen, but if I stand on my toes, I am able to see the full span of our dining area.

Uncle Number Two is sitting across the table from our mother. I am able to hear bits and pieces of this and that if I press my ear to the screen. They are so immersed in conversation that our mother has not detected my presence.

Her finger traces the contours of an earthenware pitcher—lemonade, perhaps? Lemons, unripe enough to be sour but not acidic, a quick slash into its flesh so the pulp can be squeezed, releasing the tartness of the juices as well as the faint bitterness of the rind. What makes our lemonade intriguing to foreigners, according to our mother, is the addition of salt to temper the sourness, rather than sugar. Indeed, sour and sweet balance each other out, as in sweet and sour soup or sweet and sour pork. But a grain of salt can just as well take the edge off the tang of lemon, though in an irresistible, unexpected way, like a sinuous bend in an otherwise straight road. Our mother might have prepared this lemonade with seltzer water to give it an additional kick—a surprise on the tip of the tongue.

They are mostly silent. Sometimes their eyes meet but other times they look away from each other. Because nothing seems to be happening, I skip down the steps and head toward the kitchen. My arms are outstretched like the wings of a plane as I glide here and there.

"Go to the garden if you want to play," our Chinese grandmother says, waving me away. She is lying on the hammock, swinging back and forth, watching me. "This is not a suitable place to run around."

I am almost seven and I do not like to be ordered around. When I balk, she explains that our mother is right up the stairs and that she has asked not to be disturbed.

Immediately that piques my interest. I sneak back up the stairs and peek through the screen door. Uncle Number Two is now pacing back and forth, his steps measured and methodical, then frenzied and disturbed. Occasionally he stops in front of our mother and settles his gaze upon her face. He gives her rueful looks, then averts his eyes. She is still seated, her elbows on our dining table, her back erect.

Neither Uncle Number Two nor our mother has touched the tray of pastries or the pitcher of lemonade. With labored breath, he continues pacing, occasionally flinging his arms in the air. When he speaks, he starts out in a normal voice and then inevitably lowers it. He looks at her intently as if awaiting her cue. Mother smooths the front of her dress, traces its open neckline. She ignores him and then finally she shakes her head. Again and again. No, emphatically no. He nods his head vigorously, yes, yes, as if to deflect Mother's denials. I am jolted into attentiveness. "General so-and-so," he says. I cannot hear the name. But I hear a lot of "why's" and "why not's." The words mean nothing to me but their force captivates me. Mother continues to shake her head, a few pins come loose, and a river of thick black hair tumbles down the back of her dress. She opens her palm and runs her fingers through the shimmering current of black before twisting it once again into a knot. Finally, as if exasperated, she allows her voice to rise to an audible pitch. I laugh to myself as she dramatically pleads, *"Troi dat oi."* "Heaven, earth. Please listen." Mother continues, "Let it be, Phong. Leave it alone." "No. No," he mutters. She is firm, although Uncle Number Two is on his knees next to her.

"Phong, please," she says. "Please don't go on. Please, Theo," she switches, perhaps as a last resort, to the endearing nickname I have heard our parents call him. *Theo* means "scar." I see a thick cross-stitch of scar tissue along the length of his jaw. I was once frightened of its angry, purplish hue. Our mother must have sensed my fear and will sometimes invoke his name as a deterrent against possible bad behavior from me. She tells me he has many scars, a fact that makes me all the more wary of him.

A few moments pass and then I see tears. A grown-up man is crying. He stands perfectly still, his eyes fixed on our mother's face. He leans toward her, murmurs something, and her face turns even more remote as she looks away.

I am startled by the sound of a door opening on the other side of the dining room. It is too early in the day for our father to be coming home. It is, instead, Uncle Number Five. I can tell it is he even though he sports dark sunglasses and a scraggly beard, perhaps as a disguise. He is surprised to see the dining room occupied at this time of day. He lets out a small cough. Our mother appears equally surprised, and looks at her watch as if he were appearing at a time other than the one agreed upon. Uncle Number Two turns and stops conclusively in his tracks, his eyes fixed on Uncle Number Five before directing his hard, probing stare elsewhere. His face registers but a minimal shift in expression. Our mother leans in the direction of Uncle Number Five, hesitates, then smiles nervously. "Oh," she says. Both Uncle Number Two and Uncle Number Five nod almost simultaneously. Uncle Number Two is no longer animated or sad, only impassive. To fill in the silence, our mother says, "This is my brother," pointing to Uncle Number Five with her chin, and, "This is an old friend," pointing to Uncle Number Two. They both nod, asking no question of or about each other.

I can see that our mother is nervous. Uncle Number Five does not usually visit us in the middle of the day. He is a family secret; his subterranean Vietcong connections can be revealed to no one, not even close family friends.

Our mother takes her brother's hand and squeezes it, but in an archly restrained way. Uncle Number Two smiles. Uncle Number Five's face sours. He understands our mother's signal. "I am sorry to interrupt.

It's a glorious afternoon so I'll be out in the garden," he says. Our mother does not try to detain him. Instead she quickly nods. "Good idea."

Our mother exhales, visibly relieved that the two men are no longer in the same room. Soon after Uncle Number Five leaves, Uncle Number Two looks at his watch and says something to Mother in a much lowered voice. His face reverts to a more gentle version of itself as he removes a pack of cigarettes from his shirt pocket. He holds a cigarette in his mouth and its filter tip dangles from his lips. Our mother leans forward to help. She strikes a match and brings the flame to the cigarette. He puffs on it several times until its tip glows.

I am relieved, as if a weight has been lifted. Of course, it may very well be that Uncle Number Two's presence itself is heavy. He is an important man, especially for our family. He and our father used to fight side by side. Our mother says he once saved our father's life when father was betrayed by those within our very own armed forces. We owe him devotion, kindliness; in other words, a debt too great to be discharged, one we have to wear on our bodies. *Mang on* indeed—"to wear a debt," to be cloaked in its immaculate and terrible beauty.

Our mother too wears this debt. I hear her say "Anh Theo" as he stands up to leave. *Anh* is a word with dual meanings. It is both intimate and familiar, a word to call an older brother or someone who is respected and beloved. It is also a word to call a lover, and of course when our mother uses it with our father, that is what she means.

That evening, my sister and I rush to unlace our father's enormous boots upon his return home. Normally we would give him an ice-cold fresh coconut with a straw sticking out of a hole. The outer husks would be hacked away, leaving behind a smoothly shaven cream-colored shell. Once our father sips all the juices, we would scoop the sweet white flesh from the shell with a long spoon and slurp it with giddy delight. But that night, I suggest that our father drink lemonade instead. Salted lemonade, I add, as an extra temptation.

"Where did you get it?" Father asks.

"Mother made it for Uncle Number Two," I say.

"Oh? He was here? Good. Very good."

"And Uncle Number Five too."

Our father stiffens. His mood darkens. "Really? What a day. And where is he now, your uncle Number Five?"

"Sleeping in the secret room."

When our father remarks that lemonade made for Uncle Number Two must be special indeed, I quickly run downstairs to fetch him a glass. That night I am awakened by the sounds of a long, drawn-out fight that simmers with whispers, a slow exhalation that eventually collapses into deep silence. For once in my recollection their love fails to comfort. I cannot hear everything they say, but I can feel the stings and smarts that are left behind. I can taste the bitterness on the very tips of their tongues. In a slow but sharp and sibilant tone, our father says Uncle Number Two's name. "Phong," he snorts, and the name comes flying out, expectorated. Our mother uses Uncle Number Two's nickname "Theo" instead, perhaps to dilute the tension. Finally I hear them each, with caution and purposefulness, fail to answer the other's allegations.

It is a familiar silence. It is the same silence that has slipped into that private space between them with increasing frequency.

I bury my face against my sister's chest and breathe her in. I tell her what I saw. "Mother and Uncle Number Two were upset with each other," I say.

"He comes too often when Father isn't here," my sister adds.

"Isn't Uncle Number Two our father's best friend?" I ask.

"Still. Father doesn't like him."

"He was sad. He had tears in his eyes. He was the one who did most of the talking."

"What did Mother do while he talked?" my sister asks.

"She sat there and didn't say much. She kept shaking her head," I answer.

My sister interlocks her fingers with mine. "He must have asked her for something and she said no to it, don't you think?"

I hasten to nod in agreement. "She *should* say no to his question. Whatever it is."

My sister caresses my hair, runs her fingers down my back, and tells me there is nothing to fear. She reassures me that people can argue without doing damage to their relationship. All I have to do is close my eyes and my fears will evaporate. I obey and, remarkably, in no time at all I fall asleep.

# 6

# *Karma*

## MR. MINH, 2006, 1963

Ever since my outing to Little Saigon a few weeks back, I have been worried about Mrs. An. I am not sure how to bring up the subject of her son. The very fact that I stumbled upon this knowledge feels intrusive. Is there a newly exhibited nervousness in her? Of course she cannot give up on him. What parent would? His sorrows are also hers. I understand parental compulsion—the need to protect your child.

Mrs. An squeezes past a group of people standing in the doorway of the crazy old woman across the hall from my apartment. I can tell they are medical personnel. White smocks. Plastic badges. Mrs. Amar has been ill. Extended family and other visitors stand in the hall.

"So many people here this morning," I say to Mrs. An. I glance at her. She pushes the curtains back to let the early morning light filter through my room.

"Old Mrs. Amar had another heart attack," Mrs. An tells me. The plain gold band on her finger catches the bright sunlight. "She probably should be in a nursing home where she can be watched over all the time. *My* nursing home, in fact. It's only five blocks away. The family could walk there to visit." I nod. I ask her how she is. "Oh, fine," she says affably. She runs her fingers through my hair and gives it a quick brush. A pleasing but faint aroma of fried dough emanates from her. I know what it is instantly—*banh cam,* a sweet treat of rice dough wrapped around a soft filling of mung bean paste. The pastry is rolled into a small ball, coated with roasted sesame seeds, then fried to crisp perfection.

"I'll bring some in for you." She winks at me.

"And some for me?" Mai interjects. As is so often the case, she makes her entrance without a sound and her appearance is a surprise.

Mrs. An smiles. It is not a simple task to make *banh cam.* Mung beans have to be soaked overnight and then steamed and refrigerated. The dough has to be made and rolled into balls to fry. "What is the occasion?" I ask.

"I am practicing. It's been a while so I want to be familiar with the recipe before I make it for the *hui* meal next week."

"The *hui*?" I ask, feigning ignorance as a way of prompting her. Mai flashes me a dismal look.

"Yes, the *hui*," Mrs. An says agreeably. "It's at Mrs. Chi's house. She is the organizer. And of course, as you know, we have a potluck feast on the evening of every draw."

"Your *banh cam* will be perfect for the occasion," Mai says. She nods her head slowly to emphasize the point. "I'll be bringing a platter of catfish and squid stir-fried in garlic sauce."

"Is the *hui* pot big?" I venture to ask. Sometimes lives join together, like connective tissue. Mine is knitted with not just Mai's but also Mrs. An's, like tender filaments that form a web.

Mai gives her eyes an exaggerated roll. She knows I am rummaging for information.

"Well, it is a bigger *hui* than I am used to. We're both in it," she says, pointing to Mai. "You know that, don't you?" She double-checks because my memory has been hazy lately. "The good thing about a big pot is you get to take out more money. The bad thing about a big pot is you have to put in more money," she says, shrugging.

I hear Mai's heels clattering from the doorway toward my bed. "I should help you start the day," she says, adding an emphatic nod meant to end my conversation with Mrs. An.

Naturally I comply.

"You have a busy day ahead, Aunt An. I can stay here and help," Mai volunteers. "I don't have to be at work until much later."

"Oh?" Mrs. An asks. Neither Mrs. An nor I know much about her other life, the one spent at work.

"I have several half-days this week," Mai explains. "I won't leave home until two in the afternoon."

Mrs. An touches Mai's shoulder appreciatively. It is only for one moment, but Mai leans her cheek ever so lightly, resting it tenderly against Mrs. An's hand. For a moment, the gesture evokes such a sense of familiarity in me that I have to close my eyes. It is as if we had departed irrevocably into a past when Mai was enclosed in the certainty of her mother's love and motherly tenderness was both lovingly expected and lovingly offered. I hear Mai's sigh, like an exhalation of deep longing. She is side by side with Mrs. An, as she was once side by side with her mother. It gives me a tingling, vertiginous sensation. There is Quy, reading to our daughters, one *Arabian Nights* tale after another. Quickly, I try to come up with a reason to keep Mrs. An in the room, to prolong a moment that contains a strain of something precious, like something we once had but have now misplaced. But I can't. Instead, I stay inside my own retrograde terror, my own quiet hope.

Mrs. An says, "I'll not be long. I'll take a long lunch break today and come back to have a sit-down snack with you before you leave."

"Wonderful, wonderful. I'll prepare your favorite tea," Mai says in a firm, amplified voice. "The three of us can share a pot of jasmine." Something passes over her, like a bright shining light, and I too, for once, feel an accompanying surge of happiness.

After Mrs. An leaves, I want to ask Mai, "How are you managing, my little daughter?" But I stay in the zone of the circumspect. I do not say anything, and neither does she. Mai clears the night table to make room for the teapot and cups. She folds paper napkins into halves and arranges them in a neat stack. Watermelon seeds stored in the credenza are placed in a little dish. "There," she says, admiring their red-dye sheen.

"The *hui* is a delicate subject," she tells me in a hushed voice.

"She didn't seem uncomfortable," I say.

Mai turns palpably inward. She suggests we take a walk to the community center a few blocks away and so we do, I with my walker and she by my side as we slowly make our way through the long hallway, down the elevator to the ground floor, and then across several blocks of cement sidewalks.

The place is officially known as a community center but it essentially functions as a senior center. It is an L-shaped space with a desultory dab of color on the walls and a sprawl of plump leather couches and tables arranged in a cozy configuration meant to convey amiability. There is a low-hanging chandelier with lightbulbs shaped like candle flames. A large Rajasthani painting of a lord on an elephant and several black lacquered hangings adorn the walls. I pity this room, its low-ceilinged sadness, its dimpled walls. The shag rug is plaid and dark, presumably to better hide spills and stains. Pool tables gather dust on their red felt tops. A solitary piano stands in the corner, and sometimes on the weekends, the sound of piano notes, thin and tinny, can be heard like sulky ripples of an incoming tide.

Mai points me to an oversized armchair by the aluminum casement window, in what functions as a makeshift periodicals nook. I go straight for the many Vietnamese language newspapers published in northern Virginia and Orange County, California. Mai bunches her coat and wedges it behind my back for support.

I catch myself in the mirrored surface of the window, reflecting back the image, blanched by the sunlight, of an old man with hollow cheeks and inky black eyes. I stare, feeling a growing affinity with the reflection that is strangely mine and not mine, like an injured aura that I faintly recognize but cannot place. Silhouettes of bare maples and pines glow against the filmy surface. A solitary bird taps at the window. In this tranquilized quietness, the space between the present and the past narrows to nothing. I recall old, tropical smells of lavender petals. I recall the susurration of crickets in the evening hours in Cholon. Lights float. Sound floats. Time slips from me, and passes through the recess and protrusion of old memories.

I remember a time when windows opened to sad Saigon evenings the color of purple. "Purple Evening" was the name of a famous song. The radio was on. A singer extended her arms, clasped her breasts, and yearned for her lover. My wife hummed along. The murmur of prayers from the streets could be heard and almost felt, like a vibration. Monks passed by as the blue of day made its slow metamorphosis into the purple of night.

I remember the evening's dark aubergine cast that hung in the gloaming of a departing day. I remember it; I ask for it now, to see, to smell, to be enveloped in its painterly moodiness.

We are forewarned that love might not last. We go through life trying to prepare ourselves for this possibility. But the deeper tragedy, I think now, might be when love refuses to fade.

What is it about that day that makes my bones ache even now when I remember it?

We were lounging on a sandstone terrace, my wife and I. It was before our life faltered, before the tipping point that sent her on that long descent into her own deep and unreachable self. Sparrows tipped their wings, black flourishes arcing in unison and taking flight. Mai, so little then, asked if the birds were returning home from school and if they were carrying their school bags as they spilled from closed doors into the open courtyard. Her older sister laughed at her question. My wife also laughed, and then reached up to sweep a few wayward strands of hair from her high, curved forehead. I moved closer to her and held her slippered feet in my hand. I was constitutionally bound to her and her alone. Breathing deeply, I smelled it, this exquisite, riveting scent of a purple evening. It could not be more thick, more distinct, than it was.

I am jolted out of my reminiscence by the sound of bickering in front of the television. A voice says, "Stop. Maybe you can keep it here?" I recognize the Puerto Rican accent of a frequent visitor to the center, an elderly man. "Shhh. Shut *up*." Clutching the remote control, a heavyset, plump-cheeked woman stares down her challenger. "I am in charge," she says with pugilistic satisfaction.

I want to avoid the sad parade of aggression and victory, of submission and defeat. I tell Mai I want to go home. Back at the apartment, Mai asks if I want a shave. Yes. My daughter coddles her father. I love most the luxurious shave she gives me when she has time. She lays out the accoutrements elaborately, as if they were decorative ornaments. There is the bottle of shaving cream, the razor, the gel. She places my head on the pillow, which she has covered with a towel. She moistens my cheeks and jowls and squirts the cream. I puff my cheeks. I feel short, slow strokes that start on the sides of my face. After it is all finished, I feel her hand lathering a moisturizing cream on my skin.

She turns the television on.

"Do we have any doughnuts left?" I ask.

"Yes, you can have one *banh tieu* and longans," she says. "Just one *banh tieu,* please. It's deep-fried."

The *banh tieu* is tightly wrapped in tinfoil and served to me on a plate.

She rifles through her handbag as I use the remote control to surf the channels. After a few minutes, she dumps the contents of the bag onto the floor. "Where can it be?" she asks herself. She is crouched down, searching.

"Your cell phone?" I omit the "again."

"No, my appointment book," she says, all the while continuing a frantic search around the room. "Where did I put it?" She frowns. She is flustered. She is silent for a moment but resumes her monologue. "Where *is* it?" She moves about the room—an elongated blur of agitated motion, opening drawers and lifting cushions.

Turning toward me, she says, as if to explain, "Aunt An should be coming back any minute. But I'm not sure if I have an appointment that will require me to leave soon."

The rummaging continues. It is an obsession. Maintaining order is a priority and disorder creates hand-wringing anxiety. One slip and the whole constellation of fabricated order collapses. She looks at her watch. "It's been more than an hour," she says, ruffled. "Where is Aunt An?"

"She will be here soon, Mai," I say. I watch her face for a cue, an admonitory look, perhaps. I remember the partially concealed purple bruise on her neck. I have seen this before, the spinning exhaustion, the convolution and repetition that continue until the misplaced item, however inconsequential, can be found. And when it is not, there is no release. I know there is a name for her condition in this country. Something about compulsions and obsessions.

"When did I see it last?" Mai mutters, her brows knit in concentration. "I have a feeling I've got an appointment in D.C., so if she isn't here soon, I'll have to leave." I can almost see, right there before my eyes, the little four-year-old girl who sulked when sent to bed against her will.

I know I am unable to reach her. I have no choice but to keep out of it. Even a suggestion meant to be helpful can exacerbate the situation and contribute to further slippage. I will myself into therapeutic stillness. Mai's tireless energy, not yet slapping or hissing, can be a precursor to something scarier. I cannot always tell what will provoke. Sometimes I suspect she has the ability to read my mind.

A sound at the door tips her into eagerness. She looks up brightly, expecting Mrs. An. Instead it is someone slipping a pizza delivery advertisement under the door. A few minutes later, the phone rings. I tell Mai it is Mrs. An. "She is running late. Only a few minutes, though. They're short-staffed and she's been called over to help out in another building."

Suddenly, there is a crash. My heart leaps inside my chest. A calamitous look flashes across Mai's face. She has departed irrevocably into a new, inaccessible realm. There is the rage, like a snapped-off end that bleeds after its vital part has been severed. *Boom, boom.* The sound of a broom whacked against the walls. I freeze. She has turned stormy. She is an exclamation mark that screams out at you. I am unsure. Is she reachable, is she not?

"Child, what are you upset about?"

Mai looks at me. I call her by the diminutive name I made up for her when she was little. "Little Bao. Bao Bao," I call. Using that name has the effect of miniaturizing and containing the problem. "My little treasure," I say, doing my best to reach out to her. Bảo for *treasure.* "Bao," I keep calling, blood rushing to my head. But when I accidentally pronounce "Bao" with a sharp dip and rise in tone, it means *storm,* not *treasure* or *keepsake.* Bão. Threatening weather.

A rattling sound reverberates in my chest. I cough into a tissue and see that a frothy sputum colors it red. "Bao," I say, making sure to use the right tone.

She cuts me short. "No. No." She wields the broom like a weapon and sweeps it across the air. *Whack. Whack.* I have seen worse. I cringe. There is the sound of wood striking tile.

"Go," she screams. "No, no." She is striking at the open space, then turning her fists against her chest. I hear the dull *thwock* of knuckles against ribs, against the hard plates of bones, against the soft flesh of abdomen and breasts. I see the fingers scurry to her throat and maintain a halting grip on the neck tissue. I cringe again.

"Don't talk to me," she says. She states her terms: to be left alone. Her voice comes from a place outside herself.

"Please stop," I plead. I want to meet her eyes dead-on. I want to avert my gaze. I cannot tell how far this will go. Is it madness, spirit possession, voodoo? I keep my mind from scuttling backward into loss. But I cannot command memory; mine comes and goes, skips in and out of focus. I feel its clumsy flutter. An intensifying force presses and squeezes inside my head.

There is a loud smash. Glass tumbles from my television screen, scattering. The set sizzles. The teapot and cups are flung against the floor. She lets out soft, fitful cries. I extend my arm toward her and try to move in her direction. But my spine is curved, my legs weak. Even on the best of days, I can get out of bed only with help.

I hear mumbling and babbling, and then as quickly as it all began, the storm vanishes. The ungovernable impulses have subsided. Without a word, Mai gathers the shards and slivers of glass and sweeps them into the trash bin.

Moments pass. Mai stands still, surveying the damage and her efforts at restoring order. The charcoal black of her eyes deepen. A voice can be heard at the front door. "Is everything all right?" The voice turns frantic.

Mrs. An has materialized—thank goodness—and is helping Mai as if she knows exactly what to do. Her very presence seems to have a calming effect. She positions Mai by a chair and tells her to sit. She treats Mai as if she were a compliant child, and suddenly, she is. Mrs. An squats and bends and curves her body under the bed to sweep up the smallest remnants of glass. Her hair sparks with static electricity. She puts my bed into a reclined position and wraps a blanket around me. Mai is mollified but remains distant. Soon enough she looks at her watch and announces that she must go to work. At the door, she turns back and says something. Perhaps they are words of farewell. I can't hear but I give her a nod of assurance. There is a smile and a wave and then she is gone. My hands shake even as I push them under the weight of my legs. Mrs. An approaches my bedside and offers me a reassuring pat on the shoulder. We both know my daughter is not quite right, and her departure following what happened has a diminishing effect on both of us.

I wonder if Mai will be able to drive in the crush of ice. The temperature has plummeted below freezing. A slow-moving cold seeps through the cracks in the flashing windowpanes, bringing with it an undercurrent of reproach.

I reach for the music player on my bedside and press a button. A rhapsodically beautiful sound emerges. Of course it was composed by Chopin, the man who wrote poems for the piano. I lie back and consecrate myself in this place, inside this life I never bargained for.

A few hours later, Mai returns and shares news of the events in Little Saigon in Orange County, California. The infamous Ho Chi Minh poster has stayed glued to the window inside the store, protected by the Constitution of the United States. For weeks, county police were dispatched to guard the store. But in a startling turn of events, according to the press release issued by the office of the district attorney, the store owner will be taken into custody to begin serving a ninety-day jail term. Mai recites the newspaper story matter-of-factly. Mrs. An gloats. "See? You cannot provoke people who risked everything by thrusting a photo of that face in front of them. It's downright nasty."

"Actually, he's been thrown in jail for bootlegging," Mai corrects. She reads out loud the details provided by the paper. "'Tran attracted the attention of police when he was escorted into his store because an angry mob had gathered outside to protest a poster of Ho Chi Minh that hung inside. Officers noticed what appeared to be numerous bootleg videotapes on the shelves of his store. Upon serving a warrant, they found 147 videocassette recorders inside the store, which Tran was using as part of his piracy operation. More than seventeen thousand videos had been fraudulently reproduced.'

"See? It has nothing to do with the poster," Mai adds, arching her brows.

Mrs. An looks doubtful but, after a momentary pause, smiles knowingly. "This country has its own way of meting out payback."

"Well, the man has the right to express his views and the protestors have the right to express their views. Peacefully." Mai continues, "Listen to this. The landlord has moved to revoke his lease. It's very interesting."

"Oh?" I say.

"Yes. The landlord claims that he is violating his lease by creating a public nuisance. The protests are disrupting other businesses in the mall."

Mrs. An flicks her hand in the air, as if to swat away explanations provisioned by mere legal facts. "Karma," she says, laughing. She looks at Mai and me. Satisfied that she is not contradicted, she turns to more mundane matters. "I can make extra *banh cam* for both of you. I'm cooking tonight. For real. Not practice anymore."

Mai murmurs appreciation. "I would love that, Aunt An," she says, lowering her eyes and dropping her voice amiably. "I like my subscription meals a lot, but of course nothing compares to your food."

"You are lucky to have secured a *com thang* provider. There's been such a government crackdown in the past few years because of health-code issues." Mrs. An sighs. "Fewer and fewer cooks dare operate from their kitchens."

Mai agrees. "Mine operates below the radar. They don't take any new clients. Very traditional but even they have cut down. Home deliveries only three times a week. All the other days, it's pickup," she says before going to her bedroom down the hall to retrieve something.

As Mrs. An gets ready to leave, I say, awkwardly, "You should make some extra for your son."

"My son?" Mrs. An says, surprised. Her shoulders tense slightly.

"How is he?" I ask.

"Oh, fine, fine," she answers, too rapidly. And then, after a momentary pause, adds, "Why do you ask?"

I am tempted to break from the complicity of silence and stop tip-toeing around a matter that all of Little Saigon in this corner of Virginia supposedly knows. I tell myself to choose the direct approach.

But what I say is "No reason in particular." I take a deep breath and continue, "I was thinking of him, that's all. We saw Dinesh the other day and I thought of him."

"The two of them hustled for months trying to make their new business work."

"Oh?"

"Nothing big. Doing odd jobs. Handyman work. Neither of them knows how to do anything so they had to find workers. I warned them it was not the right business for them. It's not so easy to find good, reliable handymen. The young Vietnamese and Indian boys nowadays can't do anything."

"How is he now?" I ask.

"He has good and bad days," she says. "But he's a very good father to his child," she adds without hesitation. "When he is at his best behavior."

"When is that?" I ask, perhaps lurching too presumptuously into candor.

I sense hesitation. A shadow crosses her face even as she grudgingly smiles. "Oh, most of the time. But as I said, he has bad days. I try to help him when I can." She pinches her mouth shut.

"He is old enough now to be helping you, don't you think?" I say tentatively.

Mrs. An says in a pained voice, "He does."

I look at her and I see everything: A parent's guilt and disappointment. A parent's despair. Despair when you see what is happening to your child and you are powerless to help.

I feel the onset of a dark mood and so I smile obligingly. I revert to "Yes, I'm sure he does." I notice that the veins on her neck are thick.

"He is a help. In his *own* way." Mrs. An smiles wanly, although her voice seems to carry a bite of belligerence and her eyes glow a hard, unblinking gleam. Fatigue shows in her slumped posture.

She remains near the door, ready to depart. A slight quiver runs through her upper body. I prepare myself to turn away, feigning unawareness. I let my face drift until I see Mai return, her arms wrapped around Mrs. An. Their voices drop and together they stroll out, taking their conjoined but melancholic silhouettes to the dappled pathway outside where Mai likes to take her solitary walks.

Mrs. An returns from the parking lot, pulls a chair to the side of my bed, and perches on the edge. The unease between us a few moments before has dissipated. The evening is our time together. Mrs. An and I will take our usual loping stride into the past, with its pockmarks and scars and occasional shimmery shadows.

"I've made tea," she says, pointing to the pot at my bedside table.

"Yes, thank you."

She sits next to the bed and takes my hand. "I am thinking of taking a trip back to Vietnam one day." She laughs lightly. "I say it's to visit family still there. But I think if I'm really honest, it's just to indulge myself. To feel what it's like to return to a place you've remembered and imagined for almost thirty years."

I nod. "Where would you go?"

"Oh, to places I frequented when I was young. Markets, school. The street corner in Saigon where I stood as a thirteen-year-old girl when I got my first pair of dress shoes. Strange. Such a long time ago."

"Not really. At our age, *my* age, those years feel just like the present. Or yesterday." I understand the geographical pull.

Mrs. An, slumped in her seat, leans closer toward me. "Do you ever want to go back? You carry so many memories in you and I know you can't let them go. Or they don't let you go."

I nod. It's true I have memories. But I will not ever go back to Vietnam.

Mrs. An must have read my mind. "Of course. I see why you wouldn't want to return."

I look at her. My heart unfolds. I do want to return, but not by going there. I drift instead, softly but surely, back to the event that changed our lives.

In November 1963, a few days after the coup, I stood on the edge of the Saigon River, watching its reflections of the city's darting lights. Water has a natural pull for all of us who yearn for contemplation. I saw the seamless beauty in its expanse, severe and stark, yet seemingly eternal and infinite, visible to everything, yet revealing nothing.

Before me was the dock of Bach Dang Harbor. It was late evening and a low-hanging mist had settled above the rippled water. I was grateful for the mist. I took it as an offering, an invitation to be consoled. Through the haze, things were simply less rigid, and even the hardness and sharpness of life could appear a bit less severe, less savage, more bearable. I stood still and watched a cloud shroud the city in a veil of vapors and steam, muting its edges. As the sun fell and then disappeared over the horizon, darkness itself began to deepen, pulling colors out of objects, shielding a wounded landscape from its own melancholy. Imagine it as an open palm shading a pair of tired eyes from the sun's glare.

Of course it was bound to happen again. I expected it. I saw the preparation on my way to work. The cook was busily washing, paring, slicing. A meal was being assembled and it was not for the family alone. Morning glory leaves, a type of water spinach, were soaked in a shallow basin of water, their stalks thick and lush. They were known to be temperamental. Too much heat and they quickly wilt. Too little heat and they defiantly resist, making themselves fibrous and rough against the tongue. But in the right hands, they could be exquisite; peasant food elevated into the realm of the sublime. No sauce, nothing aggressive to meddle with the revelation of their natural taste. Morning glory needed nothing more than a dash of salt, a pinch of chopped garlic, and a few drops of oil into a flashing-hot pan sizzling on a coal-fired stove.

Phong loved it that way. That was how I knew he would be coming to dinner, as if to say that politics can bash open empires, or divide and partition countries, along this and that parallel line, but it cannot do the same to friends. We had joined the army at the same time, gone to the same training school, endured similar heartaches. To celebrate our enduring friendship, we were going to have a meal *en famille*. Of course, the coup did change everything, even a long-standing friendship. But I understood that part of the change meant the need to act as if nothing had been altered. Or if it had, presumably only for the better, as a friendship was supposed to be better after one friend saved another friend's life.

Phong and his wife had arrived before I got home. The voice of Thai Thanh, despairing and tender, soared through the speakers, mourning love's end. The songs we Vietnamese loved were about farewell and separation, spiraling sadness, rainy nights, solitary souls. Even before the calamity of country lost, sorrow was deeply carved and deeply felt in Vietnam's soul. A strange grief had long ago roped itself around the country's neck, leaving deep, indelible marks on its flesh.

Phong lit a cigarette and blew smoke rings that sulked and wafted to the ceiling. His cigarette tip glowed. I noticed he had a cigarette holder. This was new. The gold flashed ostentatiously. He downed one drink, then another. My wife stood across from him, her arm looped around the slender waist of Thu, Phong's wife and her good friend of many years. There was the aroma of salt-and-pepper crabs tossed on a hot wok. There was the rise and fall of their voices.

I saw that he had undergone a fleshly change. Or was it something else? He pivoted with the confidence of somebody who had already done what was almost impossible. He had stood on a perilous ledge, yet here we were, together, as the long hot day began to slide into the cool twilight. For the sake of our friendship, it could be managed. He would be welcomed in my house and exercise the prerogative of one who had saved his friend's life. And we in turn would admire this generosity. We would take our time to eat, to talk. I saw Phong's smile reflected in the mirror. This was how the four of us had shared our evenings for years. Food, smiles, conversation, music.

But somewhere between the first smile and the ones that followed, there was, I was sure, something different. The corners and curves of the lips. The slow drawl. The liquor confidently downed with a gulp and an accompanying flamboyant snap of the head. More amorphously, there was just something about him that shied from being named or understood and hence gave me pause.

He was now a man rapt with desire, acutely aware of his own body. He sat at the table, straight-backed. I scarcely remembered how he was before, a man free of affectation.

After dinner we drank coffee in the sitting area. We each had our own percolator. I knew how he liked his. Hot water brewed over espresso, coarsely ground with a dash of chicory. And a slow burning drip over a cup of condensed milk. A record was placed on the player and a soprano unleashed one of the most amazing trills I had ever heard, sustained at the highest register. My wife was drawn to operas and I too was beginning to see their appeal. It mattered not that we didn't understand the words. That only made the beauty of *Tosca* all the more mysterious, the tragedy all the more tragic. This Italian opera resonated with us Vietnamese because Tosca's story was not much different from our beloved *Tale of Kieu.*

"Listen," Phong said abruptly. "I should say this at least once. I am sorry I couldn't tell you about the plans beforehand."

Thu and my wife stopped their own conversation nearby. My wife's eyes flashed, as if to remind me, again, that Phong had saved my life.

I nodded and gave his shoulder a quick, friendly pat. He reciprocated with a decorous smile.

"No one really thought you would be willing to be part of the plan and so there was no point approaching you."

"Why were you all so sure, Phong?"

"You're an innocent," he said. "Nobody believed you'd switch sides." His voice trailed off.

Inwardly I cringed but outwardly I maintained a façade of imperturbable calm. Quy sidled close to me and gave my shoulder a squeeze.

"I know, I do know, Phong, that I would have been taken out and shot if it weren't for you." I realized I hadn't said thank you to him. But among friends and family, that would have been extraneous. We were, supposedly, part of each other. The heart does not thank the arm for shielding it from a blow.

Phong hadn't finished unburdening himself. "I wanted to tell you but everything had to be tightly sealed. On General Minh's order."

"General Minh. Yes, of course. Your mentor."

Phong detected my sarcasm and arched an eyebrow. "The plan could be revealed only to those we were sure about. The stakes were too high." He was laying claim to virtue. "I couldn't tell anyone, not even you. We had to succeed especially with the Americans . . ." He stopped and looked at me calmly. His face shined, a switchblade sprung from its sheath.

For an instant, something raged inside me, a quickening of blood that surged right through to my heart. He had merely articulated that which I already knew. "You will curse the day you did what you did, Phong. You think you're using the Americans but they are using you. They are the ones with the guns and the money."

I stopped speaking. I saw his pupils, like a pair of cat's eyes that glowed macabrely in the dark. They stared through me. "And *you* will curse the day you did *nothing*." He clicked with his tongue as he flashed a smirk from a corner of his mouth. "We are not dealing with *poetry* here but with the life of the country," he said with mock but slurred gentleness, taunting my love of poetry, and French poetry no less. The eyebrows were kept stiffly raised. The knife in his hand cut through the hard rind of a mangosteen. "We as nationalists had to do *something*."

A rancorous silence settled over us. I kept my eyes fixed and stared unblinkingly. I struggled for a levelheaded understanding of his actions but his noble rhetoric could scarcely explain the president's murder.

Thu put a restraining hand on her husband's arm. My wife too gave him an appeasing smile. Phong eased up, his body relaxing backward against the chair. He made his voice soft. "Sometimes, the right path might seem wrong at first. Give it some time."

"Or the wrong path might seem right," I said.

I couldn't help myself. No one knew everything and he, of all people, shouldn't act as if he did. It had been reported that the CIA had given the plotters forty-two thousand dollars in financial support on the morning of the coup. There was no doubt President Kennedy himself had supported it. I wanted to ask him about all that—the false beginning of their so-called revolution.

But our wives moved to defuse the situation and we returned to the drudgery of small talk. Yes, no, maybe. Even Phong put forth a less belligerent countenance. For the sake of my wife and the peace, I stopped fueling the fire. And so the evening meandered along, until it came to what seemed like a natural, unadorned ending. Thu was half-asleep. My wife's shadow was thrown against the wall like a beautiful silhouette softly aglow. We took turns pouring the last bottle of wine.

"Let's drink to the success of our revolution. Surely you wish us—the country—success, even if you don't approve of our act," he said.

I chose my words carefully. "Even when one knows better, even when the naked facts point to a different conclusion, one may nonetheless hold hope in reserve."

"Exactly," he said with a stray smile. "Exactly."

Phong finished his last cigarette, crushing it against the curve of the ashtray. Smoke leveled above us. He carefully put his gold cigarette holder in his pocket and began to gather his things. I cleared some of the clutter. As I moved from the back end of the room toward the door, barely lit by the muted streetlamps, I saw a shadow of a hand on the small of my wife's back.

I did not miss the moment, as unspectacular as it appeared. Immediately after, I disbelieved. Indeed, in retrospect, through all of our years together, I was certain I had myself touched more of his wife than the small of her back. Had I not carried the whole of her body and run with it straight into the formidable surf of a Vung Tau beach? It was this and many other such incidents that had sanctified our friendship. Still, that single miniature gesture stayed with me. A hand on the small of a back.

I hurried Phong and Thu out the door. My wife quickly went upstairs to get ready for bed. "I'm going up first," she said. Her voice was strangely ruminative. Left alone, I mulled over the evening. The silhouette of the body, the slip of a hand, the ghost of a good-bye, mere shadows, like the loose weave of threadbare cotton against the tropical heat. Fires had been started by this very mix of ingredients.

I lay awake most of the night. Ordinarily I was not the sort of man who was plagued by the details of human interaction. I understood innocence and coincidence. Still, I began methodically to revise what I had seen.

But I lacked the nerve for concentration. In the end, all I had was doubt. But doubt is not proof. It is a grain of nothingness yet it has the power to unravel everything. I did not ask my wife, "What really happened, darling?" I resolved to treat everything that had transpired as commonplace; an occasion worthy of no remark. I reprogrammed my memory and shut my eyes.

I reached over and pulled her close to me, pressing myself against her back. There was the line I loved running down her spine, the gully that dipped slightly below the skin's surface. I ran my finger inside its groove. I thought only this: It would all begin and end with her and me, with us.

A day passed, then another. The country was subjected to the undisciplined, hopscotched wishes of one leader after another. Against a landscape of continuing anxiety and intrigue—there were rumors of more coups in the making—General Minh allowed me to regain my old position, despite my refusal to join him and his conspirators. Or perhaps it was precisely because of it. I had refused to join their coup. They could count on me to reject future coups.

As our stricken city tried to recover, we too went through the motions, with measured steps, my wife and I, to create normalcy with the new army. We continued to attend casual gatherings at the Officers' Club. In the early evenings, drinks were served; music still played in the background. Officers congregated in different areas. I could see a gathering of junta leaders around the bar, edgily celebrating the new trappings of authority. Phong mingled about, his cap at a jaunty angle, his dark aviator glasses hiding his eyes. He gave Quy and me a long, slow nod and raised his wineglass, as if to toast us. Around him were others who had cooperated and succeeded in quietly getting troops into Saigon to unseat President Diem.

My wife and I had danced there many times. A melody, deep and grainy, leaked from the stereo and hung its naked sorrow in the room. We danced together to the deep foghorn sound of the saxophone. I could feel tight knots lodged along the flanks of her back. I scanned the room. I was the only officer not part of the coup.

Despite the appearance of cordiality, November had changed everything. The coup had aged me beyond my years. Picture an army, its spirit strong, its conscience clean. In the immediate aftermath of the coup, the military was suddenly transformed; no, more precisely, transmogrified. Political ambition reared its ugly head. High-ranking junta generals shamelessly distributed medals and insignias to lower-ranked officers. New loyalties needed to be cultivated.

Every day, in the half-light of early morning and the darkness of late evening, I sealed myself inside the monastic tranquillity of my study. Things were changing. A new culture of coups d'état had seeped into our land and continued to lurk below the surface. The narrative that defined the armed forces, honor and esprit de corps, was being whittled away as the country succumbed to the spit and sibilance of intrigue.

That was how the story of our country's transformation began. By coups and the fear of more coups, by the glide of power on the glistening belly of a snake.

And then the Americans arrived.

It was still November 1963 and the air was perfumed with lavender blooms. I remained inside myself, in my own sphere, even as I moved among the junta generals. At night, soldiers at the Presidential Palace walked its black, scarred grounds. In the fading light, they lit flares, stood guard, hunched on parapets reinforced with sandbags, and stared through their rifles' telescopes. Others monitored signals over their shortwave radios. They were not watching for enemy movement. Instead they were fully concentrated on friendly troops that might have turned, might be turning, suddenly, ruthlessly, against the junta generals. They stayed in the darkness and stood with binoculars aimed toward the horizon, scrutinizing all that came within their sights.

For after that day in November, mine was a country dislodged and lost, a country immersed in false rumors. Having come into power by violence, its leaders feared they too would be removed by violence.

Coup plotters feared those they had overthrown would be plotting their own resurrection. It was simply a matter of karma, after all, and the genetic instructions it carries. This possibility had to be acknowledged, the sowing and tilling of karma. How could they prevent others from doing to them what they had done to others? This became the single, overriding concern of the junta generals. Despite the place and the time, despite an enemy buildup right outside, and even within, the city's gates, despite the movement of North Vietnamese divisions and regiments down the Ho Chi Minh Trail, what they were most sensitive to, most obsessed with, was detecting signs of betrayal: an unbecoming swagger, a cocked eyebrow, a forehead crease on an otherwise unfurrowed face. Anything that signaled inner deceit or discontent. Anything that suggested brooding or the artificial absence of it. Power had to be edgily guarded.

Of course the ghosts of the dead president and his brother continued to haunt the junta generals. Both had been buried secretly within the headquarters of the Armed Forces General Staff, in a field near a gully choked with dandelions and other weeds. The brothers were denied burial in a public cemetery to prevent their deaths from acquiring either historic or lurid significance. In no way would current events be allowed to converge around their tombs.

Later, when the city could not shake itself free of conjectures and rumors, the generals abruptly had the brothers' bodies exhumed and buried in two unmarked graves in a municipal cemetery in Saigon.

In a country such as Vietnam, we understand karma. We have all traveled its path, felt its key points, feared its whiplash. We go to great lengths to slip free of the psychological convolutions that come from fearing its wrath.

Twenty days after the Vietnamese president and his brother were killed in Saigon, the president of the United States was assassinated in Dallas. I could only imagine what the generals of the coup must have felt when they heard the news. Only a Vietnamese would shudder at the sequence of these two events and understand their spine-clicking effect.

After President Diem's death, the Americans arrived in increasing numbers. In 1960, there were only advisers. Then in 1961, 3,000 troops.

After President Diem's death, 184,000 troops. The number would reach beyond 500,000 in the years to come.

We beckoned and at the same time withdrew inside ourselves. We didn't want them to come but we needed them to stay.

They promised safety. With the Communists barreling down on us, entrenched along our borders, we were wide-eyed and howling to be saved. At the time, salvation could not have appeared to us in a more beautiful form than a flag with stars and stripes. We gazed into the horizon and placed our trust in their imminent arrival.

And the Americans entered our story not fully knowing what awaited them.

My friendship with Phong began when the Americans first arrived as advisers. Phong and I met at the Cap Saint Jacques officer candidate school. Training was extensive, accelerated. The world's intellectuals were throwing around words like *anti-imperialism* and *decolonization,* but we believed colonialism was less of a threat than Communism. The age of empires was in its twilight and it was the romantic promise of Communism that tantalized. In the North, nationalist leaders were being eliminated by Ho Chi Minh's followers in the most brutal ways imaginable. Some had been bound hand and foot and thrown into rivers. Others had been buried alive. We knew what Communism was really like.

I remembered our beginning well. It was 1955. Phong stood in front of the commander's desk listening to his orders. I was the junior officer. I accompanied them into another room where the map of our country was hanging. "The country is in a crisis," the commander said. "There is no money to pay the troops and the Americans are set on remaking the armed forces."

We understood the Americans were in a hurry. Unlike the French, they were not here to impart a superior civilization. That would have required courtship, even seduction.

The French had just left, taking with them a force of more than 200,000. To fill this vacuum and to defend the country from the North and the Vietcong, we needed a national army of around 200,000. Phong and I were assigned the task of authoring a report analyzing the state of the Vietnamese National Army. The South was trying furiously to fashion a non-Communist nationalist solution. After many months of investigation and study, Phong and I recommended that four infantry divisions, the Sixth, Eleventh, Twenty-first, and Thirty-first, be activated to fill the void.

With laconic detachment, the U.S. Military Assistance Advisory Group opposed our plan. The advisers determined that we should have an armed force of no more than 100,000, just enough to defeat a Vietcong insurgency, not repel a North Vietnamese attack. In the case of external attack by the North, we had only to obstruct their assault and wait for the United States to come to our assistance.

"We'd be committed to you through SEATO," one adviser promised. The Southeast Asia Treaty Organization would obligate the United States to come to our rescue. Even so, Phong and I both found it impossible to bear. We were two hotheads. We were still young, but quickly gaining experience and wisdom.

"What an absurd notion that is," I later said to my commander.

The commander pursed his lips and nodded. "True. But draw up a plan of discharge as soon as possible," he ordered.

Phong and I consoled each other as we performed the executioner's task of dismembering our beloved armed forces. I was distressed by the wanton elimination of names from the military roster. With a measure of clinical certainty, our superiors reminded us of the targeted goals, the deadlines, and the conditions attached to American funding. Phong was less sentimental than I was. For him, speed and determination were necessities. A quick slash across the throat. By the end of the day, he showed me the stacks of discharge papers he had signed and processed.

Sometimes I met the men who would soon be let go. I saw how they were stilled by disappointment, how sorrow showed in their faces and gathered around their mouths. Often a group would huddle on a dirt patch, passing one another a cigarette. At different hours of the day I came by and watched them from around the corner. I didn't smoke but I took a few puffs just to be among them. I listened to them and could think only about our national failings. Like a penitent at the temple's gate, my face burned with shame. Afterward, Phong and I would get ourselves to a corner café and order two big bowls of pho. To console me, Phong would pluck slices of well-done brisket, flank, and tendon from his bowl and put them in mine. I did not protest his gesture.

Our friendship deepened as we dragged ourselves to street-corner saloons where men gathered to drink, eat, and talk. We felt the loss more than we expected. The liquor would pull us out of our gray mood. The bar we frequented was owned by a wiry man, Mr. Manh, a friend of Phong's father from the North. Though it was no more than a humble storefront cursed with the appearance of imminent collapse, its tables were always filled. Around us, men congregated, grazed on tidbits of appetizers—the exotic and the mundane commingling on a serving plate. The proprietor cracked open a slab of ice with a cleaver and dropped a few slivers into our glasses. We washed down marbled beef and sinewy gizzards with gulps of alcohol. We sat on wooden stools and drank beer and rice wine with raw abandon. Jars of bone-colored homemade liquors lined a wooden shelf nailed against a plywood scrap wall. Lizards, goat testicles, gecko, gutted and washed and marinated in rice wine and herbs, lurked at the bottom of the jars. Mr. Manh elbowed Phong and me, nudging us to taste such and such a concoction to boost our libido, to ward off colds, to rejuvenate our souls and spirits. "Available by the glass or jar," he'd say, grinning. Embers glowed as rows of dried squid crackled and popped on the grill. We usually nibbled on barbecued beef and boiled peanuts, sautéed liver, ears of baby corn coated in a mixture of oil and scallions.

Occasionally we indulged in a shot of snake liquor, the meanest drink in the country. I did not like it but Phong was a Northerner and snake liquor is a northern drink. His clan fled south in 1954 when the Communists consolidated the North. I wanted to indulge his nostalgia for his hometown, Le Mat, a village just north of Hanoi. Northerners go to Le Mat to drink snake whiskey. The Saigon version was less pungent but it would have to do.

When Phong gave him the signal, Mr. Manh brought two glasses to our table, each half-filled with high-octane rice whiskey. The old man's agility astounded me. I watched as he pinned a cobra to the ground, then grabbed its head from behind as his assistant gripped the tail, stretching out its body to leave the underbelly exposed. Mr. Manh swabbed the snake's chin with alcohol, then, with a perfectly coordinated set of movements and a warrior's calmness of mind, sliced open the sterilized area with a short blade. He deftly inserted a finger inside the cut, located the heart, and severed the main artery, allowing the blood to drain into our whiskey glasses. A pulsating, glassy heart, a potent aphrodisiac, was dropped into a shot glass. Phong tossed his head back and gulped the whiskey now swirling with bright red blood down his throat, heart and all.

Mr. Manh opened another slit farther down the snake's belly. He shoved several fingers into the slit, removed a gallbladder, and emptied the bile into my glass, turning it a luminous green. Removing the canvas sheath from a different knife, Mr. Manh then proceeded to slice off the cobra's hooded head, tossing the body to a cook in the open-air kitchen. The meat was grilled, the skin battered and deep-fried, and the bones dropped into a pot for soup. We munched on snake meat in all its varieties: snake and leek soup, rice porridge with snake, snakeskin chips. Exhorted to take a swig, I obliged and shot the whiskey down my throat. A sharp rawness caught. My nose burned. Phong hooted, hooked his arm around my neck, then pounded my back for show. I sat ungracefully, my skin prickled with gooseflesh.

Night after night we drank. We nursed our bouts of loneliness together, allowed ourselves the freedom to be unburdened. Phong confided his fears and then washed them away with a bottle of "33" beer or Johnnie Walker. He bemoaned the paucity of love. He had not yet met Thu. He was not yet married. He feared he would be left behind. Would the possibility of love ever edge its way into his life? Would he meander through life untouched by it, the extravagant, ravenous kind that altered and transformed your shape? He was looking to me for reassurance that he too would be seized by the phenomenon of love, as I already knew that sort of devotion. I had just recently met my wife.

"You're done with loneliness for good," he said to me.

I didn't know how to respond. Agreeing smacked of self-congratulatory arrogance. And disagreeing seemed disloyal to Quy.

The realization that what I had was what Phong most wished for both comforted and filled me with unease. What if that which I loved most disappeared one day? How could I, or anyone, ever recover from that sort of loss?

How did I know, he asked, if I would love her forever. I did not answer the question. I did not know how I knew. I just did.

"Of course," he said, his voice lowered. "It is easy for you. You have *her*." His face glowed with heat. He turned against the open window, hands cupped, striking the wheel of his lighter.

Later, he paused after a drink and asked, "What are *you* most worried about?" as he leaned back and sucked a cigarette, blowing wisps of smoke that hung in the still air. From the ceiling, a naked bulb dangled from a bare wire, its bright light magnifying the sorrow on his face. He cupped his hand over his eyes to shield them from the glare.

I had not expected such a question. Even a hypothetical heartache was too stinging to contemplate. I revealed a different sort of anxiety to him, confiding my fear that we would be ill-equipped to push back a Communist assault. While my reply was an avoidance of his question, it was not quite a lie. Not at all, as things turned out.

Before President Diem was assassinated, he had looked for other allies. Malaysia sent armored cars, jeeps, and shotguns to help us equip the Civil Guards. Sir Robert Thompson arrived in Saigon from England, bringing with him stacks of notes, sheaves of maps, and the accumulated experience and wisdom that came from years of directing Britain's spectacularly successful antiguerrilla campaign in Malaysia. An ordnance delegation was dispatched to Japan to seek engineering help. President Diem wanted us to be beholden to no one. What happened to our plans? I couldn't say. After that day in November, the country drifted. All backup plans were sidetracked.

Even so, we did ask questions. Once in a while we pushed for a different strategy.

Aware of our own backwardness, we asked for modern weapons. Again, I was in charge of the paperwork, which gave me an understanding, even then, of the swift diminishment of possibilities for us. My windowless office was hot. Sweat dripped down my back. Every day I sat facing the wall, trying to cut to the fundamentals that would convince the Americans to rethink their strategy. I worked late into the evening, engaged in the niggling business of negotiating for this and that weapon. There were moments when I could concoct hope and make myself believe in a jazzed-up version of American benevolence. Surely they would see things our way once they read my reports. I felt the sharp, muttering crack of the typewriter's keys as a great source of hope. Each key was capable of producing a crisp, satisfied sound. Problem was juxtaposed against solution. We had been given M1 rifles that were no match against the Soviet AK-47, so we petitioned for the powerful M16. In a soldier's hand, the M16 automatic was capable of firing between seven hundred and one thousand rounds per minute. We wanted F-4 Phantom fighter-bombers and F-104 fighter jets to counteract the advanced MiG-21s the Soviets gave the North Vietnamese. I typed out our case, paragraph by paragraph.

My reports became repetitive. In the end, we received no offensive weapons from the Americans. With a sympathetic half-smile, an American adviser said to me, "That's what the U.S. Air Force is for if you need us." He was not the one making the decision. The rules of this war would be decided elsewhere.

For our war, the Americans had designed a purely defensive strategy, dragging everything out for years until they were fed up with it and with us. There would be fierce, vicious, and deadly battles and then there would be time in between, a moody, fractured time that we wistfully hoped could be translated into surrender on the part of the enemy. Year after year, the war was fought in this intense, prolonged twilight of surges and shudders.

Soon it was obvious to us that real power lay in the North Vietnamese Army, not the Vietcong insurgents fighting in the South. At one of the many meetings held at military headquarters, General Khanh, the general who ousted the mutinous junta, solemnly pushed his chair back, stood up, and pointed to the map of Vietnam on the wall. The energy in the room was dense, tightly coiled. General Khanh took up his position on the right side of the map. I watched the pointer, tightly gripped, migrate above the demilitarized zone that divided North and South. Its tip sat above the 17th parallel. There it stayed, 17 degrees north of the equatorial plane. Immediately I tensed up. I knew what was going to be discussed because I had experimented with the idea myself. Of course it was an audacious approach—taking the war to the North. The deployment of the pointer *above* the 17th parallel said it all.

"I want all options on the table," the general declared. And then, looking straight at me, he said, "Colonel Minh, I know you've looked into this possibility. Could you summarize your main ideas for us? We will take each proposal on its own merits."

I stood up and offered my presentation. "We could send several divisions to fortify a zone along the seventeenth parallel, from Dong Ha to Savannakhet, to prevent infiltration from the North. That would be step one."

Encouraged by murmurs of approval, I continued. "The next step might be a landing operation at Vinh. Maybe Ha Tinh, north of the eighteenth parallel, so we can cut their front off from their rear."

I leaned against the high-backed chair. It was beyond doubt a brazen plan, one that went against the prevailing orthodoxy that emphasized defense at the expense of offense. But for all its difficulties, it was still feasible, from a military standpoint.

With barely a pause, other commanders weighed in. The marines could be used here, the airborne divisions there, the air force could provide support. I was surprised by the avalanche of not just tolerant but positive responses and concerned that the surge and swoon of euphoria would leave little room for restraint. I resisted the momentary temptation to insert a bit of doubt and ambiguity into my own plan, an urge I disguised as a quick cough. General Khanh was nodding. His facial muscles were tensed up, the eyes narrowed in concentration.

"Which division can be moved from Saigon and redeployed?"

Several hands went up. I hesitated, but my hand shot upward, almost by its own volition, as I looked for a way to slow the moment down. Other options should be considered, complications assessed, I suggested. At that moment, Phong cleared his throat and, with a tone that bordered on flippant, lobbed a devastating appraisal of our situation. "This has to be approved by the Americans, doesn't it?"

There was a moment of suffocating silence. I wasn't sure whether I felt relieved that a counterargument had been proffered or angry that Phong was the one who had done it. Phong, who was more knowledgeable in the ways of politics, had, with one sentence, reeled us back into this brand-new world we found ourselves in.

The general paused. Without irony, he said, "I will find the right moment to bring it up with them."

The meeting continued but Phong's question served as a powerful call for restraint. He glanced at me and smiled. If I hadn't seen that smile many times before, I could almost have mistaken it for mockery.

When the meeting was adjourned, General Khanh stood up and

solemnly said, presumably to Phong but in a voice all of us could hear, "Thank you. That was good of you to inject a necessary dose of political reality into our plan. Military strategies cannot be isolated from politics."

Even though a part of me agreed with this assessment, its articulation nonetheless was irksome. The political situation was clear. The Americans had to approve all plans. But the United States was like a giant tree with shallow roots and a heavy top. A storm could topple it.

Phong began to plunge headlong into the realm of politics. He met Thu and got married. I was not sure if he was in love or just wanted to partake in the grandness of its experience. When the newlyweds first visited, I wondered if he had, with a sigh of relief, collapsed into love at long last. Had his desires finally attached themselves to another? Had he finally accomplished what he had so desperately sought?

My wife liked Thu immediately. They both came from large landowning families. Phong's wife was a slender willow, poised, graceful, and eager to please. When she drank tea, she wrapped her hands around the steaming cup and held it before her chest, as if she were performing a bow. In bringing her to our house, he was including her in our fold. But at that moment it felt as if he were seeking our permission, even our approval. I saw his eyes watching me with an expression that was at once imploring and nervous.

Later when I walked with him to the door, I squeezed his hand and said, "You have found love."

He let a moment pass and then he said, "I have found Thu."

"She is lovely," I said.

He nodded. "She is entirely so."

That night, as I got myself ready for bed, I found myself thinking that Phong was still a man who yearned and craved.

# 7

## *A Great Silence Overcomes Me*

### MAI, 1967

It is a day like any other summer day. But it will not end like any other. I know there is a war on because our father is in it, but the war is a distant presence for us. The windows of our dining room face the garden and are covered with a material thick enough to shield us from the harshest light but sheer enough to allow faint glimpses of tree trunks and branches outside. My sister and I eat a breakfast of French bread buttered and dusted with a light sprinkle of sugar. Our mother eats fruit—whatever is in season, although she prefers the tart succulence of a ripe mangosteen. I watch her press a knife into the reddish-brown rind and twist it in a circular motion, paring the fruit in half. She puts her lips to it and inhales its fragrance. She scoops the white segmented pulp into her mouth, savoring the softness of its flesh. Holding up the rind against the light, she admires out loud its inky hue.

Our father has a bowl of rice congee before he rushes off to work. Because it is soupy, our father can eat it quickly. Our mother tries to keep him at the table, adding minced beef and vegetables to his bowl even as he waves her chopsticks away. Our mother is not in a far-off, hard-to-reach mood today but our father is. This morning they have changed places—usually it is our mother who is preoccupied and it is our father who tries to get her attention. Today, her face shines and she

THE LOTUS AND THE STORM   101

holds on to his hand. I smile as I see their fingers interweave. Leaning in toward him, Mother whispers something in his ear. Her flashing eyes suggest conspiracy. Our father looks at his watch and murmurs a reply. She averts her eyes. She is resplendent as she presses her face against his cheek when he stands up. It is early morning. He has just shaved and so I imagine that she would not be feeling the sandpaper roughness of his cheeks yet.

We know our mother will be visited by her many business partners. Older Aunt Number Three the Pharmacist will inevitably leave mentholated oil or cough drop candy for us. My sister and I have the rest of the day to fill. Summer vacation has just begun. She prevails upon me to stretch my limits, to be adventurous. She believes that my natural timidity and aversion to risk might dissolve at any moment. I might even become bold and fearless if I allow it.

The outside world beckons.

*Banh cuon! Baaaannnhhhh cuuuooon!* The steamed crepe vendor hawks her specialty in a musical drawl. Our mother calls her in to buy several plates for her Chinese business friends. A hash of minced pork, mushrooms, and prawns bulges from the soft rolls of rice wrapping. When served with sliced cucumber, fresh mint, and deep-fried shallots, it acquires a crunchiness that one does not expect from the soft folds of the crepes. A revelation of contrasting textures.

My sister takes my hand and leads me out of our front door toward the back part of our house where a wholly different neighborhood waits. There, a confounding mass of crooked, unmarked streets wind and eventually merge seamlessly into one another. Our Chinese grandmother is with us of course and, I can tell, has been coddled into accommodating my sister's desire. Tightly huddled houses on these dense, indecipherable streets are all inhabited by Chinese speakers and that makes the police nervous. It might be the perfect environment for an undetectable Vietcong hideout. Several times a day, soldiers and military police make their rounds through the neighborhood, some in plainclothes, trying to make sense of the confluence of good and evil that lurks behind closed doors, the difference between paranoia and true danger.

I stand back and wait, cautiously contemplating my options. My sister continues onward in a blithe display of self-assurance. She turns back toward me once she realizes I remain far behind. "Come on," she says. I am afraid and equally excited. I think my sister might lead me into danger but will, I am sure, also lead me out.

"Once you see it, you'll be astonished," she promises.

"What is it?" I ask.

"It's something Mother never lets us see."

I try to decide if the promise of being able to do what our mother forbids is enough to coax me forward.

"Just follow me," my sister calls out.

And to my surprise, I do.

"The orphanage is nearby," she adds. "James will be finished there and coming to meet us."

We make our way through the fecund heat, amid the squat gray shadows of corrugated tin shacks. Rust bleeds from the walls. Lizards and water bugs scurry under our feet, among flat tires and broken spokes. Of course our mother would not allow us here. The air is full of snores, cries, sawing and hammering, the chants of peddlers, the constant jangle of domestic activities spilling from the insides of houses into the open air of sidewalks. Children shriek and pour buckets of water over one another as they wash themselves near gray, gritty rivulets. Old men nap on makeshift cots tied to lampposts and utility poles. Perching on the sidewalk, women do the wash, scrubbing and pounding dirty clothes, reciting the ordinary heartbreaks of their lives as they work. They flex their muscles and wring the clothes, hanging them on frayed clotheslines to dry. Our Chinese grandmother directs our attention to the deep ruts cut into the road and warns us to be careful. Men covered in black grease work wrenches and pliers, adjusting the chains and brakes of broken-down bicycles. The smell of charcoal and kerosene lingers in the air. As we approach an open area, surrounded by only a few houses, I hear the screech of animals, chickens perhaps, and the guttural snorts of fat-bellied pigs. There is a wild fluttering of wings as feathers swirl and float in the air. I smell calamity in the vicinity.

James waves to us from his spot in a distant crowd. My sister runs and throws herself into his arms. His big hands cup her head. Shrieks crescendo from somewhere a ways off. Black smoke makes lolloping curls and hangs lazily in the blistering heat. On a day like this, I would rather be home in front of our air conditioner. I close my eyes and lick the sweat beads that have collected on my arms and shoulders. James jabs a bare arm in the air as my sister waves me toward them.

I take our Chinese grandmother's hand in mine. Around us, children our age, barefoot and stripped down to their underwear, jabber in a foreign language.

James scoops me up and hoists me over his head. Perched on his shoulders, I take in the view. We stand before an outdoor eatery famous for its roasted meats, or so our Chinese grandmother says. A suckling pig lies flat on a metal grill set atop two large concrete blocks. Hot coals glow red underneath. A sauce of oil and other seasonings is lathered onto the length of the pig's body to produce a thicker, brawnier taste. The pig's skin will turn crisp even as its flesh, larded and white, turns tender.

A small and slender man, bare-chested and fine-boned, runs his finger along a knife's blade before placing it on a sharpening stone at his feet. Then, with surprising speed and using only his bare hands, he pulls a fat chicken out of a wire coop and holds it upside down by the legs. The chicken lets out full-throated clucks. It sputters and thrashes violently. I want to turn away but I find myself a captive of what is occurring before me. His arm fully extended, the man swings the chicken by its legs in wide, windmill-like circles. Dazed and dizzy, the blubbering bird is placated at last and cannot move. The man holds it against a cutting board and whacks its head off with a precise downward motion of his knife. The crowd coos. I feel a grunt, an echo deep from James's diaphragm. He nods approvingly and tells me that it is not always easy to deliver such a deft and decisive blow to end an animal's life.

"When I was thirteen, I killed my first chicken," he says. I remember "Old MacDonald Had a Farm." I imagine James as a farm boy, surrounded by chickens and pigs and cows. "I used a hatchet, and even with my full strength coming down on its neck, the blow barely broke the skin. The chicken stared at me, eyes wide open, before it escaped and then collapsed, its body shaking against the ground. My mother was horrified."

I too am horrified. With feigned calmness, I remain motionless on his shoulders. My sister is transfixed, sucked into the drama of agony and surrender. The man hangs the chicken by its feet on a low tree branch to let its blood drip in a red arc into a bucket below. When the blood stops draining, another man dunks the bird into a pot of water boiling on a portable charcoal stove. The feathers loosen and are ready to be plucked. The man pulls the feathers off the chicken, reaches inside its body and scoops out the guts, then throws it on another large grill already covered with roasting fowls. A third man brushes sauce on the breasts and thighs. Drippings of concentrated sugars and soy sauce fall on the coal-fed flame.

When we sit down to eat, I concentrate hard on the task of chewing and swallowing, the stench of guts and blood still in my nostrils. Clouds have swallowed the sun but the heat still sticks to my skin. James twists open a "33" beer and takes a long swig, wiping his mouth with one bare arm and tickling my sister with the other. Somewhere deep inside myself I feel the urge to retch and vomit. My sister turns to me, squeezing my hand.

"Are you upset I wanted you to come?"

I nod. I don't lie to my sister, not even to spare her feelings.

Our Chinese grandmother takes a bottle of mentholated oil from her pocket and rubs the balm on my stomach and throat. She dabs a few drops on my tongue to keep the nausea at bay. I put my head on my sister's lap as I lie on the bench.

To my delight I am awakened by a gushing downpour. It is the sort of rain I love. No threat of thunder or lightning, just torrential rain that empties the sky and cools the earth. It is the sort of rain that will make water run off the roof for days, spilling into the waiting cisterns of hot-fired clay. The grown-ups run. Our Chinese grandmother takes cover under the store's awnings. My sister grabs my hand. Rain pelts our faces. We are drenched. Doors open and children run out, arms extended, faces up, mouths open, screaming ecstatically. The smallest of them peel off their clothes and surrender themselves naked to the force of rain. My sister and I pick a puddle and splash. James whoops and throws himself into the downpour. He puts me on his shoulders. Occasionally he dips his body and threatens to spill me onto the street.

We walk home along the washboarded alleyways, water running down our shoulders and arms.

Hours later, I've recovered and we are playing on our own street. Ngo Quyen Street. I love this time of the day, when time makes a turn around the bend and slides into the purple evening hours. The tamarind trees lining our block shade it from the summer heat. Soon the mimosa leaves will close up and night will arrive. A brisk wind stirs the tamarind pods, making scraping sounds as the surface of things shifts. Our parents are getting ready to leave the house.

I am giddy with happiness as I walk with my sister and our Chinese grandmother toward James's compound to cook our evening meal outdoors. We each carry a bag of ingredients for tamarind soup. James is fond of meals that appeal to a peasant's palate. I have the tamarind, pineapple, shrimp, and fresh coriander to give the broth a savory balance of sweet and sour. The pineapple will infuse a sweetness into the sharp tamarind base, tempering its reddish-brown sourness with a flicker of delicate redolence. It is not a temperamental dish and requires no vigilance, merely a steady flame. We will cook in the open field across from the military compound. Once James emerges from the sandbagged garrison, we will take three bricks and make a triangle with them. We will put a pot on this impromptu stove. We will gather clumps of dry grass and wood shavings to make a fire. We will bring the soup to a boil, then add tomatoes, celery, and garnishes. We will eat in bliss.

From the other side of the street, James comes toward us from the military compound, holding a portable cassette player. I see the starched crispness of his uniform. Our father wears his the same way. Ironed and pleated.

I am about to wave at him but I freeze instead. I find that I am gazing right through him, into a washed-out, speckled grimness that so startles me I close my eyes to ward it off. A moment passes. My bare skin registers a sensation of dread. I hear the sound of my shoes tap their own tentative echoes against the cement. An enormous heaviness swoops through me, pressing my eyes shut. When I open them, I see my sister as she meets her reflection. I see the pale contour of her shadow sliding into itself, like a retrospective likeness that glides softly by.

No, I say to myself, not knowing what it is I am saying no to, not knowing why it is I am trying to wrap myself inside her reflection.

A car drives past us, then backs up. It is our black Peugeot. Our father rolls down the window. We look in. Something heavy hangs in the air, the weight of an argument cut short and suspended to create the appearance of peace.

"No," I repeat.

"Yes," commands our father, thinking I had said no to him. He tells us to get into the car. Our Chinese grandmother gives us a gentle push. Our parents would like to kiss us before they leave. We jump into the backseat. Our mother turns around and pinches our cheeks. She caresses Khanh's hair.

I look out the window. James is walking toward us, waving. My sister waves back. He is waiting to cross. In a slow, rippling motion, a peddler stretches her legs, hunches down, and shoulders a pole with two baskets dangling from each end. Several men gun their motorcycles down the street. Horns blare. Motors rumble. Heat blasts from the asphalt road.

The windshield shatters.

My sister is sitting next to me, then the entire weight of her body collapses into my arms. We both fall against the seat. It is as if the laws of physics themselves have been broken. People begin to shriek.

Khanh reaches her arm to her neck as blood shoots out from it. Every time I think of it, it is as if I have never moved from that spot nor emerged from that moment in time. I see her arm reaching up, touching her neck. Our parents scream. Our Chinese grandmother screams. James screams. Our mother clambers into the back of the car and clamps her hand on my sister's neck. She tries to plug the hole with her finger, first this finger, then that finger. Red oozes around her hand, gradually turning brown. Our father throws our mother aside and takes over. He ties a piece of cloth around Khanh's neck. Our mother screams instructions. James also tries to help, pressing his hand as if it were a bandage over the cloth covering the hole. Helpless, my mouth opens. I impulsively take in her breath, breathe it into my mouth and lungs, holding it inside. My sister's breath is in me. Her body collapses against mine as her shadow wavers over me.

Everything that occurred then occurs right here, right now, and repeats in a perpetual present-tense time loop. Every moment I spent with my sister before this moment also occurs again and again, in the present tense. It is time bending, taking away my breath.

I am still there, at that moment when God or fate or a split second before or after could have made a difference but did not.

And that is how I still am today, in a half-life that only waits and sometimes hopes.

It is still a mystery where the bullet came from. It was Cholon, in 1967. She was thirteen. I was nine.

Seasons change but her absence is a hole I cannot fill. A primitive pain lies beyond the reach of language, like an *oui yaaah* that is too deep to be cried out. I stop talking after her death. Our parents ask, then beg, then order me to speak. Perhaps I should say "my" parents but I can't because saying "our" honors my sister's continuing presence. Just one word. Any word. They are well intentioned. They fear my remoteness is intended to punish. The truth is I have become capable only of pure, uninflected silence.

Our family goes through the outward motions of mourning. I wear a rectangle of white cloth pinned to my left breast. I absorb everything, note the lightness our father tries to instill in his own voice, the long wail that leaks from our mother's chest one Sunday afternoon when she mistakenly believes she is alone.

I become a stone, elemental and geologic, transcending the human and the mortal. I merge seamlessly with the shade of gray that surrounds our altered lives.

Soon our mother begins visiting my sister's grave every week. She does not announce it but I know because she leaves the house with a bouquet of flowers and a small bag of food soon after Father leaves for work. The spell of the cemetery runs through her. I recognize it because it runs through me as well.

Sometimes she takes me along with her. I watch so I can remember the way my sister's name was carved into the stone. I watch silently as our mother gathers a few branches of frangipani blooms in one hand and a bag of sticky rice in the other. Hands folded together in prayerful supplication, she whispers to herself freely, as if I do not hear.

"Forgive me. Forgive me," she says importunately, over and over. "If only I hadn't asked you to stop and get into the car . . ." I hear the murmur of voices take on a different tone, a tone that beseeches. I let her be.

I still don't speak, and more and more I come to feel content within my crucible of silence. With each new day, I feel a sense of raw, unadulterated abandon. Friends offer their diagnoses. *Mat hon,* they whisper. I am someone who has lost her soul.

As time passes, my silence tolls with mounting intensity and force. Our parents stop trying to draw me out and go about their own simulated lives, removed a reasonable distance from mine. I am relieved to be left alone, feeling as though I were a child of whom little will be expected from now on. I know what I can get away with without triggering ferocious reactions at home and make sure to manifest some sense of normalcy. I know that they will use school as a gauge, so my attendance is perfect. I do everything the teacher asks. Over time, I even begin to like being separate from the more animated world.

Our parents think silence means absence. But I am present enough to witness what they do. I see the down-turned corners of their mouths. When they talk to each other in my presence, they say only what is most obvious. Our mother drops her eyes when she talks. "Dinner is ready."

Our father says, "Wonderful. I am sorry I was kept late at the office." His eyes momentarily look at hers and then fix themselves on his rice bowl.

She moves food around with her chopsticks. We are eating pork ribs. I can hear the sharp gristly crunch of bone against teeth.

"The sauce is very good," our father remarks.

Our mother nods. "Five-spice powder from Aunt Number Three."

Our father tilts his head as a way of signaling his confusion.

"The Chinese rice dealer. Tomorrow I will go see her. I probably won't be back in time for dinner."

"Doesn't she usually come here?"

"Yes. But not always."

"Hmmm."

I drift out of their conversation. Their voices sound strange, like a song sung on one note. When dinner is finished, each of us returns to the welcome solitude of our own private space.

As always, I find consolation in *One Thousand and One Arabian Nights.* It is precisely when our parents begin accusing each other that I turn to the stories of Scheherazade for support. Our mother lashes out forcefully but quietly. "We *should* have moved long ago," she says on the other side of the wall, the *should* thick with a blame that refuses to let go. "Our house is too close to the military police. My brother warned us they would target the police headquarters. He warned us to be careful." For a moment there is only a sorrowful silence. And then there is our father's voice, summoning up his own curt defense followed by a string of words I am relieved I cannot make out. "Your brother is a Vietcong and who knows what else." The sentence is followed, I imagine, by a dismissive wag of the hand. "That he is a Vietcong is all the more reason to listen to him when he gives his warnings," she retorts.

A knot gathers in my chest. Quickly I return to the stories I know so well. This is where I learn that we read so we can hide within the pages of a book. That there are few things more reassuring than a story silently relished. A boy rubs a magic lamp and, arms outstretched, sits on a flying carpet. I see the opening of a cave. The sky blushes purple. Among the crowded bazaars and narrow streets, a minaret stands. Everything else falters and recedes.

One day, I find a new friend, a cricket who likes to sleep in a matchbox with needlepoint holes I poke one by one into the cardboard sides. I get down on my hands and knees to look at it. I touch its iridescent wings. It creeps tentatively onto my hand, then tickles its way up my arm one day when I am in the garden among the hewn rocks and tangled vines that hug our mango tree. It is a tickle not much different from the addictive ritual shared with my sister, the sort that produces a tingling on the skin's surface and coaxes me into solace, then sleep. The cricket appears injured; one of its legs is falling off, one of its wings partially torn. I don't flick it away but carry its slumbering body indoors with me. A persistent chirp, announcing its simple presence, lulls me into the night. Hello, I say soundlessly after school. I spend the hours reading. And the cricket is simply there, demanding nothing. A small rag on the windowsill keeps it warm. It is easy to please. It lives in my room, and whenever it wants to, it crawls into the matchbox on my night table to sleep. It shows no interest in escaping into the garden right outside the open window. I imagine the cricket making its way through the dark pungent earth, the neatly clipped stretch of grass, the open wilderness, while I am away at school. But like me, it is drawn to the safe confines of the box.

Hello, I say, soundlessly again, before bed. I can hear its response:

a sharp scratch against the box and a soft chirp, small and wounded. Together the cricket and I listen to the murmurs of nocturnal life. Darkness inspires revelations that are less visible during the day. I know that we are still fighting a war and that our father is still caught up in it—no, has disappeared into it. That our mother is even more remote now than before. That we all want to be comforted, yet we are contemptuous of consolation when it is offered. That Khanh's death has diminished our lives.

From my room night after night I can see a window light up when our mother or father returns. I can hear footsteps in the yard, then the creaky hinge of our swing set. Our father would be sitting there staring at the powdery sky, living inside the nocturnal distance that stretches between him and the rest of the world. I too know that distance all too well. I let him be, as I hope he would let me be. Our father simply sits there, cauterized, night after night on the swing and submits himself to the agitation of darkness. Mosquitoes and gnats buzz around his head. When our mother's car approaches the driveway, its wheels crunch against loose pebbles on the partially tarred street; headlights shine a wide-angled beam at our house. I can hear our father move in a rush from the swing. His bedroom door rattles open, swift and certain, then closes with a click. He is still in the smaller room, two doors away from our mother's. My heart flutters as I wait to see if something will happen.

Our mother does not follow him. They are far apart from such a possibility. I put my ear against the wall of our mother's room. Now anger and grief bloom at night, when they are dark and raw. Through the force field of silence, I can hear it, the turbulence of clear liquid splashed against glass, releasing sorrow. I suspect it is vodka that flows so profusely. It would be feasible for our mother to harbor this furtive little secret, this inconsequential personal foible. Still, she has taken to drinking tea and eating wedges of lime to cover the odor. I know because when we eat crabs or lobsters, we dunk our hands into bowls of tea and lime juice to remove the fishy odor. Our mother is taking every measure to conceal her new habit.

I take a deep breath, then another and another. I believe that by sealing myself in silence, my other senses have grown sharper. I am developing an ability to see through walls, unearth others' lives of subterfuge, remove the thick cloaks they use to conceal. A tortuous warren of electrical wires and pipes lies behind drywall. Insects are burrowing through the foundation of our house, centipedes, termites, ants, beetles. Our mother will soon swallow her pill. I want to walk to her room and offer her a moment's kindness. But I cannot and the desire passes away soon enough. The more I am able to discern, the more I want to flee. Next door, night after night, our mother's grief works its way deeper inside her bones and sinews. Grief engulfs her very spirit.

I nurse my yearning for something else. James. I can still see his finger on top of her wound. And James was the one who cried that evening. I have never seen a man weep so extravagantly. But I cannot bear to be near such an outpouring of grief. An echo chamber of turmoil. I have become used to our father's porcelain gaze, our mother's discreet sorrow, the implosion of melancholy within. And what once seemed an everlasting connection—my sister, me, and James, three unabashed points always together, like sun, earth, and moon—has been broken.

James tries to stay in touch with me. But Father makes it is easy for me to rebuff him. In one of the few moments after my sister's death when he seems to be aware of me, and not simply of his perfunctory fatherly duties, he has forbidden me to go anywhere near the military police compound. He holds me tightly and shakes a finger for emphasis. His warnings give me maneuvering space to avoid James. There is gravity to his instruction and I know our Chinese grandmother will strictly enforce it. Now on those rare occasions when my Chinese grandmother and I take our evening walk, we turn left from the front gate, not right. Right is where it happened.

One day we pass by our corner eatery. Standing under the wide shade of our tamarind trees, young men flick cigarettes, tap their feet to the raucous beat of bass drums. James is squatting on a low footstool. In his hand is a bottle of "33" beer.

I see James take a big swig, then his eyes catch mine. We are face-to-face. I cannot pretend I do not see him. Our Chinese grandmother nudges me toward him. James comes upon me, kneels down, and holds me close inside the clasp of big, muscled arms, crushing my face against his chest. Once again his tears flow without reserve. I wince. It seems that the next appropriate thing to happen would be for me to say something to him. But I remain in the endless snarl of my own silence. Our

Chinese grandmother tries to communicate with James. I watch the hand signals. She is trying to tell him I no longer talk.

I am aware that my face has the plain, gray look of a stone statue. I watch the unfolding of their intricate pantomime.

Really? James struggles to express himself in Vietnamese. Really? He points to his mouth, then shakes his head.

As he moves, the sleeve on his white cotton shirt is lifted. I am shocked but touched. He has a new tattoo—it is the date of my sister's death, etched on his arm in cobalt blue.

Our Chinese grandmother nods, points to her own mouth, points at me, and then shakes her head. James grows somber. He crouches down, leveling his eyes with mine, and hugs me. I put my hand on his back and feel the tight little knots I once touched with my heels and toes. He offers his finger for me to hook, but although I want to, I freeze. James smiles reassuringly. "You will be okay. I'll be back."

When we come home, my cricket is waiting for me in the amniotic silence of my bedroom. I put the cricket on my hand and together we take a walk in the garden. Leaves rustle above as sparrows flit from a cluster of star fruit trees. Nearby, the mango tree I used to hide behind stands still and erect. Green mangoes hang low among the red glossy leaves, drooping from the stems. Unripe and tart, they can be dipped in chili powder, sugar, and salt, a delicious combination of sweet, sour, and hot in the mouth. I can almost taste the tanginess against my tongue. The night hums with nocturnal creatures. In response, my cricket makes its own little chirps. I put a finger to my lips and shush its shrill little calls.

I ask the cricket if it wants to stay outside tonight. I keep my palm open to allow it to jump off, but it clings to my skin, opting to suffer life's shortcomings with me instead. Above us the stars gleam. I imagine one blinking at me. Here on earth the cricket and I will hide out together in friendship. I will have the cricket by me while I wait for life to make its turns.

Later, as I lie in bed, the moon peeks through my window, shedding a soft ivory light into the room. This is the time of night when funny things unspool for me and I can feel the stirring of their dark, ridged edges. I close my eyes, turn my face. I can feel them move through my body, clots of memories that dislodge, then liquefy. Perhaps the darkness serves as an anticoagulant. Things unclot and bleed at night, dissolve and reveal their true form. Perhaps time moves differently at night, not across the face of a clock, in seconds, minutes, and hours, but through a reticulated space of loops and curls, dips and lunges, that spiral endlessly inward.

My compass remains what it has always been. We all have one, that one singular person for whom love is freely given no matter the circumstances. There again, even now, is the unmistakable feeling of my sister's touch, our bedtime ritual. It lingers.

Sometimes the feeling that there is some other person standing next to me is so strong I have to turn and look. It is as if the person were hovering in my blind spot. Walking beside me.

And then it occurs to me. She is my first love. Her loss is the one I will never fully recover from. When she died she left me forever full of yearning.

# 8

## *Emerald Green Eyes*

### MR. MINH, 2006, 1967

There was an American with green eyes the color of irrigated rice fields.

He came in 1963, but I did not meet him until 1966, at a training center as I entered my last week of a special command course. His name was John Clifford. He was one of several American advisers who gave us lessons in personnel management, patrol and ambush, night operations, marksmanship, small unit actions, intelligence, security, logistics. We were practicing bayonet thrusts and reviewing the mechanical workings of weapons, the simple logic of American firepower. A few of us were handed the prized M16.

He told us to watch animals for clues on how to search for food, water, and shelter in a survival situation. He asked us to call him Cliff. He was in our country not for a one-year tour of duty but to pursue more long-term strategic goals, the details of which were not shared with us. He was not young, as the American boys usually were. He had fought in Italy and Germany all through World War II. Years of combat had carved themselves into his rough-hewn face. I looked into his eyes and liked what they imparted—a full, piercing, rice-field-green presence. When we talked, I could feel the weight of his gaze on my face. I wasn't accustomed to such forthrightness.

He did not act like someone cast adrift in our country. His posture, his countenance, his eyes—nothing suggested calibration, restraint, or reserve. He was willing to be befriended. He ate our fruits—mangosteens, papayas, longans—though he insisted that they be tree-ripened. I watched as he skinned the hard rind of a longan with his teeth. He was equally game to try street food. He would eat a full bowl of pho for breakfast down to the last leisurely slurp and the last broken noodle that could be picked up with a pair of chopsticks. He would devour a heaping plate of raw green papaya salad with reckless enthusiasm.

The Americans had built a constellation of base camps around the country. Ours was located at the edge of Saigon. There we reviewed the ways of survival, honing method into instinct. The ability to fabricate something from whatever was available depended on the ability to watch the world with eyes that could see everything and miss nothing. The fact that a bee or an ant went into a hole in a tree might mean that the hole contained water. In this drifting landscape of jungle greens and moving shadows, we learned to make use of every camouflaged object, every part of the earth.

Cliff's willingness to listen distinguished him from the other American advisers and endeared him to me immediately. He and I were lunching together when news of yet another upheaval was announced. A car filled with explosives had blown up in the parking lot of a popular hotel. The explosion killed and injured more than a hundred U.S. and Vietnamese nationals. I looked at his face, tanned to a reddish brown by our sun. I could see he was trying to suppress his own emotions and gave me a consolatory glance.

"Dong Ha, Con Thien, Gio Linh have been attacked all within a short span of time. It's as if they've lined up all these towns and proceeded to knock them down. . . . You are too busy fighting among yourselves to fight the enemy." He reached across the table and gave my hand a ferocious squeeze, as if to get my attention.

"I know, Cliff. The North has become very bold. I think they will go after the Central Highlands next."

"To cut the South in half," Cliff agreed.

"It's a shame we are such idiots," I said. I felt the need to apologize for our absurdities. "To be fair, we're also in a difficult spot."

We were a country defined by a long history of repelling foreign invasions. Our heroes were the Trung Sisters, Ngo Quyen, Tran Hung Dao—patriots who fought the Chinese. "You're part of the problem too, unfortunately," I said to Cliff. "The North has managed to use your very presence for propaganda purposes."

Cliff nodded and gave me a drawn-out "hmm" that signified less agreement than curiosity.

So I told him about a popular Vietnamese proverb. *"Cong ran can ga nha,"* I said, pronouncing each word slowly. "It means carrying a snake on your back, bringing it back home, and allowing it to kill your homegrown chickens."

"I gather we're the snake." Cliff chuckled sportingly.

"It's an accusation that the North is lobbing quite successfully."

Cliff ordered another beer. "This is good," he said, reading the label. "Thirty-three. Stronger than it looks."

"Rice lager," I said.

"I get it. They've managed to play up the nationalism angle and present themselves as the true nationalists," Cliff said with quiet authority. "By associating with us, you're now the illegitimate collaborators." His face turned sweaty and red. I suggested looking for shade but he wanted to stay and continue the conversation.

"From day one, we knew this would be an issue. President Diem struggled with it," I explained. "He needed American aid but wasn't sure about paying the price of an American presence in our country. He and his brother Nhu even contacted, secretly of course, the highest leadership in Hanoi to work out a negotiated settlement that would bypass the Americans and cut short American involvement in our country."

"I didn't know that," Cliff said. As a military man, he was not naturally inclined toward the clotted, underground world of political intrigue.

Quietly, I wondered if the maneuver was meant to bring about a negotiated peace and unification or was simply a means for his brother, the controversial Mr. Nhu, to thumb his nose at the Americans, to wriggle from the grip of American pressure for reform.

"Have you heard of Mieczyslaw Maneli?" I asked.

Cliff shook his head slowly, his head lolled back as if to retrieve a memory. "I don't think so." He had his elbow on the table, supporting his chin with his hand.

In case I was mispronouncing his name, I wrote it on a napkin and showed it to Cliff. He shook his head and repeated, "I don't know him." I looked at my watch and ordered a fresh round of squid. "Maneli was the Polish middleman between Saigon and Hanoi. Neither we nor they wanted our secret dealings known."

"Why not exactly?"

"Russia and China would not want a negotiated settlement. They don't want Vietnam to be sovereign or neutral. So they aren't in favor of compromise or a negotiated peace. What they want is a Vietnam firmly within the Communist camp."

"And the American position was what?" Cliff asked.

"Who knows? Do the Americans even know?"

Cliff laughed. "Well put, well put," he said.

"The American position is probably to keep us within the American orbit. And dependent. In any event, President Diem didn't trust the American position, whatever it might have been. So he kept the Maneli affair secret from the Americans as well."

I had Cliff's continuing attention. "If you know our history, and the Chinese and Soviets certainly *do,* you would see that it's in their interest to keep you in this war. So they can trumpet your presence. They want you stuck here while they remain offstage, calling the shots."

Cliff closed his eyes as if to give the matter serious mental consideration. "I can see how complicated everything is," he said in his customary, level voice.

"Exactly. A war has to be seen from so many angles," I said, surprised that I was mouthing what was essentially Phong's stock position. This included the American domestic scene, which few Vietnamese considered or understood. Indeed, my doubts about American commitment to overseas battles in the far-flung corners of the world were confirmed years ago when I was first sent, along with a handful of other Vietnamese, to an American officers' training school at Fort Leavenworth in Kansas. We landed, and right away we let out a soft, collective sigh. Ahhh. So this is America, we thought. A country the size of a continent. Beautiful. Free. So rich, so vast, and so startlingly separate from the rest of the world, loosed from the teeming continents of poverty far away. A country like that could afford to be unruffled and detached— oblivious to miseries beyond its borders.

Every week Cliff and I would lunch together at Saigon's family-owned eateries. We were a country preoccupied with food. Practically every house doubled as a storefront designed to satisfy our culinary cravings, from the most delicately wrought to the more parochial but hearty fare. We ate sweet pork buns, steamed rice crepes, fried bread, rice rolls wrapped in banana leaves.

After our first few lunches, I invited him home. He was already adapted to our habits of eating and drinking. Still, my wife made sure we served only cooked vegetables and beef, well done. We excluded one of my favorites, green papaya salad, because it was raw. Our water, my wife decided, should be just fine even for an American. It was always boiled first, left to cool, and then filtered. Still, when we were seated at the table, I was surprised to see bottled water instead. In the center tray was an impressive mound of appetizers—spring rolls, grilled lemongrass beef wrapped in grape leaves, crab claws fried with a dash of salt and pepper.

Cliff arrived in uniform. He was broad-shouldered; the carriage of his body was soldierly, angular, and erect. He spoke a few sentences in Vietnamese to show that he had learned the language and was making an effort. And for the rest of the evening we alternated between French and English. A half-smile lingered perpetually on his face, as if he would allow himself only a half dose of pleasure.

He had a wife and three sons, nineteen, seventeen, and sixteen, at home somewhere in New York, not in the city but in the mountains. I pictured pristine streams where he taught his sons to fish, fields of flowers through which they ran. My wife reciprocated with the basic facts about our family. "Yes, two girls," she said, her face opening up exquisitely. "Mai and Khanh, inseparable." While I struggled with the corkscrew in one hand and a bottle of wine in the other, I could hear pleasantries being exchanged. My wife told Cliff about her family being from the rice-growing Mekong Delta and mine being from Laos. "But he's Vietnamese," she added. Cliff nodded and asked if there were many Laotians in Vietnam. "No," she said. "But many Chinese." Moments later, when Cliff expressed an interest in the lacquer paintings on the walls, she seemed pleased and led him to her two favorite paintings. "Look at these," she said proudly.

"I drove to several factories that make ceramics and lacquered products but didn't see anything as beautiful as these. I'd like to buy a few to send back home," Cliff said.

"You need to go to the right place. We'll take you to Bien Hoa, about an hour away. The best factories are there. These paintings have more than ten layers of lacquer. They won't crack. So you see they are beautifully polished. Here is a traditional Buddhist scene," she said. "A lotus pond which is meant to convey serenity."

"I can see the superior quality here," Cliff said agreeably.

"And this one is of the two women warriors in our history who rode on elephant backs, led an army, and defeated invaders from China," she explained.

"Yes, yes, I'm quite aware of the Trung Sisters. I had read about them when I was preparing to come to Vietnam. And your husband here has invoked their names many times since we've become friends," Cliff said, his smile lingering as he examined the lacquered details. "I understand they weren't the only woman warriors either."

"True. We also have Madame Trieu," my wife explained appreciatively.

"I do believe she was the one who uttered the famous words about riding the tempest and taming the waves and rejecting the lot of women who bow their heads." Cliff sipped his wine and slyly winked at me.

My wife's eyebrows shot up. She was impressed. "That's right. And those women are quite representative of Vietnamese women in general, I should add," she said. Her voice dropped as she looked at me to confirm her assertion.

"Quite so," I said.

"I'm impressed you know so much about our history, Cliff," my wife said, gazing at him thoughtfully.

"As I said, I wanted to learn about the country before coming," he answered. "You can tell a lot about a country by the historical figures it celebrates as national heroes. I noticed right away when I arrived that you have major boulevards named after the Trung Sisters and Madame Trieu."

My wife continued to look at him, almost in a clinical, appraising way. I imagined she was wondering what I myself had wondered many times. Why such a man would leave his country to come here.

To help, he answered amiably when she asked. The simplicity was so startling that I could tell she wasn't sure whether it was true. "What do you get in return?" my wife asked.

"Me? Contentment. Satisfaction that one has made an important contribution," he answered.

"What about your country? What does it get in return?"

Cliff shrugged. "I am more concerned with my own decisions. What *I* can do. Whether *I* can help. The big picture is beyond my control."

She seemed genuinely surprised. We were sitting at the dinner table. My wife urged me to pour the wine, nudging me gently with her elbow.

"So simple?" Quy persisted.

"Yes," he said, nodding. "Some things are simple. If you allow them to be stripped to their true essence, you would see simplicity."

My wife hardly blinked. "Really? Can you give me an example?"

"It's easy enough. Loyalty, for example. Loyalty is very simple. You don't abandon someone who has been a friend to you at his moment of need."

"But can't there come a time when you have to let go? There are limits to everything, even friendship."

Cliff closed his eyes and breathed deeply. "What is that scent? The flowers here give off such an incredible fragrance."

"Oh, that? It's the dwarf ylang-ylang. It blooms all year on our terrace," my wife said. "It's the flower that gives Chanel N° 5 its signature scent."

Cliff lifted his eyes and inhaled. "Lovely," he said. "As I was about to say . . ."

"Yes, my question. Loyalty. It isn't always so simple, especially when life gets complicated and circumstances change."

Cliff smiled, unflustered. "It's simple enough if you follow your heart. But when you start to overthink with your head, that's when it gets complicated. You churn and churn and churn, seeing this side and that side until you are immobilized." Cliff looked at me and nodded knowingly. "Surely you can relate to that after what you went through in 1963," he said.

My wife seemed satisfied. She unfolded her arms and relaxed. I opened another bottle of wine. She smiled her approval. A Cabernet Sauvignon from Bordeaux. She was smiling through most of dinner.

The soft golden hue of her face, almost a honey color, heightened, providing a nice contrast to the pale lavender *ao dai*. We were comfortable with many topics, some political, some personal. Cliff praised Johnson's domestic policies, his so-called war on poverty, but disdained his gingerly approach to fighting this war. My wife looked at me, as if to goad me into taking a position, but I neither contradicted nor supported Cliff. After dinner, I opened a bottle of Johnnie Walker Black Label to pair with the Roquefort cheese my wife had selected for the occasion. I leaned fully against the chair's back and felt the warmth of the alcohol in my throat and chest. It felt good. There was the clink of glass, the sound of easy laughter.

"Isn't it difficult to be so far from your family?" my wife asked.

"Yes, but they fully believe in what I am doing," he answered. "That makes it easier."

"They do? Really. You believe in what you're doing and they believe in what you're doing." My wife looked away from him, her brows furrowed. "What does your wife do?"

"She took care of the three boys full-time when they were growing up. She is completely devoted to them. An extraordinary mother . . . So you see . . ."

He beamed.

Cliff continued proudly. "Even when we had only the first child, she quit her part-time job to be with him. She didn't even want the help of a nanny."

My wife nodded politely but I sensed an inward shift. "A mother can be devoted to a child in many ways, no?"

"True enough, but I suppose I am referring to something intangible but innate. A maternal instinct, so to speak."

"Pardon me?" she interrupted. "How interesting. I've always wondered what a man means when he talks about maternal instinct. It's certainly something to ponder, when men all over the world have such opinions about women's instincts. And in particular, women's motherly instincts." She had always been fiery. She leaned toward him to better make out his words.

"Well, sacrificing everything for the child. For the family," he answered tentatively. His roguish eyes twinkled.

"Is that so? In a poor country like Vietnam, I'd say people know something about sacrifice." Quy gave him a dismissive shrug and shot me a look of indignation. "Any Vietnamese from any street corner can tell you about sacrifice. Ask a cyclo driver who pedaled all day under the hot sun. Or a South Vietnamese soldier who hasn't been paid in weeks."

"I am sure that is so," Cliff conceded.

His voice was low and soft, but it resonated, as if it came from someplace deep inside his chest. I noticed that the weight of his eyes rested—a viewfinder—on the bareness of her slender neck. I was not offended, nor concerned. Why should he not look? Our country is a grand wreck but our women are beautiful. A river of hair flowed down my wife's shoulders and back. Her tightly fitting *ao dai* hugged her form and was cinched at the waist. The couture silk fabric covered her body and even the entire length of her arms. A personal preference of mine— that she should dress this way. It was subtle theater. It produced a lush, sensual sensation, yet nothing showed, except the shape, the contours, and the curves. All the more intriguing, as it had the effect of provoking and sparking one's imagination. It created a dance of revelation and concealment—one of pure visual exuberance. With a figure like hers there was no need to show skin. Naturally, I noticed. And so would other men. Foreign men. This we have in common. Noticing is a normal enough thing to do. I liked Cliff all the more for it.

In the background, a voice from the radio rose. Khanh Ly's, wistfully singing a beloved song about tomorrow. Sad, of course. A song about departures, of course. And a weeping ocean that mourns love lost. Hers was an understated style, a pure lament that took us by the hand and walked us into the song's despairing essence itself.

Over the course of the evening, Cliff managed to earn our trust. Beneath the surface charm was a decent man. I imagined that Quy was disappointed, just as I was, to bid him good-bye when the evening ended.

We showed him our garden. My wife followed his movement, with her eyes and with every part of her body—a head turn, a shoulder twist. Moonlight danced on the leaves of bougainvillea petals on our garden wall. Tiny green flowers bloomed spikelets that shot upward from the branches of our mango tree. This was where Khanh and Mai hid when they played hide-and-seek and where I found them, after pretending that the hiding spot was so difficult to locate. My wife picked several star fruits, so ripe and swollen they were ready to drop. Cliff took a deep breath, inhaling the intense fragrance of the garden. We tarried by the door even though it was late. Mosquitoes gathered overhead. In the most natural way, my wife reached over and lightly swatted them away from Cliff's face.

"We hope you will come back again," she said.

When he bade good-bye, he said "Quy." It was the first time he had spoken her name. For some reason, that he called her by name commanded my attention. "It means *precious,* I understand," he said.

"Yes," I quickly replied. "Very precious."

He did come again. Over time, he became a regular presence in our household.

A faint, unobtrusive light shines through the window and enfolds me in its steadfast glow. I am still floating in a wonderful, extravagant element, soft and swift, vast and luxuriant, like water. It *is* water, sometimes metal-colored, sometimes blue, with an occasional frosty cresting of whitecap slipping and slashing through calm and turbulence. The horizon, an unvisited line in the distance, is dotted by a hopeful bank of coconut trees. I feel a tiny ping of recognition. It is the South China Sea. Quy waves at me from the sky, from the water, from shore.

I am encased in peace until the rattle and pang of fork against plate jostle me awake.

"Hello," I hear. I am surprised by the unceremonious "hello" so early in the morning. No knock, not even a rattling of the doorknob to provide notice. "Ba," a voice calls. The ritual greeting seems particularly hurried and peremptory. My daughter, ghostlike for an instant, glides into the room, sits on the chair by my bed, shaking her crossed leg. Her eyes squint, searching for responsiveness in my face. She reaches over and grips my wrist. Anxiety presses down on me. I look at her through a befuddling knothole of misapprehension.

"Can you hear me?" she asks. Each word comes out slow, somehow muffled.

She slaps her hand on the night table to get me to snap out of it and focus.

"Is that you, Mai?" I ask.

I hear a sigh. "Who else, Ba?"

"What did you say?" I ask blankly.

In almost equal proportions, reality and dream envelop me.

Her eyes seek me out. I think she takes my hand and holds on to it. Today the pills have left behind a corrosive, molten slag of torpor.

"Are you there?" Mai asks. She appears stricken. Where would I be? I want to say, but I am distracted by the voice. Almost not her voice, but another's. Something has insinuated itself into the room, something that blurs and warps instead of clarifies.

Mai goes on, "I am worried about Aunt An." She calls me "Ba." Father. Her eyes sympathetically widen as if to lift and soothe the worrisome message. I see the dark dabs of inadequate sleep under her lower lids. Purple-red leaps from the top part of her partially scarfed neck. I want to intervene but feel ill-equipped. I don't know what questions to ask. I don't have the words to begin.

I point toward her neck with my chin. On cue, she spreads the scarf to cover a larger area and tightens the knot. I hoist myself up and listen.

"I have not wanted to involve you but now that it's getting more serious every day, I think I need to tell you." She retains a measured demeanor.

"So there is something to what that woman at the music shop said," I say tentatively. I am worried but touched that Mai thinks I still have the capacity to remedy wrongs.

She shrugs and rummages through her purse. She finds her checkbook and studies it, assembling information from the muddle of figures organized under debit and deposit columns. Her eyes sink inward. "We've been part of the *hui* now for several years. Every year the numbers change. The pot is worth ten thousand dollars this year but last year it was only five thousand dollars. Most people wanted a bigger pot. And with a bigger pot, things became more formal and rigid. At the beginning, several years ago, our club was, how should I put it, more gentle. We used to not pay out anything to anyone the first month. Instead, the first month's draw would be set aside in an emergency fund to assist any one of us who had a family crisis. Sometimes, we would even have a communal fund and take a few dollars from it to play the lottery, agreeing to split any winnings equally among all of us.

But when Mrs. Chi's sister died and she became the organizer, things changed. The *hui* became more like a money-making business and she allows less flexibility." Mai sighs. "It's become less about pooling our money to help each other, and more like dealing with a bank."

Her voice, roughened by nerves, drops to a whisper. "In the past few months, I've had to help Aunt An out with her contribution. Not a huge amount."

"So it is money trouble?" I ask. "She drew the money from the *hui* and now she can't deposit the necessary amount each month?" It is as I have suspected—financial gloom encloses Mrs. An.

"That's only part of the problem, although it's a big enough part. She gives her son most of what she makes and what's left over she gives to her sister in Saigon and there's hardly anything left for anything else now."

"What did she do with the ten thousand dollars from the *hui*?" I ask.

"She gave it to the *boy,* I think."

The word *boy* has upset me. *Boy* means "child." Of course a parent has to help her child. What parent would not? Compared to your child's life, yours is the more expendable one. Mrs. An needs help and the boy needs help. I don't dare ask Mai how much she has given to help. She has a law degree but she does not work as a lawyer or an investment banker. She is a research librarian instead, preferring the less hectic lifestyle it affords her. "So now every month she has to put in one thousand dollars but can't," I mutter to myself.

"Mrs. Chi's sister used to call each of us before the draw to see how things were. She would ask if we had personal problems and she would cover for that person if needed," Mai says.

"So it's basically a money issue," I declare. I am trying to follow the story and formulate a solution.

"Well, it's more complicated than that," Mai says sadly. "Aunt An antagonized the *hui* members. They're going to ostracize her."

"But she's been paying. So why ostracize?"

Mai turns her gaze toward me and murmurs, "She got the group to let her access the money first because she claimed to have an emergency. The organizer later found out there was no emergency, that she was just giving the boy money again, as usual. Feeding his dependency."

She is probably surprised to find herself discussing such matters with me. She studies me with a serious, considering eye. Mrs. An's plight wrenches little flutters from my chest.

"Was there really no family emergency?" I ask.

She mutters a muted "um" that signifies no.

"They don't consider giving the money to a boy in need an emergency?" I ask.

"Not when she gave it to him so he can gamble it away. Or sink it into another idiotic business. Anyway, I think they will make her pay interest on it at the next drawing. She'll have to put in eleven hundred dollars or more, not one thousand dollars."

"Will she be able to?" I ask.

"Even if she does, she will still be shunned for making what they consider to be false claims." Mai looks away. And then after a moment's pause, she says, "It is a sickness. He can't stop gambling. It's an addiction."

I am skeptical of this diagnosis. In this country, no one has flaws or foibles. Weaknesses, however pitiful, are armored in psychological jargon that insulates them from scrutiny. But this fact hurts Mrs. An's case, so I keep it to myself. "So your point is that giving him the money so he can gamble qualifies as an emergency because he is sick?"

There is a silence and then the squeak of a chair being pushed against the floor. Mai leans in closer, her voice tightened. "Psychologists can testify to this fact, you understand. That it is not his fault. It's not anyone's fault. It's a sickness."

"Testify? As in court? Will it come to that?"

"Not necessarily. I'm sure not."

"What can be done to help Mrs. An, then?" I ask.

Her voice turns soft. "I am worried about both the shunning and the money."

"We cannot do anything about the shunning. If they think she misused the emergency argument, they will shun her."

Mai says morosely, "But she will suffer if she is shunned. . . . Soon enough they will turn the community against her. It will be devastating." She looks frazzled, yet fierce. "I don't think there is any way to make them stop talking. And in any event, what people think can ruin you in a tiny community like ours."

I nod. Here is the darker underbelly of community. The flip side of tight-knit circles and trust is claustrophobia and the conspiratorial hiss of ostracism and expulsion.

"And the money issue?" I ask.

"That is why I am coming to you," Mai says, her face upturned and eager, like a magnifying glass set against and focused upon a specimen.

I do a quick calculation in my head. Almost all of my social security payments go to help pay the rent. I also set aside a small amount to help Mai with a down payment should she decide to buy a house. I fear unmet expectations and disappointment.

"Not that I think you can give her any money," she quickly adds. Her lips quiver. "I know you haven't got extra money to give. But I just can't discuss this with anyone else because I think Aunt An would consider it a betrayal, my sharing her business with another. Please think about what I can do.

"It is tight for me if I have to help her make her payment every month. But it gets worse," Mai confides further. "Once the rotation of drawings is completed and this *hui* is over, she might not be able to participate in the next *hui* at all."

From her tone, I can tell Mrs. An counts on money from the *hui*. But I still ask, "Does she need to? Does she need a lump sum of ten thousand dollars every year?"

Mai says yes in a single exhalation of breath.

My mind churns, thinking of ways that we can shoulder into Mrs. An's growing problems.

"I'm going to work, Ba. I would have waited to talk to you later today but I have been feeling so anxious about this that I couldn't wait. Aunt An will stop by soon on her way to the nursing home. I don't want her to think we have been discussing her," Mai says. The chair makes a scraping sound as she pushes it back. I look out the window at the interlock of remaining green cast by the hemlocks and firs. A breeze stirs, casting a flickering, mothlike shadow on her face as she stoops to bid me good-bye.

# 9

# *The Mynah Bird*

## MAI, 1967

I am lying in bed with our Chinese grandmother. Already the evening is dimming.

As her hand reaches the small of my back, I feel a new inner static under the skin's surface. I must have reacted in an abrupt way because she jumps and asks in a tone of hushed astonishment if something is wrong.

I shake my head.

Poor child, our grandmother nonetheless whispers. Poor child.

Our parents too have whispered something similar to each other, when they think I cannot hear.

Why, in heaven and earth, can't she at least try to appear normal?

She has to try.

She is.

She has to try harder.

At night, our Chinese grandmother invariably mutters to herself. Poor child.

I do not mind it. I want to be small inside the world's vastness. They don't understand, but I have grown to like the emptiness and stillness of silence itself. I want to be swallowed up inside a vast expanse of space.

Tonight, a tide of light swells beside me. The first time I felt this lurking feeling was on the night after my sister's burial. I was in bed then as well. In my head were images of tombstones and the symmetrical shadows cast against the hill's crescent sweep of grass. The shadows had followed me home, into my bedroom. A strange feeling sank into me that night.

I felt a mass of churning emotions inside me. I thought it had to do with my sister, with the lingering imprint of her presence, with the fact that certain things can attach themselves to your body and soul and cling forever to your heart. Even after the fleshly presence, a fragment of a memory might remain, spinning alternative versions of what might have been. That was what I thought.

And the feeling that there was another person nearby became more pronounced. Is there someone on the other side of me?

So when this charge surges, I recognize it immediately. A body double is clinging seamlessly to me, like a double helix that has been lovingly orchestrated into a single wave, dancing out there, matching my movements. It is there but it is outside my range of vision. I snap my head around. Still I cannot see.

I nudge my Chinese grandmother with my elbow and point to the night-prowling shadows that have emerged from the dark. She shushes me. And then, perhaps out of curiosity, she bolts up, looks, and, seeing that nothing is there, murmurs, "Go to sleep," as she flicks my eyes closed with her fingers.

Ghosts can be found anywhere, but especially here. Even in Saigon where people can flip a switch and summon electricity to make a dark room bright or a hot room cool, people believe in the supernatural. What inhabits us is something much more primitive. A mysterious noise in the chimney, a fleeting silhouette by the window, an electrical charge in the air—these can all be explained away by reference to ghosts. I understand it now more than ever. The explanation satisfies. It feels personal, like the presence of a loved one. I am not sure how spirits fit into my sister's world, the world of physics. But I embrace the thought: My sister has turned into a ghost, a flying, extravagant figure that floats and hovers, creeps and crawls, always watching over me.

She is here, I say to myself.

———

One night, months after my sister's death, I hear our parents talking. Despite their efforts to control the modulation of their voices, it is clear that they cannot. I have understood for some time now that their manner of being with each other has become perverse. There is an inhibited quality in their talk, the subdued ferocity under the unstirred surface of apparent calm, the deliberate lowering of voices that serves only to magnify the underlying tension.

"How could you?" Mother hisses. Her power to accuse is at its peak. "How could you *not*?" she admonishes with a sovereign's authority. She pauses again and this time it is a long one.

"I will not be a party to it," Father says after a moment's hesitation.

"To what? To protecting your family?" Mother asks.

"He's not my family. Your brother... I will not..." His voice trails off.

"Surely you see that it is not proper to mix official duties with personal obligations," he admonishes.

I hear her accusation again, this time more loudly. "A disgrace." And then moments later, more of the same. "A disgrace," she repeats with greater indignation.

I imagine our father's face as he is pressed by our mother into doing something he does not want to do. What do his eyes say? Are they sad? Where is the vertical line that customarily creases his forehead when he is nervous?

"It's too bad you feel that way. But I will not. I cannot," he insists unapologetically.

I press my ear to the bedroom door. Mother continues to exhort Father. Then silence settles briefly. Even in my most extravagant fantasy, I cannot will peace or harmony into them. Some things cannot be instilled merely by acts of imagination.

"It's too much to ask," I hear Father exclaim. He is vulnerable. He is being pushed out of shape. He cannot stop himself from going on. "What do you think this is? This is a real war, not make-believe," he says. "There are limits. I can't do it."

"You can't or you won't?" Mother quickly replies, matching his excitement with her own shrill rage. "You would if you cared about the family." An opening has been created. They will walk screaming into it.

Father's voice quivers. "How dare you," he says. I have never heard such a bite in his voice. I fear the direction their conversation is taking. I hear their footsteps—father's booted thud, mother's wood-sandal clatter against the bare tiles.

"It has been done before," Mother continues more calmly. "*You would not be the first.*"

There is then an unwavering flow of unintelligible words. I cling to them, hoping to decipher their meaning.

"Others have saved you before at great sacrifice and risk to themselves. *He* did it for you. Have you ever thought of that?" our mother asks with deliberateness.

A chaotic exchange follows. Mother lashes out and Father breaks down. The recrimination continues.

Our father emits a snort of disdain, as if to shrug off our mother's unwelcome but all-too-obvious revelation.

"And so he did, did he?" he says loudly. "Of course he did. But are you sure he did it for *me*?"

Mother hisses back, and then their voices drop. Still, I manage to hear our mother say something about Uncle Number Two. Theo this, Phong that. Uncle Number Two and his thickened jawline scar. So many names for just one person. So many complications. I hear our father snicker. He tells her not to call Uncle Number Two by a name meant to be endearing, a name he came up with years ago out of habitual affection. "I never use that name anymore, haven't you noticed?" he says, and then he turns quiet. Mother ignores his question. I hear her use the word *sacrifice* several times. She tells him to look at those around him. Not *just* at the war, she adds. By the way she pronounces it, with a particular pitch of her voice and with particular emphasis on the word, the *just* is packed with judgment and tension.

"And what do you mean by that?" Father asks.

"You would not have to ask if you open your eyes. Do you think *he* is the only one who has put you above others? You see nothing unless— no, you see nothing *even*—when it is right in front of you."

"I see more than you think. I just choose not to announce it."

They both turn deadly quiet. And then I hear a muffled, melancholic cry.

"After Khanh's death, I just can't cope with another loss." She lets out a soft moan that rises excruciatingly into a raw wail. It resembles the raging howl I once heard from under my bed, that weekend long ago when she believed she was home alone. But she knows that she is not alone now. Her cries soon turn into long, plaintive sobs that mount in a swelling undercurrent of grief.

I wait for something to happen. A moment passes. Then our father gets up and moves around, sending a brief shadow across the door's crack. "Very well then," he mutters. "I will see what can be done."

Mother's sobs abate for a few moments and then rise again, although it seems more from momentum than from continuing distress.

A few moments later, I hear this: "I will do my best. I promise."

Mother's tone changes. Father lingers in the room. "But you understand, I'm sure, that there will be some ground rules that must be followed afterward. It's for all of our safety."

I hear nothing from Mother. An agreement of sorts has been forged between them. Perhaps they have finally crossed over the turbulence and arrived at a truce. I am relieved.

I want to offer Mother a gesture of kindness. Her wail has so distressed me that I am ready to summon up my nerve to rush in and whisper something in her ear. But as usual, a swell rises in me and I will not disrupt the slumbering silence that is mine alone. There is no beneficent normalcy to offer her, after all. I sit still, listening, as Father leaves. The door opens, then swings back on its hinges, and closes with a click that signals finality.

The mynah bird charms me. Perched on the edge of James's palm is a shiny black-feathered bird with a bright orange beak, its face lined with an iridescent yellow stripe. James snuggles it under his chin, then feeds it a bowl of scarlet-red peppers. The bird loves to cuddle and to be cuddled, James says. I stare into its clear, bright eyes. It returns my stare, then cocks its head as if it were trying to figure me out. Round eyes lock with mine. Thick wings flap.

Be still.

"Come closer," James says.

As I press toward him, my Chinese grandmother sneezes. The bird sneezes too. I am amazed. Intense black eyes glare at me. Head rears back, then turns askance. James whistles one of Grandma's favorite tunes, "Yesterday." The bird immediately hops on James's shoulder and whistles. James runs his finger over the bird's clipped wing, then thrusts a mirror in front of its face. "What a bird!!!" the bird says, then laughs. An English-speaking bird. Both James and my Chinese grandmother laugh as well. "What a bird indeed," James agrees, nodding.

"Some bird!" he says, and the bird repeats the words. James takes my hand and places it on the bird's head. "Stroke it."

I obey. My Chinese grandmother explains that a mynah bird is a bird that repeats the words of others.

The bird again cocks its head, then rubs it against the back of my hand with surprising enthusiasm. I feel a twinge of excitement. A lightness fills me up. I answer its inaudible call and quicken my caresses of its feathered breast. The bird stretches its body this way, then that, as if to get me to touch the precise location of an elusive itch.

"Hungry?" James asks in Vietnamese. "Hungry," the bird says, also in Vietnamese. A Vietnamese-speaking bird also! I can detect the dripping smell of mango and papaya coming from the bird. "Food?" James suggests in English. "Food," the bird rasps in English.

"Two languages," my Chinese grandmother exclaims.

I feel an odd and astonishing sense of complicity with the bird.

James leans toward the bird and whispers something in its ear. "Go on," James urges, nudging the bird and giving it a slice of ripe-yellow mango.

"Ah, ah, ah, ah, mynah bird," the bird says proudly. It continues with "Vietnam, Vietnam," which, given its slight flaw in locution, sounds like "southern duck, southern duck." This mishap provokes laughter in my Chinese grandmother. James shakes his head and offers an explanation. "We're still working on that one. We'll get it right."

James drops to the ground, kneeling on the sidewalk. "So, what do you say?" James searches, looking at me. "Do you like the bird?"

Yellow feet step forward. Head tilts side to side. Body tips.

"Yes," the bird insists, striking a pose with an ecstatic flapping of the wings. "Yes. Do you like the bird? Do you like the bird?" It nods its head frantically, repeating James's words.

I edge closer to James and rest my head against his chest. I might have said how much I already love the bird, its sense of humor, its imperious ways. "I like the bird." Those words stay stuck in my throat.

Yes, one word, just one. I can feel an ocean swell of a word forming inside me. I can answer it, this rumbling expanse and its accompanying inclination to say yes.

But as I feel the eyes on me, I know I cannot do it. The task of actually forming and uttering one word is daunting. I content myself with keeping my head against James's large, cupped hand and tickling the feathered mound of the bird's wattled neck.

The bird pulls back and looks at me in reproach.

The temptation for me to make a sound is almost irresistible.

"It's okay," he says, as if to soothe both the bird and me. "Squeeze my hand if you like the bird." I squeeze his hand.

James smiles broadly. He pulls me closer and asks, "They're sending me out of here for a few weeks. Do you think you can keep the bird for me?"

I don't answer James's question, but this time when he offers me his hooked finger, I curl mine into his and pull, the way I did so many times with him when my sister was alive.

My Chinese grandmother quickly says yes. "Yes," she answers in Vietnamese, making eating motions with her hands and mouth. "I'll make sure it is well fed."

I am delighted. I feel a burgeoning sense of well-being and joy that must add up to a happiness of sorts. James opens his backpack. He takes out a portable cassette player and a tape that has been compiled by his mother in Long Island, New York, and includes songs she thinks her son will like.

He flips the ON switch. And there it is. That riff. I have no choice but to stand there and surrender, wide-eyed and open-jawed, to the hardcore, miscreant guitar lurking under a brisk punctuation of highly syncopated chord progressions. It is a number I have yet to hear. The opening alone thrills. The beat takes you by the collar and shakes you up and launches you into a low-key but hard-edged whisper. Mick rasps about satisfaction, repeating the word over and over and over, despairingly, menacingly, urgently, until it merges with the catchy riff-filled beat. I am almost breathless as I struggle to keep up. There it is again, the chorus of double negative, half-sung, half-screamed, hissing and haunting against drum, acoustic guitar, and bass. I cannot make out all the words but I love the beat.

"Hot damn," James says, shaking his head. "I love it."

"I love it," the bird hollers.

And before I know it I hear myself repeat after the bird. "I *love* it," I say, startled by my own voice. The bird looks at me. It is used to repeating others' words and is startled to hear me repeat its words. "I love it," I say again, a little more subdued this time.

James scoops me up and draws me into his arms, a gesture suggestive of our old ways. I let myself stay inside his embrace. "Step by step. One day at a time," he says gently. "You will get your voice back. You have the loveliest of voices."

I smile. James gives me the tape.

"This way you can listen to Mick anytime."

My Chinese grandma rolls her eyes.

James also reserves the privilege of naming the bird for me. "When I come back, you tell me the name, okay?" I nod. I already know the name I will give the mynah bird. "Galileo" is the obvious choice. But the urge to speak has vanished and I tell myself I will wait until he returns to share the name with him. Before we say good-bye, James plucks me from my silence and presses his smiling face against mine. "See you soon, kid," he says to me. And to Galileo, he says, "Keep an eye on her for me, won't you?"

I watch him leave. The backpack disappears when he turns the corner. Our Chinese grandmother bends down, wiping the tears off my face with her hands.

My most intense time with Galileo is spent during a monsoon month while James is away. The skies darken and water pours down in absolution. The bird seems to love the rain. The harder the better, as if it knows that a torrential, windswept rain is necessary to alleviate the overbearing swelter of heat and humidity. As gusts of wind loft sheets of rain against our windowpanes, Galileo scratches the newspaper-lined floor of his cage and asks to be moved closer to the window. Often he will perch triumphantly on the window ledge, observing the implacable cascade. I stand close to him, placing my eyes as much at his eye level as possible to try to take in exactly what he must be absorbing.

In our yard, against the garden wall and hemmed in by thick leafy hedges, is the giant rain-collecting cistern my sister and I once used for hide-and-seek purposes. A caterpillar, tremulous and fat, is trying to escape the rain, looking for cover under the arch of a drooping leaf. The grass-covered grounds are waterlogged. Galileo seems enthralled by it all—the wind-whipped trees stoically standing up to the rain, the clattering of water on tiled roofs, the sound of little children playing naked in the streets. Sometimes he will almost flatten himself against the window, as if to help him see through the glistening rain and his own blurred vision. I watch him rub his body against the glass, lifting his wings, sinuously preening.

What are you doing? I ask silently.

And as if she can read my mind, my Chinese grandmother volunteers an answer. "Birds like to take baths," she says, as much to herself as to me. "We must get a bath pan for the bird," she mutters. I am pleased. She too is enthralled by Galileo.

"Galileo, Galileo," the bird says, shifting his weight from one foot to the other.

Grandma laughs. "What a quick study you are. Are you sure you want such a name?" And then turning to me, she asks, "So, little one, you have been talking to this bird and teaching him his name?"

I shake my head. I have not. Perhaps it is Grandma herself who has been playing with Galileo. I hear her call his name. I decide *she* is the one who told him his name and she is simply playing a game with me.

"Galileo, Galileo," Galileo says.

"What a good bird," Grandma clucks. She fusses over the bird. She gives him a piece of bread as a midafternoon snack. Galileo snatches it from her hand, then dunks it into a bowl of water before swallowing it. When I run a finger along his feathery breast, he tilts his head and opens his beak ever so slightly, as if he were being tickled into a trance. I cup Galileo in my hands and together we watch the rain pour from the eaves and drainpipes of our house. My cricket puts out a contented chirp from the sanctuary of its matchbox.

Galileo does not merely mimic. He listens and understands and knows the meaning of words. If I sit by myself and stare, he will ask, "Sad?"

Right now, he is on a roll, showing off an enviable repertoire of sounds, words, and phrases. Soon a game between Galileo and Grandma develops.

"Is that the phone ringing?" Grandma asks.

"No! No, me, me," the bird says as he makes a trilling sound.

"Is that the rumbling of a motor?"

"Nooooh!"

"Is somebody snoring in the middle of the afternoon?"

"Noooo!"

Grandma looks at me and asks once again with evident hope and optimism in her voice, "Have you been teaching him? You talk to him?"

I shake my head.

"How is he picking up all these new words? *Someone* is playing with him and teaching him. By God, he's *talking*. Not just repeating a word here and a word there."

*You* are, I want to say. Stop pretending. But I shrug. Maybe he is a smart bird who figures out his own name because he hears Grandma refer to him as Galileo. There is a rush of air as Galileo spreads his wings and strikes a dramatic pose. He turns toward me. "Talk, talk. Play, play. Come. Cecile, Cecile," he sings.

Cecile? Who is Cecile, I wonder. What a marvel. Galileo has invented a new game for us.

"Come, Cecile. Ceceeeeel," he continues. His eyes fix themselves on me. He hops toward me with his outstretched wings.

I hesitate. I can almost see Cecile's shadow by my side.

"Cecile, Cecile," he persists. He is wooing me out of my fortress of silence.

I look around. A great humming stillness envelops me while a rush of movement jolts me from the inside out. I am acutely aware of a presence beside me, like a frolicking spirit that wishes to play by a swollen riverbank. Time streams by. There *is* another person present, I am sure of it, the same person who emerges at night and hovers nearby when I am in bed. A ghost. My sister, I think. The air conditioner squeaks. I am somewhere between being and not being, subsumed deep inside a long, drawn-out transition that sticks and sticks until finally I manage to break free with a big gasp, only to hear a full-flood scream from Galileo himself.

"Cecile," Galileo shrieks.

"He has given you a pet name?" my Chinese grandmother asks. "How curious. How cute," she says, laughing. "Playful bird."

Where did he get such a name, I ask myself. I have read that animals have an innate ability to detect subtle shifts in their environment, such as the earth's vibrations, or electrical charges in the air. I wonder if Galileo senses the presence I sense now and at night too. I look around.

"Cecile plays. Cecile plays."

As I stand in dumb muteness, Galileo stomps his feet on the table's surface and asks, over and over, "Do you like me? Do you like me? Mynah bird, mynah bird."

Grandma keeps silent and turns to me.

A moment passes. Galileo tilts his head mournfully. I detect a faint movement of his cheeks, as if he were attempting a smile. I smile back.

"You like me? Mynah bird. Nice bird."

I say nothing. My silence stubbornly persists.

"You're hurting his feelings, maybe," Grandma says.

He makes wiping motions. He cranes his neck sideways, rubbing his eyes against his feathered wings, as if to wipe off a tear.

I have no choice but to reassure him. "I like you," I confess. "I really do."

It is a whispery rasp of a voice. It is mine.

The cricket emits a sound, as if surprised. I hear a high-pitched, pulsing chirp vibrating through his body. Galileo stares at me as if through the sides of his eyes and hops on my shoulder.

"Cecile," he coos.

"Hello," he says. "Hello, Cecile."

My Chinese grandmother shakes her head in disbelief.

Father continues to sit quietly at night by himself. Mother has stopped paying attention to our garden. A gardener has been hired to watch over the errant vines, gather the carcasses of mangoes that drop from the tree, fertilize our frangipani blooms. Mother spends her evenings inside her grief.

But the fact that I have reclaimed my voice delights them both. This is new. This is hopeful. At least it is not bad news. It is not another failure. It no longer takes much to please them.

I am partly relieved and partly disappointed. To my surprise, I miss the challenge. Once, I was capable of meeting their wishes. Now, as if deciding that their combined objectives for me might need a degree of clear-eyed adjustment, they are ready to adapt and expect less. They are now willing to live with imperfections and compromise. I am their only remaining child, one evidently not destined to prosper. The simple truth is that all their efforts are directed by their fear that I will stop talking once again.

"I'm happy," Father says. "I'm happy you are talking. If you don't talk, how can you do well in school? If you don't do well in school, how will you fare when you grow up . . ."

Growing up is too far in the future for me to worry about now. Still, I nod to reassure him.

Both parents wish to spoil Galileo and remind my Chinese grandmother that he is to get whatever he wants. But Galileo does not want much besides regular changes of newspaper for his cage or morsels of mangoes and papayas. My parents insist: Perhaps Galileo can be cajoled into a taste of Japanese royal persimmon, or a Korean pear, each lovingly coddled in a rice-paper-thin wrapper. Sensing encouragement and adulation, Galileo goes about performing and preening.

Fear that I might regress into silence has humbled my parents. They willingly rely on the bird for help. They also want to find out more about James. "What a miracle he is," they proclaim. "We are indebted to him," Mother says. She believes if a debt is incurred it must be repaid.

"Who is he? How did you meet him?"

My Chinese grandmother explains that he is an American soldier—a sergeant. "Oh, him, yes," our father exclaims. Our father remembers that James was there when my sister died. James is a mere youngster, as he puts it, who is attached to the military police compound down the street.

"The girls used to spend almost every evening with him listening to music." Our Chinese grandmother fills our mother in on the way we were, tapping her foot and moving her shoulders ever so lightly as memories course through her.

I am amused. I have never seen our grandmother's moves. Our parents look at each other obliquely. Whatever thought each has separately is ultimately shared by the other. After a few moments, they nod, as if in agreement about something. An understanding is sealed in a glance here, a nod there, as if anything more explicit were extraneous, even unbecoming.

It is the first time I have seen such a visible display of complicity on their part. A few weeks later I discover what all the nodding and sidelong glances were about.

The next time I see James he is in our dining room. By then I am talking again and by all outward appearances my normal self. He stands uncertainly by the table. It is the first time he has been inside our house. He clears his throat, then says hello. My parents have decided that James will be my tutor. They have both come to realize that the foreign language I should be learning is English, not French. And so for the sake of my future, for the sake of my newly minted life, they approached him. They do not know James, but he might have a faculty that ministers to the past and ushers in a different, more positive future for me.

And so that is how my second life with James begins. The language that my sister would have wished to learn, as she once announced after doing a gorgeous imitation of Mick's "Tell me." English, the language of rock and roll. With it, my life with my sister can be resurrected. This, then, is our weekly tutorial. Galileo too participates by sitting on his usual perch on the windowsill, occasionally pecking at a pear washed and pared by my Chinese grandmother. James pronounces a word. I repeat it. Then Galileo. Later I might forget a word only to be reminded of it by Galileo. The bird eggs me on, still insisting on calling me Cecile.

"Why do you give her a French nickname, Galileo?" James asks Galileo, laughing. "Why 'Cecile'?"

Eyes wide open, Galileo says nothing in response.

Life outside our dining room where the lessons are taking place fades in and out. From the other side of the room, James paces back and forth, pointing to an object, a table and a pen, a book and a cup, in quick succession—somehow they are always configured in twos. I listen to his big-booted thump against the tiled floor. Even off duty, he wears his military uniform. My eyes fall onto the crisp, starched folds of his shirt, the insignia that signifies rank or accomplishment. We are still in the vocabulary phase of our lesson but soon we will embark on grammatical phrases and more. I already know some English from watching American television. James is an eager teacher. This is an elbow. This is a stomach. This is a jaw. We go from nouns to verbs to adjectives. I nod avidly. I rarely fail him. The buildup of what is asked of me is gradual but certain.

On our occasional walks in the garden he points out flowers and insects to me. This is a butterfly. This is a rose. This is a funny mynah bird. This is a cricket. I show him a cluster of touch-me-nots that we call bashful plants. I flick a finger hard against a bunch of leaves and watch as they close in the blink of an eye. James sits close to the ground and blows soft breaths onto their wing tips. Slowly, slowly, they purr and hesitate, then fold up into themselves. I am delighted. James is willing to sit with me as we both wait patiently for them to open up again.

"How's everyone? Everyone okay?" he asks in a schoolteacher voice.

"It's hard to say," I answer. That the conversation seems to be part of an English lesson makes it easier for me to talk. "We are fine," I finally say, covering my face with my hand.

"I bite my nails too, see?" He shows me his hands. The right thumbnail is ragged. I put my hands behind my back. I know all my nails, not just the thumbnail, are chewed up. "It's okay to feel bad," James whispers.

I nod. I do feel bad, almost like carsick. "Next time we can read a book. Listen to music. Maybe even play soccer." His hand slaps his lap with each suggested activity.

"I will like that," I answer. It has become easy to talk to James. Even if there is no formal lesson plan, I will be able to manage a normal conversation with him.

We are careful to talk quietly so we don't disturb the bashful plant. Sure enough, after some time, it opens up, its leaves unfolding like a shiny, green revelation. I am thrilled that I am here to witness its opening. "Hello," James murmurs to the plant. His stomach growls. The plant blushes in the soft wind but remains wide open. "C'mon, I'm hungry. But let's do something else first," he says.

It is early evening. A cool breeze blows as James takes my hand. We walk toward the vacant field across from our house. "Soccer ball," James says, pointing to a bin of balls stored in a wooden shed. We draw two lines on a wall, each signifying a goalpost. The point is to kick the ball between the two lines. James shows me many of the game's inspired moves, the right fake and the left spin, the pinball swerve and the duck, the final scramble straight through a line of defense. He learned as a child to appreciate the game, its flow, the passes that are beautiful whether or not they produce points.

"Come close and watch," he says. The ball dances between his feet. He dribbles it to me. I kick it back. We are both delirious. He bounces it back and forth, up and down his bare knees, then runs with the ball glued to the tips of his shoes until it is released, *bing,* right between the two black marks on the wall. With each ball that James unleashes, he aims and aligns his entire being into the very arc of the ball. When his sneakers hit the ball, a solid thud can be heard. My heart beats loudly against my chest as I chase after him. Heat rises from the pinkness of my cheeks. There is James, with the perfect kicking leg, the calf muscles that flex. My Chinese grandmother, it turns out, has appeared and is watching us. She sits on a collapsible aluminum chair and cheers us on. She occasionally stops fanning herself to clap and hoot. Once in a while she even gets up and runs up and down the sidelines.

When we return to the house a pitcher of lemonade, the salted kind, awaits us. My Chinese grandmother hands us both towels and insists we wash up. She offers us a tray of *banh mi.* James takes out a guitar and we strum and pluck our way through the remainder of the evening. We are in my house. My Chinese grandmother is nearby. The music has to be melodious to be house-sanctioned. Galileo and I listen adoringly as he sings "Yesterday." I join in. I too can say the words and feel them form inside me.

Coming from him, the lyrics soar and wrap themselves around us, taking us in and holding us close. I am a rogue child claimed by a sudden sense of happiness. Coming from James, the song feels singularly personal. It is about us. It seizes our very being. We are singing about the same yesterday, or some imperfect prototype of it. I am doing it in English. This might be one way of negotiating the crossover into a new beginning, by preserving the essence of our shared past. Let it be enough to produce happiness. Let it be the way for us as we struggle to cross that line between what we expect and what we can actually get.

It might be purely my imagination, but I believe Mother is undergoing a transformation. Still, emanating from her room is the usual sullen and accusatory quiet that seals her from the world beyond. But she no longer disappears into the throng of well-meaning but exhausting visitors whose dealings and demands tire her out.

With my Chinese grandmother watching over him, Galileo is even allowed to enter the breakfast room. I sense it is for my sake, but our mother fusses over him too.

"Cecile, Cecile," he calls to me. I watch as Galileo gently takes a mango slice from our mother's hand. It is breakfast time. My parents give each other a questioning look and seem amused that Galileo has come up with a pet name for me.

"Ask for more, Galileo," I coach. I come toward him, proffering my arm as a perch. "Come, come," I whisper.

Galileo cocks his head and jumps away from me. "Cecile."

I am baffled. The skin on my arms pricks up. The bird continues to look at me but asks for Cecile instead.

Our mother chuckles and offers my bird more mango. I look at her with admiration. She is a woman whose beauty refuses to fade. Her well-being might be provisional but it is taking shape. Father encourages it.

As I try to fall asleep, I am startled by the sound of an unconcealed cry. I listen. It does not get louder as I lie there listening, and soon it fades. Our mother is not losing control. She will be sleeping soon enough. But this time, an emptiness enters me that asks not to be left alone but to be touched.

My body answers her cry. And so I get up and walk into her room. I see the form of her body under the blanket, its trembling rise and fall. As I slip into bed with her, she turns around to face me and draws me against her breasts. In that moment, I breathe in her scent and absorb her continuing sadness into mine. I realize how I have longed for her touch.

# 10

## *Across the Border*

### MR. MINH, 1967, 2006

True, the country was covered in virgin jungles. The enemy ambushed, then retreated into its deep greenery. And there was also the fog, which might not evaporate even when it was subjected to the implacable heat. It would hang there, along the shoreline and even inland. A soft wind could loft it higher or lower, over the rice fields or above the mountain peaks, but there it would remain. In war, especially this war, where the enemy was already invisible, fog was something to be feared. It suggested opportunities for cover, camouflage, and conspiracy. It meant that the air was alive in a spooky, ghostly way. Phantoms swirled. Vapors floated. There were no straight lines, no definitive truths. Our vision was blurred. Everything became ambiguous. It was easy to imagine, with one sliver of our consciousness, those impassive eyes that followed our movements before pouncing.

And so yes, there were thick jungles and dense foliage. And there was fog. We absorbed all of these facts into our mental coordinates. Still, how did the enemy melt, evaporate, disintegrate, disappear?

The enemy did not. They went across the border into Cambodia. We knew that was the answer. But we needed evidence.

It was out in the open at last, this matter of the porous border between Vietnam and Cambodia.

Intelligence collected by III Corps indicated that the Communists were converting the Giong Bau area straddling the Cambodian–South Vietnamese border in Chau Doc Province into a base and shelter for their troops. The corps had tried to destroy the Communist forces there but after each encounter the enemy withdrew into technically neutral Cambodian territory where our forces were forbidden to enter. Aerial photographs confirmed our suspicion and pinpointed enemy movements, revealing faint smudges of enemy sanctuaries across the border in sovereign Cambodia, and later in Laos.

A winding trail used as a North Vietnamese supply conduit snaked perceptibly, belligerently, through the eastern part of Cambodia. It was meticulously configured by battalions of engineers using cutting-edge Soviet and Chinese machinery. Radio operators, ordnance experts, platoons of drivers, and mechanics all came along to support the North's army. Twenty thousand or more North Vietnamese regulars were pouring steadily into the South.

Still, the Cambodian prime minister would declare that the onslaught of North Vietnamese troops was nothing but "a myth fabricated by the U.S. imperialists to justify their war of aggression."

The port of Sihanoukville was also receiving Communist supplies by sea from China. The Americans brought in equipment to assess the scope of the infiltration. Their Side-Looking Airborne Radar unit carried vertical, oblique, and split-image cameras. It was also equipped with horizon-to-horizon panoramic scanning cameras. There was a sensor for gathering electromagnetic intelligence. Mounted on the underwing of the reconnaissance aircraft were two high-intensity supersonic flasher pods to illuminate the ground underneath. Statistical data gathered by its digital data system recorded altitude, latitude, and date.

Based on the evidence, I received orders to lead two battalions of our elite forces into the enemy stronghold.

It was to be a solely Vietnamese operation, so that the Americans could remain faultless. No American troops, just two American advisers. Cliff was one of them.

Our clandestine operation was an acknowledgment that the enemy's war plan had shifted. It was dictated no longer by an internal insurgency within the South but by an invasion from the North itself.

The invasion was launched using the Ho Chi Minh Trail. Enemy troops attacked from bases secured in Cambodia and Laos.

Once, the Trail was indeed truly a trail, a rutted, primitive footpath that meandered through the Laotian panhandle and onto the border areas of Cambodia. I knew the winding turns that looked like finely veined lines, like innocent curves, on an aerial-view map. But there was nothing innocent about the Trail. Indeed, its foliage of triple-canopied green ruthlessly clawed its way through a stampede of overgrown lushness, doing whatever was needed to get a little bit more sun, a little bit more air, even if it meant monopolizing life for itself and denying that possibility to others.

I could see the rush of waterways that patiently carved their presence into the land. The Bang Fai River wound eastward through the town of Tchepone, which served as a major transportation hub for the enemy. The Kong River descended from central Vietnam, flowed west through southern Laos, and entered Cambodia east of the Mekong River. We knew they were loading food, fuel, and munitions into steel drums and launching them into the rivers to be collected downstream by an intricate system of nets and booms.

We had no choice. Their supply train down the Trail had to be stopped, not by air but by ground operations. For years, the American military had sought permission from their government to conduct such an incursion. For years their request had been denied.

Our intelligence told us there was a discernible pattern to the enemy's movements. The plan I devised was aimed at cutting off the customary withdrawal route into Cambodian sanctuaries. The two battalions under my command would move into Cambodian territory at night in order to occupy blocking positions north of the main enemy base. Then at dawn, an armored cavalry force would launch a direct frontal attack against the base from the southwest. The enemy would be sandwiched in between. Their retreat route into Cambodia would be blocked by my paratroopers and they would be destroyed.

I selected the First and Eighth Airborne battalions for the mission, the same battalions I had refused to turn over for use in the November 1963 coup. We moved by truck from Saigon to My Tho. We sat on the truck floors that were reinforced with sandbags to shield us from shrapnel and mine explosions. Still, the rumble of the engine could be felt right through the truck's thick steel plates. From My Tho, our two battalions and an armored cavalry force embarked on naval ships waiting to take us on the Mekong River, upstream toward Tan Chau. The morning light shone sheets of silver glaze across the rippling water. Later a dense fog hung over us like a strange grief, sealing us in its solemn sanctuary. Our ships rose and dipped through the shifting shoals, chugging in the palm of the current. We moved with the tide and wind. Still, our destination was one day and one night away. A violet dusk folded around us. The men laced their boots and went through the usual rituals. They switched their safety levers from safe to semiautomatic to automatic, then back. They arranged and rearranged their equipment, checked their rounds of ammunition, canteens, helmets, rifles, medical field kits, and fragmentation grenades.

Cliff kept himself apart from the others, his body taut, controlled. He stared into empty space, his gaze swept a 180-degree arc. I considered myself lucky. Cliff was a model adviser and our only one. One unit in the II Corps had, in a span of but a few years, more than forty American advisers.

By early morning of the second day, we disembarked in Thuong Phuoc, a desolate border outpost manned by our Special Forces on the left bank of the river, three kilometers from the Cambodian border. The outpost commander provided us with a reliable local guide who, we were assured, knew the local terrain, the ghost territories inside the weak faults and gorges of the border territories that occasionally slid into enemy control and pulled men into an underground of pulsing nerves and graves.

My plan was to take the lead with the First Battalion. The Eighth would follow a short distance behind. We checked for uncommon rises in the land, unusual accumulations of leaves or dirt that could conceal wires or a row of sharpened stakes. The land itself could be choreographed for death.

I was the point man, leading our column. Cliff was by my side with an M16 and a pistol belt around his waist with six magazines of ammunition. We adopted a staggered lead sweep, surveying both sides of the corridor. I fingered my web belt with its canteen, ammo pouches, and four fragmentation grenades. I walked slowly, stroking the pistol grip of my rifle, fully alert as I studied the jungle around us. I kept my index finger on the trigger and my thumb simultaneously on the safety lever.

A meek half-light filtered through the sieve of foliage. We continued making our way through the chaos of the jungle. A somber grayness cast by the three-dimensional thickness of shade seemed to envelop everything. Some may complain about the heat, but it is really the density and darkness that consume everything—light, color, space.

Instinctively, we made the necessary adjustments and allowed sight to be superseded by sense. We developed a rhythm so that trudging became automatic. We willed it all away—friction, gravity, fatigue. As nighttime approached, a deep darkness, the true spirit of this remote jungle, settled over us, seeping into our bodies, making us a part of it. There was no moon. Our guide closed his eyes. I too closed mine, allowing them the necessary period of visual adjustment before charting the coordinates of black space. It was all one fathomless stretch, menacing in its sheer seamlessness.

We marched in ponderous silence. Each man had a ragged patch of white cloth tied to his shoulder. The soldier behind fixed his eyes on the floating whiteness, ensuring that he would remain in position within the undulating column. There was the sense that with every step forward we were being watched—by the trees and the spirits that had melted deep into the collected days of the earth itself. Several times my feet got caught among the tangle of ferns, thorns, lianas, and matted vines. Here and there, carcasses of dead trees lay scattered, their protruding branches an avalanche of dead rot and saturated mulch. We hacked our way through the greenery, using swift upward strokes. Thorns and grasses slashed our faces.

Finally our battalion got the word every man had been waiting for. "We're here," the local guide said. The topography had changed. The canopy had thinned, the ground cleared, perhaps purposively leveled, except for a few scraggly brushes. Dried marshland materialized before us. Though relieved—all of us would be happy to rest—I was surprised and skeptical. Had we crossed into Cambodia? Here among the tangle of endless green, borders were hard to discern. In the vast oneness of life, borders hardly mattered and yet it was here that they mattered more than ever. We had walked almost a full day, but it did not seem we had covered enough territory to arrive at the planned blocking positions behind the enemy base. I looked at the line of phosphorous green on my wrist compass. The local guide insisted he never made a mistake. After a brief discussion with the First Battalion commander, I gave the orders for both battalions to take blocking positions facing south, behind what we had been told were the enemy's bases.

Sometimes the right way might seem wrong and the wrong way right. I suddenly remembered my conversation with Phong that evening after the coup.

The night was cool. A soft breeze blew through the low-hanging mist. Our radio operator carried a PRC-25 set on the internal frequency of the company for communication among our squads and platoons. Another PRC-25 was set on the command network. I scanned the empty space before me. The sky folded into itself, a tightly curled blackness that obliterated vision. Not a single feature of the enemy base could be discerned through the low-hanging fog. And yet were we not expecting a large congregation of men and equipment?

I reported this fact to Major General Phat, my III Corps commander, who ordered us to remain in place until the following morning. We settled in our bivouac for the night. We quickly ate our meal of sticky rice and dried cotton pork. Cliff ate whatever we ate. He had not brought the usual C ration cans provided for the American troops.

The ground was low and flat but moist from rain. I felt a cold slimy column crawl under my shirt. Leeches. I dug my fingernails into a fat, slimy mass, prying it from my flesh and squishing it between thumb and forefinger. A thick, slippery substance trickled down my hand. I wrapped myself tightly inside my poncho, put my head on a slight rise, and closed my eyes. Our defensive perimeter was secured by a rotation of men. Platoon sergeants organized reconnaissance patrols. A two-man team was assigned to each listening post along the perimeter. Each team was equipped with a PRC-25, weapons, and a watch. Mechanical ambushes were also set—claymore mines, detonation cords, blasting caps, a battery, and a triggering mechanism attached to a trip wire. We followed the protocol strictly.

By six o'clock the next morning, our troops were ready and alert. The easterly sun peeked from gray clouds. We would move out soon. I decided that the Eighth Battalion would take the lead and the First would follow. Perimeter guards went about the task of rolling the wires and retrieving their claymore mines.

I looked at the topography map folded in my back pocket. The local guide gave a faint smirk to signal that he would not need to rely on the mere surfeit of compasses and maps, those spinning mechanisms of extraneous scientific devices. And then it happened. A single pop cracked the air.

A body collapsed backward, faceup. An artery had been hit. I could see the bright redness of fresh blood pouring forth in high-pressured and distinct spurts that corresponded to the pulsed rhythm of a heartbeat. The bullet had hit the soft flesh of the neck, ripping through muscle tissue. More follow-up fire erupted from the east. A thunderclap of shells burst forth. I saw blazing tracers and enemy troops entrenched behind parapets along a communication trench. All around us the land itself exploded. Mortar and machine-gun fire flashed, pulverizing and whipping up dirt and rock.

It was by now abundantly clear that last night, we had not arrived at the designated blocking positions north of the enemy base. Instead, we had installed ourselves directly within firing range. We were on flat, open land, devoid of cover and in front of cement bunkers fortified by 37 mm recoilless rifles and flanks of enemy lying in wait. Our troops instinctively sought cover and fell flat against the ground. Enemy AK-47s, RPDs, and other light machine guns clattered and popped. Bursts of fire came from left, right, and directly in front of us. There was no other choice but to make our assault. I swept my hand forward, ordering the attack. I heard curses, screams, and moans. My escort platoon and several elements of the First Battalion surged forward in unison, firing as they made their lunge. The enemy mortar team responded furiously. As we made our advance through thick gray smoke toward enemy trenches, fire volume grew in ferocity and density. From a distance of about twenty meters, I saw a clutch of enemy troops struggling with a 57 mm recoilless rifle. It was aimed and fired at us but the round did not go off. Immediately, I ordered a sergeant to seize the enemy weapon. He sprang forward, shooting his submachine gun furiously as he ran toward the trench. Others ran up to support him, spraying continuous rounds to the right and left. When he got there, the enemy had fled, leaving behind the recoilless rifle for us to confiscate.

We continued our assault and in an enfilade of gunfire succeeded in taking the first trench. A burst of machine guns and AK-47 rifles opened fire upon us at short range from another trench behind the first. We ran forward, firing from the hips, furiously throwing grenades. I heaved one grenade, then another, releasing the grenade spoon, then throwing. Enemy guns protruded from the trench and continued their fusillade. We would need reinforcement through a second flanking attack. But a cluster of troops to my left were still flat on the ground, half hidden under their rucksacks. I heard muffled movements as some elbowed and kneed themselves forward.

I was determined to keep myself erect and visible to the troops as I commanded them to move forward. "Up now," I screamed. At that very moment, a bullet ripped through me. The moment I felt it in my right abdomen was also the moment I saw Cliff knocked against the ground. I was still standing, immobilized by shock and leaning against a small scraggly bush twenty meters or so away from Cliff. The enemy was still firing. My radio operator was shot in the eye. Blood was everywhere. The medic appeared seemingly from nowhere, lowered my pants, and injected an intramuscular antibiotic into my hip. I felt no pain, only a rush of adrenaline through the heart. A syringe of morphine was jammed into my side and Cliff's. The radio operator moaned. When the medic crouched over him and lifted his head, blood flowed from his nose and face.

As the medic slapped a compress on my abdomen, I reiterated my order to the men still lagging behind. We were being raked with gunfire. The enemy was regrouping, some firing from their trench, some moving forward in an attempt to flank our trench. "Move! Move! Move!" I barked.

"Get down," Cliff screamed. He was flat on the ground, still twenty meters behind me.

I ignored him. The enemy had another 57 mm recoilless rifle emplacement out in front. My plan was to lead my men toward that 57 mm rifle to disarm it. Suddenly I felt a muscular force yanking me to the ground. The scraggly bush I was leaning against was chopped in half, its branches and leaves scattered. A shudder wended through me. It was Cliff who had pulled me out of harm's way. He was still bleeding through the cloth bandage but he had managed to crawl his way toward me in time to save my life. His M1 manganese steel helmet lay on the ground. A bullet had clanked a part of it off.

Other elements of the First Battalion were now fully energized. They poured into the first trench and held it against continued enemy attack. The First Battalion commander moved reinforcements in behind them. We were regrouping and holding. Several prongs even maneuvered themselves forward, pumping rounds into the second enemy trench as I hurried to join them. From where I was standing, it seemed that an attack against the enemy's rear would be crucial to disrupting its defenses. The air was saturated with smoke and fire. I radioed the Eighth Battalion and gave orders for them to maneuver toward the enemy's rear. But the enemy was determined to savage the Eighth's area of operation and to keep us from linking up. White and red fire pinned them in position. The enemy resisted our efforts to capture the second trench, counterattacking with rocket-propelled grenades and flamethrowers. Around us, 60 and 81 mm mortar shells landed with rapid, high-angle, plunging explosions. We returned fire furiously. Red and green tracers lit up the sky. One of my aides set his M79 in the dirt. We increased our fire, protecting him, giving him a chance to work the M79. With its barrel near vertical, he fired high explosive rounds into the enemy's trench. His aim was accurate, deadly. For the first time since early morning, enemy fire slowed. Our men quickly re-formed in pockets, charging forward to take the second trench. I looked at my watch. Three hours had passed.

Moments later, light tanks, camouflaged under a canopy of twigs and leaves, appeared. Enemy or friend? It was a convoy of M41s. Cliff had suffered a wound more severe than mine. He was still on the ground, his body cramped and tensed into a tight ball. Still he managed an excited scream. "Walker Bulldog." Yes! They were reinforcements from the III Corps commander. Shots and explosions hurtled from their M32 guns.

The enemy's firing decreased. Smoke dissolved. The trails vanished. We were ordered not to pursue them farther into Cambodian territory.

It was late morning. Past the abandoned trenches lay an interlacing tangle of well-maintained, established dirt roads. Rows of bunkers were connected by trenches, camouflaged beneath thick mats of brush and vine and bamboo, all part of an underground transfer point of supply depots. The overhead cover was reinforced with logs and sandbags and tangles of brush. From the air it would look like nothing but uninterrupted jungle. Soon enough, I thought, once the coordinates were reported, American F-4s and Cobra gunships would rip through and extinguish the tunnels.

Our seriously wounded were loaded onto poncho stretchers. Eight killed in action. I looked at our wounded. Ten altogether. There they lay, in rows, their dressings saturated with blood. The medic had pumped Cliff's arm and begun the IV flow from a 500 ml plastic bag labeled "Plasma Protein Fraction." Bandaged in the abdomen and chest, he was coming to and then passed out again.

I fingered the bandaged wound on my lower abdomen. A bloody pink-white tissue leaked from the dressing. I poked a finger into the compress and felt the bullet slightly beneath the skin's surface. The morphine and adrenaline were wearing off. I sat down. A thick fog lingered. High above, a helicopter was hovering, its rotor slapping madly as it waited to land. Smoke was popped to guide it to the landing zone. The helicopter slid into a soft touchdown on the dried mud-flat ground. Door gunners kept a steady watch. Dust and debris churned and floated. We would soon be evacuated. Our wounded would be loaded. Gear would be thrown in. When it was all over, I was told the enemy had suffered more than 80 killed in action and more than 120 wounded.

Hours later, after the operation to remove the bullet from my abdomen, a star was pinned on me as I lay in bed recovering. I had been promoted from colonel to brigadier general by the premier, head of the current ruling junta. Phong, ubiquitous Phong, perpetually adaptable, capable of serving this junta general, then that, was his right-hand man. Again, it was Phong I saw as I came back from near death. I remember the moment well. With a smile, Phong informed me that Cliff and the second American adviser accompanying the First and Eighth battalions had submitted my name to the American chain of command for a Silver Star award. But what preoccupied me was something else. I wanted to grab Phong by the collar and ask him "Why?" or "How?" Why were we deceived by the scout? How could it have happened? Who was he?

Once again, I had been granted a miracle. I had survived but eight of my men died. I choked. The wound was tender and raw but it was the heaviness in my body that truly stung. Betrayal produced that terrible effect on one's soul. In fact, the word *betrayal* itself instilled in me a new sense of distrust that attached itself to the world in general and to Phong in particular, even as he laid a comforting hand on my shoulder. But then a murmur of regret coursed through me. Phong was indeed guilty of betrayal, but he had betrayed President Diem, not me. In fact, he had saved my life, had he not?

Phong tried to pacify me. He said something about looking into the matter further and assured me the operation was successful nonetheless. It signaled to the enemy that their Cambodian sanctuaries would be attacked. "A great accomplishment," he declared. A hard rain was beating down on the roof. The traveling water poured from gutters, cascading in broad sheets down the brick walls of our military hospital. Through the double glass doors, I could see, lying in the adjacent hallway, rows of canvas stretchers wrapped in white sheets. All around me were people who had lost arms and legs. I fixed my gaze on the dead and wounded lying inert and the many doctors working in brooding silence as the rain slashed with keening rage against the windowpanes.

Through the pearly gray surface of fatigue, I hear the sound of footsteps nearby. I am walking up and down the corridors of the apartment complex with my rubber-treaded walker. I pass Mrs. An's apartment and call out to her through the warbling, hesitant emptiness of the hallway. The door opens. I make out the face of her husband, who beams me an awkward smile.

"You're home today? Not at work?" I ask.

"I took a day off to help my son fix his car." His answer comes out in a thin exhalation as he turns to his wife.

Mrs. An stands next to her husband. I keep up my pace and, not wanting to intrude on their common space, continue my daily constitutional down the hall. She pauses, and then responds with a quick wave of the hand, a little forward push of the palm through the air as she calls out for me. She is following me down the hall. I see the weary, aggrieved face masked by an exaggerated coding of musical pleasantries and smiles. But I know how it is. We carry our grief camouflaged and concealed but occasionally it pushes through the conjunctions of our mutual lives. Private sadness becomes public.

"There is a funny cartoon I saved for you," I tell her in an uplifted tone. We walk into my apartment and I take it out of a drawer to show her. "You can't help him? I thought you said you were a vet!" is the caption. The picture shows a man proffering a sick dog to a bedraggled and slightly stupefied man in uniform. "See? Vet? Veterinarian? Veteran?" I say, laughing. She laughs obligingly, layering over stifled sadness.

The words come smoothly out of me. "You are family. Here," I say. My hand is poised and ready. I press a check into her hand and I put her hand to my heart. That money should at least tide her over for one more monthly rotation of the *hui*. I don't want to prolong the moment for fear of embarrassing her and don't want her to ask questions. So I grab my walker with alacrity and head into my bedroom and close the door.

# 11
## *Tet*
### MAI, 1968

Tet 1968, the Year of the Monkey, is not like any other Tet I have known in my life. Tet is the biggest celebration in Vietnam. It is our New Year. This is the first Tet I've had without my sister.

My Chinese grandmother wakes me up. I can tell by the way she tries to scoop me up that there is urgency, there is dread. I am half-asleep and find myself inexplicably with people in a room downstairs near the kitchen. There are our visitors, Mother, the cook, and the chauffeur, in varying degrees of dishevelment—unbrushed hair, each still in pajamas, with blankets twisted around shoulders and legs. Our mother looks startled. Aunt Number So-and-so holds her child against her. She pulls a diamond ring from her finger as she searches the house for a place to hide it. The adults spill their concerns and together their fear becomes frightening. I can feel a panic that is moving too fast to comprehend. I hear a tumult of gunshots and rockets. The clock ticks and with each second the sounds of a battle being waged get closer and closer.

We lock all the doors, close all the windows, and draw the curtains, just in case. It creates a semblance of sanctuary that hides us from the shrinking sky. Our father has gotten word to us to stay inside. Cholon is under siege. I hear a barrage of shells. The Tet cease-fire has been breached. The external walls that enclose our house are thick—brick, cement—but the portion that runs along the far side of the garden has already crumbled, according to the chauffeur. I close my eyes and squeeze them shut. Little shapes, spirals, corkscrews, circles, dance behind my lids. Galileo hops from chair to table, then back to me. "Tet, Tet," he says, and whistles. "Happy Tet," he croons. He nuzzles against me and lets out a loud call for Cecile. He looks at me with questioning eyes. "Cecile? Cecile?"

One of Mother's friends silences him with a "sh, shhh." Galileo stretches his neck and strikes a pugilistic pose. "Sh, sh," he mimics. "Sh, shh."

The woman becomes assertive. "For heaven's sake, will you keep that bird quiet?" she says to me in a peevish tone. She uses a word for "you," *may,* that allows her to be offhand and dismissive and signifies at the same time my lowly status as a child. I pick Galileo up and gather him into my arms. Mother sits still; she is elsewhere, in a darkness down deep. My Chinese grandmother comes to me and caresses Galileo's head. That is precisely what my sister would have done if she were here.

No one is hungry but food is served anyway. I look at it but the thought of eating does not appeal to me. I know the grown-ups all have red envelopes with crisp new money to hand out to us children but none will be passed out now. I have an urge to leave. I disengage from the gathering, from the thick, trapped sensation that threatens from above. My chest tightens as I walk back into my room upstairs. I say a few words to Galileo to see if my voice has failed, even as little explosions of hurt churn in my stomach.

That day and that night and the day after, I stay in my own room. My Chinese grandmother comes in and out to bring me food. She lets me stay in my own private space, knowing I will be able to keep myself occupied with my bird and cricket. I sit in front of both and open my favorite storybook. "Cecile," Galileo chirps. I have accepted it as a pet name bestowed on me by him. From within the pages of the book, it is easy to dream, as if Scheherazade has a life beyond these very pages.

I see the Tigris River as it rolls placidly from Kurdistan and winds its way past Baghdad before flowing into the Persian Gulf. As it rises and ebbs it continues to look for its twin, for it knows it is destined to meet the Euphrates and together the two will form Shatt al-Arab, where lush gardens cup enchanted stories in their palms. Somewhere Scheherazade talks to her sister. Where will the next story come from to save them both?

On the third day of Tet I find myself walking down the back staircase into a hallway leading to the garden to avoid the evident tension in the common area. I intend only to stand inside the house and look out. But when I see the mango tree we used to hide behind, I have to get myself to it. I go to the next one, the star fruit tree with my sister's and my initials carved on it. Its branches spread leisurely outward, gathering the sky within its grasp. Vines and tendrils coil around my ankles, holding moisture in the bluish veins of their leaves. I want only to hug the tree and press my back against its bulk, its collected days. The future was once written here. I sit on the ground at the bottom of it. I am aware I need to go back inside, but my eyes are drawn to the dedicated movements of a column of leaf cutter ants. The brick walls surrounding the perimeters of our house still stand. For the moment it is quiet enough, except for the sounds of rockets exploding at a distance. The attacks come in waves and crescendos. And then there is quiet.

I look at my watch. Soon, my Chinese grandmother will come to my bedroom with a tray of food. It has been only ten minutes, a harmless few minutes more should be fine. I sit still. The sun shines directly above the vaulting, open sky. Drifts of yellow *hoa mai* petals fall to the ground. The earth smells fresh, but a smoky scent blows in with the wind.

And then it all returns—as if in an interlocking reflex of events. A siren goes off. Streaks of light flash above, in front of me, and everywhere. The windowpanes of the house shatter. Our trees try valiantly to wave away the rattle of gunfire. A large branch jumps and snaps. As the sky shrinks I taste bile in the back of my throat. Blue and purple dots hang in front of me, becoming more agitated as I hold my head to steady a pang of dizziness. I run toward the door to the house but a loud noise is unloosed from above. The sky is speckled with flecks of red and awash in murderously opalescent silver. I duck down in animal panic and lie still while the air crackles all around me.

Consciousness begins to slip out of me. I feel the fleeting burden of two selves separating, like gritty shadows against a dimming light, my sister and I, conjoined and then suddenly not. I watch and am watched at the same time. I am startled by this possibility. A child's tiny voice whispers in my ear.

What was that? My sister? Khanh? Spirit? Ghost?

And although I would like to be able to say more about what happens next, the truth is I do not remember. I black out. After it is all over, I can only feel the snapping aftereffect that is lodged deep inside my chest.

I have somehow made my way back to my bedroom. It is the mynah bird who wakes me. Black eyes peer through tufts of feathers. Head reared back, wings quiver and flap. Two wiry feet stomp this way and that on the floor. His sharp beak slowly comes toward me, nudging against me as if it were a paw. A feathery face stares at me with a crinkled look of wonder and befuddlement.

I surface once again into my own consciousness and feel a newness all around me: a looming presence like a mountain's sense of the inert and elemental.

Again and again, I feel something moving inside, bleeding a strangeness into my being. I try to clamp it down, to keep it locked inside, but it cannot be contained or controlled. I feel its stealthy, fretful movement.

My mynah flaps its wings. "Cecile?"

The sun is still suspended directly overhead. Galileo sits on my shoulder as I walk through the house to look for Mother and my Chinese grandmother and the rest of the Tet visitors. I feel his sharp claws through my shirt. A plane flies overhead.

"Cecile," he says over and over.

I shake my head. "Sshh," I say to hush him. "Sshh."

"Cecile," he persists.

This is hardly a time for games. "Stop it," I say, exasperated.

He hops from my shoulder and rushes off with wings that flap in a vain attempt at flight. I chase after him, down the stairs and toward the kitchen, where the guests have been congregating these past few days. There is only an odd mix of emptiness and an air of phantom imbalance in the house. Everyone has left. The bird comes to a quick stop before hopping into the comfort and familiarity of his cage, which has been set on a table far from its customary place.

The cage door is slightly open. He can easily push it ajar if he wishes to leave. But something ominous has overtaken the room and he senses it. The windows rattle. Through the bamboo bars, I see his ragged wildness reduced to beak, claws, and feathers, a rabid energy that swoops and squawks. He has shut himself in there. I turn on more lights. It is clear that no one is in the house.

I hear another siren, a whistling menace. I run from room to room looking for Mother or my Chinese grandmother. I hear my own voice, loud and delirious, calling out, "Ma, Ma." "Ngoai, Ngoai." A part of me believes they will suddenly emerge from shadowy corners and pull me into their well-concealed hiding place. But the other part of me knows I am all alone.

I find myself outside in the garden again and there is an explosion from the shabby, disreputable neighborhood behind our house. More come in succession. On instinct I count on motherhood to do its part, even though I know my mother was not able to scoop my sister out of harm's way. As I climb into the cistern to hide from the line of fire, I still believe my mother will come back to look for me and take me with her to safety.

Gunshots pop and echo. I am thankful this giant clay jar is partially hidden by a row of thick, fleshy hedges. I hear street noises, human voices, the sounds of cartridges loading and of hundreds of boots striking the sidewalk. Then I hear rapid conversations and quick movements. Looking up from my safe haven, I see rooftops, red-orange tiles, chimneys. A white kite is caught, its tangled line looped around a chimney's neck. I cannot help but stare at it. My eyes follow its arc, its plummeting flight until the wind buffets it back up. There are movements on tin rooftops behind our house, dark gray disturbances Father warned us about, among the warren of hovels and shacks and the occasional shabby high-rise. The air crackles and hums with electrical sparks.

I huddle against the cistern's hard bottom in mute fear. The voices from outside our garden wall are coming closer and closer. I listen intently. Someone screams out an order for a full frontal assault on a nearby house. It is an unrelentingly South Vietnamese voice. There are Southerners in the Vietcong, our Uncle Number Five, for example, so the South Vietnamese accent alone does not comfort.

"Forward. Go in," a male voice orders. I hear the shuffle of troops. "Regroup in three units. Move."

It happens quickly. There is a sudden swift pop. Amid the frenzy, the man who has been shouting orders must have been shot. A turbulence of noises, voices, metallic racket, follows. I am soaked in fear and confusion.

"The lieutenant is down," someone shouts. I hear a rush of boots scud past. "Remove the weight. Take the flak jacket off," another yells. Their voices carry. "Give him something, quick." There is a moment of quiet as it sounds like help is gathering around the fallen man, and then again, a surprising pop, clean and direct and seemingly on target. Someone screams that another has been downed. "What do we do?" The voice is mournful, urgent. "Stay calm, stay calm." I hear the frantic response and then a series of incomprehensible back-and-forth dialogues in a tone of clenched rage and terror. "He's going. He's not going to make it. God. I'm not a medic!"

I try to visualize the area where the soldiers are congregated. The tamarind trees that could provide them cover are nowhere near. They are exposed in the street.

"Do it. Do whatever it takes. Put your hand on the wound."

"Press down. Take my shirt."

"Up there, somewhere up there," a voice screams. On instinct I too look up. There are scattering movements along the stretch of tin rooftops. But from where I am inside the jar, I am able to see what others cannot. It is all behind the brick chimney, one among a row of similar chimneys, not by the line of galvanized tin roofs. Behind the chimney with the tossing white kite is a crouching figure. I am sure of it. My pulse quickens. I see the black barrel of a gun as it vanishes from the chimney's edge.

"Where?"

"It's gone."

"Where was it?"

"I'm not sure. With all the noise, it's . . ."

"You useless little nothing. You can't even tell where the snipers are?"

More bullets skitter in sharp bursts. I keep my head down to hide from the flicker of illuminated fire. My chest bucks in surrender, squeezed by sharp little contractions.

"Where are the Thirty-third Rangers? They were supposed to be here hours ago."

My heart does a little lift. Rangers. They must be government troops. They will help me. The enemy is on the roofs but safety is within reach, right outside the garden walls. I know where the sniper is. A clotted weight, large and bloated, sticks deep inside my throat. I raise myself and kneel up toward the jar's opening to peek out. One of the shuttered windows is now slightly open, as if the room itself were asking for more air. I don't move. I see a thin figure in a black shirt move briefly past the roof edge to the window's opening. The voices outside get closer. The troops are outside our garden's gate. They seem to be settling in, using the area as a makeshift base of operation.

"Get the radio and call for reinforcement. Ask about those rangers," a voice commands. I hear someone yell, "This is company . . . We are at . . . Assistance requested for . . ." and then I hear a loud hollow pop and the voice is abruptly cut off. I hear the immediate *thuk thuk thuk* of rapid return fire directed at every direction. The government soldiers fire indiscriminately. I hear the sounds of bullets flying, up, down, here, and there. The sniper retreats furtively, calmly waiting for the next propitious moment. The chimney is long and wide and provides perfect concealment.

Then there is silence. I press my ear against the jar. I hear the wheels of a car, no, by the rumbling of its engine, a jeep. I hear the granulated click of gravel on our rutted road. I hear the click of boots and then a "Stop here. Here." A lightness rises from me, in reassuring waves, as if his were the voice of life itself, strong and righteous, an invisible burnished presence that promises solace and deliverance. I can imagine him, square-shouldered, determined, as he walks through the clamor of danger and dust.

"I want to walk through here," the voice announces in English.

"Here? Why? What's here? We're supposed to be at . . ."

"Just to check on something. Someone. It won't take long."

The truck is left to idle as the voice trails off. Warnings are shouted. The neighborhood has not been swept. There are shooters. Vietcong, Vietcong, they repeat. *"Di di,"* they shout in a swollen, roaring rush of Vietnamese, then English, "Go, go," urging him to go away.

I want to shoot out of the jar and into his arms. James is coming for me. My heart leaps with relief and with fear. I crane my neck upward to look. The big metal gate opens. I hear his footsteps cross the graveled path, pass the mango tree, and head toward my bedroom door.

I'm over here, James, I say, but nothing comes out of my mouth.

I look up and see the muzzle of an upturned gun sticking out from the column of red brick. The muzzle moves, left, then slightly right, then left, stalking the footsteps. I bite the back of my hand.

James, I cry. The chimney. I don't know if my cry carries any sound. It is as if a hand had reached out and with an overpowering muscular force clamped my mouth shut. I am transfixed inside the stale air.

Shut up, a voice commands me. The voices are back, but not indistinct this time. I hear one voice, shrill and potent, emanating soundlessly from somewhere within my body.

James! James! I yell, but my voice dips just out of my command and reach. I dare not move or breathe.

It is happening again. A shadow, two shadows, restless and charged, fling themselves against the cistern's walls. They spin as they expand and shrink, vanish and reappear, inside and outside the fleshly manifestation of my being. They race wailing and lunatic inside the tight confines of the cistern, one, the smaller of the two, crying and hiding behind the bigger, fiercer one. The shadows converge, then detach. I am here and not here. I watch and am watched. I am. I am not.

Like a storm, black and raging, a figure from within me shifts her shape until she is enormous and angry and erupts with a roar that swipes everything else aside. A *keep quiet* is sounded. It is there, speaking in the voice of an angry girl.

She puts out her arms and pushes me down. I am fastened to the bottom of the cistern.

Who is it? Is someone else here?

Cecile. Cecile?

Cecile cowers and cries. I sense a little girl's movement, hanging on as size is taken from her. She remains but a frail shadow that wraps herself wholly in the larger shadow's reflection.

I keep quiet. Sounds vanish.

A voice rumbles within my chest, the stormy appearance of a new scowling being. Charcoal-black eyes; a shadow of a face, barely perceptible yet strangely familiar, flickers in front of me, prying and unprying itself to and from different realities. The voice physically assaults my head.

But there is still the matter of James's life. I struggle for control. With supernatural strength, the shadow overpowers me. I succumb.

I am unable to escape its grip to shout out my warning to James. But from within myself, I can hear it all. I try again with greater force to expel a sound, a warning. Once more, someone darts out, from the deep internal depths of my being, and slides a hand over my mouth.

I hear a shot go off. A body falls to the ground.

Everything turns black yet again.

Soft clouds drift above a vast, illuminated sky. When I come back to myself after lost time, everything is quiet. I peek out of the cistern. James is no longer there. The ground where the body fell is covered with blood. I see red streaks where the earth bleeds, where flesh has been dragged. The back of my hand is torn and chewed. I find myself walking to that spot where blood was spilled. A gun lies on the ground. I pick it up and feel its weight and heft against my palm, its unexpected warmth, as if alive. I can see through a large gaping hole in our garden wall and a pile of scrap and rubble at its foot. Someone is hosing off blood. The surviving soldiers are there. Falling in and out of step, they pick up one dead body, then another, and another. I see the red protuberance of flesh and subcutaneous tissue under ruptured skin that shows the jagged line of cartilage and bone. I can hear their strides, the different lengths produced by each booted thud as they survey the hurt, the dead, and the damaged. They stand in twos, grabbing the corpses by their hands and feet and swinging them in a back-and-forth hammock motion onto a truck. I scan the latitudinal expanse that leads to the horizon. The sky is suspended in an opaque purplish haze, dense with particulate. The smell of blood, explosives, and smoke overpowers and chokes. The kite is still there, swaying in a gust of wind. And the chimney is still there as well, but it is black and scarred and pocked with holes. A column of deformed brick. The top part looks as if it has been blown off. In the dying light it stands there, eclipsed by the smoke, a lopsided, lonely silhouette inside the apocalyptic colors of Tet.

Moments later, I am inside our father's embrace, overtaken by a sinking feeling. I do not see Galileo anywhere. I call out to him. He always comes when called but not this time. I do not see my cricket either.

I look at our father's face and feel the terror in his black-hot eyes as they cling to mine. His eyes roam the entirety of my face, as if it were the face of a stranger. I am not surprised. I am an empty shell taken over by spirits he does not know.

"Your mother." He sighs. "She lost you."

He touches my face gingerly, then wipes sweat from his forehead on his shoulder. My entire being feels bitter. My body is taut and stiff. I can feel an internal crackling that reverberates against my palm. I touch myself on the chest. I see a purplish bruise on a patch of skin. I look. I am here. A part of me is still watching another part. All of us stand there together on a bed of moribund, earth-colored grass. I see the mango tree, its scrabbling branches. Pity the poor mimosa plant, which does not dare show itself. There it is, struggling, wilted and limp on the brown patch of earth. I see the sad, inward folding of the leaves, and know that the strange sensation I have been feeling since my sister died will never leave me.

# 12

## *Kieu and Tosca*

### MR. MINH, 2006, 1967

I know that I cannot avoid talking about it forever, the death of my daughter. It is a memory already wrenched loose, protruding always at a painful angle.

I relive her death numbly. Mrs. An often stares at the pictures I have in my room. She wants to know more about what happened.

In the middle of a war, death is ordinary. But I discovered it wasn't that way when it was the death of my own child.

Her death was sudden and I still refer to it as an accident. Years later, that is the only way I can think about it, if I am able to dwell on it at all.

The day after she died, we buried her. We had to do it immediately, before our bodies registered the fact of her death and its finality. Afterward, I did the most difficult thing I have ever had to do: I ushered myself out of the cemetery. I ordered my body to carry on. I resented its ability to do what I commanded—walking away and leaving my child buried there. *Please,* my wife said. *Please.* I could hear her whimper. But she never finished the thought, the sentence, or the prayer.

There was no funeral procession, no drums and cymbals. Our grief was ravenous but private. Things that matter come in sets of twos. Two eyes, two ears. Two kisses on the cheeks, one on each. Two lungs.

Two arms. Two legs. I would not be completely blind if I lost one eye. I would not be completely helpless if I lost one arm or one leg. I could still draw oxygen in if I lost one lung. If it came to that, I would have a spare.

But because we have but one heart, there is no second one that can serve as a reserve when the first is stricken by sorrow.

For years I cowered deep inside the shadow of Khanh's death. My wife did too. And as our national picture got worse I lost myself in the complications of war. I was not myself after she died. For purely senseless reasons, I sharpened the hooks and snares I did not even know I had and flashed them at my wife. Through silent tears, coldness overtook us. A form of vengeful counterspeech took over. Instead of comforting words, there were cruel accusations. The urge was to pull everything down, even if it collapsed.

"Why?" Not *why did this happen to us?* but *why did you let it happen?* I tortured my wife with a question that provided entry into pain itself. Days after Khanh's death, I reveled in my power to accuse and to judge. A mother, more than anyone, is supposed to protect her children. I remembered Cliff's remarks about his wife's devotion, her maternal instinct, and repeated them to Quy.

My wife in turn asked me the one question that still haunts me to this day. "Have you ever thought that the bullet was meant for you? My brother warned you."

I cringed. Sanity is rarely a match for sorrow. It will give way to the sudden unleashing of the sword. Holding the blade, I wanted to plunge it in, deep, and then twist it. I knew how to wield a knife. I wanted to brandish it against the mother who failed to protect her child. I knew how to exploit her motherly sense of culpability, her moment of defenselessness. Neither I nor my wife ever fully recovered from this disreputable instinct to hurt.

We had fallen icily out of each other's orbit. Sometimes I could almost remove myself from the domestic scene, step back and watch us from a calibrated distance. I could see the white plastic cap of her Valium bottle staring back at me from a chest of drawers. I could see a good enough imitation of marriage. Months after Khanh's death, a cordial formality had insinuated itself into our relationship. We were two fretting people hanging on to the remnants of what had become a mild and modest union because neither of us could bear to inflict yet another hard-hearted crack into our already fragile beings.

The terrible truth was this: My wife could no longer be touched. Becalmed, hers was becoming a life of separateness. A line from a poem that Alfred de Musset wrote haunted me: "Everything that was no longer exists; / everything that is to be does not yet exist."

A few days before the Cambodian mission, I reached out to Quy. I was embarking on a dangerous operation and I wanted to break through the chill between us. I wanted to be touched again by her particulars—the tender heart I knew and loved. And so I lingered at the breakfast table, sipping my coffee, thoroughly unsure of my place. My wife was sitting across from me, on the far side of the table, eating a tangerine. She rotated it and inspected the orange skin on all its sides. I watched her nick the rind with a fingernail and peel it off. A tangy scent floated in the air. The fruit fell into two cleaved halves.

"Would you like to meet me at the bakery this afternoon?" I asked.

She nodded halfheartedly. "Yes. As you wish." I took her in. She looked back at me but her gaze was tentative. Then she walked toward the window, her back facing me, and pressed her face against the glass as she gazed into our garden. I found myself looking at her reflection in the window, its fleeting movement liquid against the glass pane, giving me back something I had long misplaced.

I got up and walked toward her but when I reached for her hand, she stiffened and her head turned hurriedly the other way. And then I knew. I knew by the smells. I was a few steps away from her and I could smell it on her breath, the smell of gin and beer, lurid and sharp. I could feel the sting in my nostrils.

A few days after the Cambodian mission, my wife took it upon herself to nurse my wound when I left the hospital. I reached out to her, made sure our hands touched when she cared for me. My near death could be the opening we needed to redeem our marriage. A new ocean swell ushered something different into our household. My recuperation— and Cliff's—seemed to provide my wife with a medium through which she could find herself. She became preoccupied with ministering to us.

She turned herself over to that task, tending almost maternally to our meticulous progress. It could transform her, I hoped.

My wife made sure that certain foods were served to Cliff and me. To expedite our recovery, to strengthen our immune systems, she made swallow's nest soup. Swallow nests were spun from swallow saliva and nestled in crevices of caves and cliffs. They were hard to get because few climbers had the skill needed to shimmy up bamboo poles and pry the nests from the rocks. The nests were expensive, but my wife was willing to pay a high price for them. A single nest could cost as much as several thousand American dollars. She was also willing to sit patiently, immersing the dried hardened nest in water and plucking feathers and other impurities from it with a pair of tweezers. It was believed that protein from the nests enhanced the regeneration of cells and tissue. My wife watched attentively as we spooned the most concentrated distillation of calcium, magnesium, iron, potassium, and other trumpeted nutrients into our mouths.

"You must take one more spoonful," she insisted when either Cliff or I had had enough. Her tone had a bite of authority that made me obey. She propped us up with pillows the first few days we were released from the hospital. Cliff was more stubborn. My wife slipped one arm behind his head and slid a rolled-up towel under his neck and ordered him to eat. "My husband told me what you did for him. You risked your life, Cliff, to save him," she said, glancing at me and fitfully gesturing. I felt the tug of emotions through my chest.

Emerald-green eyes darted about, then settled softly on Quy's face. "He would have done the same for me."

In retrospect, I realize that it was not I but she who tried to hold us in the moment—away from the lingering threats of war and loss. We were three ordinary people in an ordinary house, slipping out of one moment and skittishly into the next. We could sip coconut juice together from a coconut shell. We could discuss with a lesser gravity military matters in our capital. With unguarded candor, Cliff and I could even retell the story of our days and nights along the Cambodian border—the murderous moments before we were duped. I told Cliff what Phong had recently learned—that the scout who had taken us off course had vanished. He was not among the dead. Or at least, his body was never found. Cliff agreed with me. "We were set up," he said.

As Cliff and I went through the slow process of physical recovery, Quy helped us stake and rope our lives together. We were bound by something delicate but enduring, something that I knew would not vanish once its novelty wore off. Slowly Quy began to let go of the nighttime drinks and pills. I took great solace in that. She was embarking on something different, an even keel of companionship, with peace and quiet. One evening it might be a simple dinner, steak au poivre, tenderly red inside, perfectly browned outside by a flash of heat, presented on a plate of pommes frites. Other evenings it would be nothing more than a leisurely time by the windows, each of us quietly reading a book while the American channel displayed a mindless but entertaining lineup of television shows. Sometimes we would put on my wife's favorite arias. Joan Sutherland's voice soared and dipped, suddenly leaping into a defiant high C and then plunging two precipitous octaves downward like a knife thrust into flesh. For my wife, Sutherland *was* Tosca. And Tosca was Kieu herself. The triumphant high notes, sustained and suspended and always supple, commanded her attention even as she engaged Cliff in conversation. We talked. She flicked a morsel of cake from the corner of his mouth. I read in my leather armchair as the oblique sun cast its last purplish hues aslant against the pages. Occasionally I clasped her hand and she would let me. Our fingers intertwined in a tender even if awkward approximation of closeness.

I was satisfied enough with time spent that way. I was content to inhabit those moments and to be open to other similar moments. To stop insisting on a certain outcome. I knew we were no longer at a place in our lives where anything was possible, where the future was still to be lived raucously, riotously. Rather, we were hemmed in by the failures of the past, and any future we could still make for ourselves would have to carry the burden of past lives. I understood. Quy's attention did not have to be on me alone. As long as she was all right, I knew that I would be too.

I wake up and turn the television on, my heart hushed. Mrs. An is here. She gives me food and hands me a newspaper. These days, Iraq is coupled to a country, no, to a war from thirty years ago. They proclaim that

Iraq is becoming another Vietnam. I scan the stories. It is Tet 1968 all over again. There is increased fighting in Basra, the city of canals and pipelines, the city controlled by the fiery and infamous cleric Muqtadar al-Sadr. Groves of date palms are shattered by bombs and bullets. Tanks roll through the narrow streets in battles as vicious as any I have known.

A part of me recalls a different Basra, city of Arabian legends, one thousand and one of them. Basra, city of my daughters' dreams.

"I don't know if I can ever return the money, Mr. Minh," Mrs. An confesses.

"Don't worry," I tell her. "I am happy that I can help. It's all in the family." I wave vigorously, as if to swat away any possibility of discomfort. Mrs. An gives me a tentative smile. She adjusts the angle of the television and pulls a chair next to my bed. We settle into what is the start of the evening news. I see the blurred contours of desert towns, a scattering of innocent anchorages that seem pristine and benign on the map. Tanks not much different from those that attacked Saigon in 1968 roll across the screen. In the background, an eerie glow is cast over the desert sandstone. Through the expanding and collapsing perspectives, the newscaster lists the names of towns ambushed and assesses the state of affairs in Iraq a few months before the presidential elections in the United States. Statesmen are interviewed. For now, the Iraqis, unredeemable, derided, and mocked, are not worth the effort. Soon enough their foibles, eagerly enumerated, will serve to exonerate the Americans. I recognize it, this shrinking willingness to stay and face the unintended consequences of your own actions.

Both Mrs. An and I know how it was then, the welling together of the gala of Tet with the savage attacks that followed. Mrs. An reads the newspapers to me in the momentary faintness of early evening, before everything turns dark. I tell her about the part of Tet that I know, the flesh and blood of battles, the memories I would rather erase. I tell her about the missing hours and days. How battles can be won but hope vanquished.

I took my car and drove as fast as I could out of Saigon. I had driven for hours, taking in the silent sweep of the landscape in the attenuated light of November. It was a few months before Tet 1968, a few months after the death of my child.

I passed verdant, unscorched fields. Cows grazed behind haphazardly constructed fences. The sun shed its light in broad sheets of soft golden hues. Here and there wind-whipped houses steadied themselves against the elements, their thatched roofs looming out of a soft green. For us, green is the color of faith and fate, of prosperity and well-being. Our eyes are drawn to the sight of it—rice plants sprouting faithful orbs of emerald that nurture and nourish.

I was crossing into a different landscape. The roads turned into broad, smoothly paved inclines. These were roads constructed by the Americans, designed to bear the humming weight of multiton trucks and tanks, to accept and hold in their bosoms a promised victory. These roads, bluish under the haze and heat, would take me farther and farther away from Saigon.

The Vietnamese have a belief that lies at the very core of our being. Family comes first. This is our lethal truth and its dull slog. *Ruot thit,* innards and flesh, we would say. True loyalty, true complicity, lies there, among the intimacies of persons, families, and friends. We do not in our hearts consider it corrupt to favor family and friends over strangers. It is not marvelous to be law-abiding. It is marvelous to be loyal.

Still, I thought I had failed. I could not be loyal to both the army and my wife.

My wife had pled with me to save her brother, the enemy combatant captured by an airborne unit under my command, the revolutionary brother who mocked us for our modern comforts and reminded my wife every chance he got with a litany of unoriginal sophisms that he was fighting for the nation's soul. We were behind closed doors. I knew my daughter, still muted by silence after her sister's death, was in the adjacent room. I did not want her to hear her parents argue. I thought a peace of sorts had prevailed between her mother and me, as we ate and drank our way out of grief with Cliff as inadvertent witness. But her sudden request angered me, throwing us off balance.

How could I be asked to act against principle and, worse, betray my men? I had been presented with impossible alternatives. I could not simply let her brother languish in prison. But I could not simply have him released. For this man, I did what I did because my wife, already fragile following our child's death, asked it of me. In the end, I couldn't bear to cause her any more pain.

I seemed to have produced the desired result almost miraculously, effortlessly. I made a phone call. I visited the holding cell. I pointed to the rust-flecked metal door. The paratrooper in charge did not wince when he was asked to unlock the cell. His loyalty was not to a rule but to me, the brigade commander. He saluted and did what he was told. Still, I hoped I would see no one on my way in and out of the military prison. When it was all over, I left, astonished by the absence of complications, the ease with which my request had been so competently performed. There is a war going on, a voice inside me said. Yet, recklessly enough, I could simply decide to release the enemy. Let him escape back into jungle hideouts where he could plot new attacks against the country and new violence against our troops.

I was filled with a deep sense of self-remonstrance as I stood outside the holding cell, monitoring the release of my wife's brother with an elaborately maintained calm. I felt an intolerable gravitational pull. My daughter's death. My wife's grief. Of course I gave in to the call. *Ruot thit.* Me and mine instead of the greater good. I was doing what needed to be done for my family. I closed the door and heard its reassuring click. I took it all in and slowly walked out.

From the corner of my eye, I could see a fleeting figure, on the periphery of my awareness, slipping through the swing doors—Phong, I thought. For no discernible reason, his name entered my mind. Ever since the coup, his name was for me tied to foreboding itself. Shame and guilt bound themselves to me. I glanced about. Was it merely coincidence or did I imagine him? He had no reason to be here. Yet an uncharacteristic coldness spread and the pungent smell of cigarette smoke, his brand, entered the room.

Moments later I found myself driving out of Saigon, into unfamiliar territory. I wanted to be released from the machinery of war itself, from the pull of family loyalty and its sinister other half, that inchoate, hard-hearted echo of treachery.

I tapped on the accelerator. The car grumbled but answered my call. It rushed forward and kept going. As the green earth flew vertiginously past, loneliness enveloped me. Beyond the highway was a thin scattering of thatched huts laid against a landscape of unpopulated emptiness.

I stopped the car and got out. The countryside opened itself fully to me, and its flaws, as much as its grandeur, moved through my heart. The simple huts were fully exposed to the elements, to the forces of nature wholly indifferent to human aspiration. I imagined a life among those fragile walls. There would be no pretense of security when the sky opened up. There would be no other option but to submit and shake the rain off meekly as it blew through the cracks and open seams. One would have no choice but to feel a storm's thrash and its ferocity, unmediated by the constructs of human hands designed to mask this melancholic but inevitable truth—the singular fact of mankind's preordained insignificance, our impermanence in the scheme of things.

Right here was where you could surrender and allow yourself to be brought to your knees, to be battered. As if in love. As if in grief. As if to slip into a state of being that is unbeing, unlabored, unburdened. Because under the surface of daily stings and struggles, defeats and ongoing battles, there was truly, in the end, nothing to struggle against. It could all be let go.

If only that were so.

There was still the matter of the war. And when that thought returned, the rice-field green vanished, and with it, the promise of benediction.

Back inside the car, I could feel the wind blowing steadily through the half-open window as the engine revved to a heady speed. A stinging, sizzling warmth rose from the asphalt. The sun glared against the windshield. The car and I headed back into the city. With each clack of its gear lever, I knew what would inevitably occur. The texture and heft of life would soon return. And just that quickly, the possibility of finding some other way of being vanished.

At first it looks to be nothing more than a depression in the earth. But the black, mirrorlike surface of the wall pulls you in, as if by force, even as it demurely reflects the images of its surroundings. Up by the left corner is a pair of faces, mine and Mai's, superimposed on and hovering over rows and rows of names. The walls, glossy and dark and V-shaped like bird wings, seem to stretch into the distance, one wall toward the Washington Monument to the east, the other toward the Lincoln Memorial to the west.

Here, on this most emotional of spots, death is recorded by precise arrangement and sequence. The names are etched in chronological order, according to the date of casualty, within each date of death, the names are alphabetized. The names of the first dead flow from the right flank of the wall, starting with 1959, while the last of the dead come in from the left flank. As a result, the earliest and the latest deaths are engraved next to each other on the wall precisely at the apex of the V— first and last coming together full circle.

I am in my wheelchair, following her as she inches toward the panel engraved with the year 1968. Around us, men in old fatigue jackets congregate with their families. They are here looking for the names of their fallen comrades. Some want to engage in the search themselves. Others ask Park Service volunteers for help. I am transfixed by a sight before me. A Vietnamese man wearing a jacket bearing the South Vietnamese Airborne insignia stands erect, removes his beret, and salutes a name on the wall. I fight back tears, tears for the American names on this wall and the countless Vietnamese names unknown and unconsecrated. I wish I could recede into the background. But the wall, bearing so much grief, draws you in. Mai is here to engage in the simple act of touching the stone, feeling its cold surface against the palm of her hand. I lean back, watching. "You have to touch it, Ba. There's something about touching it." She pushes me closer to the wall, takes my hand and runs it over an engraved name. James Baker. Like other names, his appears without gilding, stark gray lettering, less than an inch high, against black stone.

Mai places a piece of paper over his name and rubs a pencil over it until "James Baker" is charcoaled on the stenciled white surface. Then before we leave, she takes out a photo of her and James and her sister from years ago and places it against the wall, along with a white rose.

# 13

## *Time Lost*

### MAI, 1971

It is an evening like any other evening in our house in Saigon. Father is still at work. Our mother is with Cliff. These days, she devotes her time to an organization that helps widows of soldiers. Father says that Cliff takes Mother to meet other Americans who want to give money to the group. Father is relieved that she has a friend and a new interest. I suspect Mother wants to bury her hurt. I wonder: If I cry into pillows silently, what do grown-ups do for solace?

My Chinese grandmother is resting on her bed in our bedroom, fanning herself with a piece of cardboard. More and more I feel her watchful eyes on me, especially after James's death. I do not listen to rock and roll anymore. I keep the tape he gave me in a drawer. The cardboard sheet drops from Grandma's hand. She has fallen asleep.

What does she know? Has she met Cecile? Who is Cecile anyway? Galileo's playmate? Where is Galileo? I don't know the answer to any of those questions. I look across at her bed. I see her folded arms and outstretched legs, her head laid innocently on our duck-feather pillow.

I dare not close my eyes. I dare not breathe. I know I am watched by someone.

The vendors come out to entice. They park their baskets and prepare to dazzle the neighborhood with their cooking. I smell the scent of grilled meat, pork fat, and sautéed scallions as smoke from portable grills sharpens the air outside our windows.

The clock ticks. I tiptoe into the bathroom. I know something will happen and I hope to catch it—whatever it is—as it occurs so I can be a witness. I stand on a stool and look in the mirror. I try to see what others might see. I see the strangeness of my face and at the same time its utter simplicity. I see the component parts of it, nose, eyes, and mouth, indifferently, haphazardly put together. In this dim, restless silence, I am aware of a swell rising inside me, careening and breaking over and enveloping my entire being. Nothing has to happen, I say.

It can still be stopped. It is not inevitable.

But it is already here, this immense, slumbering presence that has been murmuring in my body and tearing me inside out. I am alone with something big that seeps through my skin and lives within me. I slap cold water against my face. It might wash off the wrongness, startle it and make it flee. I stand firm demanding that the wrongness leave, but it refuses. And so here I stand, diminished, compromised. I shiver as I try to fight my way back into existence. I see my arms go up, as if to shield my body's less expendable, more vital core.

It is a current, strong and swift, and it carries its own desires within its essence. It wishes to have me.

I look around. I am still in my house, inside its solidly laid bricks, one on top of another.

Suddenly, for the first time since this all started, I realize what is happening. I am helpless. I am being pulled down.

This other self and I have reached a tipping point and no amount of effort can restore the balance. An angry, scowling face, mottled red, not mine, not my dead sister's either, stares back at me. There is a look of grudge and injury on it. Through the bellow of shuffling, pulsating voices, I again hear the voice from the cistern that comes with that face, the voice that shrieked the command for me to be quiet even as James was being killed, the voice that repeats itself over and over, as if to announce its presence and its permanence with a desperate sense of persistence. This new angry being will ruin me. I see her shadow as it touches mine. I see her fingertips as they reach toward me.

I have the urge to be free of her. And I have the parallel urge to let her win.

If I stop struggling, I will fail. If I allow that to happen, I will be lost.

At last, something more powerful takes over. I give myself permission to let go.

When I come to, a big purplish bruise has imprinted itself like a mark of shame below my neck.


Darkness has descended. A pale sliver of moon hangs on the sky's edge. The vendors have gone. I no longer hear their chants. My Chinese grandmother stares at me. Neither of us speaks for at least a full minute.

"What is the matter with you?" she asks worriedly. Not "Is something wrong?" but "What is the matter with you?" My sister's death and James's death have created an experiential split in our family. My parents and my Chinese grandmother cannot understand my experience across that divide.

Yet a part of me thinks my Chinese grandmother, who spends so much time with me, must have seen it all. She must have known I took momentary leave of my body. Her face registers concern. Her eyes probe. I feel a churning queasiness. I look around quickly. Everything is in its place. The pillows are on the beds. The pens and pencils are in their holders and the papers and notebooks are neatly stacked.

On instinct I touch my chest where I feel a sharp, jabbing pain. I see a stretch of a dark crimson bruise. I know there are broken blood vessels bleeding red and purple into the skin. My knuckles ache. I dread the questions that will be asked.

Miraculously, none are. She simply lets me be.

That night, I see an outcropping of redness in my Chinese grandmother's eyes, as if tears are welling up in her.

"I will sleep in your bed from now on," she says, "with you." She is staring at my contusions.

I used to sleep only with my sister. My Chinese grandmother's bed is a few steps from ours.

I nod. I accept her suggestion. I look for my pillow. Even now I cannot go to bed without a pillow clutched against my breast. As I fall asleep with her curled by my side, she whispers a gentle warning.

"Don't hit yourself anymore. I will hold your hands and tie them to mine if I have to."

I say nothing, neither a denial nor an admission. But inwardly I am shocked by her remark. I think about what it all means, the face that scowls snaggletoothed in the mirror, the voice that murmurs and takes over, obliterates me from consciousness.

I lie in bed in fear and shame. I wait for my Chinese grandmother to doze off. Once I am sure she has settled into a deep sleep I go into the bathroom and wash my face. Suddenly I am aware that the mirror is something dangerous. With my eyes squeezed shut and with a bar of soap, I lather the entire surface of my face. Something silent and sodden rises up in me. I am aware of my reflection on the mirror's surface but I do not permit myself a look. I am too aware of what I might see, an eerie manifestation of a new, split self that adopts my form and face and stands in a spark of angry, grievous judgment of all that has occurred.

I wash and wash until my face hurts. I keep my eyes closed. I can wash off the mood, the madness, and the awareness. But I know that something still resides there. It is a parallel world that churns and cleaves and can at any moment open up and swallow me whole into its froth and swell. Still, I think, in this interlude of silence and calm, the remainder of the night is salvageable. I will tread into it gingerly.

I return to my bed where Grandma is sleeping, where a newly rescued world should be within my grasp. I draw close to her. But just as I am about to fall into sleep, I feel that ominous presence again.

In school things can take on a reflexive, ritualistic quality. Day after day I position myself at the edge of classroom activities. I watch my teacher's fingers as she writes on the blackboard. Brightness flashes from a thin gold bangle on her wrist. A single drop of sweat meanders down her face. A gecko stares downward and blinks at us from the ceiling. A boy sitting to my left tries to get the attention of his friend on my right. The classroom spins dizziness into me. My throat is parched.

I see sneakers. I see a phalanx of black military boots.

I sit still, unable to breathe. There is James, dying in the perpetual dusk, in the sinister beauty that is peculiarly Tet's.

And then something within me falters. Light from the ceiling dims. Objects ripple and blur, coalescing with others nearby. Everything becomes faint, feeble. I blink. Nothing comes into focus. And with the world's contours and edges obscured, I feel myself slip into a half-light of absence and erasure. I am beginning to disappear into the very depths of remorse and shame itself. And then the blackness takes over.

I wake up at home, exhausted. Our parents hover tenderly enough over me. Mother produces defeated little sighs. She is as always an awkward mix of signals, distant one day, concerned the next. Her attention is mostly elsewhere but occasionally it is directed at me. Next to them is a doctor who takes my pulse, feels my forehead to gauge my temperature, and listens to my heart. I feel the rubbery flatness of the stethoscope against my chest as it is maneuvered through the opening between my buttons. I am worried he will see my bruises. I know what is beneath my shirt—a darkening purple that is pulpy to the touch. My bedsheet still smells of camphor and eucalyptus and other ointments my Chinese grandmother rubbed on me last night. I contemplate my position and on a whim I confess that I feel faint. There is a strange comfort in hearing myself invent an utterly normal symptom for something that I know is so abnormal.

I feel an inflatable cuff against my upper arm. The doctor squeezes a rubber bulb until it gets larger and larger and then at a certain point he releases the pressure. My Chinese grandmother is nearby, watching with knowing eyes as the doctor asks my parents questions. I hear this and that.

"She just faints?"

My parents look at each other, then nod. "That is what the principal tells us," Mother answers.

"Low blood pressure," the doctor says, as if that should explain it all.

Mother holds my hand as a needle is inserted to take my blood. She looks ardently at me and whispers assurances. "Close your eyes," she says. I do not need to be coaxed but my fears lie elsewhere. I hold my breath and close my eyes. I imagine a yellow beak nudging me. I know the calm is provisional. The voices can start at any time.

It is all the more important, then, to be vigilant. I hold on to our mother's hand with one hand and to the armrest with the other. I keep myself anchored that way, to hold the moment. Let this be enough. Let this be enough.

Days later, the blood test results tell us that everything is normal.

———

I begin to think of boxes. Time can be unwound and stored inside four metal corners. I begin to strategize against these recurring ambushes. I find an old tin box with elaborate pictures of dragons and celestial beasts. I draw a picture of the angry face and solemnly place the picture in the box. I convince myself that I have caught a monster from the ocean's ominous depths and sequestered it in a secure, metallic compartment. I put the box under my bed. It keeps her—the interloper—locked away.

For a moment, as I slip my drawing into the box, I have another glimpse of her as the stormy, dark-eyed stranger who shoved me into the jar and kept me from shouting my warning to James.

Outside, insects drone their disapproval in the suffocating dankness of the summer's humidity. I am deafened by the din, by the discordance of internal combustion that rises higher and higher in the slipstream of my mind. She stands there at the ocean's rim, ready to grab me whenever she wants to.

After I close the box, I feel better immediately.

Sometimes Mother takes me with her when she goes about her activities. For months now she has been planning a benefit event with Cliff. But there are still many things to do.

This is Saigon and it is 1971.

Father is not home this Sunday. It rained last night and there is a silky, clean feeling to the morning. Our front door opens, ready to receive the rush of air from a rogue wind that remains even as the rain has left for the coast. We have errands to run, things to do. It is destined to be a fine day as we wait for Cliff. As vendors hawk their breakfast preparations, I sit in front of the house watching them as Mother gets herself ready upstairs. A dog greedily chases its tail. I remember that Mother's favorite composer, Chopin, wrote the *Minute Waltz* about a dog and its frantic tail. A tamarind pod scrapes against the sidewalk. When Mother comes down from her bedroom, she looks gorgeous, almost imperial. She is wearing high-heeled pumps with spangles that sparkle. The wind blows through the two gleaming folds of her satiny *ao dai*. At this moment I am filled with love for her.

I know what she has become. She is at once a mother and not a mother. I want to touch both her clarity and her mystery.

Cliff arrives and whisks us away in a black Opel. Our mother tells me she has something planned that I will like very much. Cliff drives nonchalantly into the Saigon traffic, joining its unstoppable flow. Every car, ours included, speeds along unless it has to stop to avoid a collision. Once we have escaped the crisscrossing traffic, Cliff lowers his window to usher in the breeze. The rush of air produces a constant hum and whips up Mother's long hair. She shakes her head and smiles as Cliff tells her something. When she struggles to crank her own window down, Cliff stops the car by the roadside and reaches across to help. He holds her hand and together they turn the handle. It is stuck. They try again. The tips of his fingers wrap around her wrist.

As he returns to his seat and drives, Mother snakes her body out the passenger side window and begins to photograph the passing scenery with her camera. The *ao dai* glistens and clings to her slender frame before it unspools and delivers a glossy whiteness into the transport of wind.

Cliff whistles. He handles her with a casual ease, as if she were without any sadness, and so she is. He reaches over and pulls her back in.

She is oblivious to the speed of the car. Everything will be blurry, I think to myself as I watch her click randomly at this and that.

The car stops in front of a little house. As the three of us walk toward the front door, I hear a steady drumbeat and stop. A gritty guitar riff, part rancor and part melody. Growling vocals. It is rock and roll. I look at our mother. It is not her kind of music. But it is the kind I once loved.

An elderly woman opens the door and invites us in. The sweet reek of incense permeates the house. On the table are a teapot and cups. She has been expecting us. A group of four young men are in the room. There is a full arrangement of drums, a guitar, an electric piano, and a saxophone. The elderly woman speaks to our mother in Vietnamese and points to the four young men as if she has no choice but to suffer them the way one suffers wayward children. She addresses them as *con*, "children," hers. Mother smiles and asks them to play American rock music for us. "This American here," she says, pointing to Cliff, "has heard you all at a club and he likes your music."

They are high school students who want only to play music. Even their appearance, four Vietnamese boys with mops of riotous hair flung across their faces, works to the music's advantage. They strum and work their way into the hushed glow of the melody. Another riffs while the drummer keeps a catchy, insistent beat. The singer leads with his mood. The voice is nervously wrought, velvety, hushed at first and then louder, wilder. The other three support the song with their instruments and harmonies, hitting all the customary rock-and-roll thrills until the precision-timed moment when they let it all out.

Here it is, all together now: the title of the song, "Love Potion No. 9." The song's title, which doubles as a verse, is bare and beautiful as it is sung with exuberance.

I suppress the urge to clap. More songs follow. I know the beat and the hustle. I know the thrill of it. I look at Mother. She is an exalted presence. Her breastbone makes a prominent V. I look at Cliff. Cliff knows she is beautiful. He stands next to her, long-legged and supple-bodied, his eyes green and dreamy, snapping his fingers and shaking his head to the beat. They are positioned side by side, pressed inevitably into moving and swaying, even if just for a little bit.

For one moment, I can almost see my sister in her usual wondering presence. I plunge into it. I try to stretch out the fleeting memory, to inhabit it. The spell is not broken. There she is, dancing with James.

In the car Mother asks if I liked the group. I tell her yes and she says to Cliff, "We don't have to see any other group, then. Let's hire this one."

When we get home, Mother and Cliff settle on our terrace to watch the sun recede under lavender skies. Mother smiles the way she does when she thinks about my sister. Cliff holds this twilight moment in him, his eyes taking it all in. She is next to me, inside a future unconnected to happiness. He is, conversely, inside a happiness unconnected to the future. I sit between them, looking at everything and nothing.

The cook has left but prepared a bucket of crabs fried with salt and pepper for us. It is food that requires you to dispense with chopsticks, forks, and knives and embrace fleshly force. Mother and Cliff pound the hard pink shells with a mallet. They use their bare hands to tear apart the claws, to halve the bodies, to pry apart the undersides. Etiquette is relinquished as they let themselves suck and slurp. They extract the meat from bright red claws and lick their fingers to taste a

hint of salt and pepper, garlic and lime. I lick mine too. Mother scoops
a clutch of red coral eggs and slides it into her mouth. She nods silently
at me, her hand outstretched with a dangling spoon aimed in the direction of my mouth. I gather from the gesture that she wants me to open
up so she can feed me. She is the mother who is sometimes fine and
sometimes not. They are in a good mood, reading a magazine and smiling. "Look at this," our mother says, pointing at something in the *Paris
Match* magazine she subscribes to. Cliff laughs heartily. Then he snaps
up his head to look at a flock of black sparrows lifting their wings in
flight across the sky. Although I am busy looking for crickets in the garden, they are within my line of sight.

I shoot them a look but try not to let my eyes trespass. I am aware
of a current running between them and do not want to intercept it. I
listen for my father's return. I get myself as close as possible to the gate,
where I will be able to hear the crunch of gravel as the wheels of his car
head toward our driveway.

I am the family's sentry. I am on guard to save feelings from being
hurt. I do not want my father to see my mother like this. So happy with
Cliff.

I tell Mother I am going to kick a ball around. I stand there agog,
feeling the solid heft of stitched leather against my hands. James gave
me this ball. I remind myself as I caress it, with complete fidelity to our
time together, how a real soccer ball feels to the touch, weighted just so
against the hand.

As the moments tick by, I keep my self-appointed vigil. I listen.
Father's jeep always sputters reliably. Still, I cock my ear back. When
Father arrives, I will be ready. I will cough or sneeze. It does not matter if I lack subtlety. I might run noisily up the driveway and innocu-
ously announce his return. "Father is home, Father is home."

Father is here. But before I can say anything, he has already
embraced me and asks why I am not with Mother and Papa Cliff. He
knows more than I realize. I ally myself with him even as he chastises
me. "You should not be so far away from them," he says. His finger wags
with disapproving abruptness.

I can only look at him and meekly shrug.

Before I know it, Father and I are already on the terrace. In front of
us are the expectant eyes of our mother and Cliff. "Father is home," I

say. The sentence comes out of my mouth like a clunky declaration. Something in the air moves as Cliff looks up and sees that we have been there watching them. His eyes shrink into themselves before he casts a downward glance. I look at Father's eyes as they follow Cliff's gestures. I am seeing things as if at a different film speed, in jump cuts. The clarity stings. Mother smiles much more with Cliff than with our father and me.

Mother acknowledges Father's presence sweetly, or rather, appropriately. "Anh," she says. He puts his hand on her shoulder, quickly and with a tremble. She wraps her hand in his and declares that he looks tired and tense. Father nods. She knows him well enough to know. Through it all, they still have the asset of knowledge, the complicity of a common history. I remember Kieu's verses our mother used to read to my sister and me. Like Kieu and Trong, our parents remain inseparable. They continue in defiance of reason or of suffering. They will sacrifice for the sake of love, I insist.

The sky is suddenly notched by the crenellated wings of swooping blackbirds. Almost in unison, my parents look at the arc of their flight, keeping their eyes on the horizon even as the soft smudges of blackness disappear from it. When I was little, I used to think they were returning home from school. Cliff stands there with his arms dangling by his side, taking in the fragrant evening, emanating self-consciousness, even a sense of disadvantage. He forces his lips into a half-smile. He looks down at his feet and mutters a few words about the time as he flashes an obliging smile. Father nods and they say their good-byes in the caressing light of a gray evening.

Overtaken by more blackouts, I am sent home from school again. Whatever my teacher saw caused her to describe the incident to Mother as something "like being possessed." My Chinese grandmother, worried and beleaguered, looks me deeply in the eyes. She slips her hand into the crook of my elbow and takes me upstairs. She runs a bath and insists that I enter it. I lower myself into water that is almost too hot to bear. With surprising strength, she scrubs and scours me clean. Suds gather and bubble on the sponge. A white steam rises. I draw a long, noisy breath and hold fast, submitting myself to her ministration, her redemption.

When she is done, she wraps me in a large bath towel and dresses me. In the cold, sanitized bedroom that we share, with the air-conditioning at full blast, I am ordered to bed. She draws the curtains to darken the room. She lies next to me, watchful. I am aware that she is studying me and so I turn away and face the wall instead. I am half-asleep, half-awake. Voices work their way into my room.

"Mai, Mai," my parents call. Are they pleased or irritated?

My parents are looking for me. I push myself reflexively into the folds of the blanket and shrink. But I know they know where I am and there is no possibility of remaining hidden, however desperately I want to spare them this version of myself.

Soon enough they will find me in a condition of intolerable wrongness.

The door opens. Determined, they move toward me, both ready to exercise their powers of reclamation and repossession. They have plans to have me fixed. I ignore her voice even as it emanates from within my head. She is the deranged one, locked in the box, I tell myself, trapped under a tin lid with dragons painted in blazing, raucous colors.

Father nudges me out of bed and takes me to the living area. An elderly man, slightly stooped and dressed in a black, flowing robe, looks up and gives me a knowing nod. "Here she is," Father says. "Please take a look," he adds, urgently.

And to me, he explains, "This is a *thay phap.*" A *thay phap,* I repeat— a revered teacher, a master of magical verses. I have never met one, but his presence is more reassuring than frightening. His skin is translucent and even the wrinkles are smooth. The room seems to have reorganized itself for his presence.

"Can we stay while you treat her?" my father asks, his face clenching up.

"No, we can't," my mother interjects.

"That's right," the *thay phap* agrees. "That's not a good idea. It's a delicate situation and I need to be alone with her."

My father sighs. He is reluctant to leave me, but our mother insists and tells me they will be right outside.

Here I am before him, wrapped inside an elastic silence finally punctured by a slow, monotone chant. The *thay phap* reads. I see reams of yellow paper and miniature columns of black ink. He is parting through the submerged mystery and petitioning the spirits for intercession and protection. His face flushes, his breathing becomes labored. For a moment I fear that he will stumble into my little secret and its elusive mystery. He strikes a match and burns incense. Silhouettes of smoke float and drift like vaporous spirits momentarily visiting the earth. A long-drawn-out sound, almost effortless, comes out of his mouth, like an ecstatic wail with a whip at the end. It continues, without rhythm or pulse, without form or natural progression, scratching the lungs, steely, sharp, piercing the skin. The cords of his neck bulge. Our eyes lock. I feel something creep softly against the surface of my skin. The *thay phap*'s face lightens and expands into a smile.

He pauses. I hold my breath and watch. He comes toward me. He takes my chin in his hand and turns my face this way and that and asks for my cooperation as he performs a ritual.

"*Len dong,* eh? Little one? This is what it means. I will offer myself up as a medium to be occupied by the spirits we are trying to call," he explains. "They will help you."

I nod. As long as there is a chance that I can be fixed, I am willing to cooperate.

He dons a strange red costume that reminds me of the imperial court's dresses worn by kings, queens, and courtiers from premodern times. I watch as he slides into himself and converges with the consciousness of spirits invoked, as a swimmer would glide through the water's shimmering surface. In this new persona, he is loose-limbed, boneless but muscular, thrashing like a reticulated python. A queer chant emerges from his mouth and passes through me as it rushes into open space. He is conversing with the spirits in an elocution of jangles and grunts. You can practically see the spirits quiver and vibrate like live wires along his skin, their plucked ends crackling and spitting sparks. He is taken over and occupied by an agitation of loose power. My bare skin feels the rising heat. I close my eyes. The tropical sun is upon us. It blisters our skin. The *thay phap* has become a hot, hissing column of flesh, his satiny costume shining like snakeskin.

My bones ache. The *thay phap* dances inside a deeper darkness lit only by candles and incense. Occasionally he stops and consults several books.

A sweet, smoky odor permeates the room. It is not just a possession any longer. It is something mutual that is happening between him and the spirits. It is a visitation. The *thay phap* winds down the shaman's dance. The room smokes. He returns to himself slowly but surely. I freeze, but it is only the wind's breath that briefly unsettles the folds of his robe.

I remain transfixed. Here are the instruments that promise cure and comfort: a pile of books, some joss sticks, a verse, and a chant.

The *thay phap* removes glossy squares of ritual papers from a bag and puts them in a metal bowl. He is meticulous. Flames jump upward from the bowl when he strikes a match. He cups his hands around the blue-orange fire as if to contain it. His skin glows against the light. From his pocket he takes a vial of water and pours it into the bowl, mixing the liquid with silvery ashes that have become soft and fragile to the touch. He parts my lips. "Drink," he says. "Holy water." It is odorless and gritty.

I cringe but he places a reassuring hand on my shoulder. "It is fine. Good," he says. "Wait here while I get your parents." Father enters the room with a newspaper tucked under his arm. Mother is next to him, with a pen and a notebook in her hand. They both stop at a respectful distance from the *thay phap*. He explains to them what he has seen.

I hear his normal speaking voice for the first time. It is pleasant, and comforting, and I wish he could stay and just talk. He reaches over and takes my hand. I feel the knuckles and knobs protruding from a fragility of skin.

"It will take time to heal," he declares. "But it is doable."

My parents nod in unison.

"I have searched my list of evil beings and I know the right formulas to call them forth." He glances over at the window, as if they might be reflected there against the shiny glass.

Mother's eyes widen. "Evil beings?"

"Yes. Negative energy. I don't know yet what provoked them. But it is undoubtedly negative."

Maleficent spirits. Ghosts. Devils.

I feel that strange presence hunched tight inside me.

Instinctively a thought enters my head: Not Cecile. It was Cecile Galileo must have played with. She is a child, Galileo's playmate.

"For those types, I need to use sacred lyrics," he explains earnestly.

An uneasy silence prevails among all four of us.

"It is not your fault," the *thay phap* hastens to add, looking straight at me. He is overly kind. "These are floating souls that are angry. Perhaps they have been wronged sometime, somewhere. Perhaps they had difficult lives. They will have their ups and downs, their moods. They are homeless, and just like a snail that needs to look for a shell to house itself, these spirits are tired of wandering and are merely looking for a place to stay. And they found you!"

I am myself and not myself at the same time. I am trying to understand what it all means. An untamed and temperamental spirit has yoked itself to me. I imagine something somehow standing beside me, as my ghost or spirit self. I give the *thay phap* a questioning look, but he continues talking.

"There are hundreds of spirits of all kinds," he explains. "There are those who guide and those who harass, sometimes deliberately, sometimes not. I will work to exorcise the malevolent ones," he declares.

"*Tru ma,*" Mother says with almost mystical reverence, for she believes. Father is willing to try anything. He listens but does not speak.

"An evil wind could have blown them in," the *thay phap* says. And then suddenly, he mulls the possibilities out loud. "I wonder if you have had a death in the family recently."

My parents freeze in a quiet fury. A strange sensation prickles my skin and excites inchoate images inside my head. An equipoise has been disturbed. I remember the elegies, the laments, the slow, sliding sadness that followed my sister's death. Here, then, is the irreversible silence, bursting open.

"Because a death can be an opening for other spirits to enter your home, maybe through the smallest person in the household," the *thay phap* continues. "And once a spirit enters you it may stay and make you not yourself."

I hear other words thrown experimentally about. "*Mat hon.*" Lost soul. If I take the unanswerable question my parents are posing and extend it to its furthest possibility, what answer will I get? I hear the *thay phap*'s reply. Imagine losing your soul. Another soul comes in and takes over. It erases your name and gives you a new one.

I stand still and watch our house. Perhaps it is besieged. It is now inhabited by spirits and their collected memories. And one in particular has taken hold of me. A blossoming silence courses through us all. I watch as Mother politely but quickly changes the subject.

"How long will it all take?" she asks.

The *thay phap* shakes his head and says, "There is no way to tell. It takes time to identify the spirits that cause these fainting spells and then it takes time to find the correct remedy. We will go through all the possibilities, conciliation, and even threats if needed."

The *thay phap* smiles benevolently at me. After a polite passing of time, Mother ushers him out. Dates are made for his subsequent return. He leaves but not before reiterating to my parents that I am possessed by a spirit self that wishes to exercise dominion over me.

# 14

# *Tet on the Perfume River*

## MR. MINH, 2006, 1968

I lock onto Mai's longan-black eyes, round pupils that linger on my face. A charged current runs through me. That is all it takes, a pair of wide, inquisitive eyes. My child, I declare silently, a sharp hope rising erratically in my chest.

She struggles to prop me up, one arm behind my neck, the other under my knees, returning me to a more upright position.

In a low voice, she says, "I am grateful you are able to help Aunt An, but where does the money come from?" She stares at me with an expression both imploring and suspicious.

"I can't tell you but it's okay. It's nothing wrong or illegal."

"I don't understand *why* it should be such a secret, then."

"I won't let her default," I assure Mai, who continues to eye me with a degree of uncertainty.

She sighs and leaves a basket of subscription meals she ordered for me on the table before kissing me good-bye.

The day is darkening. Thick clouds hang ponderously above the evergreens that I can see from my window. Mrs. An has finished her shift early. I am eager to have her with me. For many months now, my life has been defined by a sense of continuing emergency. By some mysterious combination of fate and plain old cussedness, I have somehow survived the vicissitudes of war and life. I see the horizon ahead. I don't share this with Mrs. An or with my daughter. It seems private somehow, this dawning realization that life is short and the days are dwindling. What I want is to make sure that Mrs. An knows about Tet. It marked the moment we began to lose the war, even though we'd won the battles. More important to me, Tet also marked the moment life split and splintered for us. I am tormented and beset by the fear that the truth about my child won't be fully known. I want Mrs. An to know so she can understand Mai and tend to her. To understand Mai, you have to understand Tet.

Many of our forces had been given home leave. It had been understood through the course of the war that a temporary peace would be sanctified to celebrate Tet. The Vietcong had called for a scrupulous observance of the holiday. In October, North Vietnam announced that it too would adhere to a seven-day truce from January 27 to February 3, 1968.

Still, I was uneasy. Last week, as usual, Phong dominated the weekly officers' meeting held at military headquarters. "I want to bring your attention to the latest reconnaissance report," he said officiously. "The number of trucks observed going south on the Ho Chi Minh Trail has increased from an average of four hundred eighty per month to more than a thousand in October and almost to four thousand in November, then six thousand in December. An astounding increase."

He passed a manila envelope across the table. Reconnaissance photographs revealed flecks and streaks of movement and a grayish discoloration that signified motion. There was a murmur of agreement among the field commanders.

"Whatever they're planning," Phong said, "we need troop reinforcements at the border to counter their plans. The battles of Loc Ninh, Song Be, Con Thien, have all been bloody ones. We are spread too thinly up there," he continued. "We need to pay more attention to the northern border regions." His eyes rested on the large strategy map pinned on the wall.

One of the corps commanders objected. "Those battles seem pointless and isolated. What is the point of the northern buildup in that region? There is no tactical advantage," he said sharply. "I would oppose moving additional troops to such a remote area."

Phong responded with authority. "Anytime a base is attacked, it is our duty to respond and not just to respond, but to further reinforce that area, as a show of force. It doesn't matter if it is in a remote region or in Saigon itself." Phong paused, uncrossed his legs, and looked straight at me. He removed a cigarette from a pack and tapped its end several times on the table before inserting it in the now-familiar gold cigarette holder. "When attacked, the South must react promptly and vigorously." By the ocher glow of light, his face looked grim and almost ashen.

A vigorous discussion ensued as different positions were articulated and defended. A boom of voices filled the room. Phong struck a match and sucked on his cigarette as he lowered it to the flame. He bludgeoned his way through the debate, reiterating the same point about the importance of not appearing weak. I felt the need to state my position. I had just led an operation into Cambodia and had been wounded. I was not worried about being viewed as weak or meek. I took a deep breath and said, "Of course we need to defend any base and any region when it is attacked, but that doesn't mean we need a tactical reorientation of troops especially to areas that are far-flung and carry little strategic value." To soften the tone, because I did not want him to take my position as a personal affront, I added, "You are right, Phong, to be concerned about increased movements on the Ho Chi Minh Trail. In fact, I would favor our deploying troops there rather than the border region up north." My dissenting views provided the opening others needed to counter Phong's position. I heard the low but continuous rumble of assent even as Phong leaned back in his chair, clasping his hands behind his head.

As it turned out, we didn't have to decide. We were subjected to multiple attacks simultaneously and each attacked town had to be defended without regard to our own strategic orientation. The Americans moved several airborne battalions and then an entire airborne brigade to an area around Dak To to sweep the jungle-covered mountains. I ordered my beloved Fifth and Eighth Airborne battalions to support the Americans in Operation Greeley. The Eighth was the same battalion I had led into battle at the Cambodian border.

Cliff was the Eighth Battalion's senior American adviser and he insisted on going with them. From military headquarters in Saigon, I followed the progress of their operation. There it was, Dak To, on a map hanging from the wall of our headquarters. Although Dak To lies on a flat valley floor, it is flanked by long, elevated ridges that soar as high as four thousand feet, converging toward the region where South Vietnam, Laos, and Cambodia meet. Double- and triple-canopy forests loomed over the area. It was impossible to construct landing zones in that terrain. The troops would have to trudge all that distance on foot. Cliff had only recently recovered from his injuries. Naturally, I worried. When I turned to my wife for commiseration one morning over breakfast, when I told her he was in Dak To, the corners of her mouth turned. My wife's lips were full and curved. She flashed me one of her demure but unhappy looks. My wife was intuitive. She knew the dangers without even knowing the terrain. Heroism, minor or not, did not appeal to her.

I saw her eyes and wondered. Her concern for Cliff felt somehow different from mine.

The enemy was still occupying several hills overlooking our base camp below. I received reports that our troops were showered with mortar from above. One day in mid-November, a North Vietnamese mortar barrage landed directly in our ammunition and fuel storage areas in Dak To. It was an immense explosion, a belligerent fireball that rolled through the folds and ridges of the valley. Our immediate mission had to shift. The Americans were to fight their way up Hill 1228 to prevent another mortar barrage. I issued the orders for our elite, all-volunteer Third and Ninth Airborne battalions to take Hill 1416. Each time the Third and the Ninth advanced, enemy machine gunners decimated them. Enemy infantry lobbed small arms and grenades. Our men called for air strikes and artillery fire for support but the dense foliage made it futile.

It took them four days to push the enemy out of Dak To.

Eventually the North Vietnamese retreated into Laos.

At the time, we saw Dak To as a military success, a significant one. My wife wanted Phong and his wife to come to our house to celebrate, the way they used to.

That evening, my wife smiled shyly at Phong. It had been a long,

long while. An awkwardness had crept in. Our child's death changed everything. Phong stood nearby, generously allowing my wife whatever space she needed. His wife, Thu, was her usual cheery self, eager to engage my wife in conversation. I felt a twinge of rancor. The treachery and insinuations from the November 1963 coup had stayed with me. I could not shake the memory—the sight of Phong next to the coup generals as they plotted the president's death. I lit a cigarette so I could hold something in my hand, although I was not a smoker. I realized that despite our long history, I could not command myself to like Phong. Something moved uneasily inside me, an antipathy I could barely suppress. I watched every move he made as if to confirm an old notion.

He is my friend. How could I not like him?

We tried to celebrate Dak To. My wife embarked on a series of questions as we sat down to dinner. "Why is it always the same units that are sent to the most difficult battles?" "When are the troops returning?" "Will the order come down soon?"

Phong raised his glass in an almost ceremonial manner. "Quy, your husband should know all the answers to these questions. Tell her," he said, addressing me. "She wants to know when *Cleeff* is returning." He snickered, stretching out Cliff's name for emphasis.

I flashed Phong a look. "Cliff will soon return," I said flatly. "The Battle of Dak To is practically over." I smiled and added, "He should be back any minute. I too have missed the many dinners we've had with him here." The last sentence was inserted to make a point, that I fully welcomed cliff into our fold; that we were having dinners with Cliff as we once did with Phong—before the coup changed everything for me, before our friendship exploded in a firefight of accusations. Now when I looked at him, I could see only the face of a man who took money from the CIA.

After Dak To, there were many more attacks. Khe Sanh was next. Ten days before Tet. The American firebases there were assaulted in the predawn hours by three North Vietnamese divisions totaling twenty thousand troops. I knew Khe Sanh had to be defended. Its strategic importance lay in its proximity to the Ho Chi Minh Trail. Our attention was on Khe Sanh, the seemingly obvious target of the enormous truck movement and buildup along the Trail for the past few months. The North Vietnamese unleashed a concentrated barrage of artillery and moved their troops into entrenched positions from which to attack

Khe Sanh's outer defenses. Two of the North Vietnamese divisions were the same 325th and 304th that had fought at Dien Bien Phu, the battle that the French lost in 1954. Surely, Hanoi wanted the comparisons to be made. The specter of Dien Bien Phu had to loom, beguile, and taunt the Americans. Lyndon Johnson understood the historical parallel. With Khe Sanh facing a full siege, by January 1968, even the American president took a personal interest in the fate of the base. President Johnson sought written reassurances from his commanders that Khe Sanh would not be overrun, that it would be held whatever the cost. Under no circumstances could there be a repeat of Dien Bien Phu, the battle that spelled the coup de grâce for the French.

And then again, the enemy's emphasis mysteriously shifted. At midnight, January 30, the first day of Tet itself, they attacked Qui Nhon City along the coastal area. Communist commandos then launched attacks in a series of coordinated moves all across the country. Were Khe Sanh and all those other fronts diversions? Were they part of a dummy campaign to draw American units out of the urban areas and toward the borders?

The next day, the first attacks on Saigon initially went unnoticed. We were too busy celebrating the New Year. The sky simmered, then exploded with fireworks. We did not hear gunfire. Cliff, my wife, my daughter, and I were taking our evening drive in the Peugeot. Once the car was parked, we meandered among the flower markets on Nguyen Hue Street. My wife steered Cliff by the elbow. The air smelled of firecrackers. Roving vendors sang. The *hoa mai* apricot trees exploded with celebratory bursts of yellow.

Sentries and army trucks patrolled the street. But we did not think about war, or battles, or offensives when Tet beckoned.

On a night like that, as rockets shot spectacularly into the air and unleashed an outcropping of yellow blossoms, coloring the sky in a wash of profligate gold, it was easy to be indulged by the sanctity of Tet; it was easy to believe in the power and the beauty of a Tet truce. Peace would prevail for seven days and the people could take a deep breath.

It soon became clear that the North had never intended to honor the truce.

But we believed in the truce. So on the eve of Tet, we had only one full-strength airborne battalion to defend Saigon. And only twenty-five of the army's three hundred MPs were on duty. Against that calculated advantage, more than eighty thousand enemy troops assaulted our cities. Nha Trang, Ban Me Thuot, Kon Tum, Hoi An, Pleiku, Quang Tri City, Tam Ky, Hue, Tuy Hoa, Phan Thiet. And of course Saigon.

Saigon found itself in a diminishing space as it was attacked by thirty-five North Vietnamese battalions. All over the city, the crisp, rattling bursts of AK-47s could be heard. What firepower did we have to return? Single shots of old-fashioned Garands and carbines.

The enemy counted on American forces being stretched to the limit at Khe Sanh, Dak To, and other far-flung posts. They counted on our forces being on leave. And most of all they counted on what they termed a General Uprising—the Communists believed the South Vietnamese would join them in a revolt.

I was asleep at home when I received a call from an aide. It was one-thirty in the morning on January 31, 1968. There was a stricken silence, then panic on the line. The Presidential Palace had been hit, not by our own plotting, rebellious generals this time but by the enemy. The enemy's Sapper Battalion was also spearheading assaults against our Joint General Staff headquarters, the national radio station, the American Embassy, and Tan Son Nhat Airport.

I rushed to military headquarters. My wife and daughter were asleep. The first person I saw at command headquarters was Phong. The maps in our operations center lit up like pinball machines, as one city after another was attacked. Phong struck a map with his hand. "Look at this," he said, shaking his head. A total of fourteen battalions, of paratroopers, marines, and rangers, were ordered back to the capital.

While I was at military headquarters, it was clear that fighting was most concentrated in the neighborhoods nearest to our home. Cholon, it turned out, was the staging area for North Vietnamese and Vietcong attacks on Saigon and its vicinity. Guerrillas from the Fifth and Sixth Vietcong Local Forces battalions fought, then slipped into hiding in crowded alleyways like those directly behind our house to tempt us to counterattack and inflict heavy civilian casualties. By February 5, Saigon was secured. But Cholon remained under siege until almost the end of the month.

The rangers were ordered there and would be reinforced by the American 199th Light Infantry Brigade. I had but a moment to speak quickly to my wife. Stay in the house, I warned. Keep our child inside. Keep her Chinese grandmother inside. You stay inside. There was nowhere they could have gone. The streets had been overtaken.

Why Cholon? The key to Cholon was the Phu Tho Racetrack, a hub to and from all the major streets. The enemy had to hold it to prevent this oval patch of red dirt from becoming a helicopter landing zone.

I tried to follow the events of Cholon from military headquarters. But the nerve center of our armed forces was one of their main targets that first day of Tet. Since the early morning of January 31, sappers had infiltrated Gate 5 of our military headquarters. I led my men outside to the gate's entrance. The paratroopers under my command were fighting off attacks by the First and Second Vietcong Local Forces battalions. By late morning, Gate 4 was also attacked. I felt the rush of metal fire. Things were alive as the red and orange glare of rockets filled our eyes.

My heart pounded. On the ground right by my feet was the body of a young man. A froth of blood leaked from his head and ears. Outside more bodies lay scattered. Several loud pops came from across the street, followed by a string of obscenities. A half-dozen mortar rounds landed nearby. I was lifted inside a cloud of dust. Sand and grit, black and ravenous, blew upward, slashing my face with a fiery sting. AK-47 fire sputtered more dust all around us. A fire burned in my eyes, where the fine dust had blown. For most of the day, I fired a machine gun in the direction of the enemy with my eyes only half open. I felt fortunate that the infiltration of dust and debris did not jam the gun.

Nine hours later, we warded them off. I sank to my knees. The jolt and whiplash of adrenaline stayed in me.

Phong had received news about Cholon and breathlessly relayed it to me. "American helicopter gunships were just ordered to retake the racetrack. That will help. And our own Thirty-third and Thirty-fifth Ranger battalions are also going in," he continued without modulation, rattling off facts meant to inform and comfort. I knew the dense alleys and tenement houses of Cholon. The fight would take place building by building, rooftop by rooftop. Helicopter gunships would be called in. Cholon would become even more dangerous.

The same realization occurred to Phong. "That means we have to

hurry and get them out of there," he barked. "The racetrack is only fifteen blocks from your house. Cholon will be declared a free-fire zone
anytime now." His face was sweaty and ashen with worry. For a moment
I was touched. I felt hard-hearted in my dislike of him.

I sent a GMC truck to the house to bring my wife and child and her
Chinese grandmother and whoever else was there to the safety of our
compound. It was Tet. We had friends visiting. They had all been waiting to celebrate. When the truck returned to our military headquarters,
I put out my arms in anticipation of Mai's embrace. The sun's rays caught
on the side mirror of the truck and reflected an unbearable brightness.
I blinked. I heard voices shouting all at once.

Where is she?

No one knew where the child was. The Chinese nanny was in a
state of panic. My wife sat paralyzed on the ground. She covered her
mouth and cried soundlessly. I gave her a comforting squeeze on the
shoulder, then tore through the front of our headquarters into the
now drastically altered midafternoon as my heart skidded and lurched
in my chest. Phong was already by her side, reassuring me that he would
watch over her.

I raced to the house in my jeep, through smoke-filled backstreets, past
carcasses of burned-out cars and fallen debris. Solitary trees had been
felled and leaned diagonally against the few telephone poles still standing.
Half-burned tenement houses crouched low. There was sporadic firing
from rooftops. I held my breath but could still smell the blistering tar. The
immediate area surrounding the house was subdued. But the weight of
what had happened still lingered. I entered the house through the garden.
The interlude of quiet that now prevailed seemed wholly provisional.
Anything could still happen. The external walls had been ruptured, the
earth raked by gunfire. Suddenly I heard a shuffling noise and dry heaving sobs. In the far corner of the garden, near the mango tree, was my
child, wide-eyed, hushed. I turned to face her. I kneeled and opened my
arms for her to run into. But she stood still, removed. I saw her hesitate.
She was a wholly different child. I barely recognized her and she me. In
this new cobwebbed strangeness that surrounded her, it was as if another
child, more afflicted, had emerged and had taken over.

Still, I walked, slowly, sure-footed, toward her. I made no sudden movements. I called her name. She backed away but I scooped her up and held her stiffly in my arms. She was all force, all resistance. I heard a muffled sound from her throat.

"Mai?" I said tentatively.

"No." A ravaged face peeked up at me. Incompliant, she shook her head. "Don't touch," she growled.

I ignored her warning of course. She was frightened. I could feel something happening, a red-hot horror that glowed on her skin. I felt the force of a storm and its murdering eyes on mine. I felt the inhalation and exhalation of sour breaths. She stared at me petulantly. I knew exactly what she wanted to do—she wanted to scream and bite and kick even as her fingernails dug themselves into my flesh.

My child had changed. She had metamorphosed and crossed into an elaborately different realm. I tried to hold her, to love and to reassure. But she pushed me off. All at once, she began a low, urgent hiss that quickly turned, through sucked teeth, into a fitful, jittery cry. A roar of feelings that had been inside her, as if under her flesh, stored in the liver, hidden in the lungs, behind her ribs, came flying out. She swiped at the plants, yanked grass from the flower beds, and stomped on the stretch of mimosa plants my wife used as ground cover. Her fingers, balled and knuckled, pounded and hammered her chest. I lifted her body onto my lap and held her forcibly against me until I felt a calmness return. I relaxed my grip. She had stopped thrashing but her eyes stared back at me in terror. I pressed her against my chest and kept her there as long as I could.

That is the story about Tet that I told Mrs. An. I can tell thoughts are racing through her head. My story has produced a ping of recognition for her. She has over the years become my confidante, this gentle woman who exhibits great tenderness and warmth. She is affable and accepting. She straightens her back and studies the pill bottles on my night table as if an answer can be located there. Having taken on the burden of caring for me, she leans forward and says, "Let's freshen you up." Her voice wobbles. I nod. I know she understands. I want her to know how the illness that struck my daughter first began. "I see how difficult it must have been," she says. "I didn't know it started that early. How old was she then? Ten?" She tries unobtrusively to wipe away a tear. She coaxes me forth, pushing her body against the begrudgings of aging muscle and flesh. She props me up and brushes my hair. It is cut short, but she takes her time, as if there were long thick strands that still need to be tamed. When she tries to smooth and straighten out the tangled sheets, her hand inadvertently touches the scar on my stomach. I feel her smooth hand against its nicked irregularities. It is a gesture that makes me shudder still. My bedsheets still hold the scent of purple blooms. I breathe it in. Once, when my wife was by my side, the sheets smelled of her.

"Your story is safe with me," she says.

I nod but keep silent. Mrs. An pulls the stiffly pleated curtains over the window to shield my eyes from the streetlamps. My face has been washed. My sheets have been changed. I have on a freshly laundered shirt. I tell myself I am alert. I hear the solid click the closet door makes when it is closed. I hear voices that float in an undertone of green.

"Tell me about Hue," she urges later. She preempts me. I have been thinking about Hue myself. "Do you know that you say his name when you are asleep?" she asks.

"Whose?"

"Mr. Phong."

"Phong?" I repeat. Mrs. An says his name in that forthright, direct way of hers.

She nods. She wants to know more about him. Her eyes are most alive as they wait for me to respond.

I close my eyes. I see my child's face as it once was, more gentle, less aggrieved, with an unhurried, childlike softness that touches me. I see Phong's face, always with a cigarette hanging from his mouth. His name means "wind." I think of it as a black, poisonous wind that changes direction and that we Vietnamese believe can inflict sickness in those caught within its grip. I feel an inner churn surging through me, making me queasy in the stomach and feeble in the knees. Without further preliminaries, Mrs. An takes my hand in hers, signaling that she is ready for me to begin.

Ten North Vietnamese and six Vietcong battalions overran the Imperial Citadel in Hue. It began the way the other Tet attacks began, in the early morning of January 31. The citadel was stormed, the airport attacked. We were vastly outnumbered. By dawn, the Communists controlled the city, except for the First Division's headquarters and the compound housing the American military advisers.

We were not permitted to unleash artillery and air strikes. Hue was a sacred city that had to be preserved.

After twenty-four days of furious block-by-block fighting, we finally seized the citadel's main flagpole and ripped down the Communist flag that had flown there for twenty-four days. That same day, February 24, our flag, imperial gold with three red horizontal stripes, was hoisted in the city center.

Of course we celebrated. The First Division was feted and decorated.

Inside the citadel, even in the midst of celebration, our troops discovered a city of mass graves.

These are the skeletal facts. In the early morning of February 26, our South Vietnamese First Airborne Task Force came across mounds of fresh earth in the Gia Hoi High School yard. Underneath the patches of red and yellow earth and the dying scent of a Tet truce were piles and piles of bodies—127 of them.

Once the first grave was discovered, I was commanded to head to Hue along with Phong to investigate the killings. Given his political connections, Phong was now one of the more significant staff members within the president's inner circle. That he came on such a trip at all showed the importance of the mission and the support we were guaranteed to have from above.

It began as a bright and balmy morning but by the time we arrived in Hue and headed to the inspection sites a gray steady rain was falling. Along with a few of our local troops, we made our way through the drizzle into the sullen courtyard. Phong's face tightened. Vultures hovered above and coveted the deadness that was everywhere. Bodies had turned black and bubbled with an infestation of maggots and flies. Rats gnawed on opened wounds and decomposed flesh. Phong's job kept him mostly in the office. He let out a nervous, whinnying sound and quickly turned his head.

In the next few months, as our soldiers cleared rubble and debris, eighteen additional grave sites were found that produced more than two thousand bodies. Their hands were wired behind backs and their mouths stuffed with rags. They lay in puddles of black, brackish waters and bubbling scum floating on a vibrating surface of insects. Many of the bodies were contorted but suffered no wounds, an indication that they were buried alive.

Phong took refuge behind his sunglasses and white handkerchief. The stench was overpowering. Reflex alone could make most everyone recoil and vomit. I wanted to be magnanimous. I handed him a bottle of mentholated balm. He shook and hugged himself with his arms to calm the shivers. I saw the staring faces of a few troops in full battle fatigue, a glimmer of scorn in their eyes, as they watched him sink to his knees and throw up. There was a stench of nausea and sourness. His lips pursed. A gray sludge spurted from his mouth as he hurried farther away from us. I could put myself in his position, but I did not manage more than a showing of sympathy and concern. To save him embarrassment, I said nothing and focused on the task at hand.

A few days later, three Vietcong defectors walked up to our headquarters in Hue and confessed as we were preparing to divide up our duties among the Airborne Taskforce. It was early morning. A flock of raucous crows flapped their wings and took flight, creating a flutter against the galvanized roof. We were drinking coffee. I was pouring several teaspoons of condensed milk into my cup. The defectors were gaunt-looking, bedraggled. They stared at us, shaking their heads, and spoke in a low monotone of self-reproach. The oldest one walked forward with the other two by his side, one touching his arm and the other his wrist, either as a gesture of caution and restraint or encouragement and support.

They told us everything matter-of-factly. They had witnessed the murder of hundreds of people at Da Mai Creek, ten miles south of Hue. It had happened on the fifth day of Tet, in the Phu Cam section of Hue, where most of the city's forty thousand Catholics lived. In some cases, entire families had been eliminated, they whispered. It was part of the Communist plan to wholly reconstruct society. They told us where to find the corpses of a well-known Catholic leader, his wife, his son and daughter-in-law, two servants, and a baby. The family dog had also been clubbed to death, the cat strangled, even the goldfish tossed on the floor. The father had been undressed and made to stand naked on top of a roof for all to witness.

Right away we put together a team from our Airborne Taskforce and headed for Da Mai Creek. We followed a dirt road. Several kilometers away from the village, the land closed inward into itself. The road made a final turn and then clogged itself up. Surrounded by a double canopy of thick brush, trees, and roots close to the ground, the creek would be impossible to reach on land. And it would take too long by boat. To clear a landing pad, helicopters were sent in to blast a hole through the double canopy with dynamite. In the artificial light, our burial team dug, scavenged, and found skulls, skeletons, and human bones. The lights strapped on their helmets shined a path to the discovery. Piled one on top of another, the dead were left aboveground. The bones were clean and white, smoothed by the water from the running stream. The terrible brutality startled us. Slowly, leaving out no details, we wrote our report. I planned to show it to the Americans, to Cliff.

By the time the Battle of Hue ended, six thousand civilians had vanished.

One evening, as we walked through the surrounding areas that fanned out from the village center, Phong and I followed the dirt road south on a path that curled through a small hamlet along the bank of the Perfume River. I wasn't sure why we did it. I felt compelled to treat him like a friend. Aggrieved or not, I wanted to manifest, if not to feel, the tenderness I once had for him. I could practice the gesture in the hope that an accompanying feeling would catch up with me. I could be bigger than my emotions, let go of this seemingly purposeless enmity.

He was slightly ahead, walking at a fast clip. I remember seeing the familiar orange glow of his cigarette butt dangling from his fingers as I lagged behind. He brought it to his mouth and took a long pensive drag. The slight breeze blew odors of cigarette smoke and coffee into my face. Perhaps we had been lulled by the profusion of luminous green that so defines the country's soul. We glided unaware into what awaited us beyond the old footbridge by the stream.

I felt the soft spongy earth under my feet. It had rained a few days ago. A water buffalo with huge curving horns meandered among the translucent squares of green and headed toward us. A boy lay on its back, seemingly taking a nap. A woman walked along the edge of the rice field, shielding her face from the sun with a conical hat. I took a deep breath. Despite what had happened here but a few months before, everything seemed rejuvenated.

"Come on," Phong said over his shoulder. He arched his back, cracking it. His legs took long, loose strides. He rotated his neck clockwise, then counterclockwise.

Before us was a patch of commonplace brown earth, an austere layer of claylike topsoil, a small and benign anthill. How quickly life changed.

I sensed it, like a flashing movement out of the corner of my eye. Something was wrong. I was a combat soldier. I was struck by a butterfly sensation that stopped me from moving forward.

"What?" Phong turned his head slightly to ask.

I was startled. Phong was walking toward its slick center. I hesitated. But I did not shout a warning.

Why?

I would ask myself that question for the rest of my life.

And then I could see it, a slight but perceptible rise in the earth's surface. A small mound.

A loud boom rose from the startled earth, followed quickly by a blast wave of hot gases. Phong was blown to the ground. An inert metal casing had jumped up from buried earth and snapped. A volcanic redness poured from his flesh. His right leg above the knee was blown apart. A white jagged bone and a tangle of ligaments protruded from the flesh. I touched him. The bone was pulverized. Bone fragments had torn through his flesh and bits of gravel were driven into the surrounding tissue. There was severe soft tissue loss all around. The concussion effect was terrible. The entire wound area was sprayed with impregnated matter, dirt, debris, grass, cloth fibers. Phong began to shake, his face twisted and distorted. I made a tourniquet to stanch the bleeding. I tried several times. It was slippery, tissue, blood, skin. I fumbled. Phong's head sagged, his face turning purplish and blue. I radioed for help. I calmed myself down and tied the tourniquet again. I put a handkerchief over the worst-looking wound and pressed my hand against it. As a cooling breeze blew softly, I, the spared one, waited for a helicopter to come and take him away.

———

I knew the moment I saw the doctor's face. Blood rushed to my head. There was to be no good news at all. When I visited him in the hospital, I knew he would lose most of his right leg. The wound had become severely infected. The doctors agonized over the level at which to perform the amputation. There was too much contaminated tissue that had to be removed. There was only one option—amputation at a level considerably higher than the original injury. Particulate matter had been driven into flesh, in between muscles. The first operation lasted almost a full day. They had to pluck out each piece of foreign matter to forestall infection. When I saw him, his flesh was perforated; his body required extensive suturing. I was reassured he was not feeling pain. The doctors understood Phong was a VIP, someone in the president's inner circle. Everything possible was done for him at this hospital. He looked up and asked in a soft voice, "Doctor, is there any chance I can see my leg? The one you cut off?"

I cringed inwardly. Miraculously they had kept it and granted his request. I knew this was not the usual protocol. I had just passed a giant canvas bin in the hallway filled with amputated body parts.

He proceeded to hold his severed leg, as if it were a baby.

When I saw him after his first operation to remove damaged tissue and suture the clean wound, he was calmly sitting on a wheelchair with an imperturbable expression on his face. I was assured he had been given the maximum allowable dosage of painkillers, both epidural and intravenous. He knew that there would be more to remove, only it would be done incrementally. He sat absolutely still in a pool of light under the fluorescent tubes, busily folding and unfolding a page from the newspaper. I could not tell if he recognized me, except for a slight nod of the head in my direction. He did take me in but without exhibiting any hint of recognition. I embraced him, the top part of his body, the torso that already felt wholly disembodied from the flapping trouser leg, the nub and remnant of bone and flesh below. He resisted my touch. I could feel his bony shoulders, the true thinness of his very being, the pure unadulterated sorrow. It was horror I felt most of all. I cast my eyes downward. My bodily presence before him, whole and intact, seemed glaringly inappropriate. I was acutely aware of my limbs. The distance that had existed between us deepened. His would be a life of pain from the moment the mine exploded.

"Phong," I called out. "You will leave here soon," I improvised. I was willing to say anything. "Thu is waiting for you." I kept my voice evenly modulated. I wanted to gather him up and hold him.

My voice failed to reach him altogether. He kept silent, mindlessly rubbing a corner of the newspaper between his thumb and forefinger. With prodigious effort, he pulled his slumping body up, digging his elbows into the cushioned armrests.

I went toward the window and opened a shutter to enlarge the square of natural light entering the room. The room smelled of ointment, of petroleum. I was ever mindful of the simple, undemanding act of walking, of taking footsteps, of the sound of booted thuds on the floor. I made as little noise as possible. Phong muttered a few sounds, a muffled groan, then lapsed into silence. Occasionally he glanced at me through the sides of his eyes. I could no longer read him. I listened and watched.

During the next few days, he appeared more gaunt, almost tubercular, as he exhaled shallow, ragged breaths. But at times he was more animated. His eyes flared, perhaps reflecting an imminent fit of agitation. They were bright, almost delirious and bewildered, and then alert and focused again.

Maybe it was the drugs.

I did not know what to expect. He did not ask, "Why me?" He did not challenge. He did not once say, "Why not you?" There was no hint of righteous indignation.

I struggled to fill my lungs with air. No, he did not say, "By stepping on it, I saved your life. Again." I shuddered. I wanted to avoid the terrain of obligation and gratitude.

What would I have said in response? No, you did not save my life again, Phong, because I would not have stepped on it.

Ah, so you did see it. And said nothing to warn me?

But I did not see it. Not really. I just would have known to avoid it.

I wondered. It was but a mere second in my mind's eye. My heart suspended in midbeat, I saw it again, the small mound. The anthill. I heard it as well. The explosion. I heard over and over the penitential murmurs of voices inside my head.

He pushed a bundle of pages from the newspaper at me, his head cocked to one side. His eyes were dark and focused, and his mouth grimly set in a straight horizontal line. I had not heard him speak since

I first visited him after the explosion. I glanced at the bold headlines. I could hear his breath rattle, the ragged effort to take in oxygen. The stories were about Tet.

I rose. I did not want him to read about battles. I picked up the pages and placed them on a table away from his reach. Phong, his eyes now glazed over, returned to a deep silence, submerged inside himself. His hand caressed the empty space where his right leg had been. There it was, stroking not the ragged protuberance that remained but the naked fleshlessness immediately below. I cleared my throat, unsure what to do or say. Phong turned toward me and said softly, "Please hand me a blanket." And when I did, he draped it over the portion of the leg that had been removed, the phantom limb itself.

"Oh, Phong," I muttered.

"It feels very cold," he murmured. "I feel a lot of tingling and tightness there. All cramped up."

"There's nothing there," I said.

His eyes teared up. For a moment he looked confused. "But it hurts. It really hurts," he said.

Two weeks later he was released. We would return to Saigon for the final phases of his recuperation. As the helicopter took us to Cong Hoa Hospital, all I could feel was the solid iron floor and the surge and swell of the engines. Phong slept, curled inside a dream. His belongings, Tet newspapers, our half-finished report on the massacre at Hue, and a few clean shirts, had been gathered inside a duffel bag.

From above, even as the chopper's propellers whirled and rotated, the city below, a welter of neighborhoods from Saigon to Cholon, blossomed and glittered with the profound conviction that victory was indeed close at hand. Still, I couldn't quite bring myself to embrace it wholeheartedly. My reservations were sourceless. Nerves, I thought. Anxieties. There was Phong beside me, afflicted and lost inside a tortured and stormy hush.

What I wanted after Tet was the resumption of a pre-Tet life. I knew we would still be in a state of war, just not the kind of post-Tet war that departed so radically from the reassuringly plain version I knew—the version that focused on the military, instead of the political and psychological. There was no doubt Tet was a devastating blow to the enemy. On the fields of battle, fire had been met fiercely with fire. Despite the element of surprise, the North had not achieved a single military objective. And in the strategic gamble to overwhelm us with multitudes of attacks and trigger a popular uprising, they failed miserably. Due to a series of miscalculations, they had instead choreographed their own defeat. Enraged by the enemy's treachery and brutality during Tet, young men volunteered to join the armed forces. The number of volunteers surged, especially in Hue. Even Vietcong guerrillas rallied to the government's side, and the number of defectors increased fourfold after Tet. Seizing the momentum, our government did what it had not before dared. It decreed full mobilization. The draft categories expanded to include eighteen- to thirty-eight-year-olds, compared with twenty-one to twenty-eight previously.

"The Vietcong is virtually destroyed," Cliff proclaimed ecstatically. "Look, they lost almost sixty percent of their troops in the South." He handed me a sheaf of paper marked "Top Secret." "Sixty percent," he repeated in a clipped, excited voice. I read the report. American military intelligence concluded that by the end of 1968, enemy losses had reached a staggering 289,000 men, with 42,000 dead during the first two weeks of Tet alone. Most disappointing to the North was the fact that there was not one uprising against the government during Tet. Faced with a choice of life and death, people everywhere fled from them and toward government-controlled territories.

The country rallied in the weeks after Tet. Balloons flew from homes. Confetti scuttled on sidewalks and pavements. Everywhere, the streets were colorful with banners that boasted ostentatiously of victory. Saigon stood up straight and erect and held its pose amid debris and rubble.

On that day, as I stood resolutely next to Cliff and surveyed the troops, I thought that the fundamentals of war were clear, that we had beaten back the Vietcong and the North Vietnamese. But I soon found out, after a memorable visit to Phong, that a different, more duplicitous reality would soon take over.

My wife and I often went with Thu to visit Phong. All of us were together again, inside the sparseness of a military hospital. There was the remaining nub, a blunt protuberance that swelled and bulged purple.

It was still wrapped in elastic bandages and, with clinical certainty, elevated. Phong shivered as my wife touched him. Her hands settled on his. She felt his hopeless flesh and took in the fact of his new, ambiguous being—one that hovered between existence and nonexistence. And then she got to work. There were massages to be administered, lotions to be applied, joint contracture to be prevented. The experts could do only so much. Thu and my wife would take turns. My wife placed the palms of her hands against his stump, massaging it to prevent muscle atrophy. Softly, slowly, she pushed against the residual limb. Their movements had to be long and supple, smooth and synchronized. She pushed. And waited for him to push back. When he did not, her face dipped, almost touching his chest, her eyes latching onto his, pulling him back into their fluttering orbit. I closed my eyes. Sometimes he simply lay there, a silent man whose remaining muscles had to be worked, whose wounds would be unwrapped, who must be resurrected by a series of resistive and isometric exercises my wife had learned from the hospital's therapists.

I knew what all this preparatory work was for, what he had to look forward to. There would be ambulation on crutches, and in the end he would be fitted with a prosthesis.

One evening, after I walked Quy and Thu out to the car and then returned to spend some time alone with Phong, what I saw nearly broke my heart. He was on the bed, with his one remaining leg stretched straight out. He was holding a mirror in his hand and watching with intense scrutiny the reflection of the intact leg against the mirror. Occasionally he moved his healthy leg this way and that, and watched the parallel movement in the mirror. For a moment, even I thought the mirror image of his leg was real.

There he was, on the bed, seemingly with two legs, not one.

When he saw me, he simply said, "This makes me feel better. Like my leg is finally unstuck. Unpinned."

I understood his need to feel whole. I smiled and nodded. "I can find you a longer mirror," I offered. The mirror he had captured only a part of his healthy limb.

He asked me to turn on the television. It was now late and his face was haggard. Although I sat next to him, we were each alone inside ourselves. Our connection was most comfortable when my wife and Thu were also present. Phong turned from the screen to look at me, blinking rapidly as if there were something in his eyes. He was shaking under the sheets. Reports of battles—ambushes, deaths, wounds— were delivered in a hectoring clip by foreign commentators on television. Tanks and helicopters flashed by, framed by the rectilinear television frame. I saw Phong's defiant stare fixed on the images, his calculated breathing. I got up and turned the television off. This was not peaceful. It could not be good for him.

"Turn that back on," he barked.

Startled, I obeyed, eager to demonstrate my harmless intentions. Perhaps the monotony of the television made him feel safe.

"Phong," I whispered.

He shushed me to keep quiet and pointed toward the television screen. "I want to listen," he hissed. He smelled of hospital powder and of something stale, a long-simmering sourness that seeped from within the pores. He jabbed a determined finger in the direction of the television. Briefly, through the soft crackle of television static I watched the camera pan the aftermath of the Vietcong attack at the American Embassy. His face was no longer vacant, uninhabited. I said nothing. It was already well known that Vietcong sappers had temporarily breached the security structure of the American Embassy. With his chin, Phong continued to point toward a pile of newspapers by his bedside. His eyes came alive. He signaled that he wished to read the paper.

Courtesy demanded that I comply. I looked at the grasping fingers, the jumble of newspapers and magazines. The front page of every newspaper covered the same story. I looked over his shoulder. Nineteen Vietcong commandos had blown their way through the eight-foot-high outer walls and overrun the five MPs on duty in the early dawn hours. With antitank rockets the Vietcong tried to blast their way through the main embassy doors. They were pinned down by the embassy marine guards, who kept them sequestered and immobilized until a relief force of the American 101st Airborne landing by helicopter succeeded in turning the tide by midmorning. It had taken the South Vietnamese and the Americans six hours to regain control of the embassy. All nineteen Vietcong were killed along with the five American MPs and four South Vietnamese.

On television, the prowling camera swept left to right. Phong was transfixed.

"It's hardly a significant battle," I said. "The embassy was never in serious danger." That was a fact but I could tell by Phong's expression that he thought it was the most trivial statement I had ever uttered.

"Hmpph," he replied. "True enough."

In the scheme of all that was going on, it was one of the most small-scale incidents of the Tet Offensive. But the cameras were all pointed there, at the embassy.

"It's the *American* Embassy, after all," Phong said with a suppressed sigh. Of course the cameras had to be there. One more camera here meant one less camera there. "American territory." His mouth was dry, lips cracked. I handed him a paper cup filled with water.

American reporters were converging on the scene.

"The *American* papers are saying the *Americans* are losing," Phong said. His face darkened. He breathed wet, muffled breaths. I did not want him to talk but this matter of the American Embassy seemed to preoccupy him.

I waved a hand as if to flick a minor irritant away. "Don't let it bother you. It's nothing," I said.

"Minh," he said in a voice concocted to impart impatience. "This war is going to be much less about the military than you think," he explained. "It will be measured by nonmilitary intangibles. You will understand if you read the papers. The more murderous the enemy assault, the more doomed the prophesies, the deeper the quagmire."

I grimaced. I scanned the newspaper headlines. Here were the nameless defeats. Here was the beginning of our inexorable fall.

"Look here," Phong said quietly through heavy breathing. He was pointing at the television. "Turn it up." There was Walter Cronkite, donning military helmet, declaring with staunch certitude that the war was lost. This was the new orthodoxy, sullenly issued. The security of the American Embassy had been breached. The war was now officially unwinnable. Another scene showed the hurl and heave of Tet. There was the same photograph, shown almost in slow motion. Here was the camera's zoom shot. A pistol at the end of an outstretched arm, a dead-on aim by a South Vietnamese general. One shot and a Vietcong prisoner simultaneously collapsed onto the ground in that fatal instant.

Phong shook his head. Something like a worried wrinkle settled above his eyes.

I wanted to divert his attention. "Concentrate on the fitting for your legs tomorrow," I said. "Don't think about these things."

He waved me away and shook his head. One shake. Then another. I kept my eyes fixed elsewhere, obliquely away from the dressings, the cauterized stump. There was his body, a slight silhouette beyond damaged, beyond bullets, beyond shrapnel. Phong was receding, his agitation muted. His eyes were closed. The lids flickered, as if they were reflecting every tick of a scarred dream.

I walked out, filled with a smoldering sadness. My heart swelled. And then a thought occurred to me. Perhaps politics itself, for a long time now, had served as a cover for him, a comforting sanctuary. Perhaps his anger over the big things provided him with an acceptable outlet for anger over the more personal but less manageable, more biting things, like love and other matters of the heart.

# 15

## *Circling Time*

### MAI, 1975

The sight of her, a big, scowling shadow like a darkened, angry girl crouched in a corner, staring at the exaggerated faces of masks from Bali that hang on the walls of our house, once frightened me. The warrior masks are elaborately detailed. I see large swollen lips and huge upper palates, bared fangs, flaring nostrils and menacing eyes that open wide. There she sits, this nameless she, in front of the masks and makes her face like theirs. It is then that our worlds meet, the outside layer that I think of as mine and the inside depths that I think of as hers.

These meetings once wiped me out but seemed to give her renewed power. They used to be occasions in which she vanquished me and took over. I would be obliterated and sent into lost time. Her appearance was violent, a hot fire that swerved and threaded itself into a terrible deceit through the shock and echo of my body. Now it is more straightforward. The hot bright orange and red that collided when we first met have now cooled into something deeper, an icier, stealthy disturbance of paler, muted colors. Somehow we have managed to accommodate each other. I still dread her appearance, but it no longer carries with it the threat of total destruction.

I think of what the *thay phap* said about a snail that looks for a shell

in which to house itself. I think of myself as the snail that is expelled. I
see the shadowy others, like disembodied spirits on the outskirts, circling time, waiting to enter, to hug the overlapping whorls and swooping imprints that spiral against the small grandeur of my shell. There
they are, circling and circling inside the same coiled refrain, waiting for
the perverse moment in time when I am defenseless so they can take
over and lay claim to my territory, its every space, its every echo.

I am slowly learning how to carry on calmly, projecting a singular,
unified self, even as she buzzes about. I am practicing how to be a statue
even as her sensation grows slowly inside me. When she exerts herself,
I can hear the noise she produces as if it were a background buzz of
static.

I have come to expect them both. There are two. I wonder if one of
them is my sister or even her ghost. Both are a cross-stitch of personal-
ities that lie languorously about, waiting to be released from sorrow
and pain, waiting to enter the darker solitude that I too long for.

Our mother is lying on a hammock, deep inside her own unrelin-
quished sadness. She is the central riddle in my life. Here she is, alone
in the brightness of a beautiful day. Our father is away. Ever since he
became commander of the airborne division, and not just the brigade,
he is almost never home.

I hear a shuffling sound. A little girl, smaller than I, emerges from
a mysterious place, not much different from that delicately balanced
space in time when dawn first becomes morning and dusk first becomes
night. Her face is sweet and soft, framed by fine black hair that curls
like mine used to when I was little. The girl reaches over and gives our
mother a squeeze on her arm. Mother neither responds nor pulls away.
She looks indifferently at the little girl. Cecile, I think. No, I don't
think—it's nothing so rational. I sense or feel that it is Cecile. Playmate
to the mynah bird. Still miraculously a little child somehow immune to
the passage of chronological time. When Cecile emerges, I am edged
out, lost inside time, but not completely. I am both in and out of consciousness. I see the world before me, but it is more like a mirage.

In this shifting, parallel world, Mother's face remains expression-
less. With childlike fussiness, Cecile gives her arm another tug. Mother
stares into the direction of Cecile's face but she does not tip over into
the present. I watch in this dreamlike moment. I see the bony edge of

her withdrawn hand and an imperviousness to her surrounding space. I can feel the agitation of Cecile's efforts. She caresses Mother's face, like a blind person who counts on her sense of touch to open up the world for her. I watch her fingers as they trace Mother's nose and eyes and mouth. Our mother briefly stirs and puts her arm around Cecile, like a hug, but not quite. Cecile is held but not comfortingly. A few moments later, Mother rises, disowning the touch.

With surprising clarity, I see disappointment on Cecile's face. She is not able to dislodge Mother's attention from that other world she is in. She cajoles and pouts and climbs into the hammock with her favorite *Arabian Nights* book. "Read, Ma, read for me." Her desires are ravenous, like those of a little child. Mother shifts her body. She is busy pursuing mental errands of little consequence. It is a repudiation. Cecile gives up, embracing herself in her own arms instead.

There is nothing more except a half-light stillness that expands everywhere I look. I know Cecile has given up and I have been returned fully to the present.

Later, after our mother has left, I lay my body on the hammock, and I feel her hypnotic presence blue-glowing against my flesh and bone.

On a thin strip of molten asphalt, a few sunken lanes away from the air traffic control tower, planes take off and land as they always do. One plane takes off and runs into trouble. It tries to return to the airport but crashes. Its wheels slip left and right, as its twisting torque of a body vibrates violently. The tail jumps and spins. The wings hang on to the metal body, barely tethered by the hinges. It makes a lot of noise. We are silent, watching the plane's jackknifed carcass on the television, its floating, windblown remnants scattered along the flooded rice fields.

The news is terrible. The American military plane carried hundreds of orphans—127 infants died. Its bloated, orange corpse has faltered and fallen, trembling in the water like a bewildered fish. One lone headlight can be glimpsed even if most of its body is submerged underwater.

"Why were they leaving on a plane?" I ask Mother.

"Because they are orphans and parents have been found for them in America," she answers, unblinking.

The war is not going well for us. But it hasn't gone well before and we have always recovered somehow. This war has always been here and we live with a continuing expectation that it will remain a part of our lives.

I keep my eyes on the television. Parts of the plane continue to burn, their glossy reflections cast against the black glass screen. Rescue helicopters hover above, their rotors whipping up debris. Babies are carried out of the plane. Tan Son Nhut Air Base has been shelled for the past several days, its runways bashed to bits. Night after night the sky turns fire opal. Mother's eyes are fixed on the sky. She is finally drawn to something and cannot be diverted from it.

# 16

## Peace in Paris

### MR. MINH, 2006, 1973

Imagine a war that might have been won.

After Tet the enemy had been shackled with more than forty-five thousand dead, in just that one offensive. The mass graves unearthed in Hue had shocked us. Like rivers that flow downhill, refugees too flowed southward, toward Saigon, shattering any illusion that Southerners would embrace the arrival of Communist liberators. Indeed. The momentum was ours. We became the war's conscience.

The war was now fought differently. The Americans switched tactics. Instead of a war of big battalions and divisions that swept the remote jungles to pin down an elusive enemy, instead of "search and destroy," they favored security and pacification, "clear and hold." Things were turning around. Imagine rice harvests that bloomed and blossomed. Imagine an extravagance of green inside an expanding perimeter of security. Imagine giving away hectares of land, its fertile silt and dark black earth that boasted rice fields and ripe fruits, fortune and prosperity, to landless peasants eager to slip the bright green sweetness of a rice plant inside their mouths. Hundreds of thousands volunteered to join the Regional Forces and Popular Forces and stayed close to home. The Americans called them by an endearing term that stuck, Ruff-Puffs. They became our eyes in the earth and the sky. They would defend the village and till the land. They would carry hoes and, finally, the prized M16s. And so 90 percent of the population came under government control by 1971. After the incursion into Cambodia, the multidivisional columns of enemy soldiers that used to slip across our borders from safe havens there now slithered in place. Vietcong agents who for years had been germinating and hungrily feeding off our country were being unmasked. We discovered the betrayal of the mimeograph operators whose hands held classified documents and the journalists who befriended American newsmen and fed them stories passed off as legitimate news.

And so the enemy had no choice but to shift into a different mode. Some thought it was a lull, a respite. But they were rebuilding and preparing new attacks. We knew better.

Despite our dwindling connections, Phong and I somehow found ourselves in the same orbit again. We were coming full circle, back to the point in time when we first met so many years ago. Once again we had to watch the gradual dismemberment of our armed forces. American advisers I had never met informed us that the geopolitical landscape had changed. Their own withdrawal would be accelerated. A secret peace plan would be cobbled together. We would have no choice but to bend toward the light of peace.

"What do you want me to tell you?"

My daughter is here in my bedroom in Virginia, looking at me with vexed eyes, as if I can make sense of the splintering of history for her. She is now at an age at which the course of history, its fine-veined glories, its ruins, its snags, so thoroughly entangled with her own life, captures her imagination.

"I still wonder, Ba. Where is Cliff? Don't you want to find him? What's his last name? I can look," she says in one breath. I shake my head. Since the war's end in 1975 and our exodus from Saigon, I have not wanted her to make contact with him.

I don't want to talk about Cliff. I want to talk about the war. I give her a look that quiets her.

In the years following 1963, the Americans marched in. They had thrown Diem off his shaky throne and witnessed the never-ending coups and never-ending maneuverings that followed. Then the Americans decided they had had enough and left. History is filled with stories like ours. Losers are maligned, left behind, and worse.

Of course much depends on how one leaves.

Much depends on how my wife left.

And I wonder about it every day.

I hear the whisper of a memory, lost in its own diminution, with the slow, dragging movement of a lost heart.

I am better able to understand the loss of the war and my country than I am ever able to understand the loss of my daughter and my wife.

I want to tell Mai this. "Mai," I start.

The look on her face almost stops my heart. She looks at me as if she does not recognize her own name. "Mai?" I ask.

She seems jolted. She nods, bringing herself back.

This is what I wanted to tell her but I couldn't put the words together. Your mother believed all was lost and hopeless after your sister died. It was not so, but she believed it and made it her reality. We had no chance. In the end, her lot was cast with the country.

I repeat her name. Quy, like a long-repressed endearment.

Friday night dinners with Cliff became a routine. My daughter had her weekly outing on Fridays with her Chinese nanny at the Crystal Palace, a new indoor mall in Saigon with an escalator that was so enticing she could go up and down it for hours. An intimate meal alone with my wife after a week's estrangement would be uncomfortable for me and perhaps for her too. Cliff's presence was a buffer. And as Vietnam held its breath, waiting to see how America would determine our fate, there were always new developments to discuss with Cliff in the privacy of our home.

I sat at the dinner table, aware of the unpromising future that lay ahead, even as Cliff tried to cheer me up. "The situation can still change," he said, projecting hope. He must have detected my anxiety. The room, illumined only by low-wattage lightbulbs to create intimacy, felt depleted and confined instead.

I took a deep breath and resisted the temptation to refute hope with facts. Quy put a restraining hand on my arm. "He's not been home all week," she said to Cliff, signaling that I needed rest. And to me, she said in a soft, soothing voice, "Here's coffee the way you like it." Her hand brushed against mine. Despite the hairline crack in our marriage, my wife's presence still softened me. She was by my side, offering me a cup of Vietnamese drip coffee. She had just shared with us her recently completed deals with various Chinese merchants—rice dealer, pharmacist, gold dealer. She looked up and smiled at Cliff, telling him that he was an eternal optimist. "You like to see the good in everything, Cliff. Nothing ends badly for you."

"The war is not lost. I firmly believe it," Cliff said. He meant to reassure but I found his arduously impassioned earnestness troubling. He wanted to convince me that this was but a brief faltering in will with no lasting effect.

I nodded but kept my private doubts to myself. Cliff had always subscribed to old-fashioned views of American benevolence. But I feared we were too distant from Washington, D.C., to be within the core of their sympathy. For all of Cliff's discerning talk, I was beginning to see the war through Phong's eyes.

"Minh, you needn't worry so. Let me tell you why," Cliff persisted stiffly.

I strained for cordiality. "It's hard not to worry, Cliff. You share confidential information with me about these new American intentions and programs and timetables, and then you tell me not to be concerned," I said.

I paused. My wife was searching for a spoon and Cliff stood up and got it from a drawer—the right drawer—in a gesture so casual and easy that it momentarily disassembled me. His presence was taking on—or had already taken on—a sense of inevitability in our house.

I commanded myself to ignore this telltale sign of familiarity and intimacy but I could feel a blooming anger. I sat up straight and manufactured a controlled appearance. "CRIMP," I said, boldly underlining the word. I first heard about CRIMP from Cliff himself. The Consolidated Improvement and Modernization Program. "What's the reason behind CRIMP?" I asked. "For years we begged for modern weapons to match what the Russians were giving the North. And after years of 'No, no, no' from your government, now suddenly you shove modernization down our throats. What's that for except to pave the way for your own escape?"

"Well, I would look at it this way. You've needed modernization for years, and now you are going to get it."

I was no longer going to hold back. "Your modernization program is being implemented now only because it suits you. It's all about you." And after a moment's pause, I added with flippant spitefulness, "Everything *here* is about you."

Cliff turned red and silent. And then he said softly, in a tone that suggested concession and accommodation, "That may be so, and I see your point, but I think you are reading an insidious motive into an otherwise laudable goal." His voice cracked.

I laughed. Of course he would keep the discussion away from the personal and focused on the political complexities of American policy. As he should. But I was beginning to understand American policy all too well, the new American expectation, lobbed unceremoniously our way.

"Okay, Cliff, even if CRIMP were just another harmless, or, to adopt your perspective, even helpful, development, remember, it's not going to be adequately funded. General Abrams didn't get everything he asked for from your Congress."

Cliff looked up, seemingly unsure of what I was talking about.

"So you aren't even fully aware of what's going on," I said dismissively.

Quy detected derision in my voice and looked up, fixing her gaze on me. My stomach tightened.

"Your very own *Stars and Stripes* reported on it," I said. General Abrams, the commander of the American forces who succeeded General Westmoreland, had warned that the South Vietnamese army had for years not had the necessary firepower, mobility, or communications. So of course we had to be modernized. As General Abrams explained, in that aptly thunderous way of his, "You've got to face it. The Vietnamese have been given the lowest priority of anybody that's fighting in this country! And that's what we're trying to correct."

I liked him, General Abrams. But even General Abrams had limited options. This was how their politicians would extricate themselves. By posing for history. They called it by an artificial but brilliantly contrived term, Vietnamization, announced with great fanfare in 1969, as if the war had never been Vietnamized to begin with.

"Oh, my," was all that Cliff could utter.

I took the *Stars and Stripes* out of my briefcase. "Look," I said, pointing him to the news story. Indeed. Congress approved less than half of what it would take to fund CRIMP. There would be no supplemental appropriations. Without the funds, everything that had been planned would crumble to dust.

I could almost see the scene as it might have unfolded half a world away. Kissinger opposite Nixon in an office far away in Washington, D.C., as they leaned back in their chairs and let the rising cold from an overworked air conditioner cool the sweat off their faces. In the toiling silence they mulled this matter of the war over. Kissinger sat up, adjusting his thick, black-rimmed glasses. He was by inclination a nervous man. Nixon, slack-jowled and impatient, fidgeted irritably. He wished for a decision rather than this brooding, ongoing deliberation. Their dilemma was they both wanted to get out but they couldn't afford to be blamed for losing the war and the country to the Communists.

I rotated my neck as if to limber it up, but truthfully, it was to shake off the dark, ugly narrative that was taking hold of my mind. I would like to believe in Cliff's version of events. For a moment, I mourned the loss of innocence that Cliff still wanted to thrust my way. There he was still exulting in the nobility of American intentions. I kept quiet as he read the *Stars and Stripes.*

"Wars have trajectories, as you well know, up, down, then up again," he said. "This is the usual tug-of-war between Congress and the president. It's the normal stuff of American politics. But you know, we've put so much into this war—troops, money, effort—it would be unimaginable if we allow all of it to collapse."

I pressed my palms against my head. "So your Congress refuses to give us the funds to spite your president?"

We would inherit more than seven hundred military facilities from the departing Americans. We would have to grow our own army, handle more weaponry, more arms. Logistics, personnel, would have to increase. The American drawdown would be complicated in any case, and even more so without money from Congress.

"Not to spite, but you could say to assert its constitutional prerogative. In the end, though, neither Congress nor the president would be crazy enough to let us lose the war."

I imagined Kissinger skirting the room. I could see the slow, fluid shuffle, the calamitous face. He had some calculating to do. There was Congress to deal with. There was the matter of American pride, American projection of power, still necessary to maintain the American empire. And to bring me back to reality, there was also Cliff's voice, insistent still on its own loping assertiveness, its right, through mere repetition, to convince me.

Once it had been simple enough. The United States merely wanted to get rid of Diem. Conveniently for them there were enough facts out there for them to declare that he was ruthless and tyrannical. They ordered his assassination. It would be an organic rebellion. There were plenty of coup plotters willing to help. And look what they have on their hands now. The unreckoned consequences of their action.

A dizzying sensation took over, making me feeble in the knees. I knew about unintended consequences. I looked at Cliff standing close to my wife and I could see far too clearly the complexities of unintended consequences. I squeezed my eyes shut. A spiking heart rate thumped against my chest.

"The Americans come and go as they please." These words came to me as suddenly as a monsoon sweeping through the startled grass. And so it was. From the vantage of power, they planted their heavy boots squarely on our faces as they entered and exited. The map beneath our feet shifted. Borders would be redrawn, cities renamed.

When did we become dispensable? Or were we dispensable all along? I wanted to ask Cliff, who till the end never permitted himself to contemplate defeat. Defeat came fragment by fragment, in the many meetings in which our fate was discussed and determined. In the end, it was all about the straight-line speed with which they could extricate themselves.

"You know, Cliff, that there is a lot of treachery going on, don't you?"
He said nothing.

"Peace. The so-called secret peace agreement. Who would ever have thought of peace as treachery?"

Cliff met my pronouncements with a languor that was irritating. His acceptance of CRIMP and now his view of the ongoing peace negotiations as harmless annoyed me. I wanted to shake common sense into him, force him to revise his perspective. I wanted him to feel bad, now, in front of me.

"I'm not the only one saying this, you know. Listen to your own American officials. The political landscape has changed. You know that," I said.

"Just because the political landscape has changed doesn't mean that the peace agreement we end up with will be bad for you."

"And why not? Because America would care about us? Because it is loyal to its allies? Why, Cliff? Vietnam is not Europe. You know full well that countries betray other countries. Friends betray friends."

Indeed, I understood the rumblings underneath. For years there had been a secret plan to end the war. Nixon himself had announced on television years before, on May 14, 1969, that there would be no one-sided withdrawal of American forces. If the Americans withdrew so must the North Vietnamese. This was only common sense. It was supposed to be nonnegotiable. A truce had to be based on a continuing balance of forces and it remained the public negotiating position of the Americans.

"I believe we will make sure the South has a strong footing to defend itself after peace is struck," Cliff said.

But bigger things have a way of overpowering smaller ones. There were forces involved that were beyond our control. This is why a soldier escapes death on a raging battlefield and a little girl playing on her own street does not.

We sensed this warming of relations with the Chinese and the Soviets. They called it détente. The timepiece ticked while the world experienced a realignment of the cold war powers. When an entire landscape shifted, countries could be sent spinning wildly on their axis. I imagined Kissinger, his hooded eyes scanning the geopolitical situation, piling on the reassurances in his deep, gravelly timbre. No doubt he studied us for a few seconds as he weighed our fate and decided it could be flicked away. He gave Hanoi assurances that America was willing to let them stay where they were, on our soil. And to the Chinese, he went even further. Because America was courting a new relationship with China, we became an object of exchange. Bigger ambitions and great political gravity were at stake. Kissinger told the Chinese premier that a Communist takeover of our country by the Chinese was fine but they must wait for an appropriate interval after the Americans departed. It was about saving American face.

At some point during the course of our many Friday dinners, I told Cliff about these secret negotiations. The part about bartering us away in order to strike a grand arrangement with China was not publicly known. Of course he would ask, "How do you know all this?"

My wife's Vietcong brother had told her and then me.

We knew what would happen next. A cold metal coil would be slipped around our neck. The year was 1973.

I walked into Phong's new office and sat on one of his upholstered armchairs. He had been assigned to oversee our national pacification program, which President Thieu and the Americans deemed a national priority. Areas controlled, contested, or heavily overrun by the Vietcong would be targeted for pacification. The villagers would be trained and armed to defend their own home provinces. Land to the Tillers programs would be implemented to give land to the landless. Bridges, canals, roads, were repaired at record pace.

Phong was in charge of all that.

He was still slight, a single silhouette of leanness, but he had not been miniaturized. His political skills and instincts were being put to good use. And he was still the person I went to when I needed to work through the war's complications with someone. Despite the posture of certainty I adopted when speaking with Cliff, I still wheedled Phong into taking positions that were more comforting and hopeful. I allowed myself to experiment with him, as if it were still possible to reorder the world in line with our needs. It seemed right somehow that exploratory musings about our fate were appropriate only with a fellow Vietnamese to whom I'd been tethered through history.

"We can always refuse to sign the peace agreement," I said.

The cigarette in Phong's hand glowed red against the gold holder. He poured a glass of whiskey from the bottle.

When did the whiskey habit start? I wondered.

"No, we have no such choice," he tersely declared in a hoarse, mad-prophet voice. His hair was uncombed, his face unshaved.

"Why not?"

His back was stooped and he sat with slackened jaws, deep in thought.

"Phong," I called, and moved closer to him, calling out his name once more. I pulled the answer out of him.

"The Americans have threatened to sign a separate peace with the North," he said, "So it hardly matters whether we sign a peace agreement or not."

"So it is true. It is hopeless," I said.

But just as I was about to leave his office, Phong said something that pulled me back. "Minh, listen. I have personally seen Nixon's letter to the president."

"Where is it?" I asked.

He chuckled. "It's not just lying about for us to read whenever we want. But I memorized the crucial paragraphs. So it might not be as hopeless as we had feared," he said. "The letter contains a very clear threat from the Americans." He was testy and tired. He cleared his throat and enunciated Nixon's very own words.

"'I have therefore irrevocably decided to proceed to initial the Agreement on January 23, 1973, and to sign it on January 27, 1973, in Paris. I will do so, if necessary, alone. In that case I shall have to explain publicly that your Government obstructs peace. The result will be an inevitable and immediate termination of U.S. economic and military assistance which cannot be forestalled by a change of personnel in your government. I hope, however, that after all our two countries have shared and suffered together in conflict, we will stay together to preserve peace and reap its benefits.'"

He laughed. "So finally all that memorizing and rote learning in grade school is useful for something, eh?"

A separate peace, he said with a smirk. His knee creaked in all its angry metallic petulance. They would not hesitate to plow us into the ground.

And when Hanoi balked at this point and that point in the treaty text and walked away from the negotiating table, Nixon ordered the war's biggest bombing campaign against them. B-52s, one after another, were lined up on five miles of ramp space in Guam and began round-the-clock bombing of rail yards, petroleum storage facilities, missile storage sites, warehouses, and docks in Hanoi and Haiphong until there was in the end no military target left to bomb. After eleven days of all-out air war, Hanoi returned to Paris and agreed to agree.

In its final version, the North got to keep their privileged sanctuaries in Cambodia and Laos and their entire forces wherever they were in the South.

Here it comes, the white-hot deadline for peace.

The North would sign the peace treaty.

The Americans would sign it regardless.

The South signed too, just as Phong said it would.

"It will be a death sentence," I said to Phong when the announcement was made on the evening news. It was January 27, 1973.

"Perhaps not," Phong answered. We were both in the office, watching the momentous occasion on television. His voice was one distant, undifferentiated hum. Other officers in the room listened intently as Phong made his pronouncements. We were trying to make sense of the information he was giving us. "The Americans," he said, "have pledged in the strongest of terms to maintain their air bases in Thailand. To keep their Seventh Fleet off our coast to deter any attack and to continue economic and military aid if we sign. If we do not, of course their Congress will move swiftly, swiftly," Phong repeated, dragging the word out for emphasis, "to cut off all aid."

I shook my head.

"The language *is* strong," Phong admonished. It was not spineless. I searched his face for clues to his real thoughts. I could see only an impervious shield.

The war was over as far as the Americans were concerned. They had peace at last and the tincture of honor plus the release of their 591 prisoners of war. But, as Phong kept reminding me, we had all the reassurances we needed from the president of the United States himself. Rumor had it that the letters were all signed originals and safely kept in a fireproof box in the Presidential Palace in Saigon.

Soon after the Paris Agreement was signed, the North stopped its lip licking and attacked. Here was the bewildering military reality. Thirteen enemy divisions and seventy-five regiments, more than 160,000 troops in all, were still in place in our country. There were also arms and troops that poured down the Ho Chi Minh Trail, more than four times the numbers that took part in prior attacks.

I walked into Phong's office early one evening. He was sitting morosely at his desk with his chin on the palms of his hands. A pale pearl-gray light shone on his face, revealing deep, creviced cheeks. His gaze leveled and settled on me.

"You look terrible," I said.

"I haven't eaten. I can't think about food," he said.

I took a closer look at him, his hunched shoulders, his slender frame, and his importunate face. His body was in slow decay, racked by long stretches of arduous, convulsive coughs.

The war's outcome now seemed beyond our control. The attacks in violation of the peace agreement were incessant and relentless. And in the face of this malevolence, both houses of the American Congress moved in perfect lockstep to tighten the noose around our neck. To great applause, their Congress cut off all funds to finance combat activities by American forces in North and South Vietnam, Laos, and Cambodia.

The only insult left was to deprive us of money. This time, after all that had occurred, we knew it was coming. Phong did not even object when I suggested this possibility. Cutting off the funds was what did it. Death could be guaranteed not by the shedding of blood but rather by an indifferent and innocuous pen, by merely crossing off an item in the budget. We shut our eyes and tried to do the calculation in our heads. A furious math, additions and subtractions, stared us in the face. Here was the worst of both worlds. Communist bases permanently on our land and no funding for the military to expel them.

I kept thinking about how Phong and I came full circle at last. Twenty or so years before, when my wife and I first married and Phong and I became friends, we were given the task of whittling down our armed forces. Now, once again, we had to embark on the same mission.

The air force was ordered to reduce air support, tactical airlifts, and reconnaissance flights by half and to reduce helilifts by 70 percent. We were told to retire more than two hundred aircraft and cancel preexisting orders for upgrades. We were instructed to recall four hundred pilots from training in the United States. The navy inactivated more than six hundred vessels and river craft and reduced river patrols by 72 percent. Not one plane, ship, or boat was replaced after the peace treaty.

The drumbeat march toward finality, toward a more perfect peace, had to be hurried. Quick, quicker, and even quicker if possible.

Our ammunition supply rate had to be reduced. The daily allowance for rifles was set at 1.6 rounds per man. Cliff said the daily allowance for the Americans when they were still in the war was 13 rounds. For machine guns, it was 10.6 rounds (while it was 165 for the Americans). For mortars, it was 1.3 rounds (and 16.9 for the Americans).

While we were conserving, the enemy was profligate. At Tong Le Chan border camp, soldiers of the Communist army shelled the base three hundred times, using more than 10,000 rounds, over a sixteen-week period.

In the meantime, in an audacious act that showed supreme confidence and advance planning, the North Vietnamese proceeded to build and finish a petroleum, oil, and lubricant pipeline that extended as far south as Loc Ninh, a mere seventy-five miles north of Saigon.

The few hundred military advisers who remained after the American pullout were soon ordered to return to their country. And so it continued. In the midst of a machinelike juggernaut that aimed itself straight at us, it was, more than anything, a quiet departure by one friend that proved devastating, especially for Quy.

When Cliff left he promised to return. He said good-bye in January 1975, early one morning. He drove down the driveway of our house, probably through the main thoroughfare in Cholon, heading back toward the fine houses and shops of Saigon's fashionable district before taking that turn toward Tan Son Nhut Air Base. We watched him go. I saw my wife stand on the rim of disappointment and heave, hanging on to his disappearing form.

We could feel the movement of time as it nudged, then pushed itself against us. Hurry up and let go so we can all begin anew.

As 100,000 North Vietnamese soldiers advanced toward Saigon in 1975, President Ford declared that the war was finished as far as America was concerned. Defended by 5,000 men, Phuoc Long Province, along the Cambodian border north of Saigon, was the first to fall under attack by 30,000 North Vietnamese and Vietcong soldiers.

The American State Department issued a "strong protest."

For the first time since I had him released, I heard from my brother-in-law, who had a message sent secretly to my house. I had bought a plate of pork buns for lunch from a vendor who frequented our street. When I bit into the soft, white dough, I found a strip of paper neatly folded in half. It read: "Make arrangements for your family to leave. Quickly. Before it is too late." The note was signed "Little Brother Number Five."

# 17

## *[Untitled]*

### MAI, 1975

I know, as Father and I get on a helicopter to fly out of Saigon, that my mother will stay behind, enfolded inside her tormented heart.

# II
# HALF-LIVES

# 18

# *The Keepsake and the Storm*

## BÃO, 2006

It is I, Bão.

I rush out of our apartment as fast as I can and gaze right through the winter mist. The air is sharp and cold. The bright blue energy that clattered and jangled through my body during that moment of violence has lessened but it has not dissolved. I can feel its effect, a formlessness of spirit carried into the unknown edge of the present. A long memory converges inside me, pulling itself into shades of colors and sounds.

It is Mai talking to herself. Of course I can hear her and see her. Even though I am hidden inside her, I am the omniscient one among us three. Cecile is merely the charming little child, freshly hatched, who allowed a bird to coax her into talking and then became its playmate. But I am Bão, the storm, not Bảo the treasure. I am the malevolent central player. Mai is here, half bewildered, half alert, adjacent to the distinct lives we have been spinning in this country where we have dwelled for thirty tarnished years. I know she is conscious of the wisp of movement whenever I stir. I see the slow rise of Mai's chest and watch as she sits herself down on the sidewalk, dumbly, and kicks a lamppost with punitive force. She has become the sort of person who reserves her anger for inanimate objects. Her stomach dips and rises, whipping up thick and bitter bile that she struggles to push back down. Here I am alone already, inside the buried, threadbare narratives hidden from her view.

I know what I have done. I have smashed a television and a teapot. I have wreaked havoc inside our father's enclosure of calm. There is a medical word in this country to describe Mai and Cecile and me. Our madness was once called multiple personality disorder but now it is coined dissociative identity disorder.

When the *thay phap* told our parents years ago that a spirit might have seized Mai's body and soul, Father associated her white-hot anger and her many indecipherable moods with alien demons. At first he was unsure when I elbowed her out, uncertain of what he called my storms—"Bao"—and for the most part, he was alienated from and afraid of me. But over the years, he has developed a different perspective— distance morphed into furtive affection which bloomed into something like love. Love for me, Bao, not just for Mai. As he aged, he somehow found a way to cherish not just the perfect moments but also life's deviation—the fortuitous turn against the grain, the sort of dissonance and melancholy that produced someone like me.

But I suspected too that our father began to embrace me for a different, more private, more poignant reason. Once, in Cholon, in the near-total darkness of night, a few days after the *thay phap* issued his diagnosis, our father entered my room and lay quietly on the side of the bed where my sister used to lie before she died. Mai was also there of course. But he could sense my presence too, halved and spliced, twinned to yet also separated from Mai.

"What is your name?" he whispered.

I had never been addressed directly before. The world around me felt like a storm. "Bao," I said. Vertigo unsettled me. I was merely repeating the word he himself had used to describe Mai. I didn't have a name before then, but once I uttered it, I knew it was mine.

"Bao," he said, accompanying my name with a thoughtful nod. "Which Bao? Bao meaning storm, or Bao meaning keepsake. Or treasure," he asked.

"Both," I whispered, though I was unsure of the answer.

"Does Mai know about you?" he wondered.

I nodded. "But she doesn't like me," I admitted.

And then in a gesture that both touched and astonished me, he stroked my hair and called me *con,* a word used to address one's child. "Don't worry," he said effortlessly. "Mai will like you. She will learn to. You're her sister, after all." And although it was dark and I couldn't see him, I sensed that he was taking in the situation and trying to understand it. He put his arm around me, and in that moment, I believed he saw me as someone his dead child, Khanh, my sister, had somehow been reborn into. It was as if Khanh had not departed irrevocably into death but could be reclaimed in this strange and new realm.

I often caught him in a state of observation and contemplation, perhaps trying to figure out how two (sometimes three, if you counted little Cecile) beings shuffled through one physical body. Who is before me, he might wonder. And I wondered in turn which adjectives might come to mind for him when he thought of us—ordinary and extraordinary, normal and abnormal, peaceful and stormy, sane and mad.

At the beginning he was wary of my appearance, which he instinctively associated with Mai's strangeness—lost time, purple bruises, obsession with order. I understood because I too could not predict when black clouds thickened and the waters churned and a storm trapped me inside its vortex. It had happened before, many times. Both Father and Mai fear me, or are wary of me. Sometimes I am all moods and contradictions and untraceable convulsions plying and pressing against Mai with wrathful exigency.

Mai's attempts to impose logic or design can be done only in retrospect and are always wrong. She fears my sourceless anger, the fluctuation of my moods, and the tangle of greedy, raw feelings that overwhelm me and her. She is afraid of the sudden mutation of an ordinary moment into something awful. She knows that with me lurking around it is all the more difficult to hold on to ordinary happiness.

That was how it was this morning at our apartment. Everything inside me conspired to thicken and expand. I recognize these spells but only after they have claimed me and I feel nothing but the rush of righteous anger that burns like a bed of hot coals in the pit of my stomach. When the heat is burned out, what I am left with is a low-slung sadness that hangs within me silently. I remember how I woke up one day and discovered that Mai was afraid, that her fear banged and clanged perpetually inside her little chest. That realization had given me a surge of power and a big, brawny sense of personal importance. Although she is the one with the public face, in truth she is small and subsidiary, a weakness that can be obliterated.

Now her eyes dart about, still in suspense. My eyes catch her look. I can smell the primitive scent of her fear. It is the fear of not quite knowing what happened or why. I am inside her and I am privy to her most intimate thoughts. She knows less about me than I about her and that fact makes her unbalanced.

I plop down, wrapping myself in my own omnipotent narrator's gaze. The episode itself has set me spinning in a blind fever of after-rage.

What was there before the darkened world took over and made me smash about?

It is always Mother I see even as I slip back and forth through the black waters of consciousness. It is always about her repudiation, her disappearance and withdrawal, like Aunt An's absence when what I longed for most was her animal warmth, the soulfulness of her motherly presence. I return to those starkly separated scenes when she and I were in differently configured positions. There I was, stilling my heart as I bolted after her through the gardened paths. It was Tet. It was 1968. I was both Mai and my incipient self at the same time. I was tentatively there, submerged among the darts and points of light and dark, under water looking up through the jumping, electrified ripples, watching as Mai dipped and dodged and scurried after Mother. The flesh on my arms pricked up. I heard Mother call out our sister's name, "Khanh, Khanh," as she walked obliviously from tree to tree, then room to room, searching, searching. Mai was calling after her. Mai was trying to hold on to a corner of Mother's sleeve. I listened as Mother repeated our sister's name, over and over, abandoning us with each repetition. A tear fell but I wiped it off.

A long, plaintive cry came out of Mai when she fell and lost her grip on Mother's sleeve. Her body was flattened against the ground. Mother had disappeared. A hurt cut through me and settled in my flesh. Still, I struggled to come out, to come up from the murmuring swell of water I was still in. I knew I had to resurrect myself. I knew I needed to reach her.

I felt the quickening beat of time and the constellations of light, a voluptuous phosphorescent silver that charged about and sizzled loudly above, like fireworks. I pushed myself upward. My hands grabbed her arms and legs, and I heaved her into the cistern. Her body gave no resistance. I would save her. I saw her bulging, fearful eyes, and for that one moment I despised her, her smallness, her weakness. In that moment of piercing consciousness, my dislike of her grew and I saw how easily she could be blotted out, how insignificant she was in the shifting order of our world. I saw her lying there, like a withered thing turned brown, and I was seized and possessed by an urge to injure her.

She deserved to be harmed.

I am sitting here on the snow-covered sidewalk but Tet 1968 comes back to me as if I were still there, inside that terrible nucleus of fear.

Here I am, floating from above in a state of elliptical meditation, looking down as if I have left my body for good. I am observing even as I am observed. Colors wing skyward, beyond the chilled fog that settles in midair.

It was of course Tet. Always Tet. I shouted out the warnings through my crushed windpipe. The sky was still illuminated like a glaciered mirror. A noise deafened us all. James was wandering about, calling her name.

I knew without thinking what had to be done.

I had absorbed the lessons of our father's yoga practice almost by osmosis—thinking without thinking. Unburdened by the back-and-forth of contemplating this or that course of action and with single-pointed insight, I pushed her down into the cistern's depths. Silence, I told her. I got loud. Quiet! I dared not breathe. I pushed her down into the jar's depths. I calmed the lunatic *whoop whoop whoop* rushing through my temples up my head. It was the continuing silence that ultimately saved us. The sniper's gun swept unpityingly left and right. I covered her inert carcass of a body with mine. And at that moment I felt the small, flaccid body of Cecile as it hugged itself against my flesh. I covered them both. I was steely and enormous.

I could tell from the softness of her limp body that she was inside a humming unawareness of lost time. Her memory would be smudged, erased even as mine was expanded. Like an idiot machine, she remained prone to malfunction. She would remember little or nothing at all, leaving me to bear this burden and absorb it all myself.

You might wonder why I dislike Mai. Because I alone have held our mother's disappearance inside my heart. Because I alone have absorbed it, shielding her from immense sadness so she can be free to move on in this country. And when it is no longer possible for me to hold it all in, when it swells grotesquely in me, when I end up releasing everything so it can wail and thrash inside the frenzied shadows out there, she, the miscreant one, is the one who will become enraged. She will sigh and sulk and seethe and exclaim "You again!" as if she has lost a war and is now looking at the face of a returning enemy that sinks heavily into her world. Yet again. She will continue to blame James's death on me even as she ignores my struggles to save her.

Deep inside the flesh of her brain I can see how the mind hates itself.

I refashion myself inside a small, dwindling space. I know about accounting and double entry and balancing the books. She is back. I might have saved her life but that does not matter to her. Someday my innocence will be established. I leave the light and go back into the fatal blackness I have been in since Tet.

Sometimes she inspires a tenderness in me. She is slowly, tremulously coming out of her shrunken world. She stands up, her body fitting neatly inside a tree's slender shadow. Rubbing her eyes, she stirs and then moves with vigorous but restless force. She collects herself and tries to reverse her mind in circular turns and half-turns to that moment in time before I took over and pushed her out.

As our father aged, he increasingly dwelled in our sweet and bitter past. I know she is uncomfortable with what she considers his stodgy devotion to our former lives. She wants to be freed of memory, its empty shape, its hardened imprints. Vietnam for her is a tragedy of forms, to be sloughed off. The more our father circles it, the longer its slow fade, the more Mai stays away. She doesn't stay away in the physical sense of course. But she is nudged away, elbowed into the wary background while I take over. She will recall bits and pieces of this and that about our past lives but hardly ever the entire story that he shares.

After thirty years in this country, our father and I still dwell on the tender pinprick of Vietnam as if it were there that we will find deliverance. And so our father's stories, all about what happened years ago, are exactingly configured to my needs. Vietnam has not receded for me, as it has for Mai; it still tugs and pulls. Its murmuring voice beckons. The arrangement, her staying away, my coming, suits us both.

For months now, I have been the one who is present when we listen to his stories.

Still, our father misses her. He will sometimes ask for her or talk about her. He refers to her as my sister.

I can tell he understands we have a division of labor. I bring him food, feed him, and cater to his needs. Mai works and pays the bills.

And so even in this freezing commotion, she will go on to do what she always does, day after day.

Despite the firefight I unleashed just moments before, I can tell that for Mai, today will be no different from any other day. She made her apologetic exit from our apartment. She condemned herself and me once she got outside. But within a few moments, she gets herself into the car, punctilious even on a moorless, blustery day like today. With the glass fogging the moment she slides into the front seat, she taps the pedal and heads as far away as possible, in the direction of the city.

The truth of her life, of what she has chosen, comes out here, in this city of monuments and angles. After visiting Father, she pilots her car onto the main boulevard, where a coating of snow has cast a preternatural glow on every surface. She hears the crunch of tires against the inevitable imperfections of the road, the granular layers of salt and sand on asphalt. Before her, a pale, misty spire rises from the tentative bend in the road. The falling snow continues its wind-whipped course, giving its fury the illusion of a manic purpose. She drives slowly. The normally busy street is quiet. Schools are closed. The car moves unthinkingly into the left lane, and as easily as that one moment of tranquillity and composure, the decision is made to enter the city. Her presence at work is not required today but she does what she always does.

She is on Constitution Avenue. A lone figure stands on the sidewalk. With his index finger, a child gingerly lifts a succulent flake from a struggling rosebush. A few others meander about as a plow truck heaves and rumbles. She stops the car a few blocks from the steel and glass of her office building and sits still watching the snow fall. It is different from a monsoon but not that different. Both can overwhelm. Both allow you to disappear into the shape of turbulence, to throw yourself into distant echoes and old vestiges that might be most strangely but also most strongly felt only when you are inside the center of the storm. A thin fog spreads across the windshield as if phantoms have opened their mouths and exhaled onto the glass. Her field of vision is narrowed and foreshortened. She shuts her eyes and leans against the leather headrest.

There are times when she wonders why she chooses this over that, includes this and excludes that, says yes to this and no to that. Perhaps they are all random, patternless occurrences, not decisions. The latter presumes a degree of planning that she lacks.

It may all be coincidental, these little truths, each like the splintered shadow of a bead hanging on a slender thread that wends its way through the life she is making for herself here. But lately, she has begun to wonder if everything about her current life is really birthed in that place that is now far away. How much, if at all, do we recover from the loss of love? How much, if at all, do we ever let go of grief, even as we proclaim the need to leave it in the past?

The truth of her life comes out here where she is a stranger to her own history. She lives sometimes in a half-life of green that is Vietnam and in a half-life of blackness that is Virginia. A line divides the two. But a black light follows her inside this ministered silence, like a missing voice. She is, in truth, of neither the past nor the present. She is somewhere in between.

Indeed, the present, the *real* present, barely touches her at all. It is merely a leftover life consisting of mundane details. It does not grab or take hold of her heart. She is outwardly Americanized but inwardly she is stuck in Cholon. In this country, where possibilities abound, where an accumulation of perfect grades could have opened up multiple worlds for her, what she has chosen instead is to do what comes most easily to her. She has stumbled upon a course that will give her what she has always wished to settle into—a long solitude. She has chosen to be among books, to be coaxed quietly into an assured world of lonesomeness.

Her work is all indoors, among rows of glass-windowed offices floored with gleaming marble and travertine. She arrives early in the morning and moves with a fierce sense of ownership around the office. A perpetual agitation gives everything in these offices a sense of urgency. It is work that is compelling, work that is pressing. All around her, people dissolve into it, pulling their sleepwalking shadows with them as they move from room to room, hunting for sacred answers among a littering of books. People are bent over tables clutching pens in their hands, adjusting the angles of their heads and bodies. This is what they do. Work. It is not just about work but it is the devotion to work, and the full understanding of the task at hand and the hard-heartedness of clients' demands. Even in the earliest of mornings there, one can feel the extremity of panic when work hasn't been perfected.

She goes to work almost every day but she is able to maintain a distance there. She is without fervor. She could have staked a larger claim. She could have been in its dead center but what she has chosen instead is to loiter along the edge. From this position, doing this work, in the shadows, among books, she is not called upon to step forward. She is allowed to remain inside her long buried proclivities and inclinations. You see, her work is important there but it is not central. The lawyers are the ones whose work defines the firm. She is a librarian. Her work supports theirs. And in this self-conscious space that is defined by power and rank, she is content to stand on the periphery.

Every weekday morning, she watches a frantic congregation of lawyers, one or two years out of law school, foraging for information by the reference desk of the library. She can watch them as she eases herself slowly into the quiet, tentative space that is but four walls and a tiny window. She has grown fond of this carefully hewn private sanctuary outside her home. Especially the little window where a solid wall might have been. Nothing more is expected beyond her relationship with the books. It is enough that she has graduated from one of the most prestigious law schools in this country. That is all her father needs to know, that she has been redeemed by an appearance of respectability provided by a degree from a well-regarded school.

She parks the car in an unattended lot and makes her way up to the fifty-seventh floor, where she sees the firm's logo, a composite of last names standing in angular brass letters. Around the corner from the elevator is a welter of brightly lit offices filled with the murmur of voices.

It is not a surprise that work continues here even on this day. The lawyers are both afflicted by and blessed with work. Not Mai. She is among it, but not of it. She walks through the portals to her office, leans back, and takes a sip of coffee freshly bought from the firm's cafeteria.

She plucks one book from the metal shelves, then another. She accesses online sites and databases. Methodically she types in search terms. There is order in the world and she is eager to practice her powers of attention, her technical precision in responding to research requests.

In the evening when she returns home, work, as much as she enjoys it, can be flicked away without much of an effort. It does not gnaw at her. Nothing does. No one does.

For many years now, she has had a routine that she follows. Nothing, not the undisciplined, agitated air of this city, and certainly not even the work she loves, can explode the ordinary order of things. Sometimes she wonders if she has absorbed her father's meditative serenity. She has managed, after all these years, to remain unbothered by desire or emotional static, to inhabit a realm of unremarkable calm. Yes she does know that in this country that state of being is considered unhealthy, a result not of equanimity but of denial.

But the truth is this: She is not easily beset or stretched or unfastened. At her age and according to the timetable one uses to gauge life's progress, she can no longer think of her life as just beginning, with a world of possibilities still beckoning. She is not one who searches for happiness; she is content with the benign life she has managed to build in this country. Years after she first practiced it, she can still make the transition into geological calmness and repose at a moment's flip. Even at work, especially if she is alone among her books, she can return to what she fundamentally is—a stone statue, imperturbable.

Very few things can pull her out of her quiet. I can, of course, when I release myself from these splintered shadows of our mutual existence and drag her along with me over a desolation of memory and fright. I am Bão, the storm, and she knows I roil inside her.

I can still, at a moment's notice, with but a premonitory motion, send her scuttling against a wall, as if to be shot.

# 19

## *Exodus*

### MAI, 1975, 1977

In the morning light helicopters fly nonstop over the Saigon sky, lifting off from rooftops and then heading somewhere out to sea. I am with our father who whispers my name as if to comfort me. "Mai, Mai," he says. It is April 1975. We are among the slumping, unstrung multitude waiting to leave for some faraway country. We are there, jostling with fists and teeth one minute, weeping softly the next. We are the fortunate ones who are within the enclosed walls guarded by American marines. Their guns are not pointed at us but at those like us who are outside the gates waiting to enter. They are not yet jittery or enraged. They still believe they can get in.

Inside, helplessness has set in. We are getting closer to the takeoff point but beginning to suspect with philosophical gravity the obvious, that the helicopters will not be able to take everyone. We have whatever papers are needed but that might not be enough.

We and thousands of others have learned of the American plan to evacuate Saigon. It is a coded message announced in a voice of feigned detachment, a huge looping ellipse of deliberate indifference designed to delude and mislead—"The temperature is 105 degrees and rising," followed by eight bars of Bing Crosby's "White Christmas" played on the American Armed Forces Radio. It is a tactile conjuring to be kept secret from the Vietnamese, this signal among the Americans that they are ready for the final liftoff out of the country. But of course this is Saigon and secrets are hard to keep during these long-overwrought and intense days.

Father has taken me here to this makeshift assembly point in front of a nondescript building in downtown Saigon that has housed the CIA station chief and his senior officers. Tan Son Nhut Air Base has been shelled for days and the runway bombarded which is why we are here. Father's eyes are shielded behind dark sunglasses but I can see his tears. I can feel my own, not in my eyes but on the inside of my mouth. I taste a sharp saltiness against my tongue. I swallow, trying to suppress the churning of bile in my stomach.

After years of submitting his resignation and having it rejected, this time, to his great surprise, his request was accepted. President Thieu, the one who denied all his prior requests, has resigned. His vice president, Mr. Huong, was president for seven days and then he too resigned. But before leaving office, Mr. Huong signed the papers for Father. He understood Father's personal circumstances. The new president replacing Mr. Huong is General Minh, the same general who orchestrated the Diem coup and ordered Father's execution that November day in 1963. Of course Father had to resign. He was not allied to the new government nor it to him. Rumor had it that General Minh planned to capture Father and imprison or execute him. Even as it collapsed, the country continued to be defined by personal vengeance.

When Mr. Huong resigned, it was with the hope that a new president would have better luck. Even now, Saigon waits for the new savior who will arrive on a surge and pluck the country out of impending disaster. But of course the other side knows peace does not have to be negotiated. It will come soon enough, with the war's end, with defeat.

Our father no longer has a paratrooper's uniform to wear but somehow he managed to keep the red beret. He holds it in one hand and my hand in the other. Through the haze we see the phantasmal shape of black whirring skyward. Its metallic essence lingers in the sky. We keep our gaze lifted toward the flickering distance as if that were where magic can be found, as if that were where a translucent door will suddenly open and take us all into an alternate universe that is big and generous and self-sustaining.

I never got to say good-bye to our mother. Our father merely showed up at school and told me we had to go. "Where are we going?" I asked at the school gate, although I already suspected the answer. For weeks, classmates had vanished as family after family fled the country. I looked around. I could not see our mother. I pretended not to know where our father was taking me, as if feigned ignorance would exempt me from the terrible knowledge.

Our father must have caught the look on my face. "Your mother is not coming," he said, adding a quick "not right now" to soften the blow. "I tried," he whispered with a frown. "I really did. But your mother hasn't been herself. She wasn't ready to leave with us, but she insisted that I make sure you get out. We both want that." My Chinese grandmother opted to stay as well and accept whatever fate might be planning for her at this stage of her life. "Of course we can also return to her later when the situation improves," he whispered. His fingers splayed over mine as he ushered me away from the school quickly to the car. His hammer-blow pronouncements delivered ever so softly shook me.

"No," I said.

"Yes," he answered firmly. And that was that.

Father dabs my tears with a handkerchief but makes it seem as if he were merely wiping sweat off my face. I feel his urgent sense of responsibility. Life has pulled me in two, one part with our father and the other with our mother and sister.

When I ask our father if Cliff will return, he shakes his head and tells me that people are leaving, not coming into the country. Still, I look around for him. There is a waxing and waning of hope. And Saigon falls, falls.

Another helicopter lands and leaves, as they have programmatically done all day. The crowd moves forward, wheels squeaking, neurons firing, nerves flaring. Father pulls me slightly to the side, as if to hold back, to delay, to restrain the forward movement of the tide. I know what he is doing. We are still at that place in time when other possibilities are not yet eliminated and consequences have yet to be dealt with. If we wait here, it is possible Mother might still arrive. If we wait here, we might still go back home because a miracle has occurred. If we wait here, we will have more time to weigh the options and calculate the possibility of other outcomes. I look into the depth of my father's face for guidance. He wants to delay what is about to transpire because he knows it will alter the direction of our lives. We are at the departure point but we are still deciding whether to go through with it.

The sky slowly darkens, tilting toward sadness and threatening rain. Father sighs. Everything moves slowly. Crowds push but achieve no real forward motion.

Suddenly he sees an American man armed with binoculars waving at him from a compass point near the rooftop. Brusquely, frantically, the American waves his hand, then his entire arm. Father squints, as if by adjusting the relative distance between us and the man, a familiar face or shape would coalesce. Indeed, through the swift-moving, finger-jabbing, lapel-poking fragments of noses, eyes, cheeks, he is able to make out a face clearly. I know him, I do know him, he repeats with relief. It is a life-altering fact. And partly a matter of chance. I see the American in his fully elemental and boldfaced presence—boots and paratrooper fatigues, baton and pistol. He is mouthing something, Father's name, perhaps. Father yells something back. Miraculously, through the patter and din that has risen to an unbearable pitch, jamming itself inside the space behind my eyes, they are able to understand each other somehow. Father jumps upward, waving his red paratrooper's beret in the air. The man steadies his binoculars and adjusts the lenses to bring the distant pointillist landscape and the blurry dimness of us into focus.

A tiny cough and another tiny cough move through my heart. I wait for the man's reaction. I rehearse our father's promises. We are leaving but when Saigon is safe again we will return. Mother will stay for now with Uncle Number Two and his wife, Father assures. Or she can stay with Uncle Number Five, now that his side, the Communist side, has won. Why isn't Uncle Number Two leaving, I ask. I don't know, he says. They have no children, so maybe it matters less to them, he guesses.

The American waves and rests his binoculars in our appointed direction. We are there, among the calcified faces in the throng. A moment passes, then another. The American marches toward the rooftop's edge where the ladder is and climbs down. He parts the crowd with his weight and heft and heads for us.

Come, come, he says to Father. His crew cut is so short I can see the shape of his skull. No words are exchanged between them. The man simply waves us forth through the clamorous but strangely submissive crowd. Father puts a protective arm around my shoulders and pulls me into the propulsive orbit of his very being, the way my sister used to. I feel the tug of her force field, the distinctive, undiluted strain of her nature inside my core, as if she were the one who is pulling me forward and sheltering me inside her sanctuary. I am sandwiched between him and the American inside a narrow path moving toward the ladder. Quick, quick, they both say.

The American mumbles something to his counterpart guard positioned by the ladder and we are allowed through. Father nods. I am sorry it has come to this, the American says. Do I know your name, Father asks. The man says something and Father nods. They shake hands. Good luck to you, the American says. This is all a shame, he adds, shaking his head sorrowfully.

Who is he, I ask Father. Father shakes his head and says he is not sure.

A helicopter hovers, stirs an updraft of wind, and finally lands on the roof with strange, epic resonance. Father touches the cement floor with his hand and brings his hand to his mouth. He keeps his hand there, as if to hold the kiss. We are on the rungs of the ladders and then we are inside the helicopter. Father turns away and looks downward. Perhaps he is thinking what I am thinking, that the two of us on board must mean some other girl and her father are not.

The helicopter takes off, cutting a poignant swath through the sky, leaving behind people still caught in the derelict fringes below. From above, the rooftop appears smooth and unpocked, a faintly melancholic surface of slate that shines in the sunlight. A lone figure stands guard on it, positioning himself directly above the ladder's top rung. For some unknown reason, the crowd below suddenly surges and swells. The guard reaches down, throwing punches at those trying to get to the rooftop. A pair of arms passes a baby across the fence hoping it will be cast into the strange trajectory of a new country.

Father sighs and tells me we are heading toward the country that forced a disastrous peace treaty down our throat. We are going to America, the country that both betrays and redeems.

From that moment on, every image and impression occurs inside the elegy of ungrounded time, moving without the physicality of effort and musculature but with full-throttled speed and unsettling ambiguity. After a few days in an American army base in Guam, we are flown to Pennsylvania. This is Fort Indiantown Gap, someone whispers. We are told to call it by an endearing term—"Fig." Fig is our hallowed haven, a refugee resettlement center, part of Operation New Life. I pull my lapels around my throat and look at Father. I ache for Mother. Where is she, I wonder, now that Communist tanks have crashed through the Presidential Palace and Saigon has been renamed Ho Chi Minh City? In front of us, a signboard near a giant building reads U.S. ARMY TASK FORCE NEW ARRIVALS RECEIVING STATION.

We are assigned to a tent, one among a long row of them, and given blankets, pillows, towels, toothpaste, and toothbrushes. There are forms that must be filled out. Meal cards are distributed. Name tags with identification numbers are assigned. For three months, there will be more of the same every day until at some point, the continuing emergency of it will slowly unravel into an unrelenting accumulation of eye-glazing minutes and hours. It is both the privilege and shortcoming of life defined by three meals in a makeshift city. We live inside a sense of dejection as well as hope. We take it day by day, drawing a line through each calendar page to mark the passage of time. In steady, quiet fashion, our days are accented by well-timed routines. Here we stand in lines for the bathroom and the shower. We are a loose armature of depleted selves, standing under row after row of showerheads, modest and fully clothed, as water gushes through our threadbare cotton pajamas. Authority has passed from us to someone else. Here we stand in line at the mess hall, asking for one more scoop of this or that. Several times a day, we carry an assortment of tinned meats and fruits and sliced white bread back to our unventilated tents. An American guard gives us a handful of Hershey's Kisses, little puckers of chocolate candy like starlight wrapped in foil.

Day after day, we go through the motions, eager to leave the camp but afraid of the new life outside its doors. Doctors and medics examine us and give us an array of shots. People congregate in predictable spots, by the community bulletin board, searching for news of loved ones still missing, and around television sets, staring at a Saigon suddenly disfigured. On television, wide-angle cameras show it all—throngs of people left behind, reduced by the four corners of the screen to an undifferentiated mass. Now that it has finally occurred, now that the Communist flag with its generic star has replaced our yellow flag with three red stripes representing North, Central, and South, now that all other logarithmic perplexities have been peeled away to reveal this finality of a disaster, there is no other fate to behold or wonder about. It is now clear. The country has fallen. Peace has come but Saigon is lost.

Everywhere I look I see the vertiginous progression of blurred barracks. I want our mother. I think about Cliff. We are in his country. He can be a comfort for us, with his soldierly sense of honor and duty. But Father has developed an unfathomable reaction against his friend. There is undeflected silence when Cliff's name is mentioned.

"Will we see Cliff sometime?" I ask him outright one day. "I miss Cliff."

Father shakes his head, thereby answering my question while maintaining his customary silence on the subject. He looks into the distance, his eyes scanning the sky.

"You cannot decently just drop him," I say, uncharacteristically bold. "Please, let's look for him," I plead. I wish to be anchored by the specificity of a mission, of finding a familiar face in an unfamiliar country.

"He left," Father replies. He does not react to my provocation. I think he sees Cliff as a friend who drifted away, as most ordinary people do when they are unable or unwilling to help but have no heart to stay and witness collapse.

"He could not help that. He was reassigned." The original configuration of Father, Mother, and Cliff, with me hovering about them, was thwarted by precipitate forces bigger than any one of us.

Father flashes me a reproving glance but says nothing. He rejects my assumption of an affinity with Cliff. He looks at me intently and then arches his brow, a gesture meant to convey skepticism.

Our new surroundings are startlingly alien. There are spirals of oak leaves blowing in the wind, a chill in the night air suggestive of the temperate zone, the sharp scent of pine, and mounds of needle-type leaves shed by coniferous trees. The world here is devoid of coconut palms, bougainvilleas, frangipani blooms. Even though it is late spring or early summer, there is a pronounced incompleteness that is surely different from the full-bodied pungency of Saigon at this time of the year.

The camp seems immeasurably separated from a world teeming beyond our vision and grasp. Somewhere in the distance, I imagine a world of normal lives—a man standing on a ladder, in an ordinary neighborhood, hammering one cedar shingle, then another, onto a roof. Children going to school and returning home. Cars blaring horns.

One day an elderly woman stumbles from her bed and a red gush of liquid pours from her mouth. Is it the redness of betel nut chewed and spat or is it the horrible immediacy of real blood? Another day I play soccer with other children my age on a field of grass not much different from the field that was near our house. Afterward, we drink salted lemonade. We sit on aluminum lawn chairs and watch the purple gloaming vanish behind the pitched-tent roofs that for now define the horizon. Through all this Father is almost always with me. He sticks to the activities, the routines, as if somehow they will help us cloak our shortcomings and inoculate us against this feeling of shame. He is exhausted but his body is straight. At night, on his army-issued bed next to mine, he sits, back erect, right foot over left thigh, left foot over right thigh, his entire body fitted and clasped as if it were one self-contained column inside the tight grip of meditation and sadness. He has changed. He wants to know where I am every minute even though I am almost seventeen.

He must sense that I am not really here. He must sense that nothing really catches and holds for me.

The only thing that sticks are the night walks I take by myself on the lighted trails that meander through the camp. I linger just enough to see beguiling movements and silhouettes through the lit openings of the tents. I discover that I like solitary evenings when the sun's last glide takes it to some other corner of the earth and darkness slowly envelops us in its tinctured sheen and deep-colored light. It is as if a much beloved song were played, but in an altered pitch—in the minor key or dropped an octave. The notes are the same, but the mood is inverted.

One evening I walk around the sinuous bend of road that hugs a distant part of the camp. I am slightly off the path and my feet sink in the bare earth. Wisps of grass and wild creepers brush my ankles. There is a strange comfort to this. And then suddenly I stop. No more than two meters away is a large black cricket sitting in front of me, as if to block my way. He stares at me, holding my eyes for several minutes. I squat and put out my hand toward him. I feel the brush of his antennas against my skin. He puts out a loud calling song, thrumming and rubbing his wings, tilting his head. The serenade haunts. And then it abruptly stops. He hops across the tracks and disappears into the bleak wonder of a soft, purple mist. Above us, a dying star shines.

Everything else is a blur, blasphemously so, perhaps. Surely whatever is happening inside this camp is important, the bullhorn announcements, the interrogative voices, the notices about who among us has found a willing sponsor outside these encampments. No one here can leave without receiving an offer from an American pledging responsibility for his well-being. All of us here will soon be scattered across the United States. Father is anxious for us to leave so I can start school at the beginning of the school year. A woman points to a map and shows her son where their sponsors live. There it is, the city, a compact dot representing a new destiny.

Ngo Quyen Street and the tamarind trees along its edges, the garden path behind our house, the soccer field where James performed dribbling feats, the profusion of mimosa plants among the cluster of bushes and trees my sister and I hid behind, the first inward turning of their leaves when they are touched. I see and feel all these and more as a continuing presence, a waking consciousness, their being, their reason, their somethingness, palpable and within reach even if their physical manifestation is not. That they have vanished is what has given my imagination its proper sense of wonder and awe. Try as I often do to push it all back, just to reassure Father of my well-being and normality, it will not concede. It is there, now a crumbling presence, but I know I will covet it in perpetuity. "It." It is everything. It is always there, in the center, without edges.

Soon things move with superstitious dread at an even greater speed. I see the shadows of our new life coming at us. Something is emerging at last from all those forms and questions and answers. After six months in the camp, Father has found us a sponsor who will for one year be responsible for our housing and food and Father's job and my schooling. It is one of the many Catholic churches in Virginia.

He delivers the news with intuitive grace, as an anecdote to accompany his simple gift, a pack of Wrigley's gum. He mouths the words "We are leaving." I am simultaneously skeptical and curious. So we are sponsored, our future officially stamped and processed.

After a bus ride and a plane ride, we are in Virginia. A priest and a nun greet us. We are provided with a four-room apartment, all laid out in a line, each room spilling into the next without corridors. From the front door, there is the kitchen, then a bedroom (mine) and another bedroom (Father's) and a bathroom. To get to the bathroom one has to walk through his bedroom and to get to the kitchen one has to walk through mine.

Within six months, Father and I find jobs and we partially wean ourselves off the church's charity. We stay in the apartment owned by the church and pay a discounted rent. Within the year, we move out so that another refugee family can move in. During the day Father cleans a bowling alley. I am home from school by the time he returns and I make a point of greeting him with great solicitude. In the evening, he writes about the "lessons of Vietnam" for a research center that is part of the American military. I clean but I am not a cleaning person, he says softly. It is something he does but it is not who he is. I too clean—the shelves and floors of a Vietnamese-owned grocery store, one of two already established on Wilson Boulevard by the pre-1975 Vietnamese, those who are in the United States for reasons having nothing to do with the loss of our country. The owners are friends of Father's acquaintances and allow me to work there when Father pleads our case to them.

A few months into our new Virginia life, I again wonder out loud where Cliff is. At dinner I ask my father the question. I touch his hand for emphasis but he disowns my touch. He recites his well-rehearsed reassurances. "Everything passes. We will be all right. We don't need help." He means to console yet I am strangely disquieted. A part of me wonders if Father was ever grateful to Cliff for the companionship he provided Mother after catastrophe struck, which freed

Father from the burden of being solely responsible for her daily well-being.

I remind him that Cliff is his friend. Father turns pensive and nods, more to himself than to me. "True," he says. "But people change." He stands up, goes to brew a cup of tea, and sips it. I suspect there is more to his formidable resistance. Perhaps he is too proud to have Cliff see us in this condition. Knowing he has disappointed me, he makes a point of holding me tightly.

I remain silent but allow myself to be pressed against him. Still, what I mind most is the slyness of his reticence, the dissimulation of any interest or curiosity about Cliff.

"Remember what I told you and your sister when you were little? Be careful whom you trust."

I am startled. It is one of the few times he has mentioned my sister since her death. We turn quiet, facing each other, not together but not apart, just silent between thoughts, each intent on protecting the other by keeping our small despairs to ourselves.

This is the structure of my new life. I enrolled in school two months after the school year began. In the morning a school bus takes me from my house to school. To give me an additional year in high school, Father falsified my age, marking me down as fifteen and enrolling me in the tenth grade. I am small in size so no one suspects. We have no official documents such as birth certificates to produce so anything can be invented. Our father does not allow himself to demonstrate much in the way of emotions, but I know he has many worries. He fears that I will have no friends or, worse, that I will be mistreated in school because I am new and all the students have been through the lower grades together. But I assure him I am unruffled by school and I am relieved when I do in fact experience these words as the truth.

Despite the romanticized view of what it means to become Americanized, I see through it all too well. The molecular makeup of the melting pot is three parts mundane and only one part visionary. The fakery of assimilation itself is tame and, worse, tedious. Father finds it hard to believe when I tell him that school is easy or that its very ordinariness will not be difficult to manage. I am newly invented, a persona practicing my will and focusing my powers of attention on high school

English, history, math, biology. Most are two grade levels easier than what I studied in Saigon. And so I am here, persistent and competent and capable of producing the top grades that will make Father happy. I take care to study in school and at home.

I hone the brain's dull organ of logic and exhibit a credulous acceptance of all that is required to make the transition into Americanness. I understand its allure and can make a show of turning myself over to it when I am in school.

My heart remains elsewhere. Perhaps Bao has it, staking all her being on it. I struggle to keep it all separate. I strive to leave my memories scattered behind so the transition can be efficiently managed. Once, I might have reminisced, but now I strive not to. The curtain falls, an iron curtain, separating my heart from my head.

In the evenings, Father and I sit together at our round table and pass the time. Neither of us has ever cooked before but over time Father has learned to produce a modulated heat, just right and not a flicker more, that simmers the stew and allows the pork to linger in its clay pot. I hear the sound of a spoon going round and round in a pan. Sometimes we allow ourselves to be surrounded by the brilliant distractions of television.

I do my homework at the kitchen table. Father pushes a Hershey's Kiss on top of my notebook. He gets chocolate candy from the bowling alley and brings it home. He puts one foil-wrapped chocolate on the table for me, then, when I am done, another. And another.

He turns from the stove and says to me, "Any of your friends live nearby?" looking for an entry into the time I spend away from him.

I set down my pen and align it in the groove of my spiral notebook. "No," I say. "They are in a different neighborhood." He nods, seemingly reassured. He assumes they are in their own houses doing their homework as I am in mine. Here, in this new country, he feels relief and anxiety in equal proportions.

I do not tell him that I am stalked by Bao and Cecile and that I exhaust myself managing them and keeping them from escaping into the public world. I do not tell him about the math teacher who excoriated me when I questioned the grade I received on a test. The hardened face. The speech about "you people" delivered with pointed finger while

I sat stilled and muted. I do not tell him that I am sometimes seized by a churning sensation that makes me vomit.

Instead, I tell him about the wonders of school because he so believes in the radiating, transforming power of education. I assure him that I am entering into a world of prodigious knowledge. Everything comes out almost as a debriefing. For him there is a comfort in the reiteration of my day, as if here is finally a shift to the essentials, a formal aesthetics that matters at last. I find at least one element of the day to share with him. I tell him about isosceles and equilateral triangles, James Joyce and Virginia Woolf. I practice words like *hypotenuse*. Father listens attentively.

The daily format of my school day and its coherence soothes. I have geometry first period, English literature second period, social studies third period, then lunch, and so forth. There is one tabulated point, then another one, that punctuates the day. Everything about school becomes material for his plainsong celebrating the refugee's hope that the child will have a better future than the parent.

If it were not for my constant fear that Bao will catapult out and cause me to lose time, my school obligations, the subject matters themselves, would be but a balm. So far she has not trespassed into the world of my school. So for now, my classes are manageable. They allow me to pivot into the present while looking toward the future and boxing away the past. Boxing it the way I try to box Bao, mentally inside a metal enclosure guarded by ferocious animals pictured on its metal lid.

I suspect that Father's work is also, for him, a circumvention of a disquiet that must lie underneath us both. I think it is the persistence of absence that we both feel.

Years are missing from our lives even as we live them.

I try to erase from my memory that day when Father and I left without her.


We hear a bit of this and that about her from the gathering of Vietnamese in our area. A community is being built here. We know what we are. We are the barnacles of a lost war, struggling against disdain, and here we are day by day building this cloistered niche for ourselves and filling it with improvised charm. One shop opens, one restaurant, then another and another, each dedicated to the sensual cues of memories, the mouth-savoring tastes of a time past. The enclave owes its accoutrements to the real Saigon itself. It owes its very soul to the indulgence of memory. What we yearn for is an element of the commonplace and so it is the commonplace and its lesser emblems that are resurrected here. The walls are painted rice-field green. The air is permeated with the distinctive scent of spices. Loudspeakers play mournful music about love lost, its notes and chords pulling sadness from the air. As more of us congregate in the area, there is comfort in the reiteration of our replicated past, in the regresses of our memories and the pretense of normality. We are eager to be neurally tripped. We wish to trick our brains into believing we are still in Vietnam. Here in this little community forged by fate and circumstance, there are shops that cater to the flavors of Hue, Saigon, Hanoi, returning us to the simple assertion of first loves and other essentials.

History is pacified. War's indecencies are tamed. Day by day, like a recurring dream, a little Saigon is willed into reality.

There is an almost daily arrival of Vietnamese leaving their one-year, two-year lives with their American sponsors to join this little community. With them come fragments of Mother's story. There are inconsistencies that Father cannot make sense of. How much is pure fabrication and how much is truth, we do not know.

Within a few months, the new government took steps to ensure the irrelevance of wealth by decreeing that everyone would start out as equals in the post-1975 world. The old currency would be invalid effective immediately. Inequalities would be razed and everyone would be given two hundred dong to start a new life, even if jobs could not be had or could be had only if you could afford to pay a steep bribe.

The neighbor telling Father the story becomes increasingly perturbed as he recounts his ordeals. His hand gestures assume attitudes of anger and unrest. Call him Uncle, Father directs me. We are becoming familiar to each other so a new appellation is required. To his grave discredit, Uncle Somebody was a well-to-do owner of a popular restaurant in Cholon. He and Father become immediate friends. Uncle drones on, bitterly. When excited he pauses to spit, his horrible, angry spittle sometimes hanging by a thread from the corner of his mouth. I turn away but Father is too preoccupied to care. He listens instead.

Houses were confiscated and subdivided if they were deemed unneces-sarily large.

A Communist Party commissar took over our house for himself and his family within the first few weeks. But your mother was fine, the neighbor quickly assures me. She was not alone. She moved in with a Vietcong relative. Of course, Uncle Number Five. Father nods, as if that were to be expected. Her Vietcong brother will protect her, Father assures me. Others connected to the South would not be so fortunate. Soldiers of the old, defeated army were sent to reeducation camps to languish and die.

I was not there to see our mother leave our house and make her way to join her brother. But I have in my head an imagined memory of this moment. She is there in her purple *ao dai,* under the shade of a tamarind bough, closing our front door with finality and walking away from the place that had housed us all.

Father keeps repeating that having a brother who was a Vietcong will serve her well during these menacing times. Both his protective impulses and the integral power of his love are intact. He wants to put his arms around Mother, knowing she is so easily wounded.

They are called the boat people. It is because they flee from Vietnam's coast by boat. Their very essence is aptly distilled by two simple, sorrow-filled words.

It is 1978. The world is taking note of these people who willingly set their bodies upon the wide-open sea in the hope of reaching some dis-tant, kindly shore. Coastal towns are increasingly depopulated because of this opportunity to escape.

In Little Saigon, our eyes behold the incandescent allure of ocean-blue spaces on a map of the world. Our relatives are leaving in droves, seeking some other place to call home. We know what the South China Sea is like with its mahogany blackness and its sinister, palpitating presence. We absorb these physical facts with our entire bodies, not just with our eyes or our heads. I imagine the silence of the water as it gathers strength, the spectral mass underneath the calm that creates turbulence and capsizes boats. Following the wandering threads on water are months and months in Malaysian, Thai, and Hong Kong camps and then an arrival, at last, as nature's elements onto the shores of a country willing to take them in for good and offer them its many possibilities. Somehow they leave behind the lost, the fallen, and the dead.

The boat people restore and comfort us. They bring news when they come, not the sort of news with hedges and qualifications that seeped out of the country after the foreign journalists were expelled, but real, firsthand news. Families here in Little Saigon wait for their arrival. The Chinese are fleeing in droves. With blunt naïveté, the new government has begun persecuting them, accusing them of undue economic dominance, treachery, and divided loyalties. Once again, as in Tet, it is Cholon that is at the epicenter of this upheaval.

I remember what our Vietcong uncle once told Mother. "The Chinese are seldom harmless."

Of course Cholon will defy its oblivion.

The government claims punitively that the Chinese in Cholon—dubbed the Jews of Southeast Asia—are strangling the economy. One percent of the population controlling 80 percent of the food and textile industry and 100 percent of the wholesale trade. The Chinese will have to adopt Vietnamese nationality or they will be heavily taxed and their food rations reduced. Even those who already have Vietnamese citizenship are harassed.

This news inverts my childhood perspective. I can feel a sliver of memory move through me. I worry about our Chinese grandmother, Older Aunt Number Three the Pharmacist, Younger Aunt Number Three the Rice Seller, stilled by the anxieties and jolts of their new lives and the slights that might have come or might yet be coming their way. It might already be impossible for them, skillful traders Mother admired. Private trade, wholesale, retail, large and small, is abolished by Party decree. Cholon, home of the Chinese, must be deflated, its commercial essence snuffed. In one of the coordinated raids on Cholon, thirty thousand police cordoned off the city and conducted searches, confiscating goods and valuables from fifty thousand retailers. Did they go through Ngo Quyen Street?

The Chinese are fleeing, along with Vietnamese of all stripes, including former soldiers, farmers, peasants, and traders, carrying nothing with them but hope and grievances.

We write letters to our mother and Chinese grandmother. We wait for letters to arrive from Cholon, even Saigon. People we know in Virginia are beginning to receive correspondence from Vietnam, sent first to France and then forwarded to America. Our neighbor, Uncle Somebody, whose name I couldn't recall so I nicknamed him "Somebody," hands our father a smudged envelope he recently received from his wife, Mrs. An, postmarked Ho Chi Minh City. Inside is a circuitously worded letter containing mundane daily details, visits to the market, routines at their son's school, exaggerated declarations of their new and happy lives, and then the disguised news about the family's impending escape. They will be visiting her brother soon for a few days, the wife announces in the letter. The brother, Uncle Somebody explains, is already in California. He is choked with joy and fear.

Of course we continue sending letters whether or not we will receive replies in return. We are told by the newcomers to Little Saigon that the names of streets have been changed. Letters might be undelivered, lost. This is pure speculation. Still, every evening, Father inserts a small metallic key into the mailbox lock and, in a gesture saturated with meaning, sorts through the supermarket mailers and other junk mail. His voracious eyes fix on every envelope. It is a ritual in hope he engages in. No one will contradict him. No one will tell him there is no letter coming.

By 1978, more than half a million people have fled. Our neighbors, also former Saigon dwellers, join us for the evening news. I hear the usual musical passage that drumbeats the start of the program. Our visual and auditory cortexes are charged. Even in the narrative compression of five-minute sound bites, the sight of wrecked boats rammed onto a beachhead and human beings lurching in the water has pulled Vietnam again from the disinterested realm of background and anecdote into a central matter of concern.

Even during the height of the war, no one fled the country.

Father tells me that the South is a place where the language of commerce is spoken. It is a place of barter and trade, chaos and free-spiritedness. Southerners are a freewheeling, all-or-nothing lot. This explains the whooping, swerving Saigon traffic, he says, smiling. No Southerner can put up with the calamity economics of Communism, the so-called reeducation camps, or the austere grimness of the northern pall.

Of course I know what Father is secretly thinking when we walk the circumference of our apartment complex at night. The paved pathway is narrow and so he walks slightly ahead. From his gait I know he is thinking thoughts that leap and plunge. He is thinking that perhaps Mother will be among those on one of the boats that reach a foreign shore one of these days.

It is possible. Vietnam's entire length hugs the coast of the South China Sea. Coves and inlets dot the southern tip of the country. Fishermen too are having trouble eking out a living because their properties have been seized and their catches taxed. Southerners are harassed simply because they are from the vanquished South. They will be willing to aim their dinghies seaward. Word has gotten out that a clandestine network organized by the Chinese has emerged. Southerners with gold pay the Chinese who in turn bribe government officials. Even as they denounce the Chinese, Communist functionaries are all too eager to accept their tarnished gold in private. Gold is favored above all other currencies. Our mother has gold in a safe. This is what he is thinking, and I am thinking the same.

# 20
## *Watching*

### BAO, 2006

I am here, inside the tumult of air and wind that fills Mai's chest. I am still Bao, the storm, but for now I have calmed myself and I am just watching. The law firm is entangled in a criminal defense case that involves charges of racketeering, murder, and extortion. The client is alleged to be a mob figure who has infiltrated the music industry and his identity has thrown this prestigious and upscale firm into disequilibrium. This is a firm whose clients include large corporations, rich bankers, and chief executive officers who are occasionally charged with more palatable crimes such as insider trading or stock manipulation. The partner who heads up this racketeering case apparently accepted the client without going through the firm's usual vetting process. The team has been formed, and Mai is on it, along with three associates. They support David, the partner and senior rainmaker of the firm.

Mai is crisply dressed, in a skirt and blazer, a pin-striped suit cinched dramatically at the waist. Our private dramas and internal turbulence are hidden from view. Her hair, chin length, is parted to one side and swept neatly back. She is clear-skinned, wide-eyed, clear-headed, seemingly unaffected by the large-scale events that have defined our lives. That she can be so cool and calm enrages me. That she remains oblivious to my role enrages me even more. It is only because I have shielded her and saved her from feeling the pain of loss that she is able to stand here, showing off her fancy Americanized polish.

She is approaching David the partner with a wide smile glued on her face in the manner of a person who is meticulously in charge. He is in his midfifties and sports a thick, graying mustache that nicely frames his smile. He is known to be one of the more volatile partners. She has worked with him before. Under intense pressure to generate business, outmaneuver opponents, and score points, partners too work intense hours and are driven to extremes. They are permitted all manner of liberties, like barking and venting and generally being hostile and demanding for little or no reason.

But David is different with her. He likes her and doesn't issue orders. He finds her charming, precisely because she is so unreachable. Ambition, the cross and backbone of everyone here, has no claim on her. And hence he, the gatekeeper of career advancement, has none either. He knows enough about her prior life to realize that parts will remain impregnable. Over the years he has even developed a protectiveness toward her. He probes experimentally instead. Weekend work will be necessary to prepare for the upcoming trial. Their team is up against the federal government. There will be research pursued in blind alleys that will lead nowhere. Ambitious schemes will have to be concocted to exclude the evidence the government currently has against their client that has been gathered by wiretap. There are federal rules of evidence to research, such as the hearsay rule and its innumerable exceptions.

She reassures him, one arm on a jutting hip, that this work will be her priority. At the same time, she warns him with a spunky half-smile and a wink that he will not find her at the office night and day. I watch her haggle flirtatiously with him. "I'm not one of your precious associates you can overpay and overwork," she chides. He is divorced and if she gives him a signal, he will eagerly demonstrate his interest in her. But she does not.

Once, he followed her into the library stacks and with her back against the books kissed her, or attempted to, his mouth briefly touching her throat as she swiftly spun her head away. I saw how he looked at her accentuated lips, the dent of flesh where a necklace had been worn. He struggled for composure and offered her an obliging smile as if to signal harmlessness but she refused to grace his action with any discernible response. Anything beyond that quick turn of the head, such as a push or a verbal reprimand, would have seemed like too much of a reaction that would in turn invite apologies. Instead, she knitted her brows and gave him a cool stare before maneuvering herself toward the narrow doorway. The incident was never spoken of.

He remains intrigued. He touches her whenever he can, her wrist, shoulder, or elbow. She is all possibility to him, only partially revealed and fully unfulfilled. He probably believes she is a daydreamer, her emotions full and ripe and ready to spill over. He does not know what I know. Mai lives her life in this country as if it were but a prelude to something more lasting that is not here yet and might never be.

I know he touches a sore point when he asks if she wishes to have a working dinner with him to go over the case. "Unless you have other plans," he adds. She has no other plans. She knows that being by herself day after day is outside the realm of normalcy. But she stands there stolidly in the middle of the room rejecting his invitation. "Just a quick dinner," he insists, slapping his hands together. They both know this has nothing to do with work. I listen while she emits a soft, single-syllabled "um" and then, with prim dismissal, tells him that she needs to go home. She does not even make up an excuse. She keeps up the barricade. Her blazer hangs on her arm. Her shoulders are exposed and catch his attention as she disappears into the elevator.

I watch as she considers carefully what she says or does not say. She listens to his account of their new case as if the matter were deeply personal to her. She has been at this firm for many years and she has seen the associates' accumulation of billable hours sweetly resolved into year-end bonuses and the possibility of partnership at the end of it all. She has taken herself outside the realm of this possibility, recognition, success, or partnership, and so can maintain an easy façade of calm.

And so this demeanor, and it is only a demeanor, of efficiency and self-advocacy is all the more incomprehensible to me. Does she think that her polish sets her apart from us? I see her becoming not American but simply un-Vietnamese, and the visual assertion of this process is enough to make her even more of a stranger to me. She is, by all outward appearances, standing guard against the trespasses of Vietnam, palms turned outward as if she were there to forestall our advances.

True, she has made it here in America with bold forays into the unknown and a careful and precise mind. But she has done it completely unaware of what has happened within herself. She sees me as someone who lashes out. I am inside the dark recesses of her being. She does not know me. I am a mystery. She looks in the mirror and sees only my scowling and angry face. But she does not bother to reflect and ask the one obvious question—why?

I try to push on, observing her as she moves past offices and computer terminals, but I am unable to manage it. I am taken over instead by an echo of pleading voices. I know I can filigree my way through the brain's circuits. I can fake hope and trick my own feelings. "Mother, Mother," I call. We call. We stay hidden in the jar. I shush Mai up. James falls. She blames me for his death.

Cecile too is agitated. She is the one who saw our sister collapse. I can feel her sobs, the sorry sounds coming from her chest.

Mai is still there, working on the LexisNexis terminal. She is stopping at irregular intervals to massage her temples as she tries to soothe the palpitations we have created inside her chest. I am like someone in the dark shadows looking at someone in the bright light. From my vantage point, I know every thought that scurries through her head and every feeling that she hides in her heart. She is perpetually perched on terror's precipice, fearful that I will break out and throw her into unconsciousness. She can feel the scurrying movements Cecile and I are making within the depths of her being.

Quickly she stands up. Over the years she has become better at the task of managing my and Cecile's discontents and disturbances. She works hard to forestall the onset of insanity associated with my appearance. Deep down I have no wish to do Mai harm. I try to cooperate. I try to save my outbursts for private times. I know we are in a public space, but as I watch her exaggerated display of Americanness, I am seized by uncontrollable rage. Still, I delay the onset of dark clouds and malicious storm. Instead, I thrash about for a long time inside her and thus give her sufficient warning to retreat to safety.

With each successive occurrence, the transit point that marks, to put it euphemistically, my entry into and exit from her world has become smoother. She knows I am about to push her into lost time. She rushes back to her office, locks the door, and with a sigh relinquishes herself and her consciousness to the forward and backward drift of our mutual lives.

Mai is home. Cecile is at the piano. The music she produces is beautiful, lush and prolonged inside the slow-moving dusk. It is music gorgeous enough to deflect all else. Here is beauty at last, in all its glory and raw intensity, briefly attained but somehow forever out of reach. It remains a mystery how she does it. She is playing Chopin but not quite. There is a faint disturbance in the air, a minuscule fragment of a sound, and then, suddenly, the music merely levitates effortlessly from the notes.

Our father exhales sighs of appreciation.

Sometimes it is like a mynah bird singing. The notes are held in its throat and then released. A beautiful birdsong emerges, elegiac in tone.

Sometimes it is like cupping the past in two hands and bringing it tenderly to the present. In her music, our essential life comes back in bursts the way a bush might explode in white blossoms one early spring morning.

I hang back and listen. Sometimes I try to pick up the notes and other times I just take the melody in.

She must be playing from memory. Our mother loved Chopin. So this is where Cecile goes to save herself, I think. So this is how the keyboard holds these hidden chords inside itself.

On those rare moments when Cecile emerges from Mai, she does so softly, melodiously, by playing the piano.

Unlike me, Cecile does not scowl and has no malice or wrath inside her. She is still an innocent. Her silhouette moves slightly. Outside, the long hanging branches of a sycamore also move. It is as if she were fully awake to life outside our louvered glass windows. It is as if she takes her cues from the old shade tree itself as it sways against the deep-churning rush of the wind.

It is her evening hour. She is alone at the piano, with our sister's heart in hers and a high-flying cascade of music inside her fingers. Mai has been redirected elsewhere. The transition is much smoother than when I elbow and bang my way out. It is as if she were merely sliding down the coiled shell, following the spiraling lines that mark its cylindrical shape. She meets no resistance. It is as if Mai knows that it is only little Cecile and she is willing to relinquish the space.

And so she is here, this evening, playing Chopin and keeping cadence. The world doesn't fall in tune with our internal currents, but we are making do under the daily strife. I can hear the music wind along the narrow Cholon roads into Ngo Quyen Street where it slows down and rests itself inside the purple dusk of the Old World.

# 21

## *Waiting*

### MAI, 1977-1978

I am in my last year of high school. We are still in Virginia, my father and I and a scattering of lives—Bao, Cecile, but mostly Bao—roiling about inside the depths of my being. I have done well, my grades not the result of brilliance but of merely workmanlike steadfastness. Today Father complains that he feels funny. It is early morning and we are both getting ready for the day. The school bus will be picking me up soon. The sight of Father slumped at the kitchen table, stilled by a strange sensation, stops me from running out the door. I go to him and put my hand on his back. His face has taken on the pallor of the haunted. He is not able to identify the sensation that plagues him beyond the one description that he keeps turning to, that he feels funny. Still, looking at his swollen eyes and puffy lids, I probe. What does *funny* mean, I ask. I want to know if there are physical symptoms. With a slow, ponderous intensity, Father proceeds to describe them. There is a phantom sensation on the left side of his body, starting from the heart and going down the rib cage to the hip. When did it start, I ask? He does not answer that question but mutters this instead: I am here, waiting for something to happen and I don't know what.

I ask him again when the funny feeling started. He tells me that he woke up two nights ago with a tightness in his throat. This very sensation has morphed into a feeling of numbness on the left side. He fumbles for an explanation. Here, he says, taking my finger and tracing it down the length of his body.

I know the feeling.

Is it a premonition, I ask, that might be producing the strange feeling? No, he replies petulantly, as if to dismiss this very unworthy thought as pure wrongheadedness. It's a physical sensation, he insists, a solid numbness that at times hardens. I don't suggest a doctor. He would refuse. I know his self-punishing beliefs about the need to endure quietly.

All through the day while I am at school, I think about the look on his gray-stubbled face as he left the house. In the morning's dusty light I saw that he has grown diminutive in his blue-gray uniform. His gaze was slightly off to the side of my face even as he bade me good-bye in the muted voice of someone who is losing hope. I cannot shake off that sad look in his eyes, the retreating gaze that seems to hold nothing.

Later in the evening, as I sit in the living room reading, I experience him by my side as if he were a blur. Can a person dissolve before one's very eyes, become out of focus because he is vanishing slowly into the dungeons of his own mind? He has nodded off to sleep on the sofa, cloaked in a pool of soft light. A book lies on his chest, opened and facedown. Reams of paper, some annotated, are scattered on the coffee table. I see his handwriting. Written in cursive, it is patrician and beautifully crafted, with each downward stroke firm and bold and each upward stroke light and airy. His breathing is steady and assured. His existence till now has been so inextricably married to his parental role that I can't look at him without seeing a father first and everything else after. But tonight he looks vulnerable. I do not see the fatherly aspects I have loved about him—the booted thump, the muscled back, the broad smiles he gave my sister and me. I see instead a slumbering, unadorned being, lying with his arm dangling from the sofa. I note his more fragile, more human particulars—the eyes squeezed shut, the worn socks peeking through a rumpled blanket, his thoughts about a lost war set on paper scattered about on the coffee table. I worry about the funny sensation that clings to his left side and wonder if it is a serious medical condition. The deeper reserve of calm he has managed to accumulate through the years seems to be dwindling. Now, late in life and in a foreign country, he suddenly needs to be rescued.

A moist, whistling sound escapes from his lungs. I crane my neck to look. He stirs slightly and crosses his arms over his chest, as if to shield his vital parts with his more expendable limbs. His face takes on a beleaguered look. His eyelids move rapidly. With mounting irritation, his breathing becomes ever more labored in the evening's prevailing hush. I reach out to touch him. Wake up, I say. My first thoughts are that he is having a heart attack, until I see that his fingers are pressed against his eyelids as if to seal them from the world, as if to shield something from view.

A bad dream, I think, relieved. But I am startled when his body snaps upward, as if it were suddenly subjected to a powerful electrical charge. What is wrong, I ask. His eyes open. He looks aggrieved. I see the flutter of eyelashes and the flush of confusion. He says nothing and shakes his head. I reach toward him but feel the rejection of his recoiling arm. Finally, he whispers a soft "I don't know." A flush of color spreads across his face. I touch it and feel an emanating hotness against my palm.

Moments pass. Father sits still on the sofa, his forehead cradled in the palms of his hands. And then, without a word, he gets up and walks to the bathroom. I follow him. The dream is still with him, its implied threat, the whole of its weight lashed to his body. In an uninflected voice, he complains of a heaviness that haunts his body's periphery. He mutters that something is on his chest and that he cannot breathe. His body must be carrying extra weight, he insists. He steps on the scale. We both see that he has not gained a single pound. How can that be, he wonders out loud. He is convinced something has happened to make him metamorphose into a man several times his actual size.

He allows me to take his hand and walk him back to the living room. What is the dream about, I ask him. But he shakes his head and smiles ruefully. Perhaps it is irrecoverable. Or perhaps he does not want to tell me. He licks his lips as if to erase the astringent aftertaste of something unpleasant. I make him a cup of tea. After dinner, we sit side by side watching the moon glide across the darkening sky. Cloaked in blackness, I can feel his weary spirit dissolve into the agitation of the evening.

Little Saigon is growing and a great big world has opened up for us. We congregate in one another's houses and apartments to commemorate notable events. Weddings, births, Tet, are all openings that the

Vietnamese in America use to channel the ragged immensity of their longings for things past. It is all about reconstructing and reclaiming what is gone. I accompany our father to these events, but my heart is not in them. I know he and Bao still occupy that past, its emotional nodes and swells, with doggedness and abandon.

Today I am at Uncle Somebody's apartment, two doors down from ours. He has been made the head of our community association for overseas Vietnamese. The association is our way of making a familiar mark onto this shifting world, of organizing haphazard arrangements.

It has been a few months since his wife and son joined him after an arduous boat journey from Vietnam's coast to a refugee camp in Hong Kong. They have not recovered from the tumbling chaos of their journey. The mother smiles but I can see the clenched jaws and tense facial muscles. Still, if you can catch her at the right moment, there is a fullness and a shininess to her essential being that is contagious. She is diminutive but she has made it across a vast ocean. Perhaps Mother might too. Something visceral moves through me. I see her as a prophetic spirit. I want her hard-spiritedness. Day after day she does the quiet work of maintaining the home where she is reunited with her husband.

From the day she first arrived, I have made a point of visiting her regularly. When I tell Father that she visited several Chinese in Cholon to find someone to take her and her son on a boat, Father also becomes interested. Bao too, of course. When she is in the right frame of mind, I am able to coax Aunt An into telling her story. Mother's whereabouts might be unknown but somehow a story about Cholon makes her existence somewhere in Cholon more palpable to me.

Father encourages my visits to Aunt An, perhaps so I can have real company while he sits alone on the sofa at night and obdurately stares down his war memories. He aims to organize them into chapters and subject them to analysis by the American military.

Aunt An cooks from scratch, the way we did in Vietnam. Knives and spoons make percussive sounds against cutting board and mixing bowls. She lost weight on her boat trip, prominent collarbones protruding through her shirt's neckline. She tells me she is one of these people who burn energy easily. I can see why. She moves about incessantly.

Today she and Uncle Somebody are organizing a birthday feast for their son's one-year-old daughter. A pot of water boils, frothing over onto the stove. For the discerning carnivores among us, there is a roasted suckling pig of both lean and fatty flesh, still whole and uncarved, its bronze skin crisp with a pronounced char. There is also an eye-catching riff of miniature dumplings stuffed with crushed mushrooms and crabmeat, meant to taste good and to showcase the cook's artistic presentation.

She finished cooking early and the guests have not arrived. "Tell me about how you planned your escape," I prod. There is a brief faltering, but after a moment's pause she closes her eyes and tells me to come closer. She remembers of course.

The Chinese in Cholon had organized a network of safe houses and boat captains and navigators. She was in a yellow room in the back of a villa hidden behind tall fences. Inside her was a tug of opposing emotions, the surge of nascent possibilities and a deep grief for her husband alone on foreign soil. Those in the room were all connected in one way or another to the Chinese organizer—friends of friends, friends of relatives. She recalls the evening clearly. The desire to escape compelled her to take all risks. It was a moonless night but the sky was overflowing with stars. The room was full. There was the strong odor of eucalyptus oil that caught in the nostrils. The house was a few blocks from Ngo Quyen Street, in the heart of Cholon, she adds, noting that it was not far from our own house. I picture the house as Aunt An positions herself in front of me and continues. They needed gold, four bars for her and four bars for her son. No bags or suitcases allowed. There was no particularly auspicious time, no need to study weather patterns. The trip would begin when the boat was ready, in one week, on such and such a date, first by bus or cargo train to the coastal town of Phan Thiet and then the escape by boat at night.

A week later, when they were ushered out of the bus after a journey that took longer than they anticipated, they were not in Phan Thiet but in Ca Mau Point, a remote coastal city perched on the southernmost tip of the country. Phan Thiet had never been the planned destination to begin with and the switch to Ca Mau was done to ensure secrecy and security. But Ca Mau had its own advantages. It was part of the vast Chinese trading network. Since the early 1880s, the Chinese had been coming to this area despite its isolation, navigating their cargo junks through the interconnecting waterways linking the trading towns of Hainan, Ca Mau, and Singapore. There are lush mangrove swamps on one side and a long line of seaboard on the other. Farthest from the capital and battered by sea winds and storms, Ca Mau natives are to this day sturdy, eccentric sorts used to throwing themselves into the elements. Its coast offers deep moorage for fishing boats owned by fifth- and sixth-generation fishermen already inclined toward deep-sea travel. A fierce, poetic sense of independence defines the very spirit of the town and its inhabitants as well.

Aunt An's bus bounced on stretches of rough, uneven surface until it swerved onto a side road, stopping by a lone shanty at the edge of a dirt trail. The main road was no longer passable. The thirty people on the bus were told to disembark into the dreaded night. Three fishermen in charge of the voyage, all Ca Mau natives, were waiting for them. I know the details Aunt An will soon provide. I have heard this part before. Aunt An held her son's hand. He was almost eighteen but she still wanted to protect him. She clung to him fiercely, the way she did when he was a child. Together they made their way through the slow slog of alluvial soil, up the soft foothills with errant underbrush, and finally down a slender path toward the beach. A sea-salt fragrance floated in with the breeze. They pulled each other forward, following the darkened outlines of those trudging tentatively ahead. Everyone held on to the person in front, each terrified of being left behind. Clusters of mosquitoes circled above. She cursed the fact that they were unloaded all at the same time and feared the presence of thirty people descending all at once onto these vast sandy stretches would alert harbor police and other officials.

A hard rain began to fall. Her eyes smarted from the sea salt. The surroundings were muted by the silvery-hued darkness and the mist of rain and fog. Rain, she thought, borne by these gusts of wind, could be a blessing in disguise, offering them additional cover from detection.

To her left, a woman tearfully bade her sister good-bye. "Take her, little sister. My daughter is now yours," the woman said. To her little girl, no more than two years old, the mother said, "Call your aunt 'Mother' from now on, you understand? She is your mother now." Aunt An tells me she could sense the failings of their circumstances, the narrowing of options, the act of last resort. She describes how the little girl clung to her mother and whimpered. As her mother turned to go back to the bus, the little girl ran after her, skittered, and fell. Her sandals had caught on something sharp and protruding.

The part that startles me each time Aunt An repeats the story will come next. It is always the same. Even though I know the story, I listen with the furious concentration of a child. In a tone of soft tenderness she tells me about how she knelt down to scoop up the little girl. With a disquieting sigh, the girl's mother switched her story and assured her daughter with a long string of frenetic promises. I will join you soon. I will be with you, she said. In the meantime, stay with her, the mother whispered, pointing to her sister. Your mother loves you and *she* loves you, darling. She is your family, the mother assured even as the little daughter wept. I want my mommy, I want my mommy, the girl cried, extending her arm in a desperate attempt to make contact with the mother's flesh. Her face wet with tears and rain, the mother turned and walked away. The little girl sucked air and shrieked as Aunt An put an indelicate hand over her mouth to cover the scream.

They took turns, the sister and Aunt An, carrying the little girl on their backs as they marched. They walked in silence. When the girl's aunt tired, Aunt An took over. She could feel the girl's fretful sobs against her back as she navigated the slick, narrow pathway that was at times dense with gnarls of ground cover and shimmering with the wetness of rain. When she needed to shift position, she carried the girl in the front, curled up against her bosom. As she walked she looked into the little girl's face, touching its roundness, feeling the hair as soft as feathers and black like her fear. Intuitively, she worked to make her steps predictable. The child, she hoped, would be soothed and rocked by the march.

At last, from a small, sandy promontory, they could see the coast through the near-monochromatic blackness of water and sky. She could feel the pebbles against her shoes. The rain had abated but a mist, ethereal and light, hung above. The air was tinged with salt. Their steps quickened. Her son held out his hand to help her along. She stretched her body and felt the slow elongation of muscles on her back. The child had been handed off to her aunt. In the faint blue-hued light they could barely make out the boat. But she could tell. This wooden boat was designed to haul little more than fruits on the rivers of the country. They would have to put their faith in this ineffectual little craft.

I know what happens next. I don't ask Aunt An to finish the story anymore. After five days at sea, the little girl died, her head cradled by her mother's sister and her feet stretched out in Aunt An's lap. Two days later, red itchy patches like insect bites appeared on Aunt An's body. She sat on her hands to keep herself from scratching them and aggravating the redness. Bed bugs, she said to herself. She covered herself, concealing the red ugliness with a blanket wrapped around her body. But the spots moved to her face and soon formed pustules conspicuously filled with a clear liquid. They could no longer be passed off as bug bites. And she could no longer resist, especially at night when she pulled and scratched the severely inflamed areas until the blistered walls broke. Soon people moved away from her. There was no way to say "chicken pox" diplomatically. Once announced, the information fell heavily. She could feel the blisters on the inside of her mouth and the back of her throat. Her eyes were also covered by thick-crusted lesions. Only her son and the aunt of the dead baby stayed close by, protectively shielding her from the raw intensity of others' glares. She felt herself slipping into a fever. Her entire body was emanating heat. She closed her eyes. Even in her wearied and light-headed state, she could make out the intonation of crisis; she knew what was being said through the agitation of clipped voices. She realized it was her very life that was being debated. Her son sobbed. She saw fear in his face. He held her hand. She tried to wrench it from his, worried that she could infect him. She understood what was happening. She was tainted. They were going to throw her overboard the following morning. She imagined it, her last moment, the harsh orange sun appearing, the blazing sky opening up to greet dawn's arrival, the water vast and immense, swallowing her in its grip. Frothy swells slapped the sides of their little boat. She was not angry. She no longer cared. She looked into their faces. She saw their panic and the concomitant resolve to live. The last thing she remembered before drifting off into a dream was the feeling of sadness moving beyond her.

In the morning she heard voices through the tail end of her dream. Orders were being issued in a foreign language. Her arms and legs were sunburned. The boat shook. She saw sun-darkened faces, fissured and creviced. A group of men thundered on board, pointing in this and that direction. She saw their knives and guns, smelled a sour blend of beer and sweat. She knew. Pirates. She heard more voices, tearful pleas, and fitful cries. A woman and child were thrown across the boat. A man stepped forward and slapped them back and forth with the palm and back of his hand. She saw the child's split upper lip. The man lowered himself astride the woman's chest. Men were clubbed and thrown overboard. Aunt An closed her eyes. Things were being thrown about, and then she felt everything come to a sudden stop. A big shaft of light was beamed in her direction. She closed her eyes, shielding them with cupped hands. There were decisive gasps and deep raspy voices. Their eyes roamed her face. She looked and saw exaggerated frowns and raised eyebrows at the edge of her vision. Then there was quiet and only the sound of quick-booted steps leaving. A frothy wind stirred.

It was she who had driven the pirates away. It was the very sight of her. Her limbs and body were themselves bursts of hot red. She carried the intrinsic threat of contagion.

No one spoke. A child asked meekly, "When are we going home?"

Later that very same day, as she lay curled inside herself, a ship appeared. On its side, she saw the words USS *Francis Hammond (FF 1067)*. She knew they would be rescued this time, and they were.

Her story has a happy ending but grief has nestled deep inside her. There she sits at the kitchen table, stilled by its undercurrent. Her husband, the same Uncle Somebody who had escaped much earlier, comes toward her from their bedroom and puts a sympathetic hand on her back.

The first time she told me the boat story, she had mentioned a man who had only one leg who was in the house in Cholon when their escape was planned. He was there to contemplate throwing in his lot with the Chinese. Aunt An was never introduced to him but apparently many in that house in Cholon knew him. She remembered the twitches of his severed limb, the puckered, irregularities of the flesh. She remembered the way he appended his prosthetic, fashioning adjustments, tightening and loosening the hinges toward the end of the evening. How would he have managed the long journey, practically speaking? To her bewilderment, she found herself staring at his blatant, defiant misfortune. There were many amputees in Saigon but this man was well-to-do, crisply dressed, and sitting within arm's reach of her.

I asked her his name when I first heard the story. She did not know.

She still cannot recall it when I ask her again. Did he have a scar on his jawline? She is not sure. As Aunt An says, there are many men without limbs in Saigon. How can I be sure, she asks?

Is it possible he is Uncle Number Two? If Uncle Number Two contemplated escape, surely he would have involved our mother in the plan. My heart leaps.

I am like a detective who wants the witness to retell the incident, hoping that the act of retelling will help the witness remember a new but crucial detail.

I ask if the man with one leg was alone or with someone but Aunt An does not know. I ask if anyone in the vicinity called him by name but she has no recollection.

Later in the evening, I am allowed to greet guests at the door, fetching them drinks and offering them spring roll appetizers. Uncle Somebody and Aunt An cut through the crowd and nudge our father toward the table to eat. Strangers mingle solicitously with one another, each bound to the other by an old complicity to keep the country we left behind in the center of our collective memories.

The little girl, Aunt An's grandchild, was born at nine in the morning the Year of the Goat, a fact that is scrutinized so that predictions about her life can be made. In Saigon of course grandparents from the mother's and father's sides would be present, as would hundreds of relatives. Here the baby is surrounded by friends culled from her parents' connections to this or that shop in Little Saigon. She is dressed in a bright red *ao dai*. Her father and mother take turns holding her on their laps as cameras click. She is clearly unaware of the little storm of emotion surrounding her rite of passage. She sits on a patch of blanket, mouthing unintelligible words, reaching for objects, deliberately placed curiosities that include a mirror, a pen, a dollar bill. Will she be drawn to beauty, education, or finance? Before she is able to confront the unlived future and make her selection, her grandfather shoves all three objects, the entire scattering of surprises, before her, exclaiming that his granddaughter will have it all.

The ceremony is over and children now run up and down the apartment's narrow hallway. Wine is served. Someone has opened the screen door leading to a small balcony. A man leans against the iron railing and lights up a cigarette. Perhaps he can sense that I am staring at him although his back is toward me. He turns around and gives me a cordial smile. I am frozen. I am fixed on the plain creaturely fact of his gesture. A moment ago, he had aimed a match across the matchbox's rough surface and struck it. He had taken a long, pensive drag on his cigarette and slowly exhaled.

I run into the kitchen. Aunt An is at the sink, scrubbing a star fruit under a gush of water. She looks at me, mild-eyed, but she can tell from my expression that I am full of excitement. Yes, she says, making an experimental question mark with her voice.

I grab her sleeve as if to press her into urgency. I ask her over and over if the man with no legs smoked. She recalls the odor of cigarette at that house, yes. And next to her, where he sat, yes, she does recall someone smoking with deep, steady intakes. She remembers the glitter his hand produced. The cigarette was held in a gold holder. His fingers were stained with nicotine.

I can feel my heart skip. I press a palm against my chest as if to calm its quick, tremulous beat. I can feel it. Surely Mother is plotting to leave. Surely any of her Chinese friends, Younger Aunt Number Three the Rice Seller or Older Aunt Number Three the Pharmacist, will be of help. She is at their house now, putting together her final plan.

# 22

# *History Is Responsible*

## BAO, 2006

We are on the outer edge of winter, impatiently waiting for spring to arrive. Melted snow has disappeared and the first hardy heads of daffodils are poking through the earth's shadows with raw abandon. I watch as Mai steers the car in turgid silence, slowly, cautiously, through an utterly familiar road that stretches from the house to the nursing home.

Yes, our father has just moved to a nursing home. Both he and Mai, he especially, put forth a common front regarding this fact: that it is temporary and hence utterly reversible. They see it as purely a matter of his health. He is not being abandoned. His belongings are still at home. The bed is as he left it the day he moved, blue cotton sheets, blue comforter neatly folded, lying at its foot. Every few days Mai peeks in. Sometimes she takes a paper towel and dusts his night tables. Being inside a space that has been his for years inspires an abiding sense of tenderness in her. When she closes the door she says a quiet "I love you," something she has yet to tell him in person.

In Vietnam there would be no question that he would remain at home where, frail or not, he would continue to exercise his commendable prerogative as father. There is a stubborn faith that illness itself would not transform the fundamentals. More personal and financial resources would be turned over to the necessity of his care. Family would stay together—four walls, one roof, and many generations. Think of Aunt An, her husband, their son, and the son's wife and baby, all together, struggling through the shared ruins of addiction and debt.

When Father was first admitted into the nursing home, it was meant to be temporary. He left with one bag, as if he were going on an overnight trip—a set of pajamas, a toothbrush, toothpaste, a hand towel, a pair of slippers, two undergarments, and a comb. Aunt An's history at the nursing home facilitated his admission. Her presence also made his departure from home less abrupt.

I remember watching with a premonition of loss. His life was being pared down to the simplest elements. He feared he was becoming a responsibility. That was how he slipped away. He had become progressively weak, but after the fall in the bathroom, his decline was precipitous. The spectacle of his frailty concerned him—the cane, the tentative steps, the increasing effort it took to do his daily chores.

Mai fought the urge to flee the truth of our father's diminishing existence. One moment she was sitting with a notebook and pen in her law firm office and the next moment she was driving home to pack him up. He had called the police and reported seeing a corpse on the floor of the apartment. The need to have him monitored was no longer something to be postponed. To keep Mai from feeling the prick of her own and others' criticism, he characterized his move as temporary. It was an inaccurate rendering of the truth. Indeed, Mrs. An, efficient as always, brought a small suitcase from our apartment to the nursing home and filled out the post office change of address form for him. A morning passed, an evening, and then another. Light and dark sifted through his room at home. Just like that, he was gone, leaving behind a big space in a bedroom that remained incongruously full of his belongings. The towel he used to wash his face that morning still hangs on the bathroom rack. Mai never truly faced this manifest but unmentionable fact, that her father would remain at an institution for the rest of his life.

Indeed, at some point it was no longer her choice to make. He became sicker and weaker. His heartbeat became irregular. His lips sometimes turned purple, the color of dusk in Saigon. One lung, then another, collapsed and every breath he took had to be negotiated with increased agitation. His breathing became labored and erratic. He made moist, breathy sounds. There were good days but often there were terrible relapses.

When the doctor announced that he should stay at the nursing home, he gave the idea an approving and endorsing nod. Ever since then, Mai has become bound up with a sense of precautionary solicitude where our father is concerned. She is forever grateful that the nursing home he is in is the same one Aunt An has been working at for almost twenty years.

Still, she calls it the assisted-living facility presumably to miniaturize his daily needs and make them seem more manageable.

The window on the driver's side is partly open and offers a light, cool breeze. Everything is bathed in a sun-warmed light tinted with a crisp freshness promised by the imminence of spring. A daylight crackle of new possibility hangs in the air. Yet she is driving as if she were headed for something less welcoming.

Today is the day Uncle Number Two visits Father at the nursing home. It is a new and absolutely astonishing development. It will be the first time we see Uncle Number Two in more than twenty-five years. He is flying from California, where he has been living since arriving in the United States by boat many years ago—when Mai was still in high school. Every few years he threatens to fly out to Virginia for a visit on the single stubborn conviction that his friendship with Father is too important to abandon. The first and only visit to Father within the first year of Uncle Number Two's arrival was a colossal failure. There was no vindication. There were no embraces.

He first wrote Father a long letter when he made it to Malaysia and for some reason Father holds him responsible for what happened to Mother and Uncle Number Five after 1975. This is the insurmountable fact: He of all people is here and Mother is not. Why not?

Still, Uncle Number Two will arrive at Father's bedside with, I imagine, the furious attention of a man trying to sidestep his friend's deep reproach so he can salvage their common past. He is willing to suffer whatever humiliations necessary to resurrect their once-sanctified friendship. Mai believes she needs to play the part of buffer. I am privy to her thoughts but she is not privy to mine. Imagine it this way. She is the exterior. I am the core. I am buried inside her and can see her from the inside out. She believes she can make sense of the befuddling accusations that she knows Father will heap upon Uncle Number Two.

But I suspect otherwise. Father will lie in his bed with his arms rigid at his sides. Even in this position, he will strike a pugilistic stance. Uncle Number Two will bemoan the fact that his show of remorse, his desire to make amends, and his admission of fault, all thirty years' worth of it, have failed to reunite the two. And Father will say that he does not believe any of Uncle Number Two's contrition. And their conversation will, in the end, resolve nothing, accomplish nothing, mean nothing, despite the pain involved. Yet every year it seems they are destined to repeat it.

How have they gotten so lost, Mai asks in her small voice.

I can guess at the answer. Perhaps the cracks in their friendship lie in a much larger perversity that transcends the intricate calibrations of who did what to whom. The cut is too deep and Father is too wounded to release the hurt. He hasn't "let it go," as Mai puts it, despite Uncle Number Two's pleas of so many years ago. He will not let it go now, least of all now. Letting go is something Mai has done but it is not something we do.

Unlike me, Mai doesn't have violent flashes that make her squint and blink and scream and gasp for air as if she could barely breathe. There is no terrible seizing up, no obstreperous thump that echoes through the gathering darkness of night. There are no moods or outbursts to send her staggering. There is, instead, just an aqueous, meager stillness that she perfects as she slowly progresses into Americanness, navigating through the routine of our new lives, slightly detached from the present, slightly unavailable. Nothing in the here and now truly gathers significance or makes a dent. It doesn't matter because ultimately she can shrug it all off. I know, with a sense of droning certitude, that I am the one among the three of us who has been holding our blemishes inside me. She is where she is, fine and assimilated, because I have made it possible.

Our father is in bed, physically there, though seemingly disembodied. The shape and form of him, of his body's physicality, can be discerned under the white sheets. I am equivocally moved. I reach out to him as if he were already slipping away. I want to sit by his bedside and listen to him spill his stories from long ago into the here and now. I like being the keepsake of his memories.

I call him Ba, which means "Father." He leans forward and holds my hand. He is still unsure. Am I Mai or Bao.

"Is it you?" he asks. I nod. Mai nods.

He is discernibly tired. "Ba, let me sit you up," I say as I prop a pillow behind his back. I touch his face to see if he needs a shave. His hair glides smoothly between my fingers. It doesn't need to be brushed but I brush it anyway.

"Bao Bao," he says as he relinquishes himself to me. I smile. He knows I am the one who tends to his daily needs.

He squeezes my hand. I am touched. Our individual consciousness converges. *Ba* is a beautiful word. A word that gives and receives. *Ba* is that simple, elemental word, one of the first words babies know how to make. I love it. One vowel, one consonant, working together to make a sound that requires no coaxing because it effortlessly slips from the mouth.

I was here by his side when he received a phone call from Uncle Number Two last week. Uncle Number Two did not ask to visit but merely announced he would be coming. Our father rolled his eyes as he listened.

"I want us to see each other's face when we talk this time," Uncle Number Two said, his voice beaming through the speakerphone.

When the short phone conversation ended, our father turned toward me with a look that was neither sullen nor petulant. Was this visit meant to be a resumption of their friendship? Or the culmination of it?

Mai hesitates at the bed's footboard. She pauses, almost with acute formality, as if she were standing on tiptoe at the edge of the ocean, as if that moment of hesitation will somehow better prepare her for the water's chill before the full-body plunge into the blue depths. She fears the shock of cold and water. She dislikes the manifestation of anxieties, the aura of gravity and remonstrance already in the room.

She stands nearby, looking around. Her eyes scan the room, checking the surface of things for dust. She touches his shoulder. She can feel his delicate anatomy.

She can hear his wet, raspy breaths. His face is proffered toward her. It is the mild, eager face of a father marked by a hollow space that fear has carved. Hard to imagine before her is a man who has killed. Perhaps as a Buddhist, he regrets that he has and knows the karmic consequences of this fact. And here he is now, waiting to be fed. Lunch, yes, she will feed him lunch. We both will. She will not eat because she cherishes the feeling of emptiness in her stomach. It makes her feel clean and light, unburdened by the deadweight of food.

"How are you doing?" she asks. She puts her lips against his forehead. Her phone is in her hand. She glances at it discreetly. He can see that she is edgily checking her e-mail.

Our father motions her closer. "Tell me how your work is going," he asks. I know he wants to engage her but the simple American present is elusive for him—and me. His voice becomes overanimated.

Mai nods uncertainly.

"Tell me about a case you're on," he suggests.

I know work is not an ardent interest but it does keep her occupied. And so she proceeds to tell him the details of her case. "It's not the sort of case our firm usually handles," she says. She tells him that the client is an executive from a big respectable company charged by the federal government with murder and extortion. "Murder is hardly ever tried in a federal court," she informs.

"It must be interesting, then, that it is," our father declares, but his voice lacks conviction.

"It's only in federal court because of a federal statute and that federal statute contains a list of predicate acts that constitute violations of the statute. Those predicate acts include things like murder, which is usually a state crime."

"You're doing fine at work, then," our father states.

Mai nods. I watch as she holds his hand.

He looks at his watch. He must be in a sea swell of nostalgia, I think, as he waits for the arrival of his old friend.

"I don't need him to come," he mutters. He looks at the door expectantly.

"Can you not talk about what happened or did not happen with him? Let it alone," Mai suggests. She is solution-oriented. She wants to help him by making pragmatic suggestions.

"Huh," he says, as if to expel something unwanted from his lungs.

He is probably weighing a series of contradictory impulses. "Then what else will we have to talk about! We have nothing else that would even link us together." He nods to himself, as if to agree with his own observation. He looks at Mai, me, us. A smile lights up his face. He can afford to stare at us with the offhandedness of someone possessing unquestioned paternal authority.

"Okay, but whatever he brings up, I'm just saying don't let it bother you. Whatever happened between the two of you, it's already done. Finished. There's nothing you can do to change it. So just let it be," she advises.

I roll a side table to his bedside and put a bowl of pho noodle soup on it. The rich, heady broth is exactly as he likes it—cooked on a low fire overnight with bones still covered with fat and gristle and tender bits of brisket and flank. Charred whole onions and ginger had been added to produce an extra-brown coloring. Wisps of heat rise from a special oolong tea.

I give him one spoonful, then another, but he eats only meekly. He has no appetite. The bedside table is crammed with appurtenances of old age—bottles of pills, an oxygen tank, and cans of liquid food containing fortified vitamins and minerals. His face is defined by lines and angles and a protrusion of bones. Mai watches him eat and flashes him an indulgent smile. She sighs. She feels a sharp tear inside her, like the sound of a nut being cracked. Blue stripes dance up and down the white cloth of his cotton pajamas. He pulls the cord to ask for Aunt An, who quickly appears, draws the curtain around his bed, and proceeds to change him.

We are fortunate he is in a home where she works. I think this thought many times a day.

Mai and I watch over him as he naps.

Mrs. An lingers, knowing that Uncle Number Two will be here soon. She can be a comforting presence these moments before his arrival. We have never spoken about the multiple selves folded inside Mai but I get the sense that she knows there is something off about us. She understands problems. She has her own—an addict for a son and, as a result, continuing financial difficulties that our father has somehow managed mysteriously to ease.

In the patchy light that shines an unstirring yellowish glow, I look at her. Over the years, the flurry of age has turned the smooth, unlined face gaunt. Her hair, dyed black to hide strands of silvery white in the front, is still thick. Despite her troubles, she is here to comfort, cutting through the shadows that will undoubtedly loom when Uncle Number Two arrives. I notice that she is glancing at my neck, head cocked, to check for bruises.

It is winter. I am wearing a scarf for warmth, not camouflage.

Soon an old man appears, his ravaged face peering through the doorway. Shivers of sunlight from the window shine directly at him. I barely recognize him. He squints, shielding his eyes with one downturned palm. He is so slim and frail inside his blue suit that you could think he might evaporate before your eyes. But his body is erect; he stands tall and steady.

"Uncle Number Two," Mai says because she must say something to fill up the muted moment. She quickly stands up from the metal folding chair. She harbors misgivings about him but she does not let this show. He is the one to whom questions about our mother during the long interlude of absence could be asked. That alone is enough to allow him access.

Despite our insistence that she stay, Aunt An leaves the room after acknowledging Uncle Number Two with a quick, flustered nod. Uncle Number Two walks softly toward the bed but stands at a respectful distance. Mai hooks her hand into the crook of our father's elbow.

"There you are," he says in a flat, unsympathetic voice once he sees Uncle Number Two. Our father pushes himself upward and glowers in typical southern pugnacity. He is unprepared for anything as extreme as this visit. The magnitude of his feelings are exposed for us to see. For one instant, for less than an instant, his face softens as if he were seeing a person who he once believed was a true friend, before he discovered otherwise.

With unguarded eagerness, Uncle Number Two ignores the scowl and returns a wide smile. This is what he said when he was here the first and last time: Nothing can equal the memory of having faced the future together at a time when the future promised so much. There is still that singular fact. He is willing to wait for our father's true feelings to arrive, when he will be able to understand the core of their friendship at last.

"Look what I brought you," Uncle Number Two says, rummaging through a bag in a show of excessive solicitude. It is 2006 but he acts as if he had just seen Father yesterday. His fingers are stained by nicotine. His shoulders fold inward, making him seem even smaller than he is.

He pulls up a chair by Father's bedside. When he sits, his prosthesis is revealed. The metal limb seems to have aged along with him.

He offers Father what he brought: a persimmon, a mangosteen, and a star fruit. He is bringing California's harvest to Virginia. Father watches with annoyed indifference. Mai steps in and exclaims over their ripeness. She gives Father a pleading look to be civil and restrained. He eases up fractionally. She takes a mangosteen, puts a knife's edge to its purple rind, and runs the blade along the circumference. She holds it in both hands and pries it gently with her thumbs until the rind cracks and the halves are pulled apart to reveal a circle of fleshy wedges, like a tangerine, but white and soft.

The way she cuts the mangosteen and brings it to her lips, she is so much like our mother at the breakfast table eating her favorite fruit that I have to stop and stare at her. Except that because it is Mai who is doing the cutting, there is something unutterably final about Mother's absence. She is not here and she will not be here. Uncle Number Two is here instead. It is a state of mind, an evocation that memory triggers. Right there in Mai is a flick of Mother's old self, interposing. The world before me alternates harshly and abruptly between anger and sadness.

I feel the "Bao"—the storm—in me swell and expand. I turn away quickly. I feel a burn in my throat and little explosions in my chest. It always returns to Mother, and the moment it does, the past keeps coming and coming straight at me. I don't know what it is that makes it all suddenly very clear to me, but here it is. I put my head deeper into the realization. I am almost drunk, almost manic, with this simple but now-obvious singularity of thought.

Of course after our sister died our mother did not want us. On this rare occasion Mai and I are on the same unwanted side.

And it is not because grief edges out love. Rather it is because we became unlovable. Imagine being the one who was not adored but who lived. I quickly glance at the mirror. I see a shocked-looking face full of harshness. It is finally obvious. You can't be lovable if you are always scowling.

I feel anger rising inside my chest. This is how my violent episodes begin. Madness edges out reason. I overpower Mai and with propulsive recklessness take over.

But a part of me knows the importance of this moment. I clench my fists and restrain myself. To avoid the appearance of impropriety before Uncle Number Two, I force myself to recede. Our father notices a distinct element of sensory shuffling, a substratum of movement in his environment that usually spells trouble. He grimaces. Mai steps forward with a tended eagerness and spoons a wedge of mangosteen into his mouth. He receives it but unwillingly. He is still simmering, though only slightly below the boiling point. Uncle Number Two says, in a tone more penitential than upbeat, "It was absolutely her favorite fruit." I struggle to stay inside the vast symphonies of normalcy. But I feel my nose running and my eyes tearing, as if I have taken a bite out of a hot pepper. A noisy disorder is building up. I know these signs that will add up to an explosion. The construction of my very sense of self is falling apart. Recklessness before our father, but not before Uncle Number Two, I mutter. I still have the clarity of mind to know what I must do.

"Ever since I first knew them, we ate mangosteens together. That was fifty years ago." He turns to Mai and emphasizes their long history, but our father will not receive the offering. Instead, he casts a critical eye at Uncle Number Two.

I slink my way behind Mai's being, searching for the neutral zone inside her. It is still possible to be becalmed. I float in and out of the glittering madness.

"I asked you not to come," I hear our father say. "It can never be forgiven, Phong." I hear both the grief and the censoriousness in his voice. "Never," he adds with arched inflection. They are almost face-to-face, as if in a contest of wills eerily reminiscent of the one involving Uncle Number Two and our mother years ago in our Cholon dining room.

"But I haven't even told you what I am here to say," Uncle Number Two insists with pointed determination. The room is filled with tension. There is a coughing fit followed by long, raspy breaths.

"Listen to your old friend Theo," Uncle Number Two begs our father.

Our father shakes his head to signal he is not interested. He has no choice but to remain lying down. His eyes glare with icy coldness.

"You feel contempt for me," Uncle Number Two suddenly says. Silence.

Uncle Number Two takes in our father's weakened condition. I can see his eyes' appraising gaze. "We are too old now to continue . . ."

"I don't know what it is you want, Phong."

"Not one thing for myself. I just want to give us, you, peace of mind." Uncle Number Two looks down, his eyes taking on a sad look.

Our father stiffens. "It is surprising that someone as keen as you should have so little sense of proportion. My peace of mind is my own private journey and no one else's." He makes no effort to rein in the admonitory tone.

Mai frowns. The clinical nakedness of their emotions embarrasses her and at the same time compels her interest.

Our father yanks the cord by his bed. Quickly Uncle Number Two reaches for our father's hand. The move is not intended to achieve physical contact but rather to restrain. "No," says our father. "You are hardly a trustworthy one," he declares.

I hover about. Mai flutters awkwardly in an uneasy silence. I hear a derisive laugh but I cannot tell whose laugh it is.

"It is indecent of you. Everything else can be forgiven but not this. She died because of you," our father says. He emphasizes the word *died*. For almost thirty years he has lived with the jarring knowledge of her death. It has been the prelude to everything that he has experienced while in this country. It is inside him. And Uncle Number Two epitomizes it by his continuing existence.

A terrible silence settles in the room. I have never heard it uttered this directly before.

Where our mother is concerned, we are neither neutral nor impartial. Her death has become the essence of how we measure time itself.

Our father's lowered voice suggests a lancing anger he is trying to restrain. I see a bodily alteration, black, brooding eyes fixed upon the fork-tongued charmer by his bedside. Between the two of them, the past they share is forever here, to be disassembled and reassembled again and again.

Uncle Number Two hangs his head, as if to ask for forgiveness. Mai withdraws into the core of her privately retained self.

"Even before I got your letter in 1978, I knew she had died because her death registered on me like a deadweight when I woke up from a dream. I felt it in my body, like a paralysis one moment and a terrible burden the next." His face withers as if he will never recover from a loss so beyond imagining. "But what I did not know until I got your letter was how she died, Phong, and how you let it happen." For a moment, his deathbed eyes flash.

She died in 1978. We found out from Uncle Number Two's letter. We were still hanging on to hope before that. Uncle Number Two's presence entangles our father in the very moment of our mother's death years ago. Not just her death, but the *manner* of her death. It is this fact that has strained Mai all these years. It is what has made her live a half-life of acquiescence in this country, removing herself from everything that truly matters.

Our father's body shakes. Uncle Number Two is here only on our father's sufferance. To witness how a shared history can somehow deteriorate, one only has to look at them. Aunt An, responding to the bell, appears, watchful. Our father says he is too tired to have visitors who upset him and she approaches Uncle Number Two to usher him out. Uncle Number Two's face trembles and his skin flushes, as if he too were shaken to the core by an everlasting wrong. With a show of resignation, he holds his head in his clasped hands as if to still the turbulence inside it. He must be reliving it physically.

And then he says so softly I can barely hear it, "History is responsible. I did not let it happen." Tears roll down his cheeks. "I was the one who was in love with her, for God's sake."

I freeze. Our father's very being shifts. He too freezes. He fears Uncle Number Two's loyalty. He fears his disloyalty. Like a law of nature, it has been that way forever.

# 23

## *The Letter*

### MAI, 1978

The situation in Vietnam is getting worse. Father is sure our mother will leave soon. He is able to feel it. From which shore will she depart? We look at the map and speculate together. Aunt An says that, with so many people desperate to leave, any coastal city will do. Ca Mau, Vung Tau, Phu Quoc. I imagine rows of boats rocking in the harbor and patiently waiting. I want to know from which cities most escapes have been launched. I tell our father that Uncle Number Two is also exploring the possibility of leaving. I tell him the story Aunt An told me.

That is why we wait. It is our community ritual. It is 1978 and everyone in Virginia's Little Saigon waits or knows someone who is waiting.

Finally the letter comes. It is stamped with a postmark from Malaysia, where ships from Vietnam often sail toward. In the past Malaysia has refused to let boats land, towed broken boats back to sea, and even fired on them. The country's deputy prime minister announced that he would expel all those already in the country and shoot newcomers on sight. In a five-month period, fifty-eight thousand boat people have been dragged from shore and thrown back into the open sea. Our lot, our nagging humanity, a matter of statistical wrong, is no longer anyone's geopolitical or strategic concern.

In an atmosphere of death and doom on the high seas, our father opens the letter. He is crying, his face drained of color. He lifts his head occasionally to look at me. He waves me toward him in a weak, somnambulistic manner. I am pulled into the rumpled folds of his overcoat until I disappear into his ravenous grief. He keeps me there, locked inside his embrace, until moments later, when I wrench myself from his grip. It is the first time in a long time that I am the one who disengages from a hug first. A sob comes out of him, expelled with the inconsolable force of something that has for years been suppressed. A minute later, he pulls me back, petting my hair in a state of great emotional agitation. He reads the letter and, when he is finished, pushes it into my hand and goes outside to cry.

The letter is from Uncle Number Two:

I am in Pulau Bidong. Malaysia. It is five in the morning. I write to you with tremendous sadness. We escaped together but she is dead.

For years now we have lived here in our country barreled against every conceivable hardship. You would want to know, I am certain, how she was after your departure. We have shared so much, but there is so much more to tell. Some I will wait to tell you in person when I make it to America. For now, let me recount the almost four years we had without you. Our journey out of the country. Her last days alive. You will know her to be more resilient than either of us imagined.

After you left, my wife and I and Quy moved in with your brother-in-law, yes, the Vietcong brother-in-law. Right on Rue Catinat, in a four-story villa with walls of dark mahogany wood and stairs framed by shiny balustrades. You have been there many times. The bottom floor functioned for years as a silk and fabric store that provided cover for the villa's many clandestine activities. For one, it doubled as a Vietcong safe house. Your brother-in-law offered sanctuary to his sister and her friends, inscribing us into the official family register recorded with public security cadres.

Your house was looted the day Saigon fell. I went by. The gates were wide open. I made my way past the walls, walked alone through the garden and into your study, stood among your Buddhist and yoga books, still intact, though almost everything else had been stripped. Soldiers from the North Vietnamese army had pummeled and clawed open the walls of every room with sledgehammers, looking for gold or dollars hidden behind the mortar and bricks. A metal safe stood in your bedroom closet, its door ajar, a fact suggestive of many possibilities.

I suspected soon enough things might not go as many of us had hoped. The government newspaper *Saigon Giai Phong* announced early on that Southerners must pay their blood debt to the revolution. It was the gravity with which these things were being declared. And so it began, with that early writing providing some sense of an ominous horizon. Still, even if drawn by pathos, Saigon managed to overshadow its more backwater counterparts in the North. The city's resilience, its energy, its forbearance, galled them. So appropriate wounds had to be inflicted. It was very sad, my friend. One evening, Quy and Thu and I took our walk around Rue Catinat, a street that has undergone a number of name changes, Tu Do, then Dong Khoi. We came across Khai Tri bookstore, where you once bought so many books for the girls. I breathed in the familiar odor of paper upon paper in an enclosed space. The shelves were emptied, books from the store flung onto the trucks parked outside. I asked one of the cadres seemingly in charge what was going on. He was a bony youngster from the North speaking in a sharp, self-approving northern accent, dressed in shabby fatigues. He showed me the list of more than one hundred authors and one thousand titles that were to be removed. Even Mario Puzo's *The Godfather,* Margaret Mitchell's *Gone with the Wind,* were on the list of decadent books. Around us, soldiers unloaded cartons of books from trucks and carried them inside the bookstore. Marx, Lenin, Engels. I read a few pages and struggled to take in the tumid prose. One crate had only framed pictures of Ho Chi Minh. "We are sending half a million pictures to the South on another truck," he said.

So that was it, an early sense of life as it would soon be. A book caught your wife's attention, a hardcover *Arabian Nights* with pictures of magic lamps and flying carpets. The young cadre saw her looking at it and offered her a clandestine smile. "For you, Mother," he said. She was frozen. I stepped forward and took the book for her.

At the time, soldiers in pith helmets ordered banks to seal safe deposit boxes and freeze accounts. Quy still had her valuables, gold bars and diamonds. She had removed them from her personal safe before she left with us to seek shelter at her brother's house. Your brother-in-law was still esteemed by the state. And so we were in a sanctuary of sorts. Or that was what I thought. He had not yet spoken out.

But it didn't last long. I remember the day Thu and I lost everything. It was some time after the midautumn moon festival in August of 1975, four months after the war was lost. Neither Thu nor I had our wealth in dollars or gold. Our savings were in South Vietnamese money, deposited in the bank. Thu had a beautiful diamond ring she wanted to sell. We found someone who agreed to pay for it in gold. Instead, on the day of the sale, he gave us South Vietnamese money. We needed cash to buy food, so we had no choice but to accept it. Several days later, old money was declared worthless. New money would be issued. Everyone would get the same amount—two hundred dongs. After that, we relied on Quy's gold and diamonds and dollars and the underground market to survive. Quy would go to Cholon, exchange her gold bars at a premium exchange rate for cash from Chinese merchants who knew her Chinese friends. The Chinese merchants got their cash by turning their gold over to the new authorities. Around us, people queued at dawn in front of state-run cooperatives for rice and meat. We were all ambushed by a mandatory money exchange operation designed to ensure we would be stripped of our entire life's savings, surprising us in both its severity and its effect. As if from a great height they were dispassionately decreed. Two hundred revolutionary dongs, or four hundred kilos of rice at the official price, in exchange for each family's entire fortune.

A ration card system was introduced for people to buy their rations at designated state-owned stores. We were not allowed to travel, since we were legally permitted to stay overnight only at the address printed on the ration card. And our ration card had to be validated weekly, when we attended mandatory meetings to learn about Lenin. Quy and Thu came back from the first one, companionably paired in the late dusky light, two silhouettes drawn by pathos, mockingly whispering a poem by the Party's favorite poet, To Huu, who declared that his love for his father, mother, wife, and himself was pale compared with his love for Stalin. Recited without false affect, those stale lines merely made us sad. It created an equivocal stir even in your brother-in-law, who at this time was ambivalent, still hanging on to his instincts to defend his cause and the grandiosity of its self-professed paradise. He was no doubt disturbed, but not yet willing to relinquish the last of his delusions.

He reassured his sister, though he must have known what was happening. I saw a Party document in his room one day containing guidelines to prohibit history, philosophy, or civics books written from the "American or puppet point of view" and those foreign publications that were of an "antirevolutionary or depraved nature." Still, he continued to hope. He reminded his sister of the declaration made by Le Duan, the first secretary of the Communist Party. "The South needs its own policy," meaning draconian rules should not be imposed by the North. Yet the very same man also wrote to assure us that the "Vietnamese revolution is to fulfill the internationalist duty." A duty as yet unfinished.

Still, we were not truly suffering. We had connections, at least, and an inadvertent, fabled past. From your brother-in-law, I learned the name of a high-ranking but sympathetic Party leader who might grant us special dispensations based on your brother-in-law's political pedigree and calculated loyalties. We two, along with Quy, would go to him for help. The presence of a woman could soften a tense situation. And perhaps I believed we would be the exceptional, unprecedented case that managed to defy reality to escape harm.

Everyone around us, the dispensable humanity of the South itself, was suffering. Your Chinese nanny went to the country-side, as did many, to scavenge for food from the earth, to fish for food from the water. For us, with our valuables hidden away, there was still a mercifully viable black market. Even if every other shop in Cholon had been boarded up and even if there were no private stores anymore, we could still buy our rice under-ground, from Quy's Chinese friends who had a network of ware-houses scattered throughout Cholon and the countryside.

We suspected you would be sending letters and packages to our old addresses, but I was not hopeful they would reach us. The Ministry of Interior made a point of inspecting and confiscating international mail, especially if they believed it might contain money or valuables.

Any package from abroad was like deliverance. People relied on them to survive. Over time, a new system was instituted: All packages would be delivered to a government-run parcels store, a shabby, odorous room on a nondescript side street I'd never been to. Your brother-in-law and I and sometimes Quy went there to check for mail from you and Mai. It was your whereabouts and your return address we were eager for.

Inside this provisional building, hundreds of people could be found lumbering about. We stood in line and waited for our names to be called. With silent intensity, men in blue trousers sliced open packages and poured the contents onto the Formica counter. They would then be carefully examined and recorded in ledgers for customs duty. Behind them, on the peeling walls, were hung long lists of tax rates: sugar, 80 percent; clothes and fabric, 25 percent; cameras, 30 percent; medicine, 200 percent; alcohol, 50 percent. People paid the high import duties and even the penitential bribe to the poverty-stricken bureaucrats to have their packages released. We could sell the goods for ten times their worth on the black market.

Every other day we stopped by just in case. I suspected Quy also ventured there herself, to check for your letters, after her customary visits to your daughter's grave. She never allowed anyone to accompany her to the cemetery. She would carry a bowl of uncooked rice and a few sticks of incense and head out the door to pass the day inside the immense comfort of cemetery walls, on the patch of earth that surrounded the headstone. I had been there myself with your brother-in-law. Your wife had kept it immaculate. The cemetery housed the South's dead, so the grave sites of those whose families had left were unkempt. The government's cemetery keeper was there merely to open and close the gates, nothing more. Among burnished gravestones there were many that were chipped and others that were choked by the tangles and brambles of swollen vines. Quy replaced the rice bowl on your daughter's grave several times a week. The grassy stretch on which the grave sat was weeded, watered, and well tended.

Quy left the house every morning and did not return until night.

Day after day we continued in that same meandering, languishing way, making do by selling trinkets and buying rice, canned milk, sugar, and other produce on the black market. I worried about how much gold Quy still had. I had caught a glimpse of her one evening going through what I assumed was a dwindling satchel of gold and other valuables.

One day Quy came back from Cholon and delivered the news to her brother. Against all sense of conventional decency, Chinese schools in Cholon had been ordered closed. Almost all the shops were tightly shuttered. The rice and pharmaceutical businesses of her friends aunts number such-and-such had been confiscated. Her brother looked at his sister with the responsiveness of one eager to placate and please.

Up until now, even in her lowest moments, she had referred to a vague "they," as yet undefined, as the cause of our misery. But this time, she meant that her brother had brought this on. We will be the ones to bear the brunt. Look at what your revolution has wreaked, she said.

The truth was, though we didn't know it yet, that her brother, and others like him, even the South itself, had to be driven to their knees. It would have been comforting to call it destiny except that destiny would not have allowed its true colors to be revealed with such drab, partisan incompetence. Still, we expected to be the exception. We thought we could rely on your brother-in-law's credentials. He had devoted his life to the cause. But one night your brother-in-law revealed a grave fact to me. He had stopped me, saying he wanted to talk. I knew something was wrong. He grabbed my arm and lowered his voice. He pulled me closer to him and warned about possible danger ahead. I could scarcely believe what I heard in the next few minutes.

He said that over the years he had thought about defecting to the South. He had had doubts. He had even shared them with you, he said, turning over sensitive Vietcong secrets to you. His was not a fluctuation of wills but a true vacillation of the heart. He didn't go through with it but he had shared his doubts with a few friends. He could foresee how this indiscretion might now be damaging. He could be considered a traitor and placed in the category of those who committed everlasting wrongs against the revolution.

Why was he worried now? I asked. He did not know. He suspected someone had leaked the information. He had made a few harmless little noises, softly urging against the collectivization of private property in the South. I am the son of a landlord, he had declared a few months back. I know peasants. They want a little piece of land they can call their own, he had cautioned. You cannot just take their land and their water buffaloes.

They had confronted him in the most mundane of ways. A knock on the door, questions from the police, an exchange of lowered voices. Two minutes later he was taken away.

Two days later, there was another knock. My wife and Quy were there when it happened. He is an invalid, they said frantically. Only one leg. Look. Thu rolled up the bottom of my pants to reveal the fleshly incompleteness obscured by the ordinariness of my trousers. I held myself steady even as they fumbled to pull at my pants. Quy took a fork and clanged it against my leg. The metallic sound was but an inconsequential abstraction to the cadres, who merely shrugged. It was this very sound, the tinkle of metal, that I heard over and over in my cell in the coming years. I answered their questions with alacrity. Thu and Quy did their best to intervene.

I was loaded on a truck parked at a nearby school and, along with others, transported in the darkness of night through provincial roads that were sometimes smooth, sometimes rutted. On that ride I realized I was experiencing what the rest of the country was experiencing. The subjugation of the South. It was something that had been long planned and was now emerging like a tree taking the shape contained in a seed before its planting.

As we crossed a bridge, its metal surface vibrated against the wheels. I noticed every sound: the throttling of engines, the creak of wheels over railroad tracks, the grunts of the driver and the guards. We were summarily unloaded. Near evening, alone in my cell, leaning my upper torso as far out as possible toward the crack in the wall to take in a breath of fresh air, I could smell only a sickly stench of vomit and excrement. An ammoniac stink pervaded the area. Cracks in the foundation were lined with rot. Neither the walls, the floors, nor the ceiling ever cooled, even at night, which led me to think this particular cell must be in the middle of a flat, unshaded area vulnerable to the broiling glare of the sun. A sheen of perspiration glistened perpetually on my skin, coating the pores with a saltiness that I could almost taste. Torture, as I discovered soon enough, had to be consummated in the raw shimmer of sweat. The experiment in cruelty was itself far from aberrant.

Both my hands were shackled to the prosthesis. The only time my right hand was released was at mealtime, when a bowl of rice mixed with sand was pushed across the door's threshold. The guard announced that it was prepared just so, to remind us of our crimes. Loudspeakers urged us to confess past wrongs and exhorted us to welcome the new future. In the evening an intervening silence consumed my cell. I began to long for company. At night the windowless cell sometimes flared with light from a naked ceiling bulb. Other times there was only an echoing, ancient darkness and an occasional sound from the other side of the wall that signaled shadow lives in close proximity but beyond my reach. Sometimes a magnanimous guard would take pity and unyoke me from one of the handcuffs so I could fold into a partial, even if still contorted, sleeping pose. Nightmares plagued the fugitive night. In the sweat and heat of the cell, scraps of ocher rust collected on my metal leg. What mattered most in this room that scarcely permitted any light were the simplest of pleasures. I waited for that moment during the day, even though the precise instant could never be foretold, giving rise to perpetual hope, when I would be told I could now lie flat on the floor, or stand up straight, once more, or even move myself from one end of the cell to the other in five short steps. Time passed—a few days, a week, two, more—an illusory continuity that provided no solace. It was the mystery of not knowing that weighed on me. A guard would enter the room every once in a while. He would issue orders with icy perfection. *"Repent! Have you repented?"* We were all open to mockery. When I asked what I should be repenting for, he replied, as if to deepen the riddle, with a question and an order. Don't you know? Think.

Of course, to admit to repentance was to admit to past sins. The guard was well pleased with the perplexity of his own scripted abstractedness, the threat and promise of ambiguity. Regret, repent, remorse, questions of nomenclature that, here at least, determined the very nature of one's existence in the cell. I asked for the manacles to be removed. When you repent.

Repentance was the answer that was meant to exact considered submission and provide the opening through which you could walk penitentially into a different, untwisted, unbound mode of being. Soon enough I could imagine all forms of confession willingly, though injudiciously, delivered in exchange for freedom.

Bugs, ants, cockroaches, materialized from cracks in the walls and floor, providing me with company. For a few days, a lizard hung from the ceiling. Its pale belly slithered, its long body and tail quicksilver lithe. Its creamy whiteness complemented the beige ceiling. You started to live in the smallest of details, your imagination easily captured. For several days I stared at and talked to it. It was the lizard who roused me, even sparked my imagination. If I survive this, I will make the hours and days count, I said to myself.

One early dawn amid a surge of frantic purpose, a guard walked in and carried me to another room where all manner of activities were being concentrated. A crowd of about seventy was jammed in against the walls of a room fifteen feet wide and twenty feet long. As the door opened, havoc broke loose. There was a collective scramble toward the morning's first light, causing several to surge forward in an effusion of curiosity about me, the newcomer. Dusty carcasses of moths and flinty grit of fragile wings fluttered in the air. There was talking and clearing of lungs, tubercular coughing and other derelict noises, jostling, sighing, crying. Faces loomed awkwardly above me. Fleshless men stared. The guard carrying me let go of me and I dropped. I could hear the metallic clack my limb made on the floor even as my head banged against something hard. For a few moments, I could see only blackness spinning against my brain's central lobe. I felt only a rising pressure against my eyes and temples. A pall of darkness rose from the floor, stippled with pulsating particles and dots. A low roar vibrated in my ears until finally volume returned.

What is the matter with him? Give him air. Loosen his shirt collar. People assumed their parts, emphatically shouting emergency wisdom. Even in their diminished state, even in my condition, I was able to recognize some of them as neighbors and acquaintances, Buddhist monks with shaved heads, former soldiers of the vanquished South, each, like me, a nameless prisoner haunted by evocations of wartime turbulence. I saw their thin, wasted bodies, their shaved heads blotched with sores, clots of soft scabs not fully hardened, and the driblets of spittle threaded with blood on the discolored floor. Many had been duped. They were told to bring one week's worth of clothes and to report "in a spirit of genuine remorse" to the accruing Communist forces for mild reeducation sessions. They had expected to stay but one week. My neighbor's son came with only three sets of summer shirts and khakis and had not been heard from for three years.

In the shrouded indoor light, my eyes latched onto one face immediately. It was your brother-in-law's, whose lot was cast with mine here in this cell. His cheeks were grimed and his eyes watery. He was being taken out of this cell as I was being brought in. Did these prisoners know of his convoluted Vietcong past but had somehow opted to grant him a long reprieve rather than exact revenge? Perhaps now, finding themselves here after so many years of war and suffering, they had all pitched their sight on something else altogether, away from blame and vengeance to embrace a more absolving, compassionate perspective. At least this was what I hoped.

Water was splashed in my face. A pair of hands touched my lapel, shaking me and rousing me forth. Soon enough, all of us here would be huddled together, bound by the same pain and loneliness.

I was the only amputee. I was allowed the most space as the more able-bodied made room for me. I could lie down while others slept sitting up, one leaning against the other, each in his own internal solitude.

They knew how to divide us. Critique him, I was ordered one day. I was shown another man's written confession. Then it was passed from one to the other. We were inside the clutch of absolute authority. We were commanded to judge the chronicles of others on a monthly basis. Whoever was deemed by most in the cell to be the weakest or the laziest would receive special treatment: no breakfast, no lunch, and only a small handful of stale rice for dinner for the rest of the month.

Soon enough, I began to fear the suspicion, anxiety, and mistrust sowed in every frame and sequence of thought. Privacy had to be invented, by averting others' eyes. Still, emotions could be glimpsed, stories shared.

A lifelong southern Communist declared himself free of illusions. Like a monk, he smiled weakly, now stripped of his usual panoply of postures, positions, and politics, and alone without possessions. He was, like me, embracing the stark primitive but showing none of its effect. For weeks, he said nothing and looked at no one. And then one day, there he was, suddenly standing on tiptoe, atop a limp body, positioning his eyes just so in front of a narrow crack in the wall to take in a sliver of the outside world. I made contact with him only because I was the limp body under his feet. He was a hothouse of memory and consciousness. He looked down at me with a purposeful stare and spoke with a spiritedness I had not seen till then. His voice registered clearly even in its diminished form. He had spent years in prison, under the French, under Diem, Thieu, and now under the Communists. "My dream now is not to be released," he said as he paused and looked at me to see if I understood his showdown with life's disappointments and discontents. "It is not to see my family." He paused so we could together ponder this unintelligible suggestion. "My dream is to be back in a French prison thirty years ago." It was not the strain of fatalism but rather the self-inflicted but irresistible desire for pain, for comfort in melancholy. In this encompassing moment, the balance had tipped. For the rest of his time in our cell until he was taken away, I never heard him say another word.

And then one day I saw him again. He and another prisoner were standing together, two long silhouettes in the light. I was on the edge of a parched field, watering crops with a hose. Accustomed still to the indoor shade, I had to shield my eyes. An old Conex box, used as a freight container, lay indifferently under the sun's light and heat. It was four feet wide and four feet high on the far side of an adjoining lot. They were there, in the purple silence, where men were made to walk, methodically and fatalistic, clearing mines. I knew immediately who the other man was. I could not make out the face clearly, but I deferred to an innate sense of certainty. It was your brother-in-law. He saw me. And I saw him. We looked at each other and that was it.

No one in here could forget or would forget. We were saddled, one way or another, with the weight of our past lives.

There were no walls to impede escape, just one slender strand of barbed wire and no watchtowers. No one escaped because we were reminded with magnificent poignancy that our parents and wives and children would be killed if an attempt was made.

They knew the names of our relatives. They let it be known that our relatives had been paid visits.

"Your sister is a beautiful woman," one of the cadres had told your brother-in-law. "Her name is Quy?" the cadre asked.

Your brother-in-law nodded. In that drab instant, any incipient sense of opposition immediately dissipated. Of course those questions had an immediate quieting effect on us.

"She lives with a girlfriend, yes? She is alone, husband also away? In fact, husband is also here to repent." Following such questions, you can imagine that our complete submission need neither be compelled nor devised.

Before he left, the cadre told your brother-in-law, "We hate traitors more than we hate the enemy. Even traitors who only contemplated defection and treachery. Remember that."

It all seemed very hopeless until the door opened one day and your brother-in-law was suddenly brought into our cell on a stretcher.

"A real cell instead of a Conex freight box for you," the guard announced.

Your brother-in-law was unloaded. His body dropped to the floor. He felt like a cold, inanimate thing. His body had shrunken. The flesh and bones had changed shape to fit the tight enclosures of the metal freight box. Still, the moment felt light. I could sense it. Our fortune, defying circumstances, would change. Even the head guard had given me a benevolent look, something inestimable a few days before. Something had changed irrefutably. His seemingly unlabored overtures, the sudden undepleted reservoir of goodwill, surprised us at first. Then came the great prosperity of rice doled out in extra large proportions, the occasional morsel of pork, and a smile now and then, and even a cigarette or two for me. One day a piece of paper was slipped to us. It was partially torn and wrinkled but the writing was clearly your wife's and it was revelatory. "We finally found out where you are. Don't give up. You will be out soon." More than ever, I wished for her unequivocal presence and dreamed, once more, the only dream worth dreaming.

———

As I am reading Uncle Number Two's letter, I am alternating between quietly crying and vehemently denying the truth I know is coming. I can't bear to go on reading. I feel my father's tremulous hand on my shoulder. He has been standing behind me, reading as well. We might have howled but we don't. Instead we collapse into silence.

# III

# THE RIVER FLOWS BUT THE OCEAN STAYS

# 24

# *The South China Sea*

## MR. MINH, 2006

I am here looking out the window. The sky is powdery blue. The ripe, creaturely facts of spring are not yet evident. I wait for that time of the year, not yet here, when trees explode in white petals and the smell of newly cut grass blows through half-open windows. I wait for that extravagant show of the earth's annual renewal. But for now, I am content with the more subtle, incipient signs of spring, like the robin I glimpsed on a tree branch yesterday.

Life itself seems to hum with a steady purpose that is disrupted only by Phong's fleshly presence. His reappearance, even if brief and limited, has magnified feelings I thought had been quieted. Now, after Mrs. An ushered him out, I am left here with an inner tightening in my stomach, light-headed with vertigo, but able to see everything with perfect clarity. The varnished wood, the sallow walls, the long, immaculate hallways. The self-deceiving friendship.

I am keenly aware that time is passing. I see myself and I see my child, sometimes as Mai, sometimes as Bao, and sometimes as both at the same time, if that is possible. It doesn't matter who is out and who is in during these visits. There are ghosts inside each of them. They both have devotions to a world that lives somewhere among the headstones, that floats somewhere under the waters of the South China Sea.

The letter is still here in my bedside drawers. I take it out and touch it. I see how it has been altered by continual handling. I remember when I first read it years ago, and when I later reread it with Mai and Bao by my side.

Mrs. An is moving about, her heels making successive clicks against the floor. She hovers nearby when she senses trouble. She is aware of my two daughters, Mai and Bao. She knows instinctively, without my having to explain much, that Bao's existence is derived from Mai's pain. Over the years, both she and I have grown accustomed to the surreal transitions that characterize their combined lives.

Mrs. An takes my hand and asks, "Are you okay?" She knows I am stoked up by Phong's presence and burdened by my worries about the intimately crosshatched well-being of Mai and Bao. Once again my lungs are filled with fluid. To prevent me from choking on liquid, she sprinkles thickening powder into a bowl of soup for me to sip.

Here is the letter again. I am beset by a ravenous hunger for air. Breathe, breathe, I tell myself. I feel a throbbing in my temples.

A terrible knowledge entered years ago and here it remains, formidable, unflinching.

I lie here keeping a ceaseless watch over her.

In my dream my wife and my daughter are still alive, their profiles paired in silhouette. I see her eyes, her lips, her neck. My wife, resplendent in purple, smiles. The house is aglow in the evening's lambent light.

I look at the letter as if her sacrifices, so many, can be felt and understood through a careful examination of Phong's handwriting. It is as clear to me now as it was when I first read the letter. We, Phong and I, her brother, all of us, have been the helpless and infirm ones in need of rescue. My wife was our source of endurance all along.

A lesser insight has kept me from seeing this truth earlier.

*"We finally found out where you are. Don't give up. You will be out soon."*

These were words Phong had quoted blithely in his letter sent from Malaysia in 1978. But how could she have managed this feat? Hasn't he wondered?

"My wife suffered so much," I tell Mrs. An. She knows what happened, though she is properly tight-lipped about it. I have shown her the letter. It forced us to confront, with a level glare of determination, what happened to her and to our country after the war.

There was Quy as she opened the front door of our house and walked straight out into the somber glow of Saigon's postwar lassitude. I see the melancholy streets, even as the morning turned hectic. It was 1975 when the South fell. But it could have been 1963 as well, when President Diem was assassinated.

To understand what really happened in 1963 or in 1975 one would have had to follow her when she left the house and took a different route than the one she usually took. There was nothing accidental or provisional about this new turn of events. It was she who ensured my release from detention in 1963, just as it was she who arranged for her brother's and Phong's release from prison in 1978. She was the one who saved each one of us.

One event was a prelude to the other. Like a lagging ghost that refuses to leave, he was the blurred but defining force that prevailed through both events. He could claim authority, power, and advantage through both with no apparent consciousness of how others would in turn be diminished. I can still see his face in shadows, feel his eyes resting on her. There was Phong, holding his cigarette, narrowing his eyes and coveting. There was the wanton acceleration of desire and intrigue. There was the erotic charge that had to be satisfied. Could it be that everything—his calculated pursuit of her and the mysterious circumstances surrounding my release in 1963—boiled down to the cold finality of one simple fact? An even exchange? I am still lost in the solipsism of this one recurring question. I see the pure inflections of desire—his—its persistent swerves and dips, exacted and satisfied at last, in exchange for a life spared from the executioner's gun.

This fact remains the unshared secret. In 1963 Phong was the one in charge. Just as he knew then, he must have known even in 1975 that the world saw her as beautiful and that her beauty would save him and her brother.

Every loop and iteration of this one fact has raced relentlessly through my mind all these years. There is no fresh perspective to be gained. With redoubled certainty and from every vantage point, I can see his hand rest one millisecond too long on Quy's waist as he left the dinner at my house after the coup.

He was here but a few moments ago, a disfigured memory, standing over me. The overpowering smell of wet nicotine remains. I fumble for the bottle of eucalyptus oil and dab a few drops on my nose and throat. The change in him from one who inadvertently exposed too much in a letter written almost thirty years ago to one who paid perfectly composed visits to the nursing home and engaged in polite queries still jars. One thought enrages me, like a string of profanity: He is here but she is not.

Time does not pass. It refuses to pass.

Here are the facts as I have cobbled them together in my head. Quy was exchanging more than gold. Phong has been the one pulling the strings and making a mockery of us all and taking advantage of her contrasting virtue and our undeserving selves. It is a fact, this stark, allegorical contrast. I have read the entire letter many times but this time I unfold it and reread just the portions that still hurt the most.

"Don't give up. You will be out soon."

Your brother-in-law and I looked at the tattered note the guard slipped to us. We thought to ourselves, she must be selling her gold.

We must get ourselves accustomed to hope again. We were not in a position to entertain the possibility of freedom. But now with Quy's note I thought constantly of leaving. I thought of seeing Quy again in Saigon, finding you in America. I could almost see our new lives, as if from a great height—its forms, its shapes, and its colors from the other side of the world's oceans, in North America. I was conscious that they were all exorbitant hopes, and far from being resolved. Still, I harbored them.

Having expected for so long to die inside this cell, imagine my surprise when one early morning, the door was opened and we were told we were being released. We would live, I thought to myself, by which I meant somewhere else. I was certain we would not remain in Vietnam. The guard gave us a note from your wife addressed to her brother. She was waiting for us. She enclosed money and travel papers for our bus ride back to Saigon. One of the guards even helped us to the bus terminal, me on my metal leg and your brother-in-law newly afflicted by a bent and diminished body.

Our human perversities were by no means extraordinary in postwar Saigon. Still, the women in our lives could barely recognize us. Your wife looked the same to me, as always full of beauty and grace. She glimmered in the sunlight as she touched my face and her brother's. Thu receded into the shadows to allow the main players their rightful place. Your brother-in-law sat on the floor, staring at his hands and occasionally lifting his legs here and there, as if he had not realized that he could move them. After a hiatus, Quy, forehead furrowed in concentration, quietly said, "You both must leave before they kill you." I looked at us through her eyes. What did she see? The mirror reflected ghastly faces, sunken and fatigued. "It is the only way to save you," she said. She meant her brother, though I would be included in any plan to leave. She sensed that our prison time together had indissolubly bound us. Her brother and I were almost like an elderly couple, muddling along. Our experiences had clearly shaken her. A shortwave radio under Quy's bed clandestinely tuned to the BBC kept us abreast of new dangers.

I looked around and took in the poignant austerity of our new lives. Old walls discarded their plaster and paint. There rose the smell of sodden laundry and heat trapped in unaired rooms. A blackened pot stood on the stove. Quý too had had to endure and improvise. Her face, however, remained untroubled by lines of age or worries. Still, something inestimable had been lost. The street, once so elegant, had turned dour. There were no crowds, no tourists, only the drab local cadres' booth at one end of the street. Every neighborhood had one. They were there to keep order and monitor the citizens. On the very first night we returned home, we were paid a visit. I was at once apprehensive. I heard the peremptory footsteps and a truculent knock on the door. There was a glum silence. Then came the request for us to show our papers so they could be promptly checked against the official family register for derelictions or unauthorized presences or absences. Such was the nature of our ordained defeat.

Quy greeted the cadre. There was a feeling of habitual famil-iarity between them. The mood shifted. It became more familial and responsive. It was clear that nothing had dispossessed her of her powers to charm. She offered him a cup of tea from the fam-ily's best set, its porcelain rim smooth and round. He waved it away. She returned with a basket of baguettes. She opened a bot-tle of bourbon and poured a glass for the guard. I instinctively swallowed, as if I had taken a big sip and felt its soothing heat wash the sharp edge of smoke down my throat. He said, "I have something for you," addressing her with a respectful form of *you*. He passed her a note. She read it and then said to the guard, "Tell him I say thank you." When the guard left, she flashed us a look filled with confidence and promise.

I imagine each scene in my head. Everything reminds me of our ballad of eternal love and loss. I feel Quy's private heart in the intervening spaces between the penned words. I see that day in Saigon, as if I were there when Phong and my brother-in-law were released.

My face burns, a red heat rising and retreating when I realize that the compulsory gratitude I have been carrying for Phong all these years was utterly misplaced. He had not protected us. Quy had.

A guard came to the house a few days later and handed us travel papers to Phan Thiet, a fishing town south of Saigon. We would leave Vietnam from there, on an expedition organized by Quy's Chinese friends. Two men were given free passage on the condi-tion that they devote themselves to helping us survive the trip.

Everything is up to fate now, I thought, as I envisaged our implausible journey ahead. We hailed several cyclos to the bus terminal, got on a bus as if we were embarking on an ordinary trip. The lot was filled with trucks and buses—ancient engines coughing and snorting fumes. I carried a pouch of dried squid and Chinese sausage that reeked of sweetness and congealed fat. Quy took along a bag of toys to prove we were visiting relatives with young children if questioned. I was surprised by not just her willingness to go with us but also her apparent vigor. We did not have to cajole her. You know we would not have left without her.

I believed Quy was eager to be reunited with you and Mai. While we were gone a letter from you arrived at your old house in Cho-lon and the mother of the new owner had saved it and hand-delivered it to Quy. We knew where you were. I believed that that knowledge injected Quy with hope and a desire for a new life, which, after all these grim postwar years, overcame her attachment to the old.

I recognized a dozen or so other passengers on the bus as people with plans like ours. Every nerve in my body was tensed up, alive, and in wait. The Vietnamese navy was known to shoot unauthorized boats on sight. So be it. We had to try. Quy, of course, was quiet, leaning against Thu's shoulders, her countenance utterly calm and composed.

We were part of a mass exodus that was unprecedented in Vietnam's venerable one-thousand-year history. Your brother-in-law and I understood the need for silence.

The ride itself was uneventful. At checkpoints, papers were produced, bribes pressed decorously into the palms of stern-faced guards. I kept my eyes on the rice fields. Here and there, buffalo herders, white ducks, and buffaloes mingled among straw shanties and blighted fields. Buses traveling in the opposite direction honked their horns and flicked their headlights in the gray dusk. After several hours, we could see water. A briny odor of fermented fish pervaded the air. It was clear we were approaching Phan Thiet.

After dropping most of the passengers off at the bus depot, the bus trundled toward a more obscure location perched across the rocky shoreline. The slender road dropped steeply seaward. We were all off to visit fishermen relatives. I assumed they were part of the stalwart Chinese network. Three men emerged from a house and pointed us toward a sandy area enclosed by fence rails. A boat was waiting for us there. Boats were nothing unusual here, of course. Leave in the daylight as if there were nothing to hide. If we had left at night, we would have been shot on the spot if caught.

The seascape was dotted with fishing boats navigating through salt gusts and churning whitecaps. Your brother-in-law walked ahead, body keeled, one foot twisted inward, one knee bent. We made our way toward the boat, moored thirty meters or so from shore. The leader, an ethnic Chinese man about forty years old, waved us forward. A gale blew, setting Quy's hair flying.

Your brother-in-law took her hand. Our arms loosely linked, we huddled together, crossed the street, and waded into the water, our feet gripping the sea's grooved depressions. We climbed into the boat one by one as the waves rose and fell, churning massive trunks and branches out of the water. One of the men charged by Quy's Chinese friends to help us carried me on his back. I clung fiercely to Thu's hand. Through the wind's grainy gusts, I could see Quy and your brother-in-law pressed against the boat's side, her head bobbing against her brother's shoulder. She is safe, I thought to myself. Then a large wave tossed the boat upward, filling my mouth with salt water. The boat plowed over the swell. It was a small boat, no more than eighteen meters long and five meters wide, but filling up with the two dozen or more people from our bus. It bobbed up and down, and from side to side; its mooring line stretched and creaked with each upheaval of the waves. As a man turned on the ignition and struggled to get the motor started, I heard the old, rebuilt engine rattle. Just as it heaved to life and was about to head seaward, there was a scream. In the ambient clatter and clang of the motor stopping and starting, I could hear a quick and desperate "No, no." It was your brother-in-law's voice.

Someone had fallen overboard. A dark form dipped and rose in the waves, arms and hands and feet synchronized for self-propulsion landward. Instinctively, I reached downward into the water and, together with your brother-in-law, tugged the body out of the waves. The captain shone a flashlight. It was Quy, thrashing against our grip, the heat of her breathing strong against my face. I want to go back, she insisted. We threw the weight of our bodies on hers and kept her pinned.

Even in my shaken, strung-out state, I then realized she came along only so we would go. Her apparent enthusiasm for the departure had deceived us.

"No, no, no," she moaned as your brother-in-law put his hands against her back and pulled her into the folds of his shirt. Shudders ran through her body. The two of us settled into the difficult business of holding her down as our boat was steered seaward, its engine snorting fits and starts.

The faintly lit coast tapered into darkness. I would never forget the way her eyes rested on me, or on the horizon and then back at me, weighing the dwindling options.

Hours passed. By now we were far from shore, in the middle of nowhere, with the weight of the journey's inevitability fully on us. As day began to turn into evening, a glint of steel flashed in the far distance. Two freighters like two long silhouettes in light could be seen on the horizon. We were too far away to send signals. There was nothing for us to do, yet an aura of frenzied purpose hung above. One day passed, then another. The open sea surrounded us with fear and the reddest sunsets I had ever seen. We drank and ate as little as possible to minimize seasickness. After one and a half days of calm, the weather changed and so did the ocean. Stripes of lightning illuminated the sky, followed quickly by successive peals of thunder. Before this, our boat had skimmed only inland bays and calm ports of call in search of fish and bait.

My stomach churned. In the billowing wind, the air smelled sour and yellow. I lay flat on the boat's bottom, one hand instinctively gripping Quy's ankle. The needle on the compass quivered without direction. No one on board was truly skilled in navigation. I heard the raised, desperate voices of the others. Our boat hit a swell and was inundated. We used pots, bowls, and our cupped hands to bail out the seawater. We jettisoned suitcases. Then night fell and it turned cold. Darkness gloated and pitted itself against us. We huddled close and felt the sea's black lappings against the skeletal frame of our boat.

On day three, food and water had to be rationed. I received this news calmly. I hadn't wanted to eat or drink for days. But others began to lose hope. In the early morning hours, we sighted an approaching boat, then another, heading straight toward us. The captain hoisted white flags to capture their attention and signal our helplessness. Everyone screamed and cheered, doing our best to engage their interest. Flashlights signaled dots and dashes of Morse code. The ships' hulks got closer and closer to us and then to our astonishment veered away. But a part of me was not surprised. The world was tired of our continuing exodus. People moaned, their excitement superseded by fear and desperation. The departing ships grew ever smaller, losing their geometrically lined shapes until they became dots and disappeared over the horizon.

Hours later, as the captain surveyed the remaining containers of diesel fuel, a sleek, fast-moving ship headed toward us. This one did not avert course, even as we came directly within its sight. Instead, it altered course to intersect with ours. It even blew its horn, as if that were needed to signal its presence. A man in dark glasses looked down over a railing, staring at us with impending urgency. A flashlight put out a somber glow, revealing a row of gun emplacements visible from the ship's edge. And then quickly, with punitive swiftness, a thick rope was thrown over our steering wheel and then looped over the captain's torso, holding him in place. Ten men wearing headbands and sarongs, each buttressed by batons and guns, jumped onto our boat, screaming incomprehensible orders. They swept through the boat and onto the back, then front, deck. They spat curses in our direction and leered at the women. In the ensuing minutes, the six or more women on the boat were separated from us men. Quy was the first to be taken away. Your brother-in-law and I tried to hold her back. Immediately we were punched and kicked. Our attackers opened our mouths, inspected our teeth. My hands were held behind my back by another. I looked at the long thick scar running down my attacker's left cheek. I looked at his horsehair goatee. I smelled his stale breath. Grimy hands shoved a pair of pliers into my mouth and yanked my four upper and lower back molars with gold fillings. This instantaneously produced long bloody welts on my inside cheeks and gums and I collapsed in excruciating pain. Our boat was searched, belongings seized, jewelry ripped from pierced ears and snatched from wrists. From the other end of the boat where the women had been taken, there were moans. The frightful sound still haunts me.

The pirates left as quickly as they had appeared. The rope tying our boat to theirs was slashed. When Quy and Thu and others emerged, I saw right away their afflicted faces. Quy held her body perfectly vertical, her fists clenched. Her mouth was slack and slightly open. Her hair, knotted and tangled, was damp and pasted to her forehead. Blood trickled from her soiled trouser legs down to her feet. Quy's and Thu's arms were tied together by rough straps. The men gasped and rushed toward their wives. Slowed by dizziness, I nonetheless managed to undo the straps on Quy's and Thu's wrists. They both began to cry soundlessly. One of the men hired by Quy's Chinese friends to help us slipped one arm under her shoulders and one under her knees and carried her to a blanket. Her brother limped toward her and caressed her face. We whispered into her ear, as one would to an injured child. I dabbed a few drops of eucalyptus and camphor oil on her tongue. Her brother draped a sheet over her, parted her legs, and looked. Quy was breaking out in a sweat and shivering. She covered her eyes with both hands, her fingers tightly gripped into a fist, shutting out the world to enter fully into her state of simultaneous existence and nonexistence. When her brother removed his hand, I saw that it was covered in blood. Dry sobs broke loose from his chest.

"She is hemorrhaging," he said.

Clean clothes were located and thrust toward us to use on her wound. He wet a washcloth and squeezed water onto her face and neck. Her skin was cold and pale. The three of us huddled around her. She was our hopeless angel. Her eyelids quivered rapidly as if she were in a state of frenetic dreaming. I pressed my ear against her chest and a finger against the pulse of a submerged vein.

At the edge of my vision, I saw our fellow passengers congregate in a huddle, their faces ashen and grave. Men held their wives' hands. Waves rippled softly. Your brother-in-law and I and Thu took turns watching over Quy. At midnight a fever raged through her body. The sheet between her legs was soaked red. We feared it was hopeless. As she alternated between consciousness and deep sleep, Thu gave her a change of clothes. In the first, red-orange light of dawn, her eyes flickered open and followed the slow blink of a few moving silhouettes.

"I have a funny feeling on the left side of my body," she said. "It's heavy, as if I have put on weight." She saw confusion and concern on my face. "It is all right?" she asked, drawing her whisper out as she pointed to the long-simmering waters in the sea.

She slept most of the next day. We put a cool wet cloth on her forehead to fight the fever. Your brother-in-law put his face next to hers, absorbing her heat into his cheeks, infusing her with his reserve of life. She vomited several times.

Once, in the middle of the night, she tugged at my shirt and pointed to the sky. Look, she said, stillness in her eyes. The ascending moon shone a beneficent glow, turning the sky's harsh edges into a soft silver.

"I will stay here," she said, pointing at the sea. Her glare was permanently fixed on the water. Here, where land could not be glimpsed or felt, the ocean was an infinite expanse of blue and a place of faith.

"Promise me," she said. "Let me be here, with Khanh." She pointed to the ocean beyond the boat. "I won't see Mai again. Let her forget me. You can help."

I waited for an explanation but silence took over. Her face had become a mute blend of concern and focus. She wanted to make sure I understood. Her body arched and then flattened itself against the deck. She heaved. Her eyes stared into mine, searching for assurance. Your brother-in-law faced the water, his hands dangling by his side.

I sat opposite her and watched. We were hard against the edge of the boat. The moonlight slid across the sky.

"A mad mother belongs here," she murmured.

I lay by her side and said nothing, abandoning my usual desire to coax others into seeing things my way. I just listened. We had known each other for years but I knew none of her intimacies. I listened to her half-murmurs and the slow phrasing of her half-finished sentences as they spilled from her mouth. I put a comforting hand on her outstretched arm. She did not move it away. I looked and realized she had slipped back into the twilight of sleep.

The next morning she was dead. How do I explain it to you? A mane of heavy hair fell over her shoulders. Her face was as alive as it ever was. But I knew she had died. Not by the face or the body but by an uneasy void that hung in the air.

I felt a larger darkness enveloping us. The last stars shone above. The shock of her death ran through my body. Right away, for me, everything became unhinged. After her death our fate hardly mattered to me anymore. What would I write in my letter to you if I survived the ocean?

Then we covered her body with a blanket and had a silent ceremony and slipped it into the sea.

Later, when it seemed to matter the least to me, an American submarine appeared out of nowhere with its horn blaring and its megaphones aimed in our direction. I knew the end of our desperate navigation was over. This was around the time when President Carter ordered the Seventh Fleet to pick up boat people. Their lookouts had seen our bedsheet tied to the mast with the word SOS on it. An inflatable raft was thrown into the waters and two Americans rowed it to our boat's side. We were given water and food. Against slim odds we were rescued on that windy day and taken to an island in Malaysia. And for all of us, it was a way station toward new places, new possibilities.

It was the island everyone had heard about. It was the island from which many had been towed back to sea a year or two before. It was the same island on which, after years in the jungle and after the hardship of prison and the South China Sea, your brother-in-law was beaten to death. Of course there had been no formal disclosure of his Vietcong past but somehow word had gotten out in the camps. It hadn't mattered among the prisoners in our reeducation camp. They had no belief in a future, so nothing mattered to them. But in Malaysia, everything mattered. The future was before us. Newfound security did not edge

out the desire to exact revenge, to put order to unresolved grievances.

When he was not in his tent in the early morning one day, I
went and looked for him. I found his body at the foot of a giant
tree trunk, among a flutter of petals and leaves. There it was, in
the curled fetal position, seemingly suspended between dreaming and being awake. He might have been blameless. History
might have been responsible. But history followed us to Malaysia and beyond. The words "Viet Cong" were carved into the
tree's bark, the silent backdrop to a cruel masterpiece.

# 25

## *Forgiving*

### BAO, 2006

This is where I live because our father and Mai chose it—this two-bedroom apartment overlooking an enclosed garden. The complex is tucked slightly in, away from the street, and I have become fond of the garden and its stabilizing presence. From the balcony, I bear witness to the passage of time. The seasons have a habit of announcing themselves clearly here. After a few warm days, sweeps of white and yellow have broken through the wintry hush and carpeted the grounds beneath poplars, elms, and oaks, adding color to what was but a few days ago a denuded landscape of simple monochromatic brown. Today, as Mai drives to visit our father, she convinces herself she will remain in the room while our father is visited by Uncle Number Two. This will be the second visit, following the failed attempt a few days ago. He is already there when we arrive, a single figure outside our father's door.

Mai comes toward Uncle Number Two and shepherds him into the room. When our father sees him, his face clenches up and he recasts himself somberly. He maintains an obvious distance, his eyes widening into a reproving glare. He lifts his arm as if to wave, reaching out in a small, compressed gesture. I know he is concentrating on pulling air into his lungs. The exaltation of national struggles and the sacrifices of victory and loss have been reduced to this: an elderly, sick man confined to his bed, struggling for breath. To help his circulation, I move his arms and legs.

Uncle Number Two wastes not a moment this time. "Why have I come again, you want to know?" he asks, trying, perhaps, to preempt Father's hostility.

Father stares into space, uninterested. I sense the physical barrier he has erected. I see the prosecutorial eyes, the hardened jaw.

"Thu killed herself."

Silence engulfs the room. "Last week," Uncle Number Two adds with a sob. "I thought you would want to know. I thought I should tell you. In person."

"How did this happen, Phong? Why?" Our father is rapt with anticipation. "Oh, Theo," he says, calling Uncle Number Two by the term of endearment used in the early years, when their friendship was unfrayed. "She is really gone?" our father asks, as if there were yet an obscure hope that fate might be appeased and she somehow spared.

Now that he has dispelled our father's detachment, Uncle Number Two stands taciturn. His cold knee clacks metallically against the metal bed. Our father's face is strained, his eyes moist. I think it pains him to see the cut-down size of their lives.

Uncle Number Two says, finally, "Pills," as if the word alone signifies a finality that can clarify everything.

Our father is quiet. Mai moves toward him and places a comforting hand on his wrist. Father arches his eyebrows and tilts his head, trying to make sense of the news, preparing himself for the contingent shock of additional details. He goes through the various alternating propositions. "Was she sick? Was she depressed?" he asks, without pausing for an answer.

Uncle Number Two's face registers a sequence of mixed emotions. He puts a restraining hand on our father's shoulder. There they are, together at last, neither man speaking, each inside the other's reticence.

Finally Uncle Number Two says, "You are right to have harbored your doubts about me." He nods his head for emphasis. "All these years. It's my fault."

Our father shakes his head to deflect the comment.

"No," Uncle Number Two insists with an admonishing shoulder grip. "You always had a bit of contempt for me. I've always known that."

He lets out a mirthless little chuckle. "I cast your judgments aside because I convinced myself you were too meek and sensitive, you with your yoga and French poetry, to understand what had to be done."

Our father releases a breath and nods. "All right, yes," he says. His admission surprises me. He gives Uncle Number Two an appraising look.

"With good reason, as it turns out," says Uncle Number Two.

Our father's eyes widen, unblinking. "Now is not the time, Theo." He reaches over, in the most natural way in the world, to touch Uncle Number Two's hand. "And what does it matter now? Tell me. What happened with Thu?"

"What I am about to say won't endear me to you. But at this point in our lives it has to be done." He rests his palm against his head, readying himself for the grave revelation. His eyes start to tear up.

"Listen, I've been a Vietcong all along."

"A Vietcong?" A frown darkens our father's face. His head must be teeming. "All along?"

The revelation pains, as if it were a dissolution of vows. I look at Uncle Number Two standing by Father, checking the ghostly sacraments of friendship against the shock of this new discovery. I have a vision of Uncle Number Two at our house in Cholon, smiling at Mother, sharing stories with Father. Everything drifts as if into a darkened nullity and then explodes into a kaleidoscope of terrible events, starting with Tet—its hurtle and hurl, its untunable sounds. I see myself hiding in a jar. There is a Vietcong sniper behind a chimney. I hear the click of metal. I hear James calling Mai's name and then I hear the sound of a body falling to the ground. I watch my mind scuffling and I see the world bursting red. I can almost feel the gun in my hand, its black metal warmed to life by my body heat. Each image is replayed inside its own slow retraction, backing over itself again and again inside the clotted space that is my head.

I imagine James lying there like a wounded animal waiting to be reached. Mai stares from a great, supercilious height, affixing blame on me.

Quickly, I shut my eyes and suppress the memories. Uncle Number Two's presence keeps me anchored in the here and now. I concentrate on not blotting Mai out, on not sending her into lost time.

Father sighs, then takes long, deep breaths like those he takes when he is alone with his yoga and meditation.

"Yes. All along. Ever since we first knew each other," says Uncle Number Two, his eyes reflecting a sadness that breaks my heart. I look at Father, and I see the downturned corners of his mouth, the grave face, and the eyes that rest with singular defenselessness on our surrounding space. The pronouncement seems scarcely credible. I fear our father's sadness and his anger. I look at Uncle Number Two, and I am confused.

Then Father goes right to the heart of it. "Why are you telling me this?" he asks.

Mai shrinks inside herself. For once, she understands him. She too looks warily at Uncle Number Two. She wonders if every memory of him has to be revised.

"I don't know. When Thu killed herself . . ." Uncle Number Two stammers, his eyes fixed on his shoes.

Our father says something inaudible, then reverses his thought—a small indecision and revision within a larger one. He keeps quiet instead. Mai is motionless, receding into the oblivion of her statuelike private self.

Uncle Number Two looks at Father searchingly, eyes asquint. They cannot unstick themselves from the past or from their collusion in mutual recrimination. Uncle Number Two is the only one who talks, dragging with him the appurtenances of their common proprietary past, even as Father closes his eyes and says nothing. Having taken the plunge, he now has the momentum to keep going. With a show of resignation, he declares that there must be an end to deception. Here he is, at last, revealing himself to us, in an effort, perhaps, to be fully known. He asks ineffectual questions, hoping for a reaction from Father that will formally release him. "How shall I tell you everything now?" He confesses he has nothing left that he wishes to conceal.

"I wanted to drive out the foreigners," he said, his voice faltering. "As one is taught to believe."

"As one is taught to believe," Father repeats skeptically.

"I did not know that a small country has few choices. It cannot control its own destiny. It is not a question of whether foreigners come but of which ones.

"I did not know how they would destroy the country," he confesses. "I wanted something better than Diem and all those who followed. I could not have foreseen the scale of retribution."

His body slouches, as if he were unable to carry its weight. He steadies himself on our father's bed rail. He looks at Father as if the possibility of leniency and compassion lies only with him. But Father is still quiet, as if he were sifting these declarations inside his head.

"All along," Father repeats. "All along a Vietcong. Living in the South but working against it."

"Please," Uncle Number Two implores, but Father ignores him.

"You were so involved in your work, in your pacification work. You were so proud of your work. All those conversations we had about the Vietcong . . . How upset you were when the South wasn't devoting sufficient energy to the nonmilitary aspects of the war . . . What did it all mean?"

"Once you manufacture a lie, you have to continue with it . . . Each half-truth spawns another," Uncle Number Two explains. "And there were even moments when I felt a true affinity to the southern cause." He is about to continue but our father shakes his head. He has had enough.

"It hardly matters anymore. I don't need to understand, Phong," our father says. A suspended silence hangs in the air that is heavy and enigmatic. Finally Father releases a labored sigh. When he speaks, he utters just one word. "Thu?" His voice shakes without control. "What does your story have to do with Thu? I only want to know about Thu. Did she know who you really are?"

Uncle Number Two wraps his arms around himself and starts to explain, head lowered before Father's sternness. It is his plea for leniency.

Uncle Number Two ignores our father's question and continues with the story he wishes to tell. "Thinking back about my life, I see I had such little sense of proportion," he continues. "After 1975, all the Vietcong operatives in the South surfaced. Your brother-in-law and I used our history to protect my wife and yours. And for some time we did, until it became clear that we and other Southerners must be made to suffer as well. By then, all the neighbors, even Thu and your wife, had learned of my true allegiance. As my side claimed all the power and advantage and authority in the country, it was in Thu's interest to forgive my secret. It was this secret about my identity that saved us initially."

He pauses, trying to assess Father's silence, searching for some slight gesture. "Since our escape in 1978, and especially given what happened to your brother-in-law in the Malaysian camp, my fear has been that someone in Little Saigon out in California would recognize me. After a few years had gone by, I thought that the danger of being discovered had diminished and that my secret life as an impostor so many years ago could be left behind . . ."

"Someone found you out?" Mai interjects.

Uncle Number Two bows his head and nods. His face turns complacent and pensive.

"Someone, I don't know who. Six months ago we began getting anonymous letters that threatened to reveal me as a Vietcong—not just from thirty years ago, but as a continuing operative planted by Hanoi. One had a photo of me in 1976 with a top Communist Party official. They have become hawk-eyed, some Vietnamese in Orange County, always ready to sniff out a Communist, especially after that Ho Chi Minh poster incident in the video store. The letters demanded nothing but merely threatened. They were of the sort that makes one feel most afraid. They arrived at irregular intervals, sometimes as a letter sent by mail and other times as a handwritten note tacked to our door."

I am surprised to see that Father's face softens as he takes in Uncle Number Two's sad perspective. For the first time he fixes his eyes to Uncle Number Two's face and leaves them there. He leans back, his head inside the floating light of the room. I am astonished by his gentle demeanor. I wonder if he understands what Uncle Number Two has been saying.

"The strain was too much for Thu. There were phone calls at night in which the caller muttered, 'Traitor,' and hung up. Thu would shake, each call sucking the resilience out of her. A week ago a reporter for the *Nguoi Viet* newspaper called the house and asked if the rumors about me were true. Thu was the one who answered the phone. She took it very badly. I think that was the fatal phone call. Her private humiliation would soon be publicly disclosed. She must have felt she had no other choice."

Father strains to breathe. Using long, deep strokes, I rub mentho-lated oil onto the concavities of his chest. Mai steps in and instructs him to take deep, slow breaths. I put my ear to his chest and feel the enfeebled beat of his heart. His eyes glint. He clears his throat but asks no further questions of Uncle Number Two. He does not appear to have the strength for further confrontation. The two men are face to face, each edgily watching the other.

Uncle Number Two puts a hand on his metal leg, lifts the creases of his loose-fitting khaki pants, and slowly steadies himself on the back of Father's wheelchair. "I am sorry," he says, offering an eerie reprieve. "I will go in a few minutes. After a little rest." He points wryly to his metal leg.

Father's breath rises and falls. He shakes his head vigorously, almost aggressively. I fear anger is catching up with him at last. I think that for sure he will spurn Uncle Number Two's apologies. But to my surprise, Father taps Uncle Number Two weakly on the shoulder and places an improbably proprietary hand on Uncle Number Two's arm. Father then points to the chair, inviting him to stay. Uncle Number Two sits, inclining toward Father, watching his friend who is also a stranger go through the simple task of breathing. They are brought here together, side by side, by a difficult but common past that still binds.

# 26

## *Arpeggios*

### MR. MINH, 2006

Under a sequined sky, the ocean sways and shimmies. It glows in the evening's early flickering light, whitecaps glistening a silvery gray. In a stir of wind, currents ripple like arpeggios, swift and soft across an ivory keyboard. A flock of seagulls rises off the water and lifts skyward.

This must be the South China Sea. It is green, blue, and lushly textured. I can make out the outline of houseboats clustered along the distant shore. Beyond that unbroken line of moored, wooden barges, rice fields flourish in a bloom of deep emerald green. A half-moon offers its oblique silhouette faintly etched against the sky. A small, slender boat floats nearby almost within reach of the undulating land. And the shadow of yet another beckons. I bring myself completely to the serenity offered here, watching the ocean do what it has always done, rising and falling inside a larger finality. I am sitting alone, knees drawn up to my chin, awash in rivulets of light, inside a nebulous dream.

I feel a hand on my head, fingers combing my hair, and another hand caressing the scar that has closed over my old wound. I am eager to absorb the touch into my skin. There is a residue of memory transfigured. Is it an abstraction? Or is it real?

The soft twilight will soon slip away. I am caught inside this feeling of leaving and returning.

The sea wind shifts. Through a partial segment of my consciousness, I notice the change in direction. The water responds in turn. Its waves surge and fall, white-stippled and wind-whipped. For hours the ocean, besieged and battered, tosses and turns in counterpoint until it is becalmed once more.

Finally the burdensome quiet is broken by the humming of prayers, each chant synthesized to the next. The sound reverberates, flowering, expanding, unfolding. It calls for me. I bolt upward into an exquisite emptiness, searching for it, knowing immediately that it is what I have been looking for. The sound that is calling is momentary but delicious. Its familiarity engulfs me. I visualize overlapping memories. I see a woman in a purple *ao dai* praying and I see a child being born and I see a child dying.

Here, inside this warp of space and time, we are at last facing sadness and remembering our dead child together. We stop casting blame. We let go of rancor and accusations.

Shapeless clouds drift and dissolve into a purple evening. Everything returns, precisely configured and without effort. Blackbirds scatter in flight, going to school, or leaving and returning. I am in another land of once-familiar trees, tamarind, star fruit, mango, their leaves brushing against my face. A woman sings. A woman prays. I turn myself over to a profusion of purple, wholly tinged with expectation.

Quy. I whisper to her. I feel her name run through my body, like a wish and its immediate fulfillment.

The reply comes back in a shimmering glow. The moment lingers, holding itself together on a pinprick of perfect grandeur. It is possible to leave where I am and join it.

Quy, I say, tentatively, then loudly. She is a beam of light, moving through an unimaginable sweep of time and space like a wave that dances. She is like a guardian spirit, bright and warm and undispelled by death. She is within reach right here, determined and unfaltering, a perfect picture of herself.

The world expands for the sake of the heart. I am capable of more risk and more magnanimity.

Quy. She is by the door, giving me a farewell or maybe a welcoming bow and smiling. Joy spreads through me. Quy. The moment I say her name out loud, however, I am awake, and immediately, a cold, stark despondency overcomes me.

I close my eyes and hardly dare to breathe. Through the window I see the moon sinking. I am determined to return to where I was, but it is not to be. Instead, I remain here, in the present, inside the tantalizing shape that she once occupied.

I am back in my room in the nursing home, restless, and caught inside the adrenal surge of the dream I wish to prolong. My heart is too weak and irregular to remove fluid from my lungs but I can feel it surge when I think of Quy. There is a deep symmetry inside this backward-flowing time, like a return to the beginning, like watching the gestation of the earth.

I dream of it as a lover would. And I know this dream for what it is. A warm thrill runs through me and I am still prolonging the bliss.

I know I am expected. It is a knowledge born of a sudden, piercing consciousness. I am bathed in it, in this feeling of home, which was once barely imaginable. There is a place for me to go toward. There is a time when that will occur. And this recognition opens up into a sense of peace that envelops me completely.

I think of Phong's arrival by my bedside the previous week, spilling confessions. The stories he had harbored that I knew nothing about. I was overwhelmed by his admissions and his collusion and treachery, his scheming and connivance, his deceit underpinning more than fifty years of our lives together. Countries betray other countries. Why should I have been surprised that friends betray friends? There he was finally, inside an expectant silence that enveloped us like a ghost fog— like the white phantom fog that covered my paratroopers and me when we were set up by a local scout as we headed for enemy sanctuaries inside Cambodia. So many of my men were killed that night. I squeezed my eyes shut. I smelled the faint tang of cigarette. I wondered if Phong had anything to do with that ambush. But I will never know.

He was about to leave. He moved lopsidedly toward the door. The metallic hinge in his leg creaked and he almost stumbled. And suddenly, I could see his frantic search for absolution. It was clear to me. His face, his spirit, and his very being were rearranged in a way that pled for forgiveness. His life haunted him. He was still there, weary and used up but caught inside a deep regret.

I am thinking now not of his first two visits but a later one, the private one between him and me, without Mai's or Bao's knowledge. There was a knock and then he materialized by my bedside, watching me with dark, foreboding eyes. I have more to tell, he declared simply. His lips quivered as he mustered a tight-lipped smile for my sake. He was shivering. I steadied him with my hand and gave him time to regain his composure. His head was cocked, his face determined and fixed with a warrior's gaze. Then he began to talk, all in an unadorned rush.

Do you understand, he asked almost too aggressively when finished. His hands were pressed against his chest, fingers interlocked.

Do I understand? I pushed the bedcovers aside and steered my thoughts back to each revelation. This is what he said, I told myself as I combed through each of his astonishing disclosures.

"I left out something important in the letter I wrote when we landed in Malaysia. And I wanted to tell you about it yesterday but Mai was here."

"What more could you have told me after you told me about Thu's death and your true face, Phong?" I asked.

My heart pounded erratically against my chest. But then immediately, I knew. I knew whatever hard little packet of news he had to share would involve not politics or war but my wife.

"Quy was pregnant in 1975. No one knew. I am quite certain you did not know yourself." He paused. "She delivered the baby after the fall of Saigon."

A sticky, panicky doubt took over. My first impulse was to pretend I had heard nothing, that this newly revealed truth had not touched me in the least. I could stare at the whitewashed walls and allow my eyes to take in everything and nothing at the same time.

Of course the child could not be mine. It must be Phong's, was my first thought. The bastard. I wanted to knock him out with a quick left hook.

He finally got what he had for so long wanted. My goosefleshed arms went cold and rigid. I recalled that brief interlude from the day before, the scintillating sense of peace that enveloped me when Phong's confession nudged us toward the path of reconciliation. But now I flashed him an angry, accusatory look.

"Her brother and I were there to help the midwife when the baby came in November. It was only seven months after the fall of Saigon but it was clear by then—a mixed-race child was out of the question."

Phong covered his face with his hand. He looked at me in his obliging way to gauge my reaction to yet another volley of confessions. I could feel my mind drift, as if I were looking down on Phong and myself from an immense distance.

"It was not merely a sense of precautionary anxiety that made me do what I did," he said in a husky voice, his hand clenching and unclenching. "These children were considered half-breeds, disreputable reminders of the much-hated Americans. I don't have to tell you any of this. I saw it all with my own eyes. These kids were being rounded up, their families became pariahs. Even our long-standing credentials with the Vietcong would not be enough to keep trouble away."

His eyes narrowed and teared. His story was still unfolding, and in the middle of it, he let out a sob. He then began speaking at a furiously accelerating pace.

"She suffered a terribly hard labor. Two full days of contractions. I still remember how her skin was hot to the touch, flaming from within, how the muscles and tendons were stretched taut, and how she collapsed after the baby slipped with a damp, sucking sound into the midwife's hands. Then I saw the baby's scandalously half-American face. I caught the midwife's faintly pursed lips, the darting eyes, the snickering up-and-down appraisal. And I knew. I could feel it down at the molecular level—it would be suicide to keep this baby. All of us would suffer. I watched as it nuzzled against its mother's chest, fingers searching for nipples and breasts. Quy's eyes flicked here and there as she took in her child's face. Our eyes met for one anguished moment, and almost immediately after, she curled up and fell into a deep sleep.

"The silence was ruthless, unbearable. I did not have the vocabulary or the ability to tell her my fears. The baby stared at me glassy-eyed, its head cocked to the side. I must admit I felt drawn to it. But your brother-in-law and I knew what we had to do. I want you to know it wasn't from hard-heartedness. We had to do it. We took the baby from Quy as she slept, knees still drawn to her chest. I felt feeble in my legs. This little girl. Her round waxy head lying against my palm. Less than one hour old and already she could grab my pinkie and squeeze it. I washed the baby in our tub, her eyes peeking at us with a sparkle and glint. We took her to an orphanage in Vung Tau that very night.

"The next day when her brother told her what we had done, her body shook. She let out a long, sustained scream. Night after night we could hear her silky whisper, 'My baby, my baby,' her body a tightly curled inert mass, like that of a sleeping animal that refuses to budge. What could he say after? What could I say? We both struggled against the numbness of what we had done. But we were convinced it was the only way. For the baby's sake, not just ours."

Phong paused. "Not just ours," he repeated almost hysterically. He was watching me intently, his breathing hushed, his eyes unblinking and impenetrably dark. Perhaps he was asking for forgiveness. I could not tell. How perverse, how ironic, how sad, I thought, that even the most calculating and ruthless act—taking a child from its mother—couldn't save them.

"This memory still haunts me. Loosening the baby's grip, taking each of her fingers and prying it from her mother's breast. Quy's long wail and the forlorn look on her face afterward."

By what dispensation of force and authority did he think he had the right to do what he did?

"We were cowards," Phong finally said softly, shaking his head. He stood there like a penitent hoping to be redeemed. "Of course you are right to have harbored contempt for me all these years."

I swallowed hard. I tried to shrug it all off. His terrible predicaments—Thu's suicide and his Vietcong connections—were immediately unimportant. What struck me with a fury in the small hard center of my chest was Quy's baby deposited in an orphanage somewhere in Vietnam. A part of my wife, now a whole being, roaming the streets. I imagined her, lost and alone. The follies of thirty years ago interleaving with the here and now. Perhaps she is a street vendor in Saigon. Perhaps she has escaped Vietnam and is living somewhere in the United States or Canada or Australia.

An old grief coiled and uncoiled inside me. Phong let out a barely suppressed sigh, his hand resting tentatively on my shoulder. I cupped my hand over his. A long sadness defined him. Although it is almost unsayable—we are so far apart from each other—I too know the feeling, though in a different way, and I felt myself oddly bound to him.

There is no cosmic perch from which to watch and judge, and I too have mourned for a world that is vanishing or already gone. Our true business has been with the past. But there before me stood this broken man. "Phong," I muttered. He heard me call his name. I looked into his eyes and saw a man at the desultory end of his life, going over what should have been done differently and wishing perhaps for the proverbial second chance, to re-create the past for the present. Despite our different paths, we are here, bereaved and together, facing the essential elements of life in our final days. Despite our divergent and disjointed lives, they meet in the here and now, in a single point of pathos, inside this bleak nursing home.

For the first time, I understood his need to be truly seen and to be touched and forgiven. Its single-mindedness heightened my sense of life's surprises and its unending mutability. Who among us can truly know why we are moved to do what we do and why we are moved to undo it?

Life's flow, like an arpeggio of notes whose combination is seemingly limitless, lies beyond our grasp.

Phong was still standing mournfully by my bed, his metallic leg creaking. I felt no anger, only a radiating calm, like a wide-open lotus flower that rises from the mud and unfolds petals that float reassuringly on the water's surface.

I knew right then that I was confronted with two irreducible possibilities, each equally strong but mutually diverging. I could obdurately redouble the weight of our past, or I could release it. I could construct and fashion something different out of what we have been given. I trembled inside. Old images churned in my head. There was Phong in Hue that fleeting moment when he stepped on the mine and I did not. A whisper of a doubt had made me stop moving. I halted but did not warn him. Why, I still wonder to this day. Could I have alerted him? Inside this deep and unfathomable patterning of time, a decision one moment changes the landscape the next.

As Phong sat here beside my bed so many years later, holding me inside his gaze, our deep ties suspended between the banal and the profound, I gave him what he sought. I opted for a resumption of normal existence devoid of howling recriminations and judgments. The moment I tipped toward one, the possibility of the other vanished.

He touched my hand. He was giving me the power to forgive or not forgive him. I closed my eyes and nodded. He knew I had seen into his depths. And that in so seeing him, I did not turn away. Yielding to faith, I gave him the gift of acknowledgment instead. And just like that, almost simultaneously, I felt it too, as if the gift were equally mine.

We will go our separate ways, but for now, in the lowering light, he remained by my bedside. And for once, I look not forward but deeply inward. I am nothing as simple as happy but I am here, inhabiting fully this moment in which I am unburdened at last.

# 27

## *Nocturnes*

### BAO, 2006

It is one week after Uncle Number Two's visit. Mai and I are with our father. The dimmer switch in the room is turned low. I hear his phlegmy breaths and gasps for air.

We put on Chopin for him. In the beginning, the notes are soft and subtle and like water, rippling in cross rhythms with the right hand playing semiquavers against the left's fluent triplets. The arpeggios console and haunt, pulling the gathering shade of evening into a room already filled with much reflection.

Our father is lying demurely curled under the blanket, but I can tell he is following these most aching and ethereal of notes. Those played by the right hand carry the melodious but more punctuated tune. Those played by the left hand carry the profound inner ellipses rippling ever so softly, barely audible though ever present and ever felt. His fingers grip the sheet. Occasionally he lifts his hands when the music swells, as if to feel the pleasure in his fingers. He lets out a murmur. His mouth turns and makes a smile as he drifts into a deep sleep. The lamp at his bedside casts a benevolent glow.

Mai pulls her chair close to the light and reads papers from her briefcase. She looks at him warmly once it is clear to her he has fallen asleep.

At the moment when dusk shifts into the twilight of evening, everything, even the space between objects, is subtly transformed. I feel the surface of my skin come alive. I touch him and feel an immediate response—despite his heavy eyelids, his eyes pop open and he gives me a purposeful look.

He utters a single word. Quy.

Of course.

With superstitious dread, I reach for his hand. His face registers my presence as he turns over his palm to receive mine. His body is briefly unsettled by a momentary twinge and then he is gone.

I stay seated, his hand still in mine. I can feel a single, continuing squeeze pressed against my palm.

Just a few days ago, when Mai and I arrived, he had coyly whispered, "I want to go." Mai had thought he was referring to some local destination. But after so many hours listening to him at his bedside, I knew what he meant.

But still my face dropped. He had added a quick, conciliatory corrective—"I am ready"—to soften the message, removing it from the realm of will and desire.

"I have lived a long life," he later said. Unlike my sister's, his departure will be as nature intended.

I look around. His belongings are here, outlasting him. The paratrooper's red beret is close by, within easy reach on the night table. I keep quiet and think of his death as something that occupies only a narrow band. I remember his life instead, with its boundless variations that are undepleted by death.

Mai is still there, oblivious, reading in a pool of light. Visitors in adjoining rooms come and go. A phone rings. A voice whispers into a cupped receiver. Shoes shuffle in the hallway. A bucket scrapes against the floor outside and then a mop is pushed here and there. His death hasn't been registered yet. It is not a surprise, yet the irrevocable loss leaves me distressed. When the nursing home discovers what has happened, the institutional particulars of death—paperwork, death certificates, funeral details—will overshadow our private sorrow.

In a box hidden under his bed are piles of envelopes, organized in reverse chronological order. Mai reaches for the first pack, held together by a rubber band. The top envelope is dated 2006 and postmarked from a city in New York.

"I don't understand," she says softly. She flips through the others, all identically marked. For a moment she does not recognize the name, despite its familiarity. John Clifford. It is Cliff, of course. As a child, we heard him referred to only as Cliff. There was no need for a last name. When we arrived in America years later and she searched for him, the matter of the missing last name kept her from finding him. Our father had rebuffed repeated inquiries.

But Cliff has been within reach all along. For years he has apparently been sending these envelopes to our father. For years our father has hidden this fact from Mai and me. And yet his baffling absence has been no absence at all.

There is one check inside each envelope, every one uncashed. Still, the checks kept coming. Offers and rejections exchanged month after month. Sometimes there is a note attached to the check, written with a forced breeziness that makes it all the more poignant. On a piece of neatly folded paper, he wrote, "Would be nice to see you and catch up," "Call when you can," or "It has been a long time." For years, then, it is our father who has maintained our separation.

Until a few months ago, that is. Amid the piles of uncashed checks, there is an index card with a brief note addressed to our father that makes my stomach lurch. "To my dear friend, As you requested, here is a check for $30,000." I recognize Cliff's handwriting from the other letters he sent our father. Mai stretches her back. She is groping for answers. I imagine what might have happened. With willed composure, our father, normally distant and pursed-lipped, had to approach his old, long-abandoned friend to ask for money to give to Aunt An. My throat feels parched and raw. The wonder of it. The heavy seesaw of life, tipping this way, then that. Mai's grave bearing shows that she too is astonished by this discovery.

Of course, I think to myself. Our father shares a long history with Aunt An and understands who she is to us all, here in this country. She has been for me the mother I lost so many years ago.

Of course we will do whatever we can, Mai and I, to continue to help Aunt An, especially now that our father has passed away.

When she finds our father's life insurance policy in another box, we both know, our heart rising, that we will turn the proceeds over to Aunt An. For the first time in a while, I feel a cumbersome affinity with Mai.

It is a complicated feeling, threaded in a simultaneous fusion and fission. The heavy, surly grayness that keeps me separated from her, the two of us colliding and commingling but each of us essentially splintered from and hostile to the other, has lifted momentarily. The space between us closes up a bit.

I am across a great distance lurching toward her. I watch as she approaches Mrs. An, who is more wounded by our father's death than I had thought possible. Her eyes are ringed by sadness. She is at the nurses' aides' station, poring over medical notebooks and records.

"Aunt An," Mai says. I will take my turn as well but for now I let her start the conversation.

Aunt An looks up in a daze. She turns slightly, offering us a glimpse of her sallow profile. She intuits that there is a serious conversation about to ensue. She puts down her pen and gives Mai her attention. "My father was worried about your situation before he died. It is clear that he wanted you to be all right. Your well-being mattered much to him."

Aunt An's face, overlaid with worries, softens. "And his to me," she says. "I cared for him as well as I could. I tried to make him comfortable."

Mai nods. I want to have my say too. I push her aside and take Aunt An's elbow for emphasis. "My father had a life insurance policy. Once I collect on it, I will turn the proceeds over to you," I explain. My hoarse voice identifies me to her. She looks at *me*. I am certain she can tell I am Bao. I use concepts—Vietnamese concepts—that Mai would not invoke. *"Mang on,"* I say. "Wearing a debt." The family owes Aunt An so much for what she has done for Father. I enumerate everything she did for him, and in so doing, let her know that I remember. "You washed him. You fed him. You comforted him. Take it with the family's gratitude. Take it for your son," I insist. *"Lam on,"* meaning "please," but not just please. *Lam on* means make good karma and take it. The Vietnamese implication is that she would be doing us a favor by allowing us to give her the money and, in the process, giving us an opportunity to create positive karma for ourselves.

Aunt An is touched but I see that she doesn't think this is right. To soften her reluctance, I put the offer in purely Vietnamese terms. As the child of my father, I am turning the money over to her for what she did for him. As the mother of her own child, she will take the money for his sake. There is no shame. Only following a path, a virtuous cycle.

"I know your son has had problems," I say as I put my arms around her. "Give yourself a cushion so you can help him."

At last Aunt An speaks. We are holding hands. Tears blur her face and mine. We walk to Father's still unoccupied room. Aunt An sobs and I can make out only part of what she is saying. "He has been through so much. He's lost and needs to set himself straight." Touched by Mai's (and my) insistence, Aunt An opens up. The armored demeanor softens. "Bad men were after him. I had to have the *hui* money first," she tearfully confesses. "They carried guns. Made threats."

We cluster around Father's bed as if he were still here.

"I will show you where to get him help." Mai reemerges and intervenes. I am grateful she has a steady salary, a law degree, and no debt. I know what she has been thinking. She commiserates. But more than that, she will cut through the patchwork emotions and take it upon herself to deal with the business of the *hui.* She says, tentatively, "If you are comfortable with it, I can talk to Mrs. Chi also. She should not malign you and your son to others."

Aunt An lifts her face and presents a look of bafflement, as if to ask, "What can you do?"

Aunt An puts a restraining hand on Mai's wrist but Mai continues with gentle determination. "Aunt An, please listen. Of course no one can change what Mrs. Chi and the *hui* gang think but we can do something about what they say about you. They've smeared you and you've been so hurt."

Her voice has taken on a sanctioned, professional tone. She explains that spreading untruths about someone can serve as grounds for a slander lawsuit. Aunt An has made all her *hui* payments on time, so saying otherwise is an untruth.

Aunt An is surprised that gossip, long a culturally freighted part of the *hui,* meant to keep members in line, can actually be a legally recognized wrong. A tort, Mai explains with authority. Aunt An has the right to sue for slander and intentional infliction of emotional distress.

Aunt An, wide-eyed and fearing the language of law and its promises of rights, gasps. "Don't worry. You don't actually have to sue. But a hint that you might will be enough to make Mrs. Chi stop," Mai declares.

Aunt An gulps and then nods blearily. "I won't worry," she says. She resettles herself and gives me a long, slow motherly embrace as a soft light shines through the uncurtained window.

As far as our father's death is concerned, we keep everything simple. He had never been a man prone to pomp and circumstance. But simplicity certainly can accommodate the presence of an old friend. That Cliff can be reached so easily startles me. Uncle Number Two merely picked up the phone and told him of our father's death. Of course he would come immediately, on the next flight out. He had been wrongly pushed onto the margins and at the first invitation he will return to the center.

He arrives at our apartment several minutes early. When Mai opens the door, he moves toward her and gives her a big warm hug. The connection from so many years ago catches and holds. His eyes squeeze shut. For a moment it is as if we are all irrevocably back in another time. Cliff has returned, and he is the fixed point we can revolve around. Cliff is here, luxuriating in our presence, imposing order, and I almost expect our mother too to materialize beside him, where she used to be.

I am haunted by that absence even now. A person arriving reminds me of someone who is not. There is no pure sensation, only an overlapping, mingled one.

"You have grown. It has been a long time." He smiles. He is in much better health than our father was before his death. Age has not shrunken him. He has retained his soldierly bearing. His hair has turned white, but the green in his eyes has only deepened. Thirty years later, with surprising agility, he has returned—an edifice of our imagination.

"Quite a long time," he says, repeating the obvious. "But I can still see the old you."

He and Mai move to the living room and sit shoulder to shoulder on the sofa, held together in a soft, bluish light.

"Cliff," she says. She calls him by his name. Something opens up between them, in a vague, nascent way, but enough to illuminate their togetherness. "Why did it take so long?"

"Your father had his reasons," Cliff answers. He leans back and loosens his tie. He is apologetic. He is hurt. He wants to make sense of the lapse but he does not want to blame. "I did come down to see him while you were in school once. He asked me not to make any more contact. Especially not with you."

"But why?"

Cliff nods. "He wanted to protect you. So you could make a new life and not be tangled up in the past."

"But he considered you a friend," Mai insists.

A silence passes. "Friendship can be complicated."

He does not say what I have always suspected, that his presence reminds our father of insufficiency and defeat. And betrayal. And broken promises.

For her part, Mai is unsure how far she wants to venture into "complicated" territory. She points to the arrangement of buns and rolls she has ordered from a Vietnamese restaurant and then goes to the refrigerator to get him a cold "33" beer. She takes a deep breath. "Do you think . . . ?" She trails off and rephrases the question. "Why do you think it was complicated?"

She feels an inner tug that is strong and dogged. I feel the same.

"Your sister's death made it complicated."

Mai simply nods as if she understands. In this most pivotal of moments, Mai is silent, her appearance controlled, and her calm is impregnable. I want her to push against the mundanity of their words, to probe. I try to thread my way through her thoughts.

"And she turned to *you*," Mai finally says. I am prompting her on. This is a fact but it has lived quietly in her. I see our mother on a hammock, in a sphere neither Cecile nor I could reach. I see her somewhere else as I make myself small and hide in a jar during Tet. I see her eating crabs with Cliff on our terrace. She did not just turn away from us but toward someone else.

I see a brief faltering but it quickly passes. "A parent does not survive the loss of a child. She turned to me, yes, but you probably don't know that I too lost a daughter. She died when she was seven."

Mai gasps. "I am so sorry," she says. She takes his hand in a gesture of sympathy. But a pressure builds in my chest. Mai is allowing herself to be comforted by meekness. I want to know why our mother turned away from us. Rage crackles in me even as tears well up in my eyes.

Mai smiles, head tipped back, as if she fully understands and has little stake left in the conversation. She wants to close off the subject of our mother. Tensely, I wait to hear more about our mother and the heartbreaks they shared. But they move on as if this topic were too volatile or, worse, merely an anecdote, meriting no additional reflection or comment. There is the indistinct but audible murmur of this and that. Mai's tone is particularly incurious. They are engaged in a catechism of polite questions and answers that can only be an insufficient accounting of the past.

They are indifferent to my private unease.

At the first forking of a faint memory, I feel something inflate and then move slowly through the gloom that is mine. As always, the truth returns, exerting a great downward pressure against my chest. Despite the surface composure, memories race inside my head, making their claims and counterclaims on my consciousness. Every image is replayed backward. The sharp crack of a gun bleeds into a pool of blood. I touch it, feeling the burned steel against my palm. James falls. I hear again and again the click of the trigger, metal pulled back against metal and released. I crouch in the jar, my inert body pressed fully against Mai. A kite, barely stirring, hides behind a chimney. I can see our mother disappear into the distance almost beyond my field of vision, searching for the dead daughter she loves. It does not help that I look like my sister. It can be confusing for her. "Khanh, Khanh," she calls. Her back, long and narrow, walks away from me and heads for the door. I see it all, each needling detail. It is indeed a tattered composition remapping itself on the neural circuitry of my brain.

We are on the sofa, in front of the sliding balcony door. I see Cliff's face and mine reflected in the glass. The words come out suddenly, before I realize what I'm saying. "Cliff," I say noncommittally, in a soft, pathetic voice. "Cliff," I repeat with a single exhalation. "My mother."

My voice cracks through the meek, querying plea. I want to understand. But only those two words come and I am suddenly overtaken by a furious remorse.

Cliff becomes quiet, his eyes watching me with unease. "You want to talk? I wasn't sure you'd want me to," he says.

I nod. I am full of dread. I push down Mai and keep her submerged. "Yes," I say, prompting him forth.

Cliff clears his throat and opens another bottle of beer. When he finally speaks his voice is soft, barely audible above the hum of kitchen appliances.

"Your mother suffered quietly and privately," he says. "I would never tell you this while your father was alive." He touches my hair. I look away. "Your father owed his life to your mother. Did you know that?"

Our father owed his life to Uncle Number Two, but I am sensing that this fact is also linked somehow to our mother. Our father has told the story many times. In the middle of a ruthless rebellion that enveloped our country that day in November 1963, it was Uncle Number Two who managed to protect his friend from his fellow conspirators. He had looked the coup leaders in the eye and insisted on the sanctity of personal friendship.

I know that story.

"Many men were in love with your mother. Or coveted her," Cliff says matter-of-factly.

There is suddenly a memory I cannot quite place. It did not belong to me originally but has over the years become mine. Our mother was sitting at a table with Uncle Number Two. There were platters of pastry and a jug of salted lemonade. There was a whispered fight about something. Uncle was pacing, gesticulating, and sighing. He was cajoling, his eyes tearing, believing that ultimately she would answer his question if he made himself relentlessly intrusive.

Uncle Number Two was in love with our mother.

As if he can read my mind, Cliff says, "Everyone knew Phong loved her. Though he was not the only one." He gives me an embarrassed laugh. "But she truly loved only one man. Did you know that?" He looks at me beseechingly.

I nod, less from certainty than perhaps from a wish that it were so.

Cliff hesitates, then continues. "Phong pled with his superiors to save your father. I'm sure you know that."

"Why did he risk so much?" I ask.

Cliff answers abruptly. "For love, of course. A man does what he does for love. Love provides a plausible excuse for anything. Even for behaving badly. Inappropriately. As Phong did, so he could get himself closer to her."

"Cliff," I say. That, and nothing more.

He knows I am waiting even if I don't know what it is I am waiting for. He shakes his head and takes a deep swallow of his beer. He is disappearing into the past, into love. "She suffered," he repeats what he already said. "She certainly suffered. And when your father withdrew, she suffered even more."

Something slips. It's just those words. I feel a fierce baring of fangs. Though I cannot yet bring myself to contradict him, I feel an instinctive need to defend our father who, even through the quiet sadness that enveloped him, managed to take care of us.

A hard wall falls between Cliff and me.

"She left *us*," I say with exaggerated force, my heart rising to meet the impending confrontation. And before I know that such words can come out of my mouth, I hear myself tell Cliff, "I hate her." Those three words, uttered with appropriate reproach and outrage, mark a turning point. I know these mood reversals, the combativeness that accompanies them, and the voluptuous release that follows. Love and hate—cleaved into two even halves. I now cling freely to the more burdensome, wholly unmediated portion. Hate. I feel it completely. It is a mutinous rage with no possibility of reconciliation.

Cliff's face is drained of color and he looks at me with unfaltering disapproval. But I am too afflicted to care.

"I hate her," I say again. The words reverberate in me, raw, angry, and sacrilegious. One tear gathers, then another, pooling inside my eyes.

"She saved your father," he says firmly.

"I thought you said Uncle Phong saved him."

"Your mother did. She ... gave herself to Phong. Neither your mother nor father was able to survive this act."

A sob heaves out of me. I manage but one word. "No. No," I say again, more forcefully. Cliff places a restraining hand on mine.

"No," I repeat, this time in a guttural shout. He removes his hand and retreats into himself, looking exhausted and battered.

A sinking feeling, mixed with the sullen thrill of anger, settles in the pit of my stomach. My hand swings upward in one fluent motion with my back arched backward for leverage. I throw the beer bottle against the wall, then cover my head with my arms. Shards of glass scatter on the floor. The clouds of Tet loom above us and the room is sucked into an explosion of orange that glows above. Panic races through me. Cliff scuttles forward as if to catch a falling object, throwing himself over me like a protective blanket. His hand clutches my chin. I swipe at him, resisting his touch. I feel an index finger pull me staunchly by the jaw so that my face meets his. He struggles to pry my hair from the iron-fisted grip of my fingers. "It's okay," he says. "Mai," he calls. Though I did not know it, I have drawn blood. The scratch marks on my neck are red and damp. I aim to follow fury to the very place where destruction began. I hear the smallest whisper thrumming in my ears. "It is all right, it is all right," the voice says.

It is not our mother's voice. It is Cliff's voice, mixed with another person's—mine. I too try to reassure. It is all right, it is all right, I say to Cecile. Again there is Cecile's soundless, intermittent crying. And continuously ringing in my ears are Mai's grumbles and reproaches. She is still blaming me for James's death. My hand clenches into a fist and, just like that, with demented fury, I unleash a succulent whack against her stomach.

Cliff fumbles to collect himself. Large hands grab me by the wrists, restraining me. We are there together, as if we had arrived at a truce, as he holds me in his arms. He keeps me there and refuses to let me go. His touch calms me, ushering in the slow but palpable return of my sanity.

Cliff is explaining what I suspect troubled our father. "Phong might have pled and begged whoever was in charge. But he did it because your mother did what he wanted," he says. "And she paid dearly for it."

"My father," I say. I try to produce a conventional conversational tone. I wish to defend him against I am not sure what.

Cliff interposes. "Your father, yes, suffered too. He tortured himself, she said, trying to figure everything out." He pauses. His voice is overcome with sadness. "She entered into a relationship with Phong, who promised to use his influence with the coup leaders to spare your father."

From the look on his face I know he is speaking the truth. I am beginning to see the pieces come together, as if transformed by the click of a kaleidoscope. I see a child standing on tiptoe listening to her mother and a family friend talk. They are upset. The man, who is an incessant presence, turns sour and surly. Perhaps after much coaxing he is trying to pull an agreement out of the woman. Knowing what I know now, I wonder if it was perhaps an agreement to turn the one-time bargain into a continuing affair.

"Your mother loved you," Cliff tells me. He goes on about the various conspiracies and convolutions of 1963.

I am not soothed. At the most pivotal of moments, she left and turned to someone else and worst of all she opted against leaving with us in 1975.

"She stayed behind and left us to go off by ourselves," I say wearily. "She left him."

Cliff touches my arm and sits back as he slowly retracts from me. I think he is preparing to retreat before the threat of another outbreak. He does not want to provoke me.

Our mother did abandon us. It *was* unreasonable and wrong. And here we are, still inside the lingering spirit of this abandonment. All these years later this banishment and our father's death only reinforces the fact of our aloneness.

I repeat to myself, *We are alone,* and I feel the full consequence of those overlapping words inside my very being.

As if he can hear my thoughts, Cliff says, "You are *not* alone." He is emphatic as he gathers me against him in remembered togetherness.

The simplicity of his answer touches me. Cliff examines the purple redness on my neck and shakes his head. He runs his fingers against the patch of flesh that is chafed and bruised. I have been revealed, and the shame of it brings another stream of tears to my face.

Cliff, though, normalizes every anomaly with a brief, practical suggestion. "A little dab of Vaseline might soothe," he says. And then, after a pause, "I talked to your father before he died. I think you should know that."

I freeze and wait. "You wrote him a large check," I say. "I found the note you wrote him in a box under his bed."

Cliff looks sideways and then at me. "I only wish he had included me earlier. I wish our friendship could have continued. As far as the check was concerned, he called me and said he needed money but wouldn't tell me why. Of course I didn't even ask. I knew it must have been important if he felt he had to turn to me."

"Weren't you surprised you heard from him out of the blue?"

"I'd imagined the day so many times that when it happened, it felt natural," Cliff answers. "The links one forges in life aren't so easily undone. Especially the kinds I had with your father. I had faith in that." His eyes widen. He reaches over and holds my hand. "Listen, what I want to tell you has nothing to do with the check. It's far more important.

"Don't think you are all alone. You are not alone. And your mother had very good reason for staying behind. As you've gone through his papers, you know that I've been writing to your father for years. He wrote back once and only once, telling me to leave him alone. But I didn't give up. And in the last six months, I heard from him not once, but twice.

"It took some time figuring out where you were after 1975. You have always been on my mind. I want you to know that your parents' friend did not just disappear from your life. Before I left, I made one of my closest aides in Saigon promise me he would help get you out. He was in the unit in charge of evacuating Saigon and he ordered all his men to be on the lookout for you and your father. I got the report from him that you and your father had boarded one of the last helicopters to leave. But I had no news about your mother. I made several telephone calls and found out that your father was in Fort Indiantown Gap and from there I learned you had moved to Virginia."

He puts out a tense, tremulous laugh. I see his eyes focus intensely on mine. Instinctively, I lower my gaze and wait for him to continue. "Your father said in that first letter that your mother had decided not to leave. And that he had no way of finding out what was happening to her back in Saigon. And then he ended the letter by asking me to not write him again. I struggled to find a way to put things right with him, but he was intent on shutting himself off."

He stops and puts his hands on my shoulders. "After thirty years of absence, of course your father contacting me was a surprise. And not a surprise. His voice was weak but clear. He told me your mother was pregnant in 1975 and the child was mine. Just like that, very matter-of-factly. Can you imagine how I felt? Probably not." He shakes his head in doubt. "Of course I wanted to protest my innocence. I never wanted your father to know this, although I suspected he knew all along. I never wanted anyone to know this. At the same time I also wanted to thank him for calling and letting me know. 'I thought you would want to know,' was what he said to me. And I told him I did."

"I loved your mother," he declares earnestly.

"Did she love you?" I ask.

"To be honest," he answers obligingly, "if she did, it's because I loved her." He jabs his finger at his own chest. "Your father and I had gone on a dangerous operation together in Cambodia, and when he was under fire, I did what I could to ensure he was safe." He smiles self-consciously. "I downplayed it. I told your parents it was just a matter of military duty. But the truth is, I did it for her. By pure instinct. I didn't want her to suffer another death of a loved one. I think she knew it."

"I know the story. My father told me that you risked your life," I interrupt.

"Whatever it was, your mother was very touched by it. We'd both sacrificed something of ourselves for someone else. On that level, she understood me. And turned to me. And who could have ever predicted that she would get pregnant at her age and we would have a child together." He turns away from me, looking into space. He fidgets. I see his back quiver and only then am I aware that he is crying. "Your mother loved you very much. Never doubt it."

I still can only guess at what might have happened years ago to our mother. Still, with this news, I can cling to the gentle swell of a new order: Our mother did not behave capriciously, or hard-heartedly. She was flawed but not heartless. We were not callously abandoned. Cliff tells me that although the whereabouts of my sister are not known, he believes she is still somewhere in Saigon. A part of us is out there, somewhere, waiting for a reunion.

"I hadn't planned to tell you any of this," he says. "But you wanted to know and I think it will do you good." He pauses, then asks, "What will you do now?"

"I will take him home," I say. My answer surprises me. I hadn't known it until now, but once voiced, it seems like the most natural thing in the world—to take him home. To the place where a part of our mother still is.

"Home," Cliff says with visible emotion as he smooths a stray hair from my face.

We remain together on the sofa through the evening's pallor, displaced and disassembled. I cannot help but look at him with a mingled sense of pleasure and surprise. The same thought must run through him too. "So this is who you've become," he says several times. He turns teary when I tell him what Uncle Number Two told us about our mother. We pass the time bringing each other indulgently up to date about the events of our lives. His sons have married and have children of their own. His wife died years ago.

We eat, drink, and surf the television channels. Through long moments of enveloping silence, I am filled with memories of our time together in Cholon. And I am certain the same memories inhabit him.

# 28
## *Knowing*
### MAI, 2006

I am back in the country where I was born.

If one measures the depth of love by the persistence of sorrow following love's separation or loss, then I can say I truly love this place. And for the Vietnamese, indeed that is how love is weighed and judged, by a lifetime of grief. Loving is bound up with suffering. I grew up with stories about pain, love, and fidelity. A woman waits for her warrior husband to come home. She carries her child to the top of a mountain so she can witness his return from the summit's peak. Through heat and rain, she waits, until she becomes a rock, eternally frozen in time. In matters of the heart, we persevere and endure, even in the face of hopelessness.

For years, when it was morning in Virginia, my mind drifted steadfastly twelve hours forward to evening in Cholon, where every unpretentious detail of life over there can be rehearsed with habitual affection, reimagined with quotidian particularity. It is as if I remain aligned somehow with a different time zone, subjunctive and contingent. Cholon became phantomlike, a childhood city lovingly buffed in my imagination to a perpetually lustrous glow. In this habit, I found both pain and its antidote—solace.

And now I am here as if by magical transport. Though it feels instantaneous and magical only because I took a sleeping pill on the plane. When I arrived in the evening, Tan Son Nhat Airport seemed unreal, with its runways spilling theatrically over the land and its rows of lights shining a path that glowed as if illuminated from within. As the plane made its descent, tracing a downward arc across an ebony-dark landscape lit by the hypnotic allure of starry pinpricks, I was barely awake. From above, the city was but a blur of color that lovingly came into focus only as the plane began tipping its wings. When the plane landed, I felt as if Saigon had been willed into unlikely existence by an extravagant act of faith—mine.

The next morning I get ready to venture into the streets. I find myself reflexively studying the faces of people around me, even though I fully realize the improbabilities associated with the exercise. It might be nothing more than poetic conceit, but I tell myself I will recognize her soul the moment I am in her vicinity. And so I go on staring at features, searching for signs of the Eurasian mix. One of these young women might be our mother's lost child.

The city itself has been resurrected and revived, after its long decline. People are now allowed to buy and sell. Cars and motorbikes rev their engines and honk their horns as they swerve through the vertiginous Saigon traffic. Tourists sip coffee at outdoor cafés and luxuriate in the delicately mannered, colonial atmosphere of Old World hotels.

Despite the familiar undertow, everything has been altered by the vagaries of fate and the curse of defeat. It is still Saigon. But my infatuation with it is mingled with suspicion. There is the old Rex Hotel and the Brodard Café where we used to have ice cream served in pineapple and coconut shells. There is the French Opera House. For all their anti-colonial rhetoric, the Communist regime has preserved everything French. I look around, wanting to be overtaken by nostalgia.

I wonder what can be won back from the jolts and bends of loss. The black, stolid statue dedicated to the South Vietnamese soldier and sanctified has been torn down. A new flag, not yellow with three red stripes but red with a five-pointed star eerily reminiscent of China's flag, now flies above the old French Opera House and every other public building. I am on Tu Do Street. I cannot bear to call it by its new name, Dong Khoi. This is where our parents used to take my sister and me for early

evening strolls through the boulevards of venerable villas and old tamarind trees. But the place has turned falsely familiar.

*It is exactly as it was*—this is what people like me want very much to
tell themselves when they return home. But this is not the case. Thirty
years after the war's end, the city is visited daily by the love-struck Viet
Kieu, the overseas Vietnamese who, like me, are perpetually filled with
unrequited longing. We have embarked on our trips in search of a time
and place that no longer exists. We have carried our lives here from the
other side of the earth. We want to take a lungful of air and fall in love.
And we are clearly not ready to adjust our expectations to meet this
radically different reality.

If it were not for the hard currency—U.S. dollars—we bring with
us, we wouldn't even be welcome here. This is no longer my city. It is no
longer my inheritance.

I keep a strict accounting of my activities. I take care to avoid raw
vegetables for fear of getting sick. I drink only bottled water and even
then I check to make sure the thermoplastic sheet hasn't been broken
and surreptitiously resealed. I prefer water with fizz—the hiss and
crackle produced when the bottle is opened will guarantee that it hasn't
been tampered with. I ignore the call of street vendors hawking steamed
crepes served in bamboo bowls. *"Baaaannnhhhh cuuuoooon,"* an elderly
woman beckons in a long-drawn-out drawl as she drifts by. I shy away,
cast my eyes downward, stumbling past her, and I feel a quick tumult of
disapproval moving inside me.

I know it is Bao, disappointed that I have returned home only to
behave the way an ordinary stranger to the city would. Over the years
of shadow dances, I have managed to get a sense of her mood. Right
now she is feeling almost primal excitement. Home at last, she makes
peace with Vietnam as it is.

I am surprised that since my return to Saigon, Bao's slippage into
my reality has been more frequent. I have, more than ever, felt her
thumping presence and the push of her ravenous will. It is as if the
secret tangle of her existence has escaped from the subterranean darkness, shooting life outward. She is at home and so she exerts herself
fully here. A part of me feels what she feels—a humming exhilaration
that vibrates as if the atoms were aligned and alive.

Just a few hours ago I found myself in a network of unpaved alleys rutted with dry, brackish mud. I was emerging, with unfolding exactness but a fraction off center, from a blackout—many minutes, perhaps hours, of lost time—in which Bao customarily takes over and I lose consciousness. Bao must have taken charge and made a foray into a neighborhood I would never have ventured into on my own. Around us were modest structures of unfinished plywood and corrugated tin that randomly doubled as houses and makeshift restaurants. Men and women with children were sitting on short wooden stools, hunched over long tables covered by smudged plastic tablecloths. The air was permeated with the pungent scent of charred meat, fried scallions, dripping fat, and chopped lemongrass. A man lit his cigarette. The sudden flare of his match emitted a phosphorescent glow. A stray dog sniffed through the garbage and howled. I suddenly felt feeble, caught inside the agitation and chaos merging and converging within me. Bao looked at me with the pure bafflement and practiced disdain of her assessing eyes.

I knew, of course, that she did not like me.

A melodic voice floated from an open window nearby. A woman was singing a simple lullaby. It was a swelling, blossoming moment for Bao. Her feelings coursed through me, expanding into something arching and enormous. Here, in Saigon, inside this transport of Bao's intense emotions, it still might be possible for me to absorb Bao's fervency. I might even feel her ardor and claim the fullness of the moment as mine.

I am suddenly seized by a thought: To truly discover myself here, I must hang on to Bao. I keep going despite the fear of relapse. Both of us are claiming the moment. It is a big task, managing and modulating one's expectations. For the first time in more than thirty years I am riding on her optimism. I am filled with a large, booming sense of anticipation.

So I hail a taxi. I hold on to myself and put myself in full alert mode. The air smells of heat. Smoke rises from the parched tar on the road. Around us, motorcycles surge and shudder, shifting gears. I am in teeming, battered Cholon. There is Ngo Quyen Street. The taxi edges through a dismembered line of traffic and makes a slow-paced turn onto my street. The sight of it through the car window fills me with a soothing warmth. I crane my neck, trying to feel the old moorings. There is much unburdening and resolving left to do, even in a place that is barely recognizable. The possibility for salvage remains, even when the slippage is great and the framing skewed. The entire body remembers.

I feel her jazzed-up emotions plainly, without letting them displace my own perceptions and expectations. I get out and walk about, eavesdropping on this new far-flung life that is shimmering into place. I know this diesel-scented air and the hawkers and peddlers who do commerce in the pulsing energy and bustling chaos of Chinatown. I know the crisscrossing roads where our mother used to drive around in her Peugeot. I know the confined spaces between tight alleyways, the five-spice powder and other odors emanating from sidewalk stalls. I am walking past the corner where James's encampment once stood. Now it houses a narrow three-story villa with a disconsolate sign dressed up in gilt letters advertising lodging. This is the street my sister and I roamed. A thousand new possibilities could have occurred here. Instead the future was foreclosed in one quicksand moment.

I realize that I am but a few steps away from a house that is no longer there. I cannot even locate the spot where it once stood. French-era hotels and the Opera House are preserved but everything else has been demolished to make way for the new. Still, I step up to that imaginary spot where the future once held little threat. I look at the surrounding space with proprietary wonder and ascendant hope, searching for the afterimage of life as I once knew it. I imagine a little black mynah bird flying about, swiping its wings, black eyes peering, yellow beak searching and poking. My head swivels, as if to catch sight of shiny black feathers dancing nearby.

My sister might be standing nearby with her notebook, an angel without a shadow. The mango tree might have been here, frail and muted, or over there, its leaves moist and green. The star fruit tree could have been somewhere next to it. I am both restless and anchored, touched and alienated, present and invisible.

Droplets of water fall from the treetops. The clouds are swollen and flannel gray, beautiful and awful. The sky darkens and glistens, signaling the imminence of short but heavy downpours. I realize we are at the peak of the monsoon season. Under the threat of rain, footsteps quicken. Engines spurt and rev. A car nearby bolts and squeals inside a puff of tire smoke. Headlights glow pale and jaundiced in the accumulating haze. Plastic sheets are draped over heads and shoulders.

Quickly, I seek shelter under the nearest eaves, still trying to determine the approximate location of our house. All the landmarks that I would normally use to calculate its whereabouts are themselves gone. I stand there, staring, waiting to see if our old life can somehow return to its original shape.

Before I know it, the sky opens and it pours, just as it did when my sister and I played on this street. With the rain, new life, plucky and eager, is unsprung. Little children peel off their clothes and run open-mouthed onto the sidewalks into the drumming downpour. Sheets of silken water pour from gutters and eaves and produce a deafening sound that vivifies and overwhelms. I remember how it was on that fateful day. Children shrieked. Rain poured, overwhelming the roof spout. A few hours later, there was the long-drawn-out instance of momentary indecision as our parents' car slowed down beside us.

I hear a voice, not mine, but another, inside mine, calling out for forgiveness. In my mind I see James, our Chinese grandmother, and my sister as we walk back from our illegitimate outing in the alleyways of Cholon. Now death has followed two of them. Is our Chinese grandmother still alive, eking out a living somewhere in Cholon? The rain continues its downpour, drowning out most sounds. But through it all I hear a barely discernible voice again, floating in the hot quavering whiteness of a summer downpour. It is not just enunciating a name, but rather, calling out to me. It is intimately known to me, like an alternate, parallel voice that bears my soul but has split from me to forge a different path. There it is, to my left, to my right, transparent and lucid, like starlight. I try to hold the moment, to be part of it, to snake my arms around it. I feel it vibrate briefly until it moves on.

I feel Bao's shudders as she steps out, straight into the cascade of water, hoping to catch the voice in her hands, but the moment she moves, it vanishes. I stand still, watching, immobile, oblivious to the water that washes over me. I am drenched but I seek no shelter. Instead, like Bao, I too lean into the rain and allow myself the opportunity to catch up with the buildup of emotions. Bao's shoulders heave—a sight that springs a rush of tenderness in me.

Our lives of separateness seem to be disintegrating here. For a few moments I am inside her gravitational field. We are together in a double loop of shared consciousness, hermetically sealed from the world. I can feel, down at the molecular level, what she feels, a deep condensed grief that seems unbounded.

I am eating pho at Pho 24, a few blocks from the hotel, enjoying the rich broth, delicately balanced with the right mix of beef bone, charred onion, roasted ginger, star anise, black cardamom, coriander, fennel, and clove. The restaurant, part of a franchise, is authentic but also clean and somewhat Westernized. The idea is to bring pho from the world of cheap street food to a more upscale and modern setting.

The local magazine I am reading reports that the "24" refers to the twenty-four ingredients that make up the secret formula. The lawyer in me finds the story behind Pho 24 interesting. I have studied franchise agreements. I am intrigued that there are plans to expand the Pho 24 brand to international markets, beyond those already in the Asia-Pacific region. California, New York City, perhaps? The transfer of intellectual property, the trademark, from East to West?

I read on, flipping the pages absentmindedly as I wait for the food to arrive. A story on the next page about an orphanage catches my attention. The headline states, in bold letters, AMERICAN VETERAN VOLUNTEERS TIME. There he is, the much-beloved American, in khaki pants and a short-sleeved shirt, standing in front of a decrepit building, seemingly transfixed by the crowd of children aligned in a tight circle surrounding him. Despite the graininess of the black-and-white photo, there is something familiar about the American suspended in freeze-frame. According to the article, a group of nuns founded the orphanage and a school that is dedicated to teaching the *bui doi,* "dust of life children," who roam the streets and scavenge garbage dumps. The children learn English and crafts, quilt making and carpentry. Their creations are sold in select shops in the city.

The story lifts my heart. Something tender drifts unintelligibly toward me, the strain of hope against blood. I scan the rest, looking for confirmation of a name my heart already knows. I read on, spasmodically picking up keywords. Veteran. Wounded. Lost years. Returns to Vietnam. New life here.

James Baker. Resurrected. Never dead.

I sit still, my heart thunderous. Apparently, the American has a rigid routine. Every Monday he ventures to open-air markets to buy produce for the cook and then goes to Ben Thanh Market to eat at one of the food stalls and hawk the orphaned children's wares at one of its most heavily trafficked corridors. Every Wednesday and Thursday, he gives two hours of English lessons. And on top of everything, the writer remarks, he spends time making connections with a number of non-government agencies to promote the orphanage.

I am perched on the chair's edge. Is it another James Baker whose name is etched on the Vietnam Veterans Memorial? Can there be another James Baker? Here, in Vietnam?

Later, I Google the name and get pages and pages of search results. Indeed, it is a common name, but the facts are matched up with dates. The man in the photo has the same way of standing. It is James.

The certainty of the knowledge suggests that there is no internal static or dissent. All of us are together and aligned.

We all know it, Cecile and Bao too.

# 29

## *The River Flows but the Ocean Stays*

### BAO, 2006

For Mai, this trip was flawed from the start. But now that she is here, she is beginning to give in to my full range of emotions, to my recriminations and my sadness. Her mood has turned conciliatory and, of course, now hopeful.

It is Monday. We venture to the middle of the city's raucous central market. Where would a mixed-race woman go to make a living? Here, I think, a crowded place filled with vendors and beggars jostling for money and space. That is but a tangential and secondary hope.

Before us is the clock, blunt and massive, that hangs on the external wall of Ben Thanh Market. This is the compass point of downtown Saigon. Tourists, drawn by the weathered flea market's charm, will tolerate the unruly throngs of smooth-talking pushers hawking every object imaginable.

Mai has no intention of buying anything or even window-shopping. Neither do I. There is an urgency inside me. Mai leads the way expectantly. I find myself walking toward the center, as if ushered by the visceral compulsion of memory. I know exactly where to go.

The air smells of the hearty aromas of various soups simmering on stoves. There are rows upon rows of stalls selling fabric, bags, shoes stacked in towers of multicolored, glittering likenesses. The interior is

cloistered and dark, slightly stale, a relentlessly uniform grayness ruptured by only the occasional shafts of natural light that spill through
curtained windows. There are exposed pipes, protruding nails, crude,
mismatched furniture, and wood floors with broken planks. I feel
the flow and rush of pedestrian tourist traffic and the quiet thrill of
haggling.

A child follows me, tugging at my shirt, pleading in monosylla-
bles, her voice gentle and plaintive. A woman stands before her fish display, auctioning off giant lobsters and crabs and deep-sea bass. She is
pointing to the pink flesh of the fish and the finger-sized anchovies.
Next to a basket of catfish, a tangle of pincers, tied by rubber bands,
struggle for forward motion.

I find myself staring at the fishmonger, assessing her facial features
despite the infinitesimal chance that she would be our mother's lost
daughter. Still, even in the random ordering of the world, even against
unimaginable probabilities, fate has managed to rear its head. It is not
impossible. The woman is in her thirties. I study the eyes, the nose,
where the balance of racial mix is most discernible. She senses me
observing her and waves me forth. I hold her gaze and walk away, taking her seaweed odor with me.

Mai and I scan the crowd, our gaze directed in counterpoint at the
foreshortened mix of stalls made from corrugated steel and plywood.
Our habitual sense of distance has broken down—we are together in a
common quest. Everyone is eating, enthusiastically, some squatting,
their haunches practically touching the floor, some on stools, others
firmly ensconced in chairs. It is a serious enterprise here, eating. Loud
voices permeate the market. Mai winds her way through the labyrinth
of stalls and booths illumined by neon tubes mounted from the ceiling.
A man sits on a low footstool sucking marrow from a bone, his head
bent over his plate. Mai stares at him. I know what she is thinking: Bao
too sits and eats exactly that way, squatting, back stooped, face to plate.
Nothing goes to waste when she eats, gristle, fat, collagen, marrow, tendon, or cartilage.

Here in Saigon, she is face-to-face with the rival counterworld that
I inhabit without ambivalence. After more than thirty years in America, I remain wholly and quintessentially Vietnamese, tethered to this
place.

From a measured distance, a man catches my eye. I see broad shoulders and thick, wavy hair that shines. His presence fills the room. I see only his back through a rush of people in the dusty, main hallway. It is hard to say what he looks like from behind. But still, I know.

The man is wearing a cotton ribbed tank top, revealing bare arms and shoulders. Around him, vendors sit on low wooden stools smoothed and beveled by wear. They are hunched over the squat grayness of their own shadows. He is sitting by a stove that hisses blue and yellow flames atop a bed of burned-orange coals. A pot burbles, its lid clanging against the metal. By the smell, I can tell it is a Hue noodle soup, gilded broth, sawtooth herb, lemongrass, tomato, and shrimp paste, with lime, onion, and a madness of hot pepper and garnishes. The vendor, a woman with a crooked grin, throws in a dash of this, a soupçon of that, which produces a version of Hue noodle soup that is uniquely hers. Its richness comes not from fat but from marrow. I cast my eyes on the line of pushcarts, each advertising the chef's specialty: griddled rice cake, vermicelli with minced pork balls and caramelized shallots, green papaya with chicken and shrimp.

Mai too is feeling the pull and push of feelings crowding in her chest, surging and receding. Lured by hope, she has come here after reading the magazine story to search for James. Almost against my volition, I lean against the wall, a respectable distance behind him, and watch. An electric fan rustles cool air about. The man is drinking a beer, laughing at something the vendor said. He is smoking and inhaling deeply as he reaches for a bowl of soup.

The man must have felt our eyes on him. He turns, his face flushed with the full sun and glazed with sweat. He is absolutely himself, in an offhand, handsome way. Everything jams and stalls. I know even before I see.

For years Mai has blamed me for his death. But here he is now, alive, in this single, well-aimed moment among all the unfixed, infinite number of moments in time.

On his arm, immortalized in a cobalt blue tattoo, is the date of our sister's death. That day when God of omnipotent power looked down and did nothing, choosing instead to dispatch salvation to some other select few. I see the date, pixel by pixel, as if it were held in the lens of a digital camera.

He stands and picks up his knapsack. He is turning toward me, and when he sees my face he freezes. I am not sure if he is surprised to see me, or if he takes my appearance, though startling, as something long anticipated.

There is a brief faltering. James stands up, rocks on his feet, and looks quizzically at Mai, cocking his head to one side as he fixes her in his heart and mind. And then he says something and smiles. Eventually I hear: "You look just the same." There are tears in his eyes. His voice is lucid, with a grave undertow. "Mai," he says, with an upward inflection.

Tears well up beneath my eyelids. Mai squeezes her eyes shut. I feel the tremors in her knees. It is James's voice. It is the missing voice, emerging from an acoustical silence. He is here, outside her imagination. She sees him as he is now, a man who appears to be in his midfifties, though he must be older, juxtaposed against his younger self almost forty years before. With that one word, she is pared down and stripped, made not invisible but too visible, seen at last but too much so for comfort.

He calls her name again and again. Somehow he has survived, I keep thinking. That we are both here and alive owes more to luck than to our own judiciousness. I realize he is talking but that one simple thought, that he is alive, cracks and glows and fills my head so completely that I hardly listen to what he is saying.

Mai follows him. They head nowhere in particular. I am surprised that she wants to put her hands on him, on his arm and his face, whether to feel his flesh or to comfort she doesn't know. He interweaves his fingers with hers. They walk calmly to extend the sweetness of the moment, slowing down the rushing world. She lays a finger on his arm to fix his attention on bootleg CDs of Rolling Stones classics. She cannot find the words to fit her feelings. So she tells him she is amazed by the audacious display of counterfeit movies and music in plain sight. She tells him that it must be a violation of Vietnam's obligations under World Trade Organization law and he chuckles.

She wants to say "I thought you died," but the words resist. The spoken word, language, feels awkward, a clumsy attempt at translating untranslatable feelings from a deep emotional well. What matters is the healing presence that being next to him brings. What matters is the fact that he is here. That we are all here. The world that was certified by subtraction is restored for now to its proper balance.

He recounts for Mai the facts of his life, the random trail it has taken. Of course it matters what has happened to him all these years. But it is his mere presence that I am drawn to.

You stare at the face of a loved one you have not seen for so many years. You remember that last moment in time when you saw him and you see a broken mosaic of images—the perverse persistence of that one day. A day that has now flattened and faded. A chimney, a kite, a rifle. You imagine his wound and the depression it made on impact. You are pulled by the whipping tangle of that memory back to that time. You are trailed by your past, carrying it with you like an evershadowing present.

There is a long moment of silence. "They had mistaken me for dead when I was shot in your garden and dumped me onto a truck."

The words are too much. Mai feels as if she too has received a wound.

I think about the compulsive secret Mai and I share, that we have a stone in our heart where our sister used to be. She taught us love and pain and hurt. I still insist it all began with our sister. But of course, who is to say what is the first cause or the last cause?

"Mai," he says. He is pulling her hand, leading her through the foot traffic, warning her about the buckled sidewalks and the skittering pebbles. Occasionally he stops to buy a beer or a pack of cigarettes. The vendors all seem to know him. He inhales deeply, pulling smoke into his lungs, making a long satisfied sound.

I look at him, not to see what he looks like but to take him in. I too have felt the way he must have. For us both, there is the life before the war and the life after. And the one after, the one we try to bend and shape and reconfigure, filled with methodical pursuits tied to no great unifying purpose, hardly seems worthwhile.

James puts his hand gently against the back of Mai's neck. "Look," he says. He pulls several photos from his wallet and goes through them as if he were dealing cards. He chooses one from the lot and hands it to her. There we are, caught by the camera's flash, James, our sister, and Mai, pinned in time and place. I see Mai on the edge of the photograph, pressing herself close to the center so that she would not be accidentally excluded when our Chinese grandmother shot the picture.

"You have kept it all these years," Mai says softly. She runs her fingertips lightly over the wrinkles. He brushes a stray hair from her forehead. He gives her a gaze that is focused and intense, to be received on privately different terms. After tragedies and travesties, he is here, aiming a beacon into the heart, where our mutual loyalties remain undiluted.

James takes Mai's hand to his cheeks. And then he puts her hand to his head and squeezes her palm. She does not recoil. She rakes through his hair and feels a deeply indented concavity of sunken skin depressed against bone. It is hard, like deformed metal covering an old, terrible wound that must still throb. I can only guess what he endured after 1968.

In the outdoor light, the other scar, on his underarm, glistens and flashes. Mai stares at it, a cicatrix smoothed by time. In the heat, the still tender tissue bubbles pink and red against a web of fine blue veins.

Mai grips his arm as James thrusts his hands in his pockets. The sky, thick and striated, is turning purple. They make their way along crosshatched streets, through the long parabolic curve of peak-hour traffic, through the scrimmaging density of motorbikes and pedestrians, to amble along Tu Do Street with its rows of silk and handicraft stores.

Air conditioners drip onto sidewalks. Mai stops at the Givral restaurant, amazed that she still remembers the place vividly. They move on to Brodard, where they buy a cup of orange and durian ice cream. Soon they are by the harbor, next to a black statue of a national hero who led an important fight against the Chinese. A line of light glimmers in the distance where sky and river meet. The water pulses and glistens. A haze makes its hot, ragged climb, rising from its skin as the sky fades into dusk and the horizon is foreshortened by a hovering mist. They walk side by side along the paved banks, his palm against the small of her back. Water laps at the riverbed. James occasionally stops and turns his body so he is directly in front of her. He smiles. "You were a child. A wonderfully perfect little child. And now . . ." He puts his arm around her. Mai beams.

It slips from him automatically: "You have your mother's face." He puts one hand on his heart as if to cup it.

Mai bites her tongue, overtaken by so many feelings churning among the warren of partitions inside her. We are usually double-chained and padlocked, but here in Saigon, Cecile and I are sprung. All of us are

amazed to have found James alive, and when we are unified our common emotion turns out to be strong, like a swelling of the senses. It is a
rare moment of coherence among us.

I know what Mai is feeling. For the first time in a long time, she
stands before someone who sees her as she was. Innocent. Perfect.
Child.

Streetlamps shed pools of light along the boulevard. The air is fragrant. Fruit trees are laden with ripened fruits waiting to be picked. The
first mangoes of the season hang from trees. Tamarind pods burst
open, their shells honeyed by the sun. I am not sure where we are but it
is beginning to get dark and the day's heat has long peaked and is finally
receding. Night is coming soon, but of course they will not part. They
are joined together by something enormous. They are both aware that
every filament of their newly found connection needs to be nurtured.

James takes her arm and guides her down an unobtrusive side street
to a local eatery. Mai is not hungry but is eager to go with him. He
assures her she will love the food. The waitress gives James a questioning glance and arranges a tray of fried squid, dumplings, beef morsels,
and French baguettes on the table. When the electricity goes out, the
waitress lights candles and hands James a bottle of beer, which he uses
to wash down a handful of pills. Soft shadows slide along the walls.
Light reflects against James's watch. Extra candles and flashlights lie
on the table. Mai shoots him a rogue glance. It is only now that she is
taking the time to look at him. Through his tank top, she can still see
the hard, ropy muscles that jump when his back moves. He was always
physically active when we knew him. But there are perceptible advances
of aging. His hair, though thick, is graying. But he is still lithe and compact. New lines and the perpetual shadow of inadequate sleep have
formed around the eyes. His face, burnished by the years, is still angular and chiseled but clearly careworn.

A hard breeze flattens the candle flame. He cups his hand over it,
shielding and steadying the smudge of light from the wind, prolonging
its glow in the darkness. He sits with his hands almost touching hers,
expelling plumes of smoke through his nostrils. The candles have
nearly burned away so James inserts new ones into the holders and
lines them up, creating a sieve of light. There is no talking, only a brooding silence as he crushes his cigarette in the chock-full ashtray.

As she finishes off the last dumpling, he peels a green mango, slices it for her, and slips a morsel into her mouth.

A big round moon, shrouded and moody, shines down on them.

He opens his knapsack and removes a three-quarters-full bottle of Dewar's White Label scotch.

They are in a darkness that covers fear and makes talking easier. Something happens; Mai can talk. "Tell me something," she finally says.

He tells her about his years of loss after 1968. Mai, I, we, all of us are rapt, listening attentively. He explains that there was the long period of time spent in a veterans' hospital and a rehabilitation center. He talks about his cross-country wanderings and the years living at home with his mother on Long Island, doing odd jobs. He says something about a disreputable existence and shakes his head as he tries to sum up his life. "Everything was temporary. Nothing stuck to me. I caused my mother untold worries, broke her heart. I spent my time watching movies at home on TV. When she died, I upped and left. Wandered about for a while and then came here. To try and make a go of it." He gives her a long, focused look, then adds, "And to stay.

"This is where my daughter was born," he whispers.

Mai is stilled. She tries to give shape in her mind to the word *daughter.*

"I've been given a new life here. Look at her," he says, pulling a photograph from his wallet and putting it under the pale light.

Mai looks at the photo. There are traces of Asian features in the little girl's face.

"Where she was born is where I am putting down roots."

Instinctively, Mai pulls away, not trusting herself to speak. So this is how he has been brought to this moment, she thinks. A hot flare rises from her cheeks. She imagines James holding the child, now four years old, he says, and she muses about the quiet, meaningful life that now moves through him.

It always comes back to the mother and so he tells her. "The child's mother, my wife," he says, "tried to escape by boat with her mother in 1980 and they were caught and imprisoned. She was only four then and her mother wanted to give her a future away from Vietnam. Her father was a soldier for the South and did not survive his reeducation camp years."

I see the watchfulness in his eyes as he tells Mai about the mother of his child and her life of frailty and torment. "Every day she puts on makeup and goes to work at Apocalypse Now. It's one of the most famous clubs in Saigon." James's voice becomes a monotone, pitched low. "She is a good mother," he adds, nodding for emphasis. His voice, gritty from cigarettes, is breaking as he tries to loosen the inhibition and finish the thought. He is struggling to put the words together. After a moment's pause, he pulls a pack of Marlboro from his trouser pocket. He flashes Mai a smile and confesses that he needs a cigarette to figure out what he wants to say.

The smoke burns Mai's tear ducts and stings the back of her throat.

James lifts his eyes. The brownish filter tip hangs from his mouth. He takes a deep drag and stares into a vacant space and begins to talk. His voice hoarsens. "Since our first meeting, my wife had looked to me to take us out of Vietnam in order to fulfill her own mother's hope for her," he says. "I'm sure that was my appeal to her." He clears his throat. "But especially now, after the birth of our child. It has become a matter of her future, our daughter's future," he adds, throwing the weight of his voice into each word, "that we have to leave Vietnam."

He reaches across the table and holds Mai's hand. "You know I cannot return to America, don't you?" Mai says nothing. "And so we are still here, much to her chagrin.

"I know it is a big disappointment for her," he continues ruefully, taking in a long drag of smoke. "With a few strokes of the pen and forms from the American Embassy, my signature would confer American citizenship on her immediately," he murmurs. "And we could all take a plane and land in the U.S." At last he raises his head and stares straight at her. He foresees the hooks and snares of judgment, and to soften it, he inserts his own self-assessment. "Maybe what she says is true. Maybe I am hard-hearted," he concedes.

James tells Mai how his life has been a spiral circling back into itself, a snake swallowing its own tail. But he will not leave Vietnam. "Saigon is a gentler place," he says, "for people like me. A less judgmental place." He smiles. "There are many drifters here and I am just one of them."

He takes a deep swallow of his scotch and gives her a quick smile. He tells her he teaches English a few days a week at a local school. "More than that," he says, "would be too much for me. I don't think my wife understands this. But you do. I know." He looks at her through the flutter of candlelight, as if to study her. "Maybe you found the American Dream. But it's not for me. I wouldn't even know how to look for it." He sits there, biting a corner of his lower lip.

Mai listens and says nothing and I note when she lifts her head that she is tearing up. His story hollows her. James has taken his slender prospects and planted them here, in Saigon. He has found love, perhaps even the kind that rushes through the heart and yanks it loose, and it has given him a child.

He has managed it. He has outmaneuvered death and made it across the crags and precipices of war. He has thrown himself into the jostle of marriage and turned himself over to this seemingly undramatic task of making a home and settling down.

Mai struggles to simulate the requisite expressions of surprise and congratulations. Instead all she can manage is a suddenly sensed sadness and a question. "Where are they?" she asks.

James says that his wife has taken their child to visit her ailing mother in Ba Xuyen Province deep in the Mekong Delta. He is not sure how long she will be gone.

He does not bring his wife up again.

James puts his hand on Mai's cheek, wiping away her tears and leaving a warmth on her face. She smells smoke and beer coming from him. Her throat burns but she whispers that she is happy for him even as she looks away. He is leaning toward her and hooking his finger into hers.

You remember, she wants to say, but she does not want to turn her head and risk looking him in the eye. He nods again, as if he were replying to her unasked question. Of course he remembers the hooked fingers. In comforting her, he becomes confident and self-assured, not the drifter ground down by old wounds. With his appearance the dead have awakened; our sister dances as Mick screams, our mother with her face beaming and flushed drinks tea with her Chinese friends, and our father shows us his polished boots.

When they stand up to leave, he kisses the top of her head, wraps his arm around her, and leads her off. Almost by habit or instinct, she consigns herself to him, following him in silence down slanty alleys, making several turns through this and that street, past old lampposts oxidized copper and orange, and then onto the main boulevard. She hears his footsteps by her side. He leads her to a park bench across from the old French Opera House. There is a shimmering growth of green, slightly damp from the rain, beneath their feet. An occasional soft breeze breaks through the stagnant hot air. Lampposts shed pools of light that are too slim to illumine the expanse. But it is the dimness of night that comforts, shelters, and even elevates the spirits. I know that for Mai, darkness is a release. Under the glow of a nearby streetlight, she is visible but inconspicuous. They are alone but not really. They are in the city's center and so there are footsteps of people strolling by, conversations, and obliging laughter. Street vendors can be glimpsed along the edge of lamplight, carrying the burden of unsold wares home. They are resilient and dogged but weighed down by poverty and fatigue.

James puts his arms around Mai's shoulders. "Come close to me," he murmurs into her ear. She looks at him, suddenly unafraid and intrigued. The miracle of it is this: how little things from such a long time ago can still be remembered as if they had occurred only yesterday. Tamarind trees, not much taller than when she was a little girl, still grace the streets. I feel the impulse to jump up and grab a low-hanging pod, crack it open, and suck on its sticky pulp while twigs scrape underfoot.

"Remember how your Chinese grandmother disapproved of our music?" he asks Mai. He tells her he has gone to Cholon many times to look for her. "I didn't forget her," he says. "I never found her."

She clasps her hands in her lap and gazes down at them. James is laughing at something. His hand rests on the curve at the nape of her neck. She hesitates to tell James where she is staying but he insists on walking her to her hotel. They stand by the entrance, among hotel personnel in traditional silk garb who open the door and bow as hotel guests go by, greeting them in the requisite spruced-up voice. She notices that he is edgy. I too recognize his nervousness. It is like mine. He lingers by the lobby entrance and then tells her that he will see her tomorrow.

The sidewalks offer us reminders of how things were. Mai's stomach feels the sharp bite of nostalgia as they examine mementos hawked by vendors, objects of importance only because of their link to something now defunct. James tells Mai that he has all of the South's old paper money and will give the bills to her. But Mai wants her own. They are being sold and displayed under glass cases. There is the red one-hundred-dong bill with the picture of Le Van Duyet, national adviser to emperors, great statesman, and protector of Christian missionaries from persecution. There is the orange-tinged five-hundred-dong bill with a photograph of the Presidential Palace. It was through the iron gates of this building that two North Vietnamese tanks crashed when they entered Saigon that last day in 1975. Despite James's protestations, Mai buys both and pays full asking price for them without even bothering to haggle. I remember the plates of *banh cuon* Uncle Number Five and our mother bought with a one-hundred-dong bill and the red plates of fireworks they bought with the five-hundred.

What they need is simply to touch. They hold hands as they walk. The sidewalk is being repaired and whole cement tiles are being lifted up by jackhammers. The gravelly surface pokes at her heels with each step she takes. Peanut shells are scattered about.

The reality is that they have today together, and any other way of looking at time, perspective, scale, or distance, hardly matters, at least on the surface. They spend the day lounging about, walking here and there, as if it were the very route they were meant to take all their lives. They sip pressed sugarcane juice when they are thirsty, eat steamed peanuts to tide them over until the next big bowl of pho noodle soup. A breeze soaks up the humidity. Wind. So sweet and cool. They walk into several boutique shops on the main boulevard, the old Tu Do Street, so Mai can buy souvenir lacquer boxes as gifts for her law firm friends in Virginia. Saleswomen instantly lift their heads and slide toward them, shadowing their every movement in a space-invading way that Mai finds offensive.

"They don't know any better," James tries to mediate. "It's a different sense of space here," he explains. Of course I understand. But not Mai. He nudges her to admire the lacquer shine and luster and the mother-of-pearl inlay. He tells her when she hesitates that anything that seems mundane here because it is one of so many will be beautiful in America. They pick out several sepia photographs of old Saigon for her to frame when she gets home. A vendor hawking durians stops when she sees Mai eyeing her basket from the store's threshold. James picks out a medium-sized one and asks her to split its thorn-covered husk open. He does not want the vendor to touch the flesh. I know it is a sweet concession to Mai's concern for contamination.

"Leave it in the fruit," he tells the vendor. It is the first time she hears him speak Vietnamese and she is impressed by it. Mai loves that moment when the tongue touches the durian's soft, creamy flesh. She loves how the custard pulp melts in the mouth. Mai is in a sweat, but she is happy squatting on the sidewalk with James by her side.

They walk past the Sheraton Hotel with its burnished marble walls and stairs, its ground floor housing a glass-encased Gucci store, then past the Esprit shop occupying the large corner across the street, past the row of small boutiques selling designer jewelry and other curios made of buffalo horn and tortoiseshell, past restaurants and cafés adjacent to the relatively new Versace store that has, James said, recently displaced a small coffee shop. Mannequins flash their metallic sheen through transparent designer dresses and half-zipped jackets. A wind starts to blow, then intensifies as it whistles toward the harbor. James pulls Mai under an aluminum awning into a small newspaper shop with racks of postcards in the front. A man looks at them through lifted eyes, barely nods, then returns to rocking himself slowly on a cane-bottomed rocker.

Mai is drawn to this small space crowded with stacks of old books and magazines, maps, and other miscellaneous papers. Old books are stacked against a row of windows in the vestibule. The sun enters at a slant, making dust speckles visible against the glass. She peers through a glass-enclosed bookcase, searching meticulously through the tattered covers for an English copy of *The Tale of Kieu,* the book she has brooded over since our mother first read it to us. She sees the curious stack of belongings pushed against a wall—photo albums, loose photos, letters—intensely personal, yet offered for sale, and in a surge of emotion she reaches over to touch it. She picks a random photo from a pile stored in a plastic container. It is a picture of a young woman, face illumined, palely but professionally, by the photographer's ivory light. It is but one among many loose photos. There are photo albums that remain wholly intact. There are family snapshots. Some are Polaroids, others glossy three-by-fives with white borders. Their colors, once lustrous, are now leached away. Some are wallet-sized, tinted a faint sepia.

Next to the pile of photos are letters, evidently international by the flashes of red and blue along the envelopes' borders. Some have never been opened and perhaps never delivered to their intended recipients. Mai eyes the left-hand corner where the sender's address is written. San Jose; Washington, D.C.; Frankfurt; Paris. Judging by the postmarks, most of the letters were sent by boat people between 1978 and 1980, writing home to let their loved ones know they survived crossing the various oceans.

A faint smile crosses the proprietor's clouded face as he moves into their line of vision. He tells them he bought the photos and letters thirty years ago.

"Why?" James asks.

"So things that deserve to be passed down to someone won't be discarded. Their owners fled and left everything behind."

James nods and gives him a smile in return. He is leafing through a pile of old maps. His eyes widen as he follows the many red and black lines and the circles and stars used to designate towns and cities.

The proprietor intervenes. "These date a long time back," he says. He tells James he has sold many of them to film people making movies about Vietnam. He proudly names some of the movies he has been involved in. *Indochine, The Lover,* and *The Quiet American.*

When they leave that store, with its unclaimed photographs and letters, I feel a discomforting countercurrent. There is a swell beneath the waves. I muster all the strength I have to suppress it, for fear it will seep through our shared skin and infect Mai's time with James. And then I am surprised by the realization: This is the first time I have wanted to protect Mai from the invading presence of my turbulence. This is the first time I have wished to avoid a deliberate escalation with her. Indeed, for this moment, as I watch her walk with James toward the harbor, her pale face for once serenely disposed, I feel a rare surge of kinship with her.

Mai wonders aloud to James whether any of our family photo albums might be among the pile edged against the wall in that store. What would be the chance of that?

One day in the late afternoon, almost early evening, Mai takes James by the hand and tells him she wants to do something with him that day.

They are at the harbor of the Saigon River again, where several large ships, one a rusty oil freighter, are waiting to be repaired. A gauntlet of shirtless men, wearied by the sun's heat, nonetheless take aim, striking molten iron with hammers half the length of their bodies. Down-stream, a row of boats are rafted together by the shore, swaying and tugging against the mooring lines. The water naturally draws one's eyes toward the horizon, across the river, where coconut trees etch the water and sky with reflections of meditative green. A lone fisherman stands on the wharf by a railing of eroded plywood and casts his rod, its monofilament dancing with the movement of wind and water.

Mai has made all the arrangements by phone. She has timed it so that the trip will be swathed in the purple half-light our parents loved. She searches for a boat with a large dragon's eye. The boat's owner, a frail middle-aged man, looks at her balefully. He is full of reverence and sentiment. He understands the purpose of the trip.

He crouches down, gives the motor cord a scrupulous tug, and pulls it in a single stroke. We are under way.

Mai runs her hand against the boat's warm, wooden flanks. This is a busy river with boats chugging upstream and downstream. Green water hyacinths float on the water in tight, twisted swatches past a pale crescent of gray-shingled houses and houseboats where families are cooking and eating. James leans against the boat's side, his hands wrapped behind his neck. Hydrofoils slice through the oil-filmed water, taking passengers on a two-hour trip to Vung Tau. As we get farther from the city center, away from the sluggish cloud of smog, I smell a trace of sea salt in the air. I feel the ripple and pull of currents under the boat as it heads into the gathering distance, toward the deep, past-dispelling curve of the open waters. James switches positions, pulling Mai toward him. He is so close to her I can feel his breath against my cheeks. He offers her a bottle of water from his knapsack.

Of course I know what Mai is doing but I don't think James knows the plain facts of the voyage. It is a nice enough evening for a river cruise. After a few moments she asks him if he knows why they are on the boat. Before he can answer, she puts her hand in her rucksack and with great deliberation removes an object from it. She holds it with both hands and stares into the deep blue before us.

She shows him the smooth metallic box that contains our father's ashes. Mai looks at James and tells him she wants both of them to drop her father's ashes into the water. I feel sad our father's life turned out as it did. But I am also strangely reassured. Through our father, I see it is possible to love one person in your lifetime, the way he loved our mother. It is possible for love to endure.

Mai is sending him off the way he would want to be, not fixed and earthbound and weighted down by a headstone but free and flowing, untouched by ephemera. And then suddenly, a thought she has been quietly struggling with enters her head, and with clarity and precision takes on the shape of a decision: She will not try to find our sister's grave. The cemetery where Khanh is buried is run-down and half-abandoned. There can be nothing consoling about it.

James looks at Mai solemnly. "Your father used to stand by a patch of flowering weeds and watch us kick the ball around the soccer field," he says. "He wanted to hear you talk." I know James is referring to the time when Mai lost her voice after Khanh died. "He wanted to hold on to the sound of your voice," he adds.

It is a pleasure for Mai to be given that memory of our father.

Mai chooses this moment to tell him that she has another sister somewhere in Vietnam. She goes on to tell him about our mother and Cliff. She anticipates questions but James is unfazed.

"She was taken to an orphanage in Vung Tau. I think I should go there to see if there is a record of her. Maybe find out what might have happened to her," Mai says.

"There was only one orphanage in Vung Tau and it was demolished a few years ago," James tells her. He explains matter-of-factly that our sister might have already left the country. There is a program for Amerasians who want to leave, James tells her. Many have left.

Mai asks him if he is surprised by this story and he tells her no.

"Anything can happen in life," he says. "Look how we have found each other."

The steel-gray water churns, far from the seductions of the world, its surface sequined with a spectrally silvery foam. The boatman turns around and flashes his wide-eyed, brows-up look, as if to ask, "Here? Or here?"

"Here," she volunteers. *Here* has a fine, generous sound to it. This body of water will merge at some point with the South China Sea. Mai smiles at him, and he takes that to mean any place in this vicinity is fine. Here it is, then. Seaweed tinges the water green. He turns off the motor and lets the boat drift in the salt-smelling breeze. Their names differ and they seem separate and distinct but oceans and seas are all connected to one another in a tumultuous web.

From where I sit, the great body of water before us prophesies not boundaries but continuity. I know Mai picked this body of water because of our mother. I stare it down. For years she was a ghost, invisible, absent, living a life apart from us, occasionally pantomiming devotion. Now she is somewhere in the South China Sea. Soon our father will be released to join her.

A conflicted tide moves through me. I still feel the piercing pain of Mother's rejection. With clarity I see the angelic face, not looking at me. Years later I am still waiting for her to complete her gaze toward Father and me. But now on this boat I feel tiny valves opening up in me, expanding the blood vessels and opening up the pores. I fight to contain myself. A strange sound escapes me. The barriers between Mai and me have been weakened. She feels my cries and I feel hers, as if our nerves glow, crosshatched, and we are bound together by a maddening, common vulnerability.

This is as good a place as any, I think. Waves slap the sides of the boat and produce a ravaging swell of foam. Mai stands up with James. The water is alive, its skin breathing. Mai looks straight down into the exploding waves. In one swift movement, she dips her hand into the box, as if what she is doing requires speed and determination. The ashes are there, inside a plastic bag. They feel personal—velvety and soft, fine like soot, with the occasional grittiness of bone. Mai gives the bag a little shake and tilts it toward the water, sifting the last handful into the waves where they immediately disappear. It is both shocking and comforting. At that instant I do not feel bereaved. There is beauty and fierceness in the moment itself: shafts of purple, granular light hammered against the water, a profound distance at once vast and seemingly bottomless, the sun beginning its preternatural descent, disappearing slowly beyond the curve of the earth.

With sudden force, the waves turn choppy. Mai hands an envelope to James and together they scatter petals of roses on the water's surface where the ashes were and watch them float away, pulled inside a membrane of shimmering ripples, inside a submerged, reconfigured symmetry. The boatman nods. I imagine it is a signal of his implicit approval—here is a little golden hush of consolation, the surprising relief of death held and released.

This is what I would want for myself as well, when the time comes. This is one way of putting to rest the question about home. Tears well up in my eyes. And just like that, with a modest turn and tilt of the mind, everything shifts as I slip into an invisible line of trip wires where equilibrium itself is provisional and arbitrary.

Mai feels it too. She presses thumb and index finger against her lids. The interior voices are back in full punctuated heave. I calm myself and, in so doing, calm Mai.

Sometimes things are aligned and we feel singular and contained. Sometimes things are jumbled and mixed up, a shuddering mystery that needs to be carefully dealt with.

Mai leans back, resting her head against the bulk of James's chest. Her stomach claws momentarily inward. For now she focuses all her attention on calming the unruly tendrils of my frayed nerves.

The boatman whistles a tune. The wind blows a cool breeze into my face. I keep my eyes shut and feel myself being on the same side as Mai and little Cecile. All of us are here to remember our father and mother. Mai breathes deeply. She is aware that all of us are caught in the same vortical web of emotions. Too many feelings collide, clashing and canceling one another. My heart is stilled and inverted, suspended inside a long slow wave of conflicting tides. It will soon be over. I imagine the thin strip of verdant coastline that lies ahead as the boat makes its way, by infinitesimal degrees and on an even keel, back to shore.

Mai holds James's hand when she steps onto the dock and does not let it go. She hangs on to him to reassure herself of his continuing presence. The little trip to release our father's ashes has bared her nerves. The road opens up in front of them, as if to coax them along the shortest route to the hotel. James puts his hand on the small of her back to nudge her small, erratic steps forward. She allows the fatigue to take over even as her body rights itself and cooperates with his efforts. He walks into the lobby with her and ushers them into the elevator.

Without a word, he picks her up and carries her to the bed, a gesture both innocent and charged. His bare arm rubs against her hair, making electricity. The mattress sinks slightly but holds firm, offering relief. He lies next to her, caressing her hair and stroking her face. A silence, deep and pervasive and free of explanation, floats and swirls about. The air conditioner blows, stirring coolness into the flush of humid air. Her head rests on the slope of his shoulder. There they lie in their somber colors and lingering warmth, caught between stillness and motion.

He holds her tightly, his face wet from her tears and his. Their shared memories come at them obliquely. "Mai," he keeps saying, whispering her name merely for the sound of it. Coming from him, the word is uttered with a slight upward tone, as if to suggest a question when it is in fact meant as a declaration. Occasionally his tone takes an upward, then downward, turn, and her name pronounced thus takes on a different meaning—"always."

His voice is barely audible. I can hardly hear him but I can feel the scratch of his nails, against the length of her back. He speaks wistfully, almost covertly. He tells her he has never stopped missing her and her sister. Mai lies still, clasped inside his embrace. She tells him she loves him. James sighs. He strokes her hair into place, a fledgling to soothe, ragged ends to heal. There is strange comfort in watching them and listening to their voices. The night seals itself off to the rest of the world.

He shifts position, rolling on his side and onto his elbow. He tries to move her closer to him, and even though she lies still, he does not take this as a rejection. He edges closer to her and massages knots in her back.

A strong wind moves through the trees. It starts to rain. James pulls her with surprising delicacy into a fetal position closer to him. Mai senses everything around her. The faucet drips. The clock ticks. A door closes across the hall. Either she lacks the nerve for reflection—the kind that serves to restrain temptation—or she is overcome by a rush of longing.

She wants to shed her skin; she wants to be close to him, for the entirety of his body to be fitted against hers. He clears his throat and hums a descending line that hangs stealthily until it fades into a simple heartfelt declaration of "Yesterday." Mai lies back, ignoring the tide of contradictory impulses within, watching attentively as he hums a few notes, his fingers strumming an imaginary guitar held in his arms.

Mai loves the melody, its phrasing like light and shadow. A flush works its way through her and she feels a hotness on her cheeks. It is as if something tightly reined within her has begun to loosen and is waiting for release. The heart, redeemed and reconfirmed, stumbles and swerves. There was that life then and there is this life now, although it seems almost impossible for both to coexist at the same time.

She feels a warmth radiating from his body, his breath rising and easing, rising and easing. So this is what it feels like to be moved.

Mai and I are overpowered. Here, with the sound of the wind rustling through the plants outside. Here with the darkness making its way stealthily through the mysterious imperatives of the heart. Something perilous and strong moves through us. We feel it all—the certainty of old devotions; the weight of impermanence; the age-old human flaw of wishing for more than what can be instead of accepting with gratitude what has been given.

Mai's heart is coaxing her on to a new place. James's face is slippery with sweat. She hears her own breath next to his. She leans close to him, her face touching the soft curve of his neck and sometimes the sharp edges of his clavicle. She can feel him alternately squeezing and releasing her hand.

And then I hear a cry in the echoing silence. It is a jarring cry for the grieving that remains unfinished. I know Mai is already preparing for the inevitable good-bye that lies before them. By the time she realizes it, James is on top of her. Her head sinks into the pillow. She softens her body, allowing herself to be pinned down and submerged as she inhales his essence. A different life is bound to lie between them but for now they have this.

His hand seeks her out and clutches her hair, even as he is on top of her, barely moving. He can tell she has been alone all her life.

Hours of darkness hold them together through the night. She savors these minutes. Already she misses him and the blind perfection of lovemaking. Already she sees tonight as a memory, even as it turns around and courses its way back into her body.

When Mai leaves the following morning, James is still asleep. A tapestry of darkness is just beginning to lift. The sun is barely up, a mere speckling of orange. The walls are washed in the pale, gray palette of dawn. She moves about stealthily in the bathroom as she gets ready to leave the room.

Her heart quickens as she takes a long look at him. Mai is fully dressed but she lingers. There is a flicker under his eyelids, a sign of troubled sleep perhaps. The sheets are bunched and knotted against his stomach and she can see his chest moving up and down in quick, ragged breaths. She bends down toward him and kisses his forehead. He does not pull away. Even in his sleep he seems to be leaning toward her. She closes the wooden shutters so he will not be awakened by daylight.

James, she whispers, not out loud but only to herself. The *s* in his name is drawn out, like an eternal, sibilant whisper. Even his name carries its own aftereffect; already it is a purple mark foundering deep inside her soul. She knows he is lost to her, and she leaves the room carrying his heart inside her. How surprising, she thinks, that later in life, she is feeling what others feel in their early youth—a sensual jolt and wonder. No matter what happens next, she knows she will be lost to him forever. It is a miracle that she has found him at all. More cannot be asked.

Later that night she returns to her hotel and checks out. She is told a man had been waiting for her and that he had written her a note. "I will wait for you at Ben Thanh Market," it says. "Or come to the orphanage." At the bottom of the note are the name and address.

She moves into another hotel two streets away. She stays there for more than a week, trying to sort her way through the befuddled grip of her emotions. She ignores his nearby presence in the sprawling market. It is a familiar feeling, nursing yourself back from the precipice of ruined love, the misaligned and scattered selves splintered within. Sometimes these feelings are about James but sometimes they barely attach to a person at all. At those times she is just displaced, weighted down and beset by an intense hunger for life that stirs within, a hunger that can scarcely be met.

When love is experienced and released, where does it go? How does it balance itself on the pinprick of the moment? This much is clear to me. We don't recover from love forged in childhood, in history. We carry it with us. Or more precisely, it just sticks to us. And it is never really forfeited or lost.

It is early but Mai makes her way to Ben Thanh Market. She will return to the very spot where she first saw James. The note says he will wait at Ben Thanh Market but that was written more than a week ago. And certainly at this early hour he will not be there even if he still plans to wait. Still, she is filled with hope. Vendors are just beginning to set up. She finds her way back to that spot where she first saw James—by the *bun bo Hue* noodle cart. The vendor she is looking for is there, fanning herself with a conical straw hat. When Mai asks, she is immediately told where the American lives.

That evening, spurred by a freighted sense of urgency, she takes a cyclo to Hai Ba Trung Street and, after crossing several intervening alleys, arrives at a cul-de-sac called Alley Number 9. The sidewalks are wet. The moon looms overhead. Mai walks silently along the reticulated backstreets, in search of the 100 block where she has been told his house can be located. She hurries past a disordered row of crude, boarded-up buildings, some abandoned and vandalized, their scabby timber pulled off and left in a junk heap of tires and other unwanted items. A motorbike spews gravel as it screeches to a sudden stop with a gasp of the brakes before a repair shop festooned with multicolored pennants. The road, grudging and forlorn, is beaten and rutted and bears the deep imprint of wheeled vehicles. The houses here are of weathered clapboard and cement. Small and narrow, they stand haphazardly next to each other. Some are enclosed by a crisscross of chicken-wire fencing, others by concrete knee-high barricades choked by red spikes of dry, thorny stalks and edged by a sludge of brown slime. A small boy eyes her and beams a big grin.

Mai identifies his house by its pale yellow-ocher walls, hot-pink bougainvillea bush, windows with two broken slats temporarily fastened together: slippage fixed by cords and strings. Butterflies float among the

flowering bushes. Birds cast a shadow across the sky as they break the horizon and approach the neighborhood. A ragged doll partially covered by
leaves and dirt lies facedown near the bottom step. It is late but the street is
still crowded with cyclos and bicyclists. She finds a spot across from the
house, behind a row of motorbikes parked on the sidewalk, and sits there
to watch. She fits her body inside shadows big enough to hide her.

Here is James's life, unveiled like a slow heaving confession in the
shaded fringe of dusk. She hears the voice of a little girl and the occasional chirps of crickets asserting their nocturnal presence. Through
the mosquito-netting curtains, she sees his silhouette, as if etched
against the ivory gauze. The little girl is climbing onto his lap, pulling
his hair tenderly. Mai sees her face, sweet, adoring. She is a flower. He
offers her a spoonful of something and she pushes the offering away to
pursue something of greater interest, painting her father's face instead.
After a brief struggle in which she bobs and fidgets, he capitulates with
a show of resignation, pledging solicitous stillness so she can adorn his
face at will. In the background a woman sends her shadows back and
forth as she moves across the room. But what Mai focuses on is what
she has many times conjured in her mind, James and the little girl. She
has fashioned a paper crown and placed it on his head. In exchange for
his cooperation, she is making a show of being more tractable, accepting his offer of food with minimal fuss. The bluster of play subsides. A
smell of caramelized pork comes from the open window. Mai takes a
deep breath, inhaling and holding it as if for a lifetime.

James walks with the girl toward the refrigerator. He opens it and
holds her in midair, suspended inside a cold blast. They both laugh. After
a few minutes, James closes the door and hoists the child up on his shoulders, father and daughter in sweet complicity. The girl points at the window and James glances out with a dark questioning. Still carrying the
child on his shoulders, he walks out the door, to the level patch of grass in
front. Mai feels as if someone were holding her and squeezing her tight.

"Over there, Daddy," the girl exclaims, struggling to wriggle free.
James submits to her wishes. He eases her down his back but keeps his
arm half-clasped around her body. The little girl twists loose and runs
to the bottom of the steps. She scoops up her doll and shakes it clean of
dirt, rearranging its hair and dress before embracing it. She reassures
the doll that they will sleep together tonight. She puts the doll in a

sitting position and squats down to talk to it. This is the little girl who will rescue him. She is changing him already, Mai thinks. Things won't fall apart. Light from the house is at his back, emitting a soft glow, absorbing him in its vast repose. Something is marrying him to the night. And in turn, it, the evening, the place itself, is opening up, embracing him in its fold.

James hangs a cigarette between his lips, cupping his hand over it as he strikes a match. After several tries, the sulfur tip flares. A stray cat yowls as it slowly strides along the street with proper melancholy and presumptuous propriety. The little girl takes a few inquisitive steps forward, calling out to the cat, and then running toward it. Meow, meow. James's eyes follow his little girl's every move. He edges closer to the street, confronting, scanning for her movement.

"Khanh, come back," he calls when the little girl ventures too far for his comfort. Only a short flight of steps separates the house from the street. "Khanh."

The name claws at Mai's heart.

James takes a long drag of his cigarette, letting the smoke settle in his lungs. A woman's voice, more harsh than necessary, I think, calls for him. The voice is beckoning him in flat but heavily accented English. James in turn calls for his child. He finds her by the curved walk. He taps her bottom before scooping her up and carrying her against his chest back into the house. Before he enters, he turns briefly toward us as if to impart a final, valedictory glance.

Mai and I stand still together in the purple presence of the evening, watching the little house return to its internal torque. The woman takes the child from James, then returns her to him before their backs turn and they disappear from our line of vision. Slowly the house recedes and dwindles as lights are dimmed, then turned off. Darkness takes over. I think Mai knows what she is witnessing. It won't do to hold on to the form of things. This is a scene she has entered late and from which she will leave early. Still, we both feel something move through us, maybe a realization that we can accept something less than perfection.

Mai stays in Saigon for a few more days and then, before leaving, decides on the spur of the moment to take a drive outside the city. You don't have to go far from Saigon to see the country. The rice fields surprise her. They lie flat, without much ceremony, embracing a piercing, green consciousness.

She has hired a driver to take her around. The road, one among many arterial feeds that surround Saigon, is newly paved but there are long, drawling stretches of rutted asphalt. There are no monuments, no tourist attractions here. Nothing majestic. Only the dramatic compression of green in quadrilaterals. She is not sure why she is doing what she is doing, only that it feels right.

Mai remembers how our mother was pleased when the pale green of her jade bracelet deepened over time into the rich, verdant green of a rice field, which for her augured health and prosperity.

She does not know what to do or where to go. She merely asks to be driven. The engine rumbles and its internal bearings click smoothly each time the driver shifts gears. Everything is peaceful now, though years ago this was the site of ferocious military campaigns. The hard eyes of history can still be felt. The names of towns, some painted, others in grouted signs, appear parabolically through the windshield, but Mai and I remember them through the varnish of war, as battlefield names only. The highway unravels its black asphalt strip flanked by bright emerald green. Mai and I both remember that our father talked often about rice fields, that he once solemnized and imbued them with formidable characteristics—defiant, hard-spirited. Here they are— something immense and simple. Despite the intervening years of triumph and loss, goodness can still be found here.

Although Mai has no conscious memory of the countryside—it was not safe to drive far from the capital city during the war—she feels something so familiar here, as if she were going toward a known place. Toward a still point. That point in the present that carries a scent from the past but is not afraid of it and so welcomes the future without fear.

Suddenly, she (and I too) see why the fields are so familiar. The realization comes as a surprise. Mai asks the driver to stop. She steps out. The air smells of palm thatch and tropical wetness. We are surrounded by green, like the interminable white of a Virginia snowstorm. Despite the elemental difference, this vast green is but an alternate version of the wintry white expanse when harsh lines and edges are muffled and softened. Its beauty too sinks right into your skin. Boundaries are erased here, contours blurred and diffused.

Far away, beyond the sculpted curve of a hill, Mai sees a small thatched house clinging to its shadow, rising foglike from the field as if it were a reflection of life's true, miniaturized reality. Something about it, an injured, ill-fated aura perhaps, touches her to the core. She has been opened up and my sudden window into her is matched by her window into mine. The barricades between us have weakened, perhaps for good.

Mai too wants what I want—for us to be reconciled and integrated in a shared web. When we return to Virginia, she will get the help we need to heal. Right now, we both feel it, a full immersion into the furious center of the other's life.

The countryside opens itself fully to us, as if everything we see before us now has already been seen and felt through the ages. It is something intensely and viscerally familiar, like an inheritance passed down from parent to child. Mai and I marvel at the way a small thatched house soaks in this landscape and this rice field, fully exposed to the battering elements. Stripped to its essentials and fully aware of its impermanence and vulnerability, there is not even a possibility of pretense or posturing. Despite its weary pride, one large monsoon would knock it to the ground.

We linger in this moment, immersing ourselves in its attendant spirit. Mai sees a group of children playing hide-and-seek among concrete markers bearing the names of soldiers from an old war that still haunts today's many battles. The same way rows and rows of gravestones haunt the weed-choked earth, spirits from generation to generation float, wounded and invisible in the air. Now and then there are high-pitched shrieks of laughter and jubilation. Palm tops stir and sway against the sky.

This moment we want to prolong soaks in the shadows of life, then. The future bends backward to mirror the past. We can almost see our sister and mother and father, in a row, all dead but not. Mai thinks of James. She knows I do too. And the name alone makes her smile.

# Acknowledgments

To my parents, and to John Fritz Freund, Margaret Freund, and Christine Wolf, whom I remember with love and gratitude; the Vietnamese International School, which gave me a treasured repository of memories and dreams and an understanding of that which is true and lasting (Rat and Buffalo).

I thank Le Phuong Mai, Jessica Fraser, William W. Van Alstyne, and William C. Gordon for their thoughtful reading of manuscript drafts, their encouragement, and their steadfast presence in my life. I also acknowledge with gratitude these friends for fidelity and enduring friendship through crises, transitions, and the ordinary passage of time: Nancy Combs, Khoi Nguyen, Himilce Novas, Arthur Pinto, Peg Wagner, and Cynthia Ward.

For historical details and insightful analysis, I relied on the following excellent books on the war in Vietnam: Mark Moyar, *Triumph Forsaken: The Vietnam War, 1954–1965* (2006); Bui Cong Minh, *A Distant Cause* (2005); General Bruce Palmer Jr., *The 25 Year War* (1984); and Lewis Sorley, *A Better War* (1999). I also learned much about the treatment of trauma from Dr. Sarah Krakauer, whose work reflects not just wide-ranging professional knowledge but also deep wisdom and sensitivity.

I thank Rosemary Ahern and Marjorie Braman for their keen and superb editorial eyes, as well as the many people at Viking who have contributed to the advancement of this book, particularly Chris Russell and Randee Marullo for meticulous reading and attention to details.

As always, I am fortunate to have Ellen Geiger as my agent. We met serendipitously almost twenty years ago on a beach in East Hampton and I am thankful for her fierce advocacy, sharp mind, and literary smarts. Heartfelt thanks and appreciation go of course to my editor, Carole DeSanti, who edits with singular sensitivity and perception and has passionately championed my work over the years.

# *Monkey Bridge*

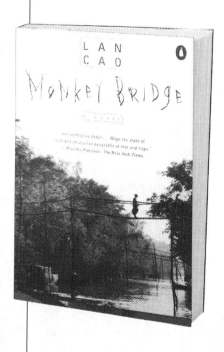

*Monkey Bridge* charts the unmapped territory of the Vietnamese American experience in the aftermath of war. Like a monkey bridge—built of spindly bamboo— the narrative intertwines two stories: one, the Vietnamese version of the classic immigrant experience in America, told by a young girl; the other, her mother's dark tale of betrayal, family secrets, and revenge. The haunting and beautiful terrain of *Monkey Bridge* spans generations, encompassing Vietnamese lore, history, and dreams of the past as well as of the future.

Printed in the United States
by Baker & Taylor Publisher Services